P9-CRK-570

"Written by two major actors of the New Age drama, *Reimagination of the World* is a historic document. But it is more: both sobering and inspiring, this book cuts through the frills and points to a New Age that is age old. If the good news proclaimed two thousand years ago is still good, still new, then the Gospels are a New Age manifesto. That's why I agree: 'The New Age is not optional.'"

—Brother David Steindl-Rast, monk, lecturer, author; coauthor with Fritjof Capra of *Belonging to the Universe*

"An explosive, provocative duet by two imaginative and innovative voices of our times—one a mystic, one a cultural historian—in a dance of opposites, each with a critical eye to the 'New Age' story. The result [is] a synergistic and highly valuable critique from within the 'movement' of a major cultural phenomenon. A book for anyone attempting to sort out the wheat from the chaff of the New Age."

—Elizabeth Campbell, Ph.D., president of the Association for Humanistic Psychology

"William Irwin Thompson's perspective on cultural change in the world today is absolutely unique. No one else, to my knowledge, joins the expertise of first-rate social science to poetic imagination and religious insight like he does. These conversations with his friend and mentor, David Spangler, provide perspectives upon personal and social transformation that are completely original. I don't know anyone else in the world today who can relate esoteric psychology, America's GNP, and new theories in biology with such brilliance and sweep."

—Michael Murphy, founder of Esalen Institute, author of *Golf in the Kingdom*

"The cross-fertilization of two such fecund minds was bound to yield an abundant harvest. This book fulfills that promise. For those who cherish hopes for a future that is not just more of the past, but who are disheartened by the cultish and faddish aspects of 'New Age' phenomena, this volume helps illuminate what is of value and what is trivial in the gathering movement for cultural transformation."

—Andrew Bard Shmookler, author of *The Parable of the Tribes*

"These are two masters, speaking informally, who know firsthand the weaknesses of the New Age, and they know also the thrilling, inspiring beauty of its possibilities. It's easy to imagine that you are there with them, picking up on the wisdom and life experience that their presence can catalyze."

—Willis Harman, president of the Institute of Noetic Sciences

REIMAGINATION OF THE WORLD

David Spangler and William Irwin Thompson

REIMAGINATION
of the
WORLD

A Critique of the New Age, Science, and Popular Culture

*The Chinook Summer Conferences of
David Spangler and William Irwin Thompson
July 1988 and 1989*

BEAR & COMPANY
PUBLISHING
SANTA FE, NEW MEXICO

LIBRARY OF CONGRESS CATALOGING-IN-PUBLICATION DATA
Spangler, David 1945-
    Reimagination of the world : a critique of the New Age, science, and popular
culture / David Spangler & William Irwin Thompson.
        p.   cm.
    "The Chinook weekend workshops of David Spangler and William Irwin Thompson,
July 29-31, 1988; July 22, 1989. Chinook Learning Center, Whidbey Island,
Washington"—Cover.
    ISBN 0-939680-92-0
    1. New Age movement—Congresses. I. Thompson, Willim Irwin.
II. Title.
BP605.N48S66   1991
299'.93—dc20   91-12395
                                                                       CIP

Bear & Company, Inc.
Santa Fe, NM 87504-2860

Cover & author photos: Crispin Currant
Cover photo enhancement: Glen Strock
Cover & interior design: Glen Strock
Editing: Gail Vivino
Typography: Casa Sin Nombre, Ltd.
Printed in the United States of America by R.R. Donnelley

9 8 7 6 5 4 3 2 1

This book is dedicated in love and brotherhood
to our mutual friend
John Cutrer.
His passion to reimagine and heal the world
inspires us both.

CONTENTS

SEMINAR I
Friday, July 29 – Sunday, July 31, 1988

SEMINAR II
Saturday, July 22, 1989

ACKNOWLEDGMENTS

We wish to acknowledge Fritz and Vivienne Hull, the founders of the Chinook Learning Center on Whidbey Island near Seattle, Washington, and all of their associates who have labored long and lovingly to create a special educational and spiritual center in the Pacific Northwest. We have each had an association with Fritz, Vivienne, and Chinook for nearly fifteen years now.

Since its founding in 1972, Chinook has brought an outstanding collection of modern thinkers, philosophers, spiritual teachers, scientists, environmentalists, and political activists to the general public through a wide range of classes, workshops, and seminars. Fritz and Vivienne's vision of a new emerging paradigm, a creation-centered spirituality, a planetary—as well as a Christian—mysticism, and an active discipleship of public service has been an inspiration to many. We are grateful for the kind effort Fritz, Vivienne, and the Chinook staff put into organizing the summer conferences that formed the basis for this book. They continue to show such kindness and graciousness to all who come to their center for learning, sharing, or simply a time of retreat.

We also wish to acknowledge the hard work and kindness of Barbara Hand Clow, Barbara Doern Drew, Gail Vivino, and others at Bear & Company for seeing our manuscript through to this final form and giving us valuable advice along the way.

Finally, but far from least, we acknowledge our families, whose support was—and continues to be—beyond value.

PROLOGUE

David Spangler
April 1991

This book is based on two seminars that William Irwin Thompson and I gave together for two consecutive summers at the Chinook Learning Center near Seattle, Washington. When the last seminar was finished in July 1989, the Iron Curtain still covered all of Eastern Europe, the Berlin wall still divided that city, there were two Germanys, and the Cold War was still in effect between the United States and the Soviet Union. In the Middle East, Iraq was a friend of the United States and Syria was an enemy. The idea that there would be military bases for American troops on Arab soil was out of the question. If the world were to go to war, it was assumed it would be fought on the plains of Germany and that the enemies would be NATO and the Warsaw Pact.

Now, two years later, all that has completely changed. Communism for all practical purposes is dead; the Cold War is over. The Warsaw Pact no longer exists, Germany is one country again, and the Berlin wall has been torn down. The Soviet Union teeters at the edge of civil war and collapse. The United States, along with more than thirty other nations, has gone to war and won a victory, but the battlefield was the desert; the enemy was Iraq, not Russia; and Syria was one of our allies. As a result, it appears there will be a permanent American military presence in the Persian Gulf, while, conversely, troops have been withdrawn from Europe.

More is said about these events in the Epilogue of this book. I mention them here by way of affirming the transformational nature of our times. Furthermore, there is nothing stable about the present situation. It is entirely possible that a year or two from now, the entire political, economic, and military situation in the world will have changed again as drastically and amazingly as it has over the past two years.

Yet, all these outer changes should not obscure the comparable inner changes—the psychological and cultural transformations—going on in our time. Indeed, in many ways the outer changes simply reflect the inner changes. New ideas and insights are constantly emerging, challenging older worldviews. We live in a stewpot boiling with new spiritual, religious, scientific, technological, and cultural energies. Who knows what will bubble forth next or what the final mixture will taste like?

We live in the midst of ferment, victims of the ancient Chinese curse "May you live in interesting times!"

When we cook a stew, what finally emerges is more than just the sum of all its ingredients. Flavors, spices, juices, and textures blend in a gastronomical synergy; the final product is an alchemical transformation of all that was added to the mixture. It is no longer just water, meat, carrots, potatoes, onions, parsnips, salt, garlic, coriander, bay leaves, and so forth. It is something new: *stew.*

Similarly, something new is emerging synergistically in our world. Every culture, religion, philosophy, economic system, political system, artistic sensibility, and technology adds something to the mix, as do all the forces and beings of nature. The resulting dish will be something new, something for which, as yet, we do not have a name. Whatever we end up calling it, it will be planetary—globally embracing, interconnected, interdependent, synergistic, holistic, and mutually empowering—in a way we have never experienced. Also, just as a stew is not a final product, meant to sit forever as a monument to our creativity, but a nourishment from which we derive energy and sustenance for our bodies, so this new planetary sensibility or culture will be less a thing and more a process that nourishes our creativity and wholeness and provides sustenance for building the bodies of our tomorrows.

This book is about this emerging planetary stew. It is not about the final product so much as it is about the process of the cooking. Stew does not exist naturally. We do not harvest it from the fields or find it in the forests; it does not graze in pastures. It emerges from our imaginations. We *reimagine* water, meat, vegetables, and spices into this thing we call a stew. Similarly, we are reimagining our world. We are taking hunks of ecology and slices of science, pieces of politics and a sprinkle of economics, a pinch of religion and a dash of philosophy, and we are reimagining these and a host of other ingredients into something new: a New Age, a reimagination of the world.

REIMAGINATION OF THE WORLD

SEMINAR I
Friday, July 29 – Sunday, July 31, 1988

Whidbey is an island in the Pacific Northwest, thirty miles north of Seattle and an easy fifteen-minute ferry ride from the mainland. Mount Baker is to the north, Mount Rainier to the south, the Olympic range to the west, and the Cascade range to the east. At the southeastern tip of the island is a forest, and within that forest is Chinook, an adult learning center focusing on issues of spirituality, ecology, and service. In the shadow of a nineteenth-century farmhouse in the middle of a meadow within the forest, people often gather to look ahead to the nineties and to the twenty-first century beyond.

An open grassy field is surrounded by trees. In the center, a tent canopy covers folding chairs arranged in a wedge-shaped formation. At the point of the wedge are two high stools where Bill and David take their seats, feet upon the lower rungs. These two are veterans of the New Age movement of the seventies, the former through his work with the Lindisfarne Association and the latter through his work with Findhorn, Lorian, and Chinook. They are no longer young and not yet old, but somewhere in the middle.

SIXTEEN YEARS
OF THE NEW AGE

William Irwin Thompson

Since this setting is so informal, I propose that we do not give academic lectures but have a more casual sharing of ideas in which we can explore together the cultural work of the New Age at this moment when it is being vulgarized, debased, and degraded in the commercial marketplace. Is there anything of intellectual worth or spiritual value left? What kind of spiritual search is it that brings us together in cultural centers such as Chinook?

One of the best ways to learn is to recognize one's mistakes and admit the reality of one's stupidities, even when one's conscious motivation or ideality might have been the highest. When one compares the ideality of one's intentions with the social reality that one actually serves to bring forth, one can learn a great deal about that peculiar oxymoron we like to call "human nature." So let me begin by telling you a story about my mistakes and sharing with you the ways in which I was naive, for perhaps in this transparency we will be able to see some of the general political and cultural problems of the New Age and the popular culture at large.

In the seventies and eighties, I was vigorously involved in an effort to reachieve "the sacred" in architecture as one project of the New Age movement. I had several conversations here with Fritz and Vivienne Hull about possible sites for a Chinook meditation chapel, for at that time we were building one in Crestone, Colorado, for Lindisfarne. Some of you may have seen the cover-article about the Lindisfarne chapel written by Jamake Highwater in the May 1988 issue of *Omni* magazine. I spent a whole seven-year cycle between 1976 and 1983, from Manhattan to Crestone, deeply involved in the effort to reachieve the sacred in architecture, and I threw myself passionately into supporting a faculty of teachers at work in the field of ancient Egyptian and Greek geometry.

What came of this was the emergence of a kind of British Neo-Platonic mystery school in which Keith Critchlow, Rachel Fletcher, and Robert Lawlor were the teachers, and the poet Kathleen Raine was the poetic voice for the Western esoteric tradition.[1] After teaching at Lindisfarne in Manhattan and attending conferences there in which Keith Critchlow brought over his work in London with the Society for Research into Lost Knowledge (or RILKO), Kathleen Raine returned to London

3

quite energized. She decided to found a new journal, *Temenos*, one that would be devoted to "the arts and the imagination of the sacred."[2] In fact, this period of Lindisfarne in Manhattan and Crestone (1976–1983) was dominated by teachers from England: Gregory Bateson, E.F. Schumacher, John Michel, Warren Kenton, Keith Critchlow, and Kathleen Raine. We were something of an intellectual colony, so to speak.

It is appropriate that this summer school for sacred architecture featuring the work of Keith Critchlow, a school that I established in Crestone in 1980, has now returned home to Britain and is going on as a summer school at Oxford University under the patronage of His Majesty the Prince of Wales in furtherance of his new "vision of Britain." It takes princely patronage to build chapels, temples, and mosques, and it was rather naive of me, a working-class Irishman from Chicago, to get involved with these ambitious projects. I had a vision of a simple underground "kiva" for silent meditation in which people of all faiths could set aside their rituals and languages to face one another and the center in equality and profound silence. I saw people seated on petals that were very much like, as I discovered later, the petals of Dante's *rosa candida* from the *Paradiso*.[3]

Visions, however, are not meant to be taken literally, for in that way lies manic paranoia. So when I was not smart enough to recognize that the vision was of the etheric dimension—a vision of the meaning of meditation but not necessarily its physical form—I became not an initiate, certainly, but the initiator of an ambitious spiritual project in which everyone else joined in with their spiritual ambitions. A humble underground kiva for silent meditation soon became the magnifying lens for everyone's religious self-image.

Keith Critchlow's dedicated students jumped into the project, rolled up their sleeves, and went to work on what soon became a million-dollar temple to the mystery school of sacred geometry and New Age spiritual desires and ambitions. The more I observed this project, the more I began to be dissatisfied with this attempt to go back to theocratic Egypt or Platonic Greece. Something didn't feel quite right, but at the time I thought it was only the economic cost of esoteric constructions, and I wasn't thinking of the political cost as well to my own working-class background and my commitment to a Whitmanesque celebration of democracy and the mystical body of Christ.[4]

As a teenager in the fifties, recovering from surgery for cancer of the thyroid, I had had a year away from school (after high school and before college). During that time I read A.N. Whitehead's *Science and the Modern World* and had an intellectual mystical experience in which I felt that Whitehead's process philosophy was the right way to put Humpty Dumpty together again. Descartes had separated egg and yolk; in effect, he had thrown away the yolk, the genetic material of the ancient tradition, the Perennial Philosophy, and with a new technology he had whipped up the egg whites to give us the very French and sweet meringue of materialism. It takes up a lot of space, considering the little that's in it, and it doesn't exactly nourish body or soul.

Now, in this conversion experience I had while reading Whitehead, I formed my life, as only adolescents can do, within his mold of rejecting scientific materialism to embrace a process philosophy in which physics and biology were brought back together in a new kind of higher order animism or a more cosmic form of pantheism. Since Whitehead had said that "all philosophy is a footnote to Plato," I was open to accepting Platonism as the appropriate mystery school of the intellectual elite. Down with Ayer and Austin; up with Whitehead! So I set myself to work fundraising and supporting sacred geometry as part of the curriculum of Lindisfarne. I gave lectures at Lindisfarne in Manhattan titled "The Future of Knowledge and the Return of Hieroglyphic Thinking,"[5] but in spite of the title of Whitehead's book, I had insufficient appreciation of where science was actually going in the modern world of the seventies.

The problem was that this Lindisfarne mystery school of sacred geometry was not a vision of life as process, as flow and change. The mystery school expressed a mentality in which change was looked upon as a threat to the unchanging values of the eternal. I was being drawn back to an understanding of the New Age as only a rejection of modernization—a rejection of the contemporary world, a rejection of the profane, the secular, the changing, the lively, the threatening, the novel. Unfortunately, these British intellectuals were singing the swan songs of vanishing cultures and were not invoking the prophetic emergence of the new. Some even looked upon the Beatles as the Antichrist, and for someone who had been in his twenties in California during the sixties, this rejection of popular culture violated my whole sense of how wonderful it was to be young and alive in that period of spiritual revelation and cultural revolution.

I suppose I had no one to blame but myself for becoming mired down in British versions of reactionary thinking. After all, I had given my imaginative project of cultural transformation the British name of "Lindisfarne." Although I used the word as a symbol of a small group of people effecting a transformation from one world system to another, the word also brought with it the archetypal associations of a small group of monks holding onto ancient knowledge in a fallen world, a world that would soon overrun them during the Viking Terror. [Lindisfarne was founded in A.D. 635 by St. Aidan and was the first monastery to be attacked in the beginning of the Viking Terror in 793.] So, by invoking images of a spiritual elite holding on to

5

knowledge in a dark age, I had energized not a new age with an appreciation of the emergence of a radically new level of human cultural evolution, but an old age in which a mystery school of reactionary sensitives hated the historical time in which they lived.

RILKO was, of course, not the only theme that Lindisfarne was playing. It was more the music of the left hand, for with the right hand I was exploring the relationship of lost knowledge to the frontiers of new knowledge and was playing with melodic lines taken from the world of science in the work of Gregory Bateson, Francisco Varela, James Lovelock, and Lynn Margulis—all of whom were Lindisfarne Fellows.

To shift metaphors from music to architecture, which I guess is not inappropriate since architecture has been called "frozen music," the bridge I tried to build between the esoterism of the past and the science of the present was one of architecture and the design of the meta-industrial village.[6] If one could bring sustainable agriculture and energy conservation—the work of Sim Van der Ryn, Amory Lovins, Wendell Berry, and Wes Jackson—together with sacred architecture and a new vision of life in a new biology, then, I figured, we would have something big enough to be worthy of the term "planetary culture."

The trouble was, the ingredients didn't mix. Sacred architecture was lofty, ungrounded, and enormously costly. After all, it came out of a culture in which serf or slave labor was cheap, but I was doing all the fundraising to pay the workers normal wages. On the other hand, solar architecture was earthy, humanly supportive, and energy efficient; it worked well for the physical body, but it was not esoteric and did not serve the energetic mysteries of the subtle bodies. We simply stuck the solar collectors on the roof, and nobody worried about golden rectangles and harmonious proportions in the shapes of doors, windows, or collectors.

So at Lindisfarne in Colorado, we ended up with the celestial lattice of a bent Pythagorean *tetractys* in the shape of a dome, but no funds with which to put a floor on the ground or finish the last two-thirds of the building. Keith Critchlow's dome is truly beautiful, but to force wood to bend in that fashion you have to use highly toxic glues. Thus we ended up with the conventional Western division of a lovely Platonic form and a dump of ugly cannisters of toxic waste. Across the path from the unfinished dome in the sky, we had its opposite in the form of a half-underground and bermed seminar building that was not especially concerned with the esoteric resonance between the subtle body and the harmonics of the residential space. Although I worked to fill the living room with philosophical discussions after the manner of Lindisfarne in Southampton and Manhattan, the local people and the spirit of place wanted little part of that kind of urban culture and responded only

6

only to traditional handicrafts and shamanic sweatlodges. So I ended up, through the small-group dynamics of our community, with the old conventional splits of Earth versus heaven, mind versus body, esoterism versus exoteric technology, rich versus poor, patron versus artist, and urban high culture versus the "idiocy of rural life."

Intentional communities seem to attract strong women and weak men—the children of alcoholic parents, or children who had been sexually abused by parents or physically abused by siblings, or both. Though we thought we were coming for the life of the higher mind in the New Age movement, the unconscious mind still had its unresolved emotional life to work out. Thus, many of us who chose to live at Lindisfarne in New York or Colorado came to redeem the vision of family and to work out a hidden agenda of revenge for unhealed wounds.

Whatever the conscious philosophy of an intentional community may be, the unconscious agenda usually becomes what Jung called "possession by an archetype." You get the community as Great Mother and the leader as "the king who must die" to fructify the fields. Men who are dominated by their mothers and who hate their fathers are drawn to intentional communities as a theater in which they can act out their oedipal aggressions. They try to drive out the father and take over the land, for they experience the earth as the body of the Great Mother. Often they are afraid of the outside world and its harshly competitive standards of masculine excellence, so they seek the more maternal and nourishing atmosphere of a smaller community. But once they are securely positioned within the community, their unresolved feelings of inadequacy and inferiority become projected onto the leader, who then begins to serve as a screen for their projections of rage and resentment. This is why in places like San Francisco Zen Center or the Farm in Tennessee or even Rajneeshpuram in Oregon, the leader is driven out.

For abused women, community provides an occasion for revenge against the abusing male, but for strong and more individuated women, community provides an alternative to the isolation of the suburban home. It gives them a chance to reenter the stream of ideas and visions that pass through a home that is now within a cultural center.

In my case, being Irish and therefore not exactly ignorant of the unconscious and the psychic, I transformed the mythic pattern of expulsion into the ancient Irish pattern of voluntary exile, the *peregrinatio* of the Irish monk Columba or the "exile and cunning" of James Joyce in Switzerland. I turned over the place to the community of construction workers and students of Keith Critchlow who had worked on the chapel with such admirable dedication, because I hoped that by doing so I could demonstrate some sort of working-class integrity and avoid what my oldest son

Evan called the "intellectual feudalism" of my living in the big house and holding forth in a salon of intellectual chamber music.

Perhaps the greatest split we encountered was not between soul and body, but the traditional one between rich and poor. By turning the land over to the workers, I was hoping to keep the property from becoming a scene for "Lifestyles of the Rich and Famous." Class does seem to continue to play an unadmitted role in the New Age movement, for I have noticed that the people who do well in this movement generally tend to have trust funds and inherited wealth. Had I my own independent means, I would have been able to hang on in Crestone, but Lindisfarne had no endowment and therefore was always more a figment of my own imagination than an enduring institution.

Since the local people and the spirit of place did not seem to want to have Lindisfarne in Manhattan transplanted to the wilderness of the Sangre de Cristo Mountains, I turned over Lindisfarne's monthly allowance to the construction workers and took to the road in an effort to survive as a writer and lecturer. Unfortunately, it was the Reagan era, with its takeover of society by the new culture of greed. Intellectualism was not exactly in, so there was no chance to survive outside the university as an intellectual idealist or return to Manhattan, where the rents had quadrupled in response to the demand of all the new yuppie stockbrokers and accountants. If I had been more socially skilled as a popular writer, I might have been able to produce the more fashionable kind of books that people liked to buy and thus been able to make a living back in New York. But I was being drawn toward even more remote areas of culture in poetry, philosophy, and cognitive science, and that couldn't cut it in the Trumpish eighties when the phrase "literary essay" had become a term of derision in the big publishing houses in New York.

My Swiss wife, Beatrice, came to the rescue and found a teaching job and an apartment in Berne. I became a refugee from the American New Age and started up a new life as a stranger in a strange land by becoming a housewife and an artist. Perhaps this was more truly New Age, for instead of writing about the role of the feminine in a prepatriarchal culture, I became a housewife in a postpatriarchal age and my wife became the breadwinner. And instead of working out an unconscious agenda concerning the archetypal family, I began to work most consciously with my own nuclear family. Instead of serving as a father figure for strangers, I began to spend much more time as a real father for my own kids. Instead of trying to build a solar village with some lunar collectors in the Rockies, I designed and built cities out of *Leggos* and made up stories to go with them for my six-year-old son.

In the mornings before the time of cooking, cleaning, and shopping, I worked as a solitary artist and I wrote myself out of the Neo-Platonic mystery school of sacred architecture by working on the science fiction novel, *Islands Out of Time*[7] In a fury of trying to understand what it was that I found missing in the mysteries of sacred geometry, I dashed off six hundred pages of writings and rewritings of the novel in three months' time.

When I looked up from my typewriter, it was spring in Berne and I was no longer a member of the New Age movement. In the summer, I returned to Crestone and, at the request of the local residents, had dinner with Shirley MacLaine, who had been invited to consider Crestone as a possible site for her Ariel Ashram. I tried to envision what the new zeitgeist had in mind for the future of Crestone, but I simply could not accept what the local residents wanted to do with Lindisfarne. So I worked to give the place away to another sacrificial victim of intentional community, the Lindisfarne Fellow Zentatsu Baker-roshi, who lived nearby in Santa Fe. The site now stands as a small but beautiful Zen mountain retreat, and under the care of a fastidious couple from Germany, it is in much better shape than it ever was under my direction.

Zen, as it turns out, has had much more experience than I have had in figuring out the relationship between the mundane details of life and an esoteric practice of meditation. The opposed buildings of the celestial dome and the underground house are now beginning to find a way of life more appropriate to their time and place.

The Crestone community has had many different designs on the finishing of the dome, but most people want it as a place for magic, rituals, psychic empowerment, and magnification of their religious self-image. One group preferred to use the chapel as a place to channel Earth spirits. Even though the founding principles were "Be still and know that I am God" [Psalm 46:10] and "No iconography, only geometry," they preferred to put in a candelabrum that had images of extraterrestrial faces, bow to it, and chant aloud as these magical beings embraced their consciousness. Others preferred to have Native American peace-pipe ceremonies, concerts, or community meetings. Some said they would like to lead in a procession of world leaders and help them lift their consciousness to a higher level so that the world could know peace. In short, what stopped the Lindisfarne chapel from becoming a truly New Age chapel was precisely the New Age movement and its takeover by the old psychic mentality of magic and religion.

At the time of the early eighties, when all these old battles between matter and spirit, mind and body, rich and poor were going on within Lindisfarne in Crestone, the New Age at large in American culture was becoming, thanks to Shirley MacLaine and José Argüelles, more popular and widespread than ever. Psychic channeling had become suburban; in fact, it seemed so suburban that the new psychics appeared to me to be trash compactors of the astral plane who could take in the whole debris of the unconscious and compress it into an idol for a cult—a Ramtha or a Lazarus.

To lift myself out of that murky orbit, I ignited the second stage of my rocket and blasted into the outer space of science and philosophy in Paris. Replacing Platonic geometry with Chaos dynamics, nineteenth-century agriculture with twentieth-century microbiology, and shamanism with Buddhism and cognitive science, I set myself to relearning philosophy in collaboration with Francisco Varela and Evan Thompson.[8] The sins of the fathers were to be redeemed by the apostolic acts of the sons. Lindisfarne in Manhattan became a much smaller and more convivial Lindisfarne in Paris.

Paris was a safe place to escape the New Age, because the French were having no part of it. They were not about to exchange their pâté for tofu, their wine for herb tea, and their smoke-filled cafés for zendos. As for environmentalism, nobody ever talked about it. With more than forty nuclear reactors in tiny France, the French didn't even want to think about alternative technology and certainly not about Fritjof Capra's post-Cartesian, new-paradigm science. As a city, Paris was so artificial and so much of a human artifact, with its linear trees and formal Luxembourg Gardens, that it felt like the right way to design a space colony.

Only the Germans were into the New Age; the old American counterculture of the seventies was just catching up with them in the eighties. But, as is normal for them, they were into it in a very serious, humorless, and slightly fanatical way. Their guru of choice seemed to be Rajneesh (whom they called Bhagwan), and you saw red shirts and *malas* everywhere. It is not a long way from the brown shirts of Hitler to the red shirts of Rajneesh, but it is a long way from Findhorn in 1972 to Rajneeshpuram in 1985.

On the other hand, I guess that's how culture works, for it is a long way from square Dr. Hoffmann at Sandoz Labs to hippie Jerry Garcia, or a long way from elitist Aldous Huxley in his study to Timothy Leary on the road. Perhaps now that the New Age has become so commercialized in such things as Lynn Andrews's Hollywood workshops on how to become a Beverly Hills shaman, it is a good time to stand back and take stock of the whole movement.

The first thing that strikes me about the New Age is how hardly any of it is new. Witchcraft, dowsing, palmistry, astrology, geomancy and Chinese *feng shui*, shamanism, astral projection, pyramids and stone circles, extraterrestrials and elves, neolithic agricultural communities, Tibetan Buddhism, Sufism, Zen, Cabbalah— what is new in all of this? In terms of the *content* not very much, but in terms of the *structure* in which this content is held, everything is new. The first phase of the New Age is really *the planetization of the esoteric*. It is the release of "secret oral teachings" from medieval societies into mass paperbacks and rock music albums.

The first phase of the planetization of the esoteric, or what Freud might call "the return of the repressed," works to dissolve the linear, rational dominance of Western civilization, with its simplistic dyadic splits between nature and culture, female and male, unconscious and conscious, sacred and profane, body and mind. In the really new culture that is coming not simply out of New Age communities but also out of scientific laboratories in which genetic engineering, immunology, and artificial intelligence are soon to be crossed, we will begin to experience a shift, a metanoia that so far has been only intuited in science fiction, in works by Arthur C. Clarke or Stanislaw Lem, for example. Now we live in a situation in which technology is the *structure* and spirituality is the *content*, but what we are heading into is a reversal, in which technology will become the *content* but the *structure* will be cosmic life, and cosmic life is simply another term for what, I think, David Spangler means by spirituality. This reversal is precisely what you see taking place in the Tarkovsky-Lem film *Solaris* or the Kubrick-Clarke film *2001*.

To understand this reversal, in which the split between the sacred and the profane is overcome, we need to understand the meaning of the word "religion." *Religare* in Latin means "to rebind together, to reconnect." Basically, it means to reconnect the part to the whole. A fragmentary vision, whether of ambition, hate, greed, or envy, is not a religious vision. So when the chimpanzees studied by Jane Goodall stop their daily activities to have a rain dance, they are setting up a *cultural* ritual that serves to connect their society with the larger cosmos of nature in the thunderstorm. Religion, therefore, by its very nature and definition, comes into play when a split has already occurred. If a warrior culture has dispossessed the culture of women, then a priesthood comes in to take up the old symbols and become men playing women in the culture of patriarchy.

Religion is the way spirituality expresses itself in a civilization, a society built on literacy, hierarchy, and warfare. In the new planetary culture, we are all more intimately bound together in a world in which the mystical body of Christ becomes not Jesus wearing a gold Rolex and white polyester robes and giving sermons on TV, but the entire biosphere in which humanity lives in "a new heaven and a new Earth."[9]

This new human settlement requires that we see our buildings, not as objects to be located on the ground, but as processes that first have to be constructed out of what they excrete. To do that, we have to make peace with the whole and reconnect to the elemental world of bacterial pollution (the new Earth) as well as to the angelical world of pure mathematical topologies (the new heaven). As elemental and angelic are brought together in the human domain ("As above, so below" is an ancient Hermetic axiom), then the biosphere of the planet becomes the Second

11

Coming of Christ as the New Jerusalem emerges as a bride adorned for her husband. All the old splits are overcome and the opposites are wed together. In the tower and city of Babel, the symbol of the period of civilization, *man*kind attempted to dominate the skies. He failed, and his consciousness broke into the many languages of the specialists of civilization. But when the city of the New Jerusalem comes down from sky to Earth, the emergence of the Christ, the Second Coming, is not one of domination but of marriage, of erotic coupling in a new "nature," a marriage of the artificial human city and the transcendental Christ.

If we try to build these biospheres (such as Biosphere II near Tuscon) in the mentality of dominance and control, as multinational corporate banks for the storage of genetic capital in a polluted world, then these biospheres will simply become new towers of Babel as languages blossom out of control and the wild reasserts itself in unexpected viral and fungal growths. If, however, humanity prepares for this marriage of heaven and Earth not through systems of technological domination, but through forms of cooperation in what John Todd calls "living machines,"[10]—by re-uniting itself with the elemental (bacterial) and angelic (mathematical) domains— then civilized religion with its priesthood and priestcraft will no longer be needed, and life will become the spirituality of the ordinary and everyday cosmic life.

In this sense, the archaic content of the New Age is like the old-fashioned 1910 small town that welcomes you to the electronic world of Disneyland. The *content* is camouflage for the *structure*. We humans like to back into the future, so we rescue the Middle Ages in the Crystal Palace of 1851 in London, or we rescue the Midwestern small town in the midst of Los Angeles freeways. We move into an industrial revolution by celebrating the return to nature in romanticism, and we move into a culture of artificial intelligence by celebrating "the transpersonal consciousness movement." Like Olmstead's Central Park in the midst of the financial capital of New York, so is the mind in the midst of this new planetary wiring in which we are all brought together through music and electronically shared images and fantasies. In the new cybernetic world, the sci-fi world in which neurons are wed to silicon chips (think of the novel *Neuromancer* by William Gibson), the mind becomes the park.

In the terms of anthropology, the archaic aspects of the New Age show that it has many of the characteristics of a "nativistic movement." The nativistic movement is a tribal movement against modernization. When a smaller culture is being overrun by a larger one, the smaller culture attempts to go back to the sacred values of the past. It is a pattern of tribes against the empire: the Ghost Dance of the Plains Indians in America, the revolt of the Métis under Louis Riel in Canada, the revolt of the Mahdi in the Anglo-Egyptian Sudan, the revolt of the Irish with Padraic

Pearse in the 1916 Easter Rising in Dublin, or the revolt of the ayatollah in Iran against the Satan of America in the seventies. The pattern of the leader of a nativistic movement is often one of a man who has learned the ways of the overlords but chooses to return to the culture of the underdogs. Think of Moses, Quetzalcoatl Topiltzin, Louis Riel, Padraic Pearse, Jomo Kenyata, Gandhi, and Malcolm X. The nativistic leader rejects the routinization of success in the empire for a glorious failure with the tribe.

It seemed curious to me, considering that I had written a dissertation on the Easter Rising and had lectured about nativistic movements in the university, that I should find myself serving as a leader of a nativistic movement for the tribe of humanists versus the empire of behavioral scientists: Lindisfarne versus MIT. In resigning from the New Age, I gave myself the necessary perspective to see that all these unconscious patterns lacked a sense of humor, an ironic self-awareness, but were certainly overloaded with a sense of sacrifice and martyrdom. With that kind of unhealthy and unconscious program manifesting itself in social activities, one could not really expect to achieve a healthy culture. Small wonder that so many of the New Age communities turned out to be psychological toxic dumps! And small wonder that Findhorn has managed to survive, decade after decade, for Findhorn has a sense of humor and always makes fun of itself. Taking itself "lightly" is something it takes literally.

Linear thinking, whether normal or paranoid, lacks the multidimensional complexity of a sense of humor. In fact, most forms of linear thinking are too simple and too pious. In the sloppy syncretism of the New Age movement in the early seventies, I thought that all the religions were simply different paths up the mountain and whatever path you took would bring you to the same pinnacle of mystical experience, for all the religions were really one. Therefore, I thought, planetary culture had to be a miniaturization of the great universal religions in their esoteric seeds. Instead of having Hinduism, we would have yoga; instead of having Shin Buddhism, we would have Tantric Buddhism or Zen; instead of having Judaism, we would have Cabbalah; instead of having all of Islam, we would have Sufism; instead of having all of Christianity, we would have the kind of esoteric Christianity one found in Thomas Merton or Brother David Steindl-Rast.

I worked to bring all of these esoteric schools together at Lindisfarne, and we would sit together in silent meditation in the meditation room. Indeed, it was profoundly moving to see a Cistercian monk and a Hopi elder, a rabbi in a prayer shawl and a dervish in a turban, a Japanese roshi and an Anglican bishop, a Quaker and a Gelupa lama, all seated together in the meditation room in a silence so thick and powerful that it felt as if an angel or bodhisattva had entered the room and enve-

13

loped us in a new body politic of light. We came together right at the time when the newspapers were full of reports of religious warfare all around the world.

Because of this experience of the esoteric harmony of the world's religions, I was moved to try to construct a Lindisfarne chapel as a place where this kind of experience could happen continually. I suppose the project was "misplaced concreteness," for the spiritual dream became an economic and social nightmare, and I was not able to finish it. I guess since we were building this dome as our constructed heaven, it was more of a Tower of Babel than a New Jerusalem descending out of the sky to the Earth. And I guess again that the lesson to be learned is that nothing less than everything is enough—that the chapel is the planet.

Clearly, the notion that all religions are one was too simplistic and linear. It ignored the fact that, in religious experience, what you see is what you think. If you believe that Jesus was crucified through his palms rather than through his wrists, then in your intensive meditations you can bleed through the *stigmata* out of your palms rather than your wrists. [Historical evidence suggests that crucifixion was done through the radius and ulna bones in order to support the weight of the body suspended on the cross.] The great Catholic ecstatic saints of history who experienced the *stigmata* always bled from the palms, because this is what they saw in the pictures that surrounded them. Similarly, if you are a Hindu and believe that Sanskrit is written over your brain in the thousand-petaled lotus of your sahasrara chakra, then that is what you will see when your third eye opens in meditation.

In fact, meditation creates a personal and portable psychic neighborhood through the visualizations of the creative imagination. This neighborhood becomes a form that you inhabit to experience a particular reality—even, perhaps especially, in the death experience. What you get is what you have built up over the years through your practice. The paths up the mountain are self-created paths, and people's experiences vary profoundly according to their different cultural and historical traditions.

It expresses too sloppy a syncretism to say that all the religions are one. Given the conditions of the planetary cultural transformation we are now experiencing, some traditions with their particular ideas and imageries may be more historically appropriate and open to a planetary culture than others. In the religious violence of northern Ireland, the Middle East, the Punjab, Bangladesh, Sri Lanka, or even here in the shoot-out of the Aryan Nation on Whidbey Island, we can see forms of culture crystallized into religions that are completely inappropriate for the epiphany of a new planetary culture.

The more I reflected on the New Age in my exile from it, the more I began to be concerned about the explosions of hysterical religious warfare on the one hand

and the neurotic implosions of New Age cults and communities on the other. Rather than being prophetic of the future, the religions were stuck in the past; rather than being evolutionary harbingers of a new dawn, the intentional New Age communities were actually quite regressive and were not really open to a radical sense of planetary interconnectiveness, but were moving into a life of "us and them."

Small wonder, then, that during my days inside an intentional community I had latched onto the rigid medieval structures of sacred geometry and architecture. Sacred geometry split the world between the sacred and the profane, the *us* and the *them*; it saw motion and change as a threat, as evil. It envisioned a small esoteric elite that alone knew the mysteries, while the rest of the world was fallen and filled with noise. And small wonder that while one part of me was energizing the mystery school of the rigid crystals of sacred geometry, another part of me wanted out, and was energizing the world of the living in the biology of Bateson and Varela, Lovelock and Margulis. That part of me was constructing a philosophy of cultural change that confronted noise and evil. Small wonder again that Buddhism, with its emphasis on impermanence, would seem to hold forth a way out of the traps of the soul in the Platonic solids.

In the radical shifts from Hinduism to Buddhism, and from Judaism to Christianity, these reform religions took a quantum step forward by proposing reforms that were not sacralizations, but radical *secularizations*, in the literal Latin sense of the word, of making something secular by making it belong to the *generations* outside the temple, outside the priesthood. The Buddhist path can be seen as an antisacerdotal movement in Vedic life. It was an innovation that threatened the monopoly of the Brahmanic caste and their control of sacrificial rites, as well as the monopoly of the teachings of the pandits. Buddhism was a radical analysis of the psychological roots of human suffering. Technically speaking, as the Dalai Lama has explained, Buddhism is not a religion. It is a way of life, a philosophy and a practice of right consciousness.

Similarly, Jesus' teaching was a threat to the Pharisees. Jesus did not work at building temples; rather, he spent much time in prophesying about their destruction. His was not really a sacerdotal institution; it was more a radical secularization of life in which he was even willing to associate with women. He cared little for priestly dignity and would talk with taxpayers and prostitutes.

Sacred geometry is the knowledge of the past, but biology is the knowledge of the present. I believe that what Christianity was to Judaism, science is to Christianity. Science is reform Christianity; it is a community of members who must tell the truth to one another as they explore their faith in the inherent intelligibility of the universe. These roots of science in Christianity are the ones discussed by Whitehead in his classic, *Science and the Modern World*.

One of the things that has always attracted me to David is that he is a mystic who comes out of a scientific background and has a playful love of electronic technologies. David started out as a student of genetics at Arizona State University in Tempe, and he has always had a very scientific orientation in his spiritual imagination. This is something that connected the two of us from the start in 1972, when I was an ex-MIT professor wandering around the world in search of the sacred.

Science did not seem to me to be inherently evil, for it was a community of people committed to the truth. If you lie in science, the whole enterprise becomes nonfunctional. You can lie in religion for a long time, and the priesthood will still be able to make a go of it in society. You can rail on about baptism—about whether baptism has to be done by sprinkling or by total immersion—or whether the guru is the avatar or the Antichrist. You can create communities of mutual deception and shared fantasies. The fantasies will proliferate, and the religions will divide and subdivide until they end up in the cultural entropy of the religious warfare of sect against sect, single fanatic against single fanatic. Science, however, has more compassion for the human condition and does not render itself absolute; it is committed to providing the conditions for its own disproof. And that is a very generous and compassionate act indeed, one quite different from the absolutism of religion that gives the true believer a license to kill the infidel. If you start lying in science and publishing lies in the journals, or slaughtering those who disagree with you, you no longer have science—you have religion.

This epistemological sense of compassion for the mind that is basic to science seems to indicate why Buddhism and Western science have a natural affinity for one another and why people like the Dalai Lama and Francisco Varela have been drawn together. In 1983 when the New Age movement was becoming degraded and commercialized, I found myself much more attracted to Varela's work in synthesizing cognitive science and immunology, and Lovelock and Margulis's work in synthesizing bacteriology and atmospheric chemistry, than to the last dregs of the planetization of the archaic that José Argüelles was interested in distributing to the multitude. For me, Harmonic Convergence in 1987 was the sunset effect of a cultural process of the planetization of the esoteric that had dawned in nineteenth-century Theosophy and come over the horizon with the Boston Congress of World Religions at the turn of the twentieth century. Rather than signaling the beginning of something new, Harmonic Convergence for me signaled the end of the psychic era of human consciousness, that magical modality of being that the archaic cultures so beautifully exemplified. Of necessity, this popular involvement contained

16

an extension of the message in a media mass in which ritual noise overwhelmed the transcendental signal.

The vulgarization of the New Age indicates that the New Age is over, that its *kairos* is finished, and that now is definitely the time of its degradation—when anaerobic bacteria can digest it and break it down. In this digestion process, what you naturally get are broken-down ideas. When I was observing these phenomena from the perspective of wintertime exile and introverted reflection in Berne, I felt a sense of desiccation, of a dropping away of the lush and luxuriously irrelevant.

At the Lindisfarne conference on the political implications of the Gaia Hypothesis, held at the Cathedral of Saint John the Divine in New York in 1985, Lynn Margulis explained to me how she saw Lindisfarne and the work of John and Nancy Todd as "planetary propagelles." Part of the life of a spore is the ability to overwinter and endure desiccation, for in this phase its information gets very finely packed and it survives this period of desiccation until the new *kairos* comes along with its season of new water. Then, wham! The hidden and underground mushrooms spring up everywhere, and the very capacity of having spent a winter as more information than mass allows the spore to survive into totally new historical circumstances. So in letting go, in eliminating the unnecessary and drying down to the essential, minimal, genetic information, the tiny spore takes part in a larger and longer cycle of life.

My own sense of cold and wintry desiccation involved a need to deconstruct the New Age, to strip away the glamorous and excessive in two ways. One was negative, as in this critical assessment I have been sharing with you, but the other was a appreciation of what was positive, of what was truly the genetic information for the future—a necessary horizon to our imagination. David has written about this in *Yoga Journal* in his disagreements with Ken Wilber.

When you look at this phenomenon of the vulgarization of the New Age, it is interesting to notice how little a sense of its own history the New Age has, even when it is claiming to be recovering ancient mysteries. In America, we have electronically erased our literary sense of history with its expanded horizon of time. We are a broken machine with fast forward, but rewind always seems to erase the tape to make room for the recording of new television shows. Even in my generation I have seen a perceptible lowering of standards of literacy. Thirty years ago, even *Time* magazine had to be half-literate, but now it is at the level of *People* magazine. Thanks to television, journalism has now lowered its standards to *USA Today*. You can't call it conspiratorial, but it does seems like a move toward lowering the mentality and level of civilization of the United States to make it easier to rule a nation of dumbos with television. I need only point to the presidential campaign of Bush and Dukakis to rest my case.

In this dumbness we North Americans seem afflicted with a collective amnesia. I remember once in a class in communications at the University of Hawaii in 1985 a student said, "Who is Marshall McLuhan?" and I nearly fell off my chair! During one generation McLuhan is on the covers of *Time* and *Newsweek* and his phrase "the global village" is on everyone's lips, and in the next generation even university undergraduates in a course on communications are asking who Marshall McLuhan is. It was just astonishing to see what an amount of generational knowledge could be lost within fifteen years. New kids could come along for whom Prince erases Bob Dylan and Madonna erases Joan Baez. The music of the sixties seems to linger, but the thinking of the sixties—the works of McLuhan, Norman O. Brown, and Alan Watts, since their storage seems to require the preelectronic activity of reading—has not survived.

Then I began to realize that this loss of popularity is an inherent part of popular culture, and that before Alan Watts came on the scene there was Gerald Heard. How many people here know of Gerald Heard?[11] No one, and yet he was tremendously influential in the founding of Esalen. He had his own New Age experiment called Tribuca in California in the forties. He was a friend of Nancy Wilson Ross, the author of *Three Ways of Asian Wisdom*, a woman who had been a young student at Bauhaus in the days of Kandinsky and Klee and had been influential in the founding of both the San Francisco Zen Center in the sixties and Lindisfarne in the seventies.

Beyond Nancy Wilson Ross and Gerald Heard there were his friends Aldous Huxley and Christopher Isherwood. Beyond them there were D.T. Suzuki, Jean Gebser, and C.G. Jung. Beyond Jung was W.B. Yeats, and beyond Yeats there were Rudolf Steiner, Wassily Kandinsky, and Nicholas Roerich. Beyond that constellation of geniuses, who turned the nineteenth into the twentieth century, there were the giants of the nineteenth century, Goethe and Blake. In the eighteenth century there were the Freemasons Mozart and George Washington; they were inspired by the English and German Rosicrucians, who influenced scientists such as Boyle, Newton, and even Bacon.[12] Beyond Blake there were Swedenborg and John Dee. Beyond Swedenborg there was Boehme, and beyond Boehme there was Paracelsus; beyond Paracelsus there was Hieronymus Bosch, and beyond Bosch there were Pico della Mirandola, Marsilio Ficino, and Gemisthos Plethon in the Platonic academy of Renaissance Florence. Beyond them were the Cabbalists of Spain, Dante, the Sufis, Ibn Arabi, the Cathars, the Islamic alchemists, the Neo-Platonists, the Gnostics, and the Essenes. Before the time of Christ there were Pythagoras and Daniel and the

Chaldean astrologers of Mesopotamia. Beyond them was the prehistoric darkness of myth, with its legends of Enoch and the Sons of God, or the lost continent of Atlantis.

The New Age as the esoteric horizon of exoteric military, patriarchal civilizations has always been here, and we need to remember that many of the past New Age groups, such as the Hermeticists, the Rosicrucians, and the Freemasons, were not reactionary cults trying to set up theocracies or caste systems, but liberal groups working for political liberation. It is precisely because of this that they were seen as a threat to the church and the aristocracy as the forces of repression in the Counter Reformation were brought to bear on them in an effort to wipe them out through inquisitions and witch hunts of many kinds.[13] The *Novus ordo seclorum*, the Great Seal, the symbol of Freemasonry that is still on our dollar bill, is part of the revolutionary horizon of the eighteenth-century Enlightenment's battle against the ultramontane powers of crown and cross, king and pope. As long as we are not enlightened, and as long as there are forces of violent political suppression and endarkenment, there will always be a New Age pointing to a horizon of freedom and exploration that lives at the edge of the known and the controlled.

The New Age is always new and always ancient at the same time. It is the necessary horizon to our imagination. As we run toward it, it recedes, but as we run away from it, it follows us. One can neither thoroughly live with it nor thoroughly live without it. It is a Zen paradox. Christopher Lasch, in his article on the New Age in *Omni* magazine, presents the New Age as a kind of mindless fad of people caught up in purple crystal dowsing and investment channeling, but if you take a more historical look at the tradition of the New Age and consider the work of Aldous Huxley, W.B. Yeats, Rudolf Steiner, Blake, Goethe, and Ficino, you realize that you cannot throw these people out without pulling apart the architecture of Western civilization. These writers are not your Shirley MacLaines and your J.Z. Knights; they are major figures of Western civilization. And they are certainly more important to cultural history than the work of fashionable critics like Christopher Lasch in America or Fritz Raddatz in Germany.

This misrepresentation of the New Age in the negativity of journalistic critics came home to me when I went through the Frankfurt Bookfair in Germany in 1985. The Frankfurt Bookfair is a very depressing thing for any author to experience. It is huge—a city unto itself. Imagine several hundred thousand people in an area that is about the size of a downtown Seattle, and there are just millions of books: more books than anybody could ever hope to read.

To be a writer and to be involved in this form of cultural entropy is really depressing, for it shows you clearly that no civilized consensus is possible, that all there is is a jumble of competing subcultures. You walk through all the pavilions, and the differences between national cultures are quite pronounced. When you walk through the German pavilion, everything you see is about high culture. You see woodcuts of Hegel in a wig, profiles of the Brothers Grimm, and, of course, Goethe. The whole place seems to be a survivalist's intense celebration of the German language and culture in the face of its eclipse by television and the global dominance of vulgar American English. Then you walk through the French pavilion, and everything is very cinematic: there are black-and-white photographs of authors everywhere, and all the authors seem to be gesturing with cigarettes. You see Camus, Jean-Paul Sartre, Simone de Beauvoir. Everything is very stylish and intellectually pretentious. Then you walk into the American pavilion. There are no writers, no authors, no culture—nothing but movie stars. There are books by movie stars and ghost-written biographies of television celebrities. No Melville, no Hawthorne, no Jefferson; just Jane Fonda, Shirley MacLaine, Bill Cosby, and that is it. It was really depressing.

DAVID: And don't forget Donahue's history of Western civilization!

BILL: Yes! Phil Donahue, who is now being presented as a major philosopher explaining the mysteries of human nature.

AUDIENCE PARTICIPANT: How was the Japanese pavilion?

BILL: I remember going through the Chinese and Japanese pavilions, but since I can't read the languages, I don't have any visual images in my mind. One of my books has been translated into Japanese, but I certainly can't tell whether it is a good translation or not.

Because I had a couple of books coming out in German translations, I was more involved with the German pavilion. Hazel Henderson, Brother David Steindl-Rast, Morris Berman, Robert Mueller—there was a whole bunch of us Americans whose books were being presented to the German public for the first time. So the snide and patronizing German critics were trying to find ways to put down all this mushy-headed New Age kitsch from America and keep up their own higher standards of intellectual critique as expressed in such ravishingly enchanting philosophers as Jurgen Habermas. Goldmann Verlag had made the mistake of printing up campaign buttons to launch their new series of New Age books, so the critics were out to beat back the invasion of American barbarians. It was the usual sort of human situation in which both sides were silly—a war in which one side threw pink confetti and the other side threw the dry-as-dust ashes of their philosophical ancestors. We were herded by the publishers into a press conference room where a hundred journalists had come to fight it out. And, of course, as the intellectuals of Europe and Japan always seem to do, they were all smoking in this ghastly, fluorescent-lit room with no windows. It was a gas chamber of the German sixties fighting the American seventies in the eighties of that *bardo*-dead zone called the Bookfair. It was truly depressing.

At any rate, the paradox of our American erasure of history is that we are impoverishing ourselves, not only by losing our high-culture heritage but even by erasing our pop culture. Rock music erases jazz just as much as television erases literature. Part of this erasure seems to occur when a message is extended to a mass audience. Americans are always concerned about "getting the message out," as if there were no appropriate scale to cultural expression. However, when a message is over-extended it becomes more mess than message. We can all sit here because Chinook is small and on a human scale, but if I were Shirley MacLaine and David were J.Z. Knight or Chris Griscom, this place would be a madhouse—like a Madonna concert or a Frankfurt Bookfair.

Half of me thinks that this degradation of the New Age is repulsive; the other half of me thinks it is healthy and necessary. The democratic process of communication is noisy, vulgar, and messy, but that's life. A healthy garden needs a compost pile; and if one considers the teeming and abundant life within a compost pile, then one begins to understand that degradation is actually a signal that the *kairos* of a thing, its "appropriate season of action," is over and that it has to be broken down and digested and turned over. At any rate, these are my reflections on "the imagination of the New Age" as a way of looking back over the sixteen years that David and I have been working together from Findhorn in Scotland to Lindisfarne in New York and Colorado to Chinook here near the border between one country and another, one age and another.

IMAGES OF THE NEW AGE

David Spangler

Bill has given us a marvelous and important critique of the New Age. I want to offer some additional perspectives. In particular, I want to back up a bit and give some personal definitions about the New Age.

I was struck by Bill's remarks about our cultural forgetfulness, about how we erase our past. His experience and observations echo my own. Our Western culture is stuck in something like an "eternal immediacy"—not the "eternal now" of the mystics but a much lesser condition in which the horizons of time collapse around a black hole of impatience. We want it all now. As Suzanne Vale, the lead character in Carrie Fisher's marvelously funny novel *Postcards from the Edge*, puts it, "Instant gratification takes too long."

We see this manifest not only in the kind of historical amnesia mentioned by Bill, but in the variety of ways we sacrifice long-term well-being for short-term goals. Not for our culture the requirement of the Iroquois Nation that any governmental decision must have beneficial consequences for at least seven generations. Can you imagine what our society might be like if Congress had to think through a law's consequences and effects over the next 140 years before it could pass that law? Similarly, American businesses generally think only of short-term goals and the next quarter's bottom line. This, as we all know, is one reason we're falling behind the Japanese corporations, who plan in at least twenty-five year cycles.

Another example of our fixation upon the immediate is the way our culture often wants progress but not change. We want life to get better but not different. We want our culture to grow indefinitely, to become richer, more powerful, and so forth, but we don't want it to move from where it is.

Such concentration upon the short term cannot help but erase our sense of the past. It also erases our sense of the future. We do not really imagine a new future as much as we project our present into our tomorrow. As the Dutch futurist Fred Polak wrote in his seminal book *The Image of the Future*, Western culture does not have an image of the future. Instead it has an image of progress, which is really an extrapolation of the present, a continuity of the familiar.

This is where the idea of the New Age comes in. It restores our imagination of the future by confronting us with images of transformation, not just of change. It asks us to consider a break with the present. It asks us to imagine a future that is not just better but that is different. It asks us to be creative in the face of the unknown, to embrace the unknown. It confronts us with an image of death and discontinuity in order that we may move through it to a deeper understanding of rebirth and continuity. The New Age idea calls us to replace projection with vision. It is prophetic not in the sense of precognitively describing our future but in calling us to live with a transformative vision that opens us to the metamorphic and regenerative qualities of life.

I see the New Age as a call to learning. It is through learning that we break the bonds of amnesic immediacy. We need to learn about our past and to remember our heritage as a race. For this reason, I see the archaic elements in the New Age movement, which Bill referred to as acts of remembrance and recollection, to be important as we stretch our collapsed sense of time and enlarge our awareness of who we are and where we have come from. We also need to learn about the future, which in part, at least, means learning about the imagination—our power to create and shape images—and learning how to embrace the unknown, the unpredicted, and the unexpected.

Probably because of my background as a student of science, I see science as a metaphor for this learning. Bill spoke of science as reform Christianity, as the pursuit of truth. I was very moved by this. In a similar way, I see science as a spiritual path, as a yoga of learning. By science, I mean more than a particular technical content; I mean more than just physics, biology, chemistry, and so forth. I mean an attitude of life, an approach to life that is open to learning, to changing, to being transformed by the truth, just as Bill was describing. I also mean more than a reductionistic, materialistic approach to the universe. That is not science as much as it is a cultural choice about the boundaries within which we will apply science. Particular scientists may be reductionistic and materialistic, but science itself need not be.

Perhaps this is why my mysticism and my sense of science are intertwined. Mysticism, to me, is not a retreat from the world into some metaphysical space. It is the path of embracing the world, of knowing the world ever more deeply and lovingly, of striving to know the world as God would know it, for in that sharing of perception and perspective with the divine, we become one with the divine. So mysticism is for me a path of learning, as is science.

The New Age is an image of transformation. True learning is also transformational, so I equate the two and see the New Age essentially as a metaphor for a state of learning. The emergence of a New Age would be—will be—the emergence of a learning culture—a society, a planet, dedicated to unfoldment through learning.

23

Please note I am not saying "education," for education (read "schooling"), as unfortunately defined by our culture, often has little to do with imagination and transformation and much to do with cultural conformity, obedience, and control. I suppose, then, based on my own definitions, that I see the New Age as a culture of science and mysticism: the age of science as a spiritual path and of spirit as a scientific path. In this definition, both are dedicated to truth, the enhancement of life, and the pursuit of excellence and emergence, all of which are the products of learning.

Now we are getting into my subject matter for the evening, which is to define the New Age or at least to look at various ways in which we imagine it and thereby reimagine our world. Over the years, I have often been asked for a definition of the New Age. In responding, I have become clear that no one definition really suffices to describe an idea that encompasses so many different activities and visions. So I have several definitions or at least images, and here are some of them.

Let's start with what I call the "experiential New Age." I call it this because we are all experiencing the transformation of the status quo. Actually, if you think about it, there has hardly been much status quo for several decades. Only sixty-six years separates the first powered heavier-than-air flight at Kitty Hawk in 1903 from Neil Armstrong's first human step on the moon in 1969. That is well within the lifetime of an average person in Western society today. There are people alive today who were babies or children when the Wright Brothers first flew. Consider all that has happened during their lifetimes: flight, space travel, nuclear power, a world depression, two world wars, the development of radio and movies, Einstein's relativity theory, quantum physics, the invention of television, computers, and the complete redrawing of the world political and economic map. During that time, for example, we saw the birth of state-supported communism with the Russian Revolution, and apparently we are now seeing the death of that system with the effects of *glasnost*, *perestroika*, and the Gorbachev revolution, although the book is still open on how that process will turn out in the Soviet Union itself.

All of us living today are experiencing a time of accelerating change. We are living in a flux of transformation—so much so that it has become a cliché. We tend to overlook just how quickly change is taking place around us. Since the turn of the century, we have already gone through two or three "new ages" in the sense that we have witnessed the emergence of technologies, ideas, social patterns, geopolitical alignments, and the like that could not or would not have been predicted only a few years or even months before they appeared. Those emergences have transformed or are transforming the world as our grandparents and parents knew it, and as we know it even today.

It used to be that significant change of the kind we have witnessed in the past

24

ninety years took several generations to unfold. Thus, in ways unimaginable to most of our ancestors, we are living in a world in which transformation has become one of the dominant characteristics. This is one reason, I believe, that we can talk about a New Age and how a sense of planetary transformation exists in our culture. We can imagine such a transformation as a reality because we have already been experiencing it. Given the amount of change that has already taken place in this century, it is not far-fetched at all to consider that change of an even more radical nature may be probable.

The New Age is often used as a way of talking about the future, as a vision of a new world still to be born. However, we can use the term in another way—a way that is descriptive rather than prophetic. Just as the advent of nuclear power brought us the Atomic Age, and flights into space initiated the Space Age, and the development of computers takes us into the Computer Age or the Information Age, so in this century we have come to experience novelty and change as real and present factors in our lives. Largely driven by science and technology, we have entered a world in which we are increasingly experiencing newness and transformation. For this reason alone, the whole twentieth century deserves to be called the New Age. Thus, the New Age is not something yet to come. It is the character of the time in which we are living! It is the age in which we encounter the new on a yearly or monthly or even weekly basis.

Furthermore, we now anticipate more rapid change and evolution in the various cultures of the world than ever before. It is entirely possible—and most analysts and futurists I have read or talked to agree on this—that the most profound transformations are still unfolding or have yet to appear. In their view, and in mine, the whole twentieth century and the first part of the twenty-first century represent a vast metamorphosis of human consciousness and behavior whose only historical equivalent would be the invention of agriculture and the rise of civilization itself thousands of years ago. We are in the midst of a process of reimagining and reinventing ourselves and our world.

There is another side to the experiential New Age as well. All the change that has taken place and is taking place—all the new ideas, inventions, discoveries, technologies, and so forth—all create problems and opportunities. They all alter some environment in some manner, which means that adaptation becomes important. Consequently, there is a constant activity to initiate structural and institutional alternatives, to develop new strategies for the future, and to create new ways of living and being. There are activities to deal with the problems and rise to the opportunities, as well as activities whose main purpose is adaptation. So when Japanese industry begins to overtake American industry, American companies begin to adapt. They look for ways to change that will make them more competitive in a world market. When new technologies, such as the computer, come on line, individual entrepreneurs and large institutions look for ways to change that will make use of these new tools. As planetary communication and travel continue to mix up the cultures of the world, we look for new ways of engaging different cultures to minimize the threat of conflict. When pollution threatens the very biosphere that sustains us, we look for ways to deal with that problem.

Now, there are also many reactive activities as well: efforts to resist change and maintain at least an illusion of the status quo, like a person trying to prop up a house in the middle of an earthquake. My point is that transformation is not a passive affair; it doesn't just happen to us, leaving us with the choice either to accept it and flow with it or to react to it and resist it. It is also a creative strategy. People seek to meet problems, adapt to new situations, take advantage of opportunities, and generally shape the future to their liking—and hopefully to the well-being of the world as a whole. This creativity could also be called New Age, since the sum total of all these efforts is transformative.

Simply put, thousands of people have a vision of a better world, understand the dangers and problems confronting us, and are seeking to create viable ecological, social, technological, and cultural alternatives that can deal with the problems and embody the vision. These people are in politics, economics, business, the arts, education, science, engineering, the military, and religion, to name a few basic cultural activities, and while most of them would not call themselves New Age, especially not at the moment when that phrase commonly denotes crystals, channels, and chakra-readers, what they are doing is the very essence of New Age. They are experiencing the vision of a New Age and are acting to manifest it. They are also part of the experiential New Age.

Likewise, as new technologies develop, new information is discovered by science, and new experiences and insights are gained through the increased intermingling and intercommunication of different cultural viewpoints, our understanding about ourselves and our world is changing. New worldviews are arising. These worldviews are sometimes called "paradigms," and the New Age is often referred to as a "paradigm shift," or a change in the dominant worldview. This change is generally regarded as one in which the worldview is moving from a materialistic, industrialized perspective to one that is more information and consciousness oriented, more decentralized, more ecological, more holistic. There is nothing prophetic about this shift. It is not something to wait for, something that will happen in our future. In science, in politics, in business, in the arts, in institutional structures, in individual behavior and relationships, it is happening right now. There are currently scores of books out detailing this paradigm change in one way or another. This shift in worldview—and the transformations in the ways we live that it can bring about—is another facet of the experiential New Age. It is a vital, challenging, disturbing, exhilarating part of the dynamic flux we are all experiencing right now.

So, the New Age is the effort of people to be midwives of a better future within the womb of the present, in spite of the character of the past. It is the present, not the past—not our history—that holds the key to the character of the future. The mother may be an addict, but this is no prediction that the baby will also be an addict or that the child cannot grow up to be a healer, a liberator, or a saint. The possibility of transformation is always present. The New Age is the spirit of that possibility.

For me, another definition of the New Age is that it is a spiritual phenomenon. As such, it has three aspects: it represents a fundamental formative force, an essential component of life; it represents an inner condition or state of mind; and it represents a particular spiritual and initiatic impulse inherent in the incarnational processes of Earth.

In the first instance, the New Age may be seen as a symbol of the spirit of renewal and creativity rooted in the ground of all being. It reminds us of the process of emergence and discovery by which the universe unfolds and reveals itself. In this sense, the New Age is not an event but a process. It is not a particular period in history as much as it is the force behind the unfolding of history. It is the spirit of becoming! It is a verb rather than a noun!

Life exists through processes of self-regulation and self-organization that provide and maintain a continuity of being. To avoid stagnation and entropic collapse, life also requires processes of self-transformation and emergence, that is, means by which unfoldment and evolution may take place. In other words, life is an open-ended system, not a closed one. At the boundary of that-which-is, a transformative force is actively exploring and giving birth to new and perhaps unexpected and unpredictable manifestations of being. The New Age is an expression of the spirit of that transformative force.

That force is not separate from us. It lives within us, and we may give expression to it. We may become one with it and be agents of emergence. When we forget that this is so, we may identify solely with those forces that maintain the status quo. Then, while changes may occur, no fundamental renewal takes place; there is no emergence to liberate us from the dangers of stagnation. The New Age as an image challenges this stagnation. It challenges the tyranny of the familiar and reminds us of the transformative, creative, renewing force within us. It can empower us to take steps so that we may once more be one with that force.

The New Age idea reminds us of the presence of change and the possibilities of transformation in our lives and in our world. It reminds us that such possibilities are natural, not to be feared, and are part of the dynamic process of life itself. Therefore, when we attune deeply to the idea of the New Age, we are really attuning to the transforming, renewing, spiritual core at the center of life. Life in all its power and creativity is continually expressing a New Age. Whatever enables us to experience life more abundantly is New Age. Whatever enables us to empower the kind of emergence that further enhances the regenerative, holistic, compassionate, creative, and revelatory capacities of life is New Age.

The second aspect of the New Age, when seen from a spiritual perspective, is that it is a state of mind. By this I do not mean a particular set of beliefs or even attitudes. It is a way of looking at the world, an inner architecture that structures how we process our information about the world and how we set up our relationships with others in the world. I would like to talk about this at greater length later this weekend. For now, I will simply say that it is a perspective like "beginner's mind" in Zen, the kind of perspective that allows us to see the world always as if for the first time, aware of its possibilities and vibrancy. Beginner's mind does not deny memory or familiarity, but it does not project that memory or familiarity inappropriately upon the present. New Age mind also includes compassion, by which I do not mean a sense of feeling sorry for others but the ability to empathetically feel *with* them and *be* with them in both sorrow and joy. It includes a sense of the interconnections and synergies between us, a sense of the wholeness of the world. It is a mind open to creative possibilities, a mind that is both empowered and empowering in its capacity to support both emergence and the appropriate status quo. It is a mind that is sensitive to and aligned with the spirit of emergence, the fundamental forces of renewal and creativity of which I have just spoken.

I shall have more to say about New Age mind later. For now, let me move on to the third aspect we encounter when we consider the New Age as a spiritual or inner phenomenon. This is the New Age as a specific spiritual force acting upon humanity and the world. This spiritual force acts upon us from two distinct sources, both of which reflect the deeper presence and influence of the sacred. One of these sources exists within the collective psyche of humanity. I call it the myth or archetype of the sacred world. The second source is within the evolving life of the planetary spirit itself.

The myth of the sacred world is an image of a set of relationships between God (or Spirit), Humanity (or Civilization), and the Earth (or Nature) that are symbiotic, communal, synergetic, empowering, and co-creative. It is an image of a condition where harmony reigns, where the interconnectedness of life is understood and wisely acted upon, and where the well-being and potentialities of each of life's expressions are nourished and supported.

This image of a sacred world, it seems to me, has been a driving force behind the development of civilization. However imperfect its understanding, its vision, or its actions may have been, each society in history has attempted to bring some aspect of this sacred world into being. Whether the specific vision has been called Shambhala or the New Jerusalem, Utopia or the American Dream, capitalism or communism, behind these lesser images lies this archetype of a planetary condition in which the planet-soul itself achieves a deep level of integration and synthesis, allowing a fuller incarnation and sharing of its life and potentialities.

This archetype transcends any particular historical expression of its possibilities. Its origins may well lie in a deep biological memory of the formation of the eukaryotic cell, which is a peaceable kingdom of interacting, symbiotic organelles creating a place of life and emergence. Such a memory, and the mythic or archetypal images it generates, can be ignored or distorted as we try to manifest it, but it cannot be killed. In many ways, the images and activities that coalesce around the New Age idea are all related to this greater image of the sacred world and represent a specific modern alignment with its possibilities and an attempt to manifest it.

The second source from which the spiritual force acts upon us emerges from the processes of planetary incarnation itself. I see the planet as a living being that possesses an evolving spirit. From an inner perspective, the New Age represents the emergence of another stage in that evolution. These stages are millennia long; the entry into a new one is a process that can last for hundreds of years. However, at certain moments in this process, special formative and transformative forces can be brought to bear that encapsulate, heighten, and advance the process as a whole. That is what is happening now and into the next century.

These formative forces emerge from the soul of the planet itself as well as from sources outside the pattern of specific planetary evolution. They are mediated and directed by purposeful entities whom we might call angels or archangels, along with other beings both human and nonhuman who work out the specific application and incarnation of these forces. Thus, there are spiritually activated and directed currents of will and creativity with which we may align and that impact directly and indirectly on human affairs. The presence of these currents and the transformative nature of their interaction with ourselves and our world is one of the factors bringing a New Age into being.

My final image of the New Age is that it is imaginary. By "imaginary" I do not mean "unreal," of course. I mean that the New Age is an image of the future—one that we hope will align us with the deeper spirit and empower us to create a new world.

Before going into this in more detail, I will offer a word of warning. I view an image as a tool. As long as the New Age as an image successfully mediates between spirit and Earth, as long as it does not impede the flow of life's creativity and empowerment, then it is useful and important. But when it becomes an obstacle— when the image becomes more important than either the world or the spirit behind it—then it ceases to be New Age. It loses its connections either to the actual experiences of change going on in our world or to the spiritual possibilities and forces that coincide and, in many cases, I believe, direct that change. Over the past decade, I have heard a number of folks say that the New Age has died. What actually dies is a particular image's capacity to reflect and mediate between the experiential and spiritual components of the transformations going on in our world. It is a death of the imagination.

The imaginary landscape of the New Age generally is divided into two regions. One focuses upon events, opportunities, challenges, and processes within the world at large, while the other focuses upon inner changes and esoteric issues. So, for example, the former sees the New Age as representing the cutting edge of human scientific, technological, spiritual, and social development. I include within this region of the New Age landscape such things as space travel, computers, chaos theory, the new physics, the convergence of cultures and emergence of a planetary sensibility, the idea of Gaia and the deepening of our concern for the Earth, alternative energy technologies, changes in political theory and practice such as experiments in decentralization and nonadversarial politics, changes in how business institutions are structured and operated, and transformations in medical and therapeutic techniques and modalities.

The second region of the New Age landscape includes psychic investigations and studies; the quest for new religious experiences, including investigations into postmortem and past-life memories; the resurgence of interest in occultism and esotericism; transpersonal psychologies; and the whole slew of workshops and seminars about channeling, UFOs, crystals, and the like. At a deeper level, this region may also include research into and work with the planetary formative forces that I spoke of earlier, though such work is open to distortion and glamour when improperly approached.

There was a time during the seventies when it looked like the dominant image of the New Age might be derived from the first region. However, with the media hoopla around channeling and psychic phenomena over the past few years, it now appears that the New Age is being defined by its inwardly oriented elements—and particularly by the most sensational and bizarre of these.

The effect of this, of course, given the suspicion and silliness that seem to go along with anything of a psychic or esoteric nature, is that people who were comfortable with the term *New Age* are now feeling put off by it. Now to identify oneself or one's work as being New Age is to risk being categorized with activities and ideas that have little spiritual, intellectual, or social credibility. To identify a book as being in some manner about the New Age, no matter how scholarly or insightful its content may be, is to consign it in many bookstores to sharing shelf space with works on how to develop your cat's occult powers or how to use crystal magic to repair your secondhand car. Rather than an image of hope and inspiration, this version of the New Age becomes one of ridicule and irrelevancy.

I am reminded of an event that took place a year or so ago. I was awakened at 6 a.m. one day by a phone call from a *Time* magazine reporter who had forgotten about the three-hour time difference between New York and Seattle. "What is the New Age?" she asked. I sleepily rattled off my usual philosophical answer, to which she replied, "Well, that's very interesting, but what about crystals? Isn't it true that all New Agers believe in and use crystals for various purposes?" "No," I replied, "*I* don't use them." "Well, in that case," she said, "I can't use you. My editor is quite clear that the New Age is about crystals, and that's what I need to write about." She was nice about it, but I knew a rejection when I heard one. Whatever New Age I represented, it wasn't the one that *Time* magazine was interested in.

Many colleagues of mine, including Bill here, now have difficulty with the image of the New Age and don't want anything to do with it. Whereas ten years ago they might comfortably have called their work New Age, in that it was directed at the serious and informed transformation of our culture toward a better world, to be called New Age today is the kiss of death intellectually, academically, and professionally—unless, of course, you are selling something to a New Age market. The image of the New Age may well have died as a useful tool of the imagination for anyone seriously attempting to work with civilizational change and betterment.

This would be unfortunate, for the image has many good connotations, as we have seen, and is quite a useful one. There *are* deep patterns and cycles of unfoldment and transformation that operate within our world and within our lives. The image of the New Age relates to those patterns and calls them forth into our imagination and awareness. It enlarges our perspective in ways that other images of the future do not. I have never found another term that can substitute for it in a satisfactory way.

However, there is another side to all this. The fact that many people are interested in channeling, psychic phenomena, new meaning in their lives, or an experience of the transcendent is not itself a bad thing. If anything, it is an indictment of our culture in both its secular and religious aspects that it has failed to provide for and nourish the mythic and spiritual needs of its citizens. Within many New Age activities lies a genuine quest for new spiritual meaning and for new ways of being in the world.

If the strength and appropriateness of a particular image of the New Age lies in its capacity to blend the experiential and spiritual components of the transformational process, then each of these regions alone has flaws. Often, the worldly side of the New Age does not seriously address the spiritual needs of individuals, while the inner-directed, often psychically oriented, aspect of New Age thought and activity fails to connect with real planetary issues and needs. In fact, as in the case of the so-called New Age teaching that we each create and are only responsible for our own reality, sometimes there is a lack of compassion and any sense of involvement in the sufferings and needs of the world at large. It is the seeming self-involvement, the narcissism, of some interiorly directed New Age elements that seems most irresponsible and open to criticism by an intelligent public. However, these elements in no way represent the whole sensibility or thrust of those who seek new inner direction and perspective under the rubric of New Age explorations.

The July/August 1988 issue of *Yoga Journal* contains a dialogue of sorts between myself and Ken Wilber. Ken wrote a critique of the New Age, basically saying that it is an expression of baby-boomer narcissism. There is no question that there is an aspect of what is now being called New Age that does manifest baby-boomer narcissism. It does so precisely because it has been isolated as a marketing strategy designed to appeal to a consumer attitude that is narcissistic and wants it all. Ken, in his usual erudite way, has great fun ripping that image to shreds, and I applaud his effort. But is his analysis of the New Age generally valid? I think not. In my thirty or more years of experience in dealing with people who are interested in New Age thought, there have been very few of them who would fit Ken's description of narcissistic baby-boomers. By far and away, the majority of the people whom I have known are individuals who are experiencing a heartfelt need to give birth to something in themselves, without always knowing what that might be. They are looking for something that will restore for them a sense of power, a sense of worth in themselves, and an ability to make a meaningful difference in the world. Most of them are motivated by both personal and selfless motives. They may become involved with psychic exploration, but less as an end in itself and more as a pathway toward the transcendent—toward filling an empty place in themselves that our modern culture has forgotten how to fill.

Ken suggests that the New Agers are wrong in supposing that we are on the brink of a spiritual transformation—that at best our culture is learning how to truly deal with the realm of the mind and the intellect. He has a point there, particularly when he states that the new paradigms represent changes of mind rather than new expressions of spirit. Yet in drawing on a rather linear cosmology for spiritual development, I feel he misses a larger point. We may or may not be experiencing a collective or planetary spiritual transformation, but at the individual level it is precisely a spiritual transformation that is the goal. It is a reclaiming of a lost spiritual and mythic dimension, and it is a breakthrough into a new relationship with spirit. This is what I have found most motivates people I have known within the New Age movement over the years: the spiritual quest. It may have its narcissistic and silly stages; it may take on selfish forms for some people; but on the whole it is a reaching out for, an invocation of, a genuine spiritual dimension. It is a quest for a new relationship with the sacred and an accompanying sense of empowerment and value— a sense that now I can make a meaningful contribution in service to my world.

My main point is not that the New Age is about a spiritual transformation rather than a mental or physical one. Reality is not that neatly divided for me into levels and planes—with clear demarcations as to where the earthly ends and the spiritual begins. What is important to me in considering the New Age as an evocative, inspiring, and empowering concept is whether a particular image of the New Age successfully enables us to blend the spiritual and worldly aspects of our lives and see them as one. Can we translate our spiritual alignments and values into incarnational strategies and connections? Can we align our worldly activities with a higher purpose and make them transparent to the light of a greater wholeness? I propose simply that when any image of a New Age prevents us from doing that, then the spirit of the New Age dies within that image.

DISCUSSION 1

Entry into the New Age,
Illusion, Delusion,
and Paranoia

AUDIENCE PARTICIPANT: Bill told us something about his history with the New Age idea, David. I'm curious about your own. I've read in a couple of places that you are the one who initiated the New Age movement, but I gather you don't agree with that. How did you and the New Age get together?

DAVID: I first heard about the New Age in the late fifties when my parents introduced me to a friend of theirs who was a trance channel. The entity she channeled spoke quite a bit about the coming of a New Age. Not long after, I discovered other channels and psychics who were saying or channeling the same message.

I must say that at that time I paid less attention to the idea of a New Age than to the whole phenomenon of channeling and psychic contact with other levels. I had already had several years of experiencing my own contact with the inner, or spiritual, worlds—a contact that began for me when I was very young and continued throughout my childhood and adolescence. I thought everyone had this inner sensing, and since it seemed perfectly natural to me, I never thought much about it. Meeting these psychics taught me that this was not a usual phenomenon and made me look at my own contacts in a new way. This led to a more deliberate practice of developing my inner awareness, which I have never thought to be a psychic awareness but more an intuitive and mystical one.

I began my career as a lecturer and teacher in 1964, when I moved from Phoenix, Arizona, to Los Angeles. Then a year later, I moved to the San Francisco Bay area, where my work expanded and developed. My interests were not so much in the New Age as in how we might develop a co-creative relationship with the spiritual dimensions. I was interested in the integration of the personal and transpersonal aspects of ourselves. The New Age, if I mentioned it at all, was usually a peripheral topic.

This changed when I went to the spiritual community of Findhorn in northern Scotland, which identified itself as a New Age community. Until I arrived, its garden had been the primary focus of attention and activity. This changed about the same time I arrived. I came in 1970 as part of a wave of new members. Over a period of six months, this wave swelled the ranks of the community from 15 people to 45 people and then, six months later, to 150 people. This population explosion brought people of diverse talents: artists, musicians, actors, gardeners, craftspersons, teachers, and many unskilled but enthusiastic young people. To meet these new folks' need to understand what Findhorn was all about, an educational program was created that initially consisted of my giving weekly lectures on spiritual philosophy, esoterics, and especially the New Age and Findhorn's role in "midwifing" the emergence of a new culture.

Most of these lectures were collected, edited, and published by Findhorn during the seventies as a series of books. One or two, including *Revelation: The Birth of a New Age*, which I had written while still living in the community, even came out before I returned to the United States in 1973. Consequently, when I did come home and began lecturing and teaching in the States again, the two topics most groups wanted to hear about were the creation of intentional communities and the birth of the New Age. In this manner, I became fully identified with and part of the New Age movement in the seventies and early eighties and was even described at times as the one who had created the whole idea of the New Age! In that strange ahistorical immediacy that many Americans seem to live in, I had the distinction of erasing everyone else who had ever thought about or taught about a New Age, all the way back to Neolithic times. Not bad for a Midwest mystic from Ohio! Of course, as far as envisioning a New Age goes, I am really a David-come-lately. The idea itself is at least two thousand years old, while I've only been talking about it for thirty years or so.

AUDIENCE PARTICIPANT: You mean the idea of the Age of Aquarius is two thousand years old?

DAVID: Well, astrology is well over two thousand years old, and the Age of Aquarius is one of the traditional twelve ages that make up the zodiacal great year. However, I don't necessarily identify the New Age with the Age of Aquarius. Each of the zodiacal ages is a "new age" to the one that preceded it. When I think of the New Age, I am thinking of a deeper mythic image: the capacity of both an individual and a culture to transform, to experience metanoia—or a radical change of mind. It is the capacity to shift to a new level of perception and action. It is the emergence of a new life. Such a shift may be accompanied by other phenomena, such as Earth changes or social changes, and these secondary changes might be seen as the New Age. The real New Age, though, is an inner reorganization allowing a greater wholeness to manifest in our world. It is an inner phenomenon that need not have a lot of dramatic, sensational outer effects.

For example, you might experience an inner shift of perception. Let's say you have an experience that convinces you of life beyond death, so that the fear of death leaves you. The fact that you no longer have this fear may not be all that apparent to people observing you from the outside. You still look like yourself, and you may still do many, if not all, of the same things you were doing before your experience—but you are not the same person. Energy that was tied up in fear is now freed and available to be used. You feel lighter. A new spirit flows through your life and activities. Changes do happen as a consequence, but they are graceful. You may become less pressured, kinder, gentler.

Dramatic outer change can accompany the shift into a New Age, but the New Age is not defined by such change. As I define it, the New Age is that inner place where we touch our own boundaries and accept transformation into our lives as a creative, natural, and organic part of living. It is the place of our co-creativity and our deepening in attunement to a larger wholeness. The Age of Aquarius may also be a New Age as I am defining it, and certainly the cyclical change Aquarius represents is one of the contributing factors to the potentiality of transformation and the birth of a new consciousness in our time, but the New Age transcends the Age of Aquarius. They are not, in my mind, synonymous terms.

Actually, a study of European religious and social movements over the past fifteen hundred years will show you just how often the New Age has been spoken of and how many New Age movements there have been in our past. I might recommend a couple of books for those interested in further investigation. One is *The Pursuit of the Millennium* by Norman Cohn, and the other is *Disaster and the Millennium* by Michael Barkun. I might also suggest *The Apocalyptic Vision in America* by Lois Zamora. The idea of an emerging New Age is not unique to our generation, even though it may have new power for us because of the unique planetary circumstances in which we find ourselves.

AUDIENCE PARTICIPANT: I gather you haven't been talking about the New Age much lately, either.

DAVID: That's right. I lectured on the New Age for ten years after leaving Findhorn, but by 1983 I had come to a point, much like Bill, where I felt a need to move away and reconsider the whole idea from a distance. There were a number of reasons for this. Perhaps most important personally was that my wife and I were starting a family, and I did not want to be on the road lecturing for two weeks out of every month. I wanted to devote more time to being a parent. Secondly, I simply needed time away from the public to reflect and think and return to my own inner well for new insights.

I had also discovered that there was a new wave of audiences coming forward. The New Age they wanted to hear about was one filled with psychic phenomena and the glamour of crystals, channels, and ascended masters, much like the audiences I first started lecturing for in 1964. There is certainly nothing wrong with this; we all start somewhere. But I had already been through that cycle, and I didn't feel the energy to do it again. To address the needs of those who, like me, had also been through all that and were looking for something more, something deeper and more relevant to their lives, I felt I needed to take time to research and deepen my own understanding of our planetary spiritual journey.

BILL: I agree with you, David, in your disagreement with Ken Wilber's analysis of baby-boomer narcissism. Your sociology of knowledge analysis of these religious groups corresponds to my own experience as a poor kid in Los Angeles, going to occult meeting after occult meeting in 1953 and 1954. These folks were the dispossessed, the lower middle class; this was not your affluent yuppie class with Gucci loafers—that came later in this generation with Wall Street brokers who go to psychics to help them channel their portfolios. That is new. [Laughter.] Yes, that literally happened! That does go on in New York.

I was in Manhattan during the stock market crash of 1987. There were a few articles in the *New York Times* before the crash about various stockbrokers consulting channels and astrologers and people like that. However, the occultists and psychics from thirty or forty years ago were very much the powerless. They were not the people from the country clubs or from Harvard or other Ivy League schools. They were people who felt afflicted and imprisoned in history, and they were looking to the flying saucers for deliverance into another space.

In their paranoid literalness, these people expressed both a failure of imagination and an inadequate data base. Paranoia is a funny kind of concreteness, because on the one hand the intuition is correct, but on the other hand the intuition doesn't have enough knowledge to take the insight from the higher dimensions and actually render it into the effective knowledge of an incarnation.

I remember once talking to a teenage kid who came out to Lindisfarne in Southampton fourteen years ago. This teenager felt that he had the messianic role in life to teach people how to have *the* proper bowel movement. I had about an hour and a half discussion with him, for when a paranoid goes into monologue, he really goes at it! If you think I'm bad, you should hear one of these! It is nonstop for two or three hours. But the data base is very narrow—the whole thing is very repetitive—its loops spin over and around very quickly. There is a poetry to the narrative, however, if one understands it symbolically as a metaphorical diagnosis of our situation. The central problem of our time is indeed that we don't know what to do with our shit! Here was a sixteen-year-old kid who was talking about a world of leaking nuclear reactors and dioxin spills in Seveso or Bhopal. He was picking up on it all.

I remember when David first came to speak at Lindisfarne in Manhattan when we were on the corner of Sixth Avenue and Twentieth Street. He was picketed outside by a local Greenwich Village cult. This cult really resented the fact that we had been given four buildings in downtown Manhattan. They had been running their little business in Greenwich Village for years and nobody had given them any buildings. It was a cult in which everybody had to sleep with the leader, and everybody had to be absolutely open and transparent to the leader and to each other; you were not allowed to have any secrets. It was an implosive intentional community in the most caricatured form.

They came and picketed David because they didn't like the idea that there was this new cult, Lindisfarne, that had hit town and moved in on their own neighborhood. And here was this guru, David Spangler, this New Age prophetic figure, moving into their turf. They really locked onto David with all kinds of projections of rage and resentment and hatred. When I look back on that group and think of everything I have seen around the world concerning the phenomenology of communities and the explosion of all these groups in California and everywhere around the world, I can see in that group a kind of paranoid caricature of the worst qualities of implosive intentional community and the worst qualities of sexual predatoriness.

At any rate, paranoia is a kind of tragedy of failed connections; there is sensitivity to the other dimensions, but there is no actual empowerment beyond the three ordinary dimensions. There is not enough knowledge; there is not a broad enough data base; there is not enough hard work; there is not enough common sense or ego strength and conviction. Therefore, all that sensitivity ends up having a destructive, implosive, and flattening effect in which the individual becomes crazy and hysterical. At the same time that there is not enough data, there is not enough imaginative suppleness, humor, or self-irony to understand how not to take these things literally. Everything is concretized, and the category mistake is made over and over and over again.

If we look at history and try to imagine how people a thousand years from now will talk about what is going on in our time period, we can imagine that these people will probably see all kinds of things that are happening right now that we actually don't see reported in our newspapers. But the paranoids are reporting on some of these things, in the sense that they are giving us political cartoons of the unreported news. If they had more knowledge, more imagination, and more of a relaxed sense of humor, they would not have to go crazy.

This quality of peripheral vision is, of course, not restricted to paranoia. When it was my turn in 1976 to be picketed at Lindisfarne in Manhattan by this group, I was giving a lecture on "The Future of Knowledge and the Return of Hieroglyphic Thinking."[14] At that time, I didn't know about Smale; I didn't know about Lorenz; I didn't know about strange attractors; I didn't know anything about chaos dynamics. I wasn't making prophecies—I was just picking up on what was actually going on in the mathematics of the seventies that I wouldn't learn about until the eighties. I think that is characteristic of how imagination can be sensitive and can be the porous membrane at the end of our three-dimensional world. In order to make the intuition or hunch real, however, there has to be a considerable amount of knowledge and data and hard work carried on with a sense of humor and compassion for others who don't agree with you. These are all things that paranoids simply are not able or willing to do. That is why they explode, and things become tragically insane and messy.

AUDIENCE PARTICIPANT: Bill, you were talking about the dispossessed in the 1950s, people in the lower middle class who felt they had no power and so on, and you said that of course they aren't the yuppies with the Gucci shoes. I want to say that maybe they are not so far apart. The yuppies feel just as powerless to know where to go forward in the instability of what we are seeing on our cultural horizon. I think they are not finding, perhaps, a lack of basic survival needs, but I think they are facing a lack of vision.

BILL: I think anybody who is alive in our time has to be a little scared of the enormity of the global problems we are confronting. You can read this week about the death of the oceans in *Time* magazine, or watch the daily news and try to deal with all that stuff coming in. What I find with the yuppie is a kind of parallelism with the punks. The punk working-class thing in England and the upper-middle-class affluent thing in New York are two sides of the same coin: both are saying, "It's all coming down, so I am going to get mine while the getting is good." It is a gesture of despair and fear. It is a response of fear and not a response of confidence or a sense of adequacy. With the lower middle class, I found a different kind of sociology—one of class resentment, class warfare, and a feeling of hate.

I noticed this hatred when I set up Lindisfarne in Colorado, for we began to receive a lot of hate mail from the fundamentalists, the Aryan Nation, and the Posse Comitatus—you have some of these people here on Whidbey Island. A lot of these paramilitary groups were preparing for the end of the world and practically had bazookas in the back of their pickup trucks. Basically, they did not like, in a class sense, people coming from Manhattan and moving in on their corner of the world. It didn't seem to matter who we were as individuals—but if we were educated and we were people from New York, we were just hated as a class. It was almost like contact dermatitis, an allergic reaction, and it had little to do with personalities. That seems to me more what was going on in the 1950s.

The flying saucer contactee movement was coming from the lower middle class, from those who were not highly educated. Scientology doesn't attract scientists; it attracts those who have a superstitious, almost peasant's worship for the glamour and power of science and want to take some of that to themselves. For example, it is the machinist who would like to work in a scientific laboratory instead of a car garage and has visions of a larger horizon for himself—who is attracted to L. Ron Hubbard; that kind of person *is* L. Ron Hubbard.

There is a deep longing for connection to a larger world of fantasy. Television, actually, when it came to dominate our culture in the late fifties, took up a lot of that lower-class longing for connection and institutionalized it in the new electronic society. The UFO cults were replaced by "Space Patrol" in the fifties and then "Star Trek" in the sixties. Television became an electronic version of Plato's cave—images on the wall that kept people in line and in place. Television took all that yearning for connection to other dimensions and locked people into a collective illusion. It worked because the economy was expanding into post-industrial society with its subdivisions, freeways, shopping malls, and credit cards.

When you have damaged economies in recession, then you tend to get a lot of things such as the Ku Klux Klan after the Civil War or the Posse Comitatus during the Carter stagflation. Reagan deflected a lot of this by lowering interest rates, playing to the religious fundamentalists, and offering "Dallas" as the TV saga of the poor white trash getting their own Wall Street in Texas. He deflected the class hatred by giving the poor white trash a sense of their own empowerment; he did for the Moral Majority what Kennedy had done for the intelligentsia—he gave them a sense that it's OK now to be poor white trash (as long as you're rich) or it's OK now to be intellectual (as long as you're from Harvard). Reagan performed the collective unconscious for the American public and created this new kind of electronic politics, this consensual delusion of shared fantasies that we call an election.

AUDIENCE PARTICIPANT: What strikes me is my own personal process. In 1983, I left a spiritual community that I had managed for eight years. I left and let go of all the glamour, the excitement, the magic, and began to raise my family very quietly. I was struggling to endure, not falling back to grab onto the next spiritual community that I thought might be interesting with its trendy process of zazen, or crystals, or swimming with dolphins, or whatever. I feel now as if I am just hovering, just having to endure the negative input of the death of the oceans—the kind of feeling that the world is falling apart and I am aching for some refuge. I have become very conscious of living and enduring at this edge. This edge is an important area, I think, to explore in a process that helps people.

BILL: I think that the sense of endurance is important. For me, 1983 was more like a death experience in that this period was also the explosion of the San Francisco Zen Center. During the 1970s, I think, with the San Francisco Zen Center and Lindisfarne in New York, we were really "bicoastal"—we were truly cooperating and trying to bring forth the entire national alternative movement. So, I was really depressed by the explosion of the San Fransisco Zen Center, and I felt that it was really a great loss for American Buddhism and the whole national alternative movement that had been spotlighted through Governor Jerry Brown. My own personal experience was one of simply meditating and feeling a complete experience of death—of dying to the whole New Age, to the school of sacred geometry, to the thoughtform of "Lindisfarne," to the thoughtform of the mystery school, and to all the archaic esoterism that I had been energizing.

Then I left Colorado and wrote the science fiction novel *Islands out of Time*, with its deconstruction of sacred geometry and the male chauvinist mystery school—the boys'-club kind of sacred architecture. At this time, in 1983, the New Age movement was crystallizing, literally, into crystals. What began to be much more alive for me were *fractals* and not crystals, the whole scientific imagination of chaos dynamics, Ralph Abraham's work and the Santa Cruz Collective, as well as the biology of self-organizing systems with Maturana and Varela. I moved from setting up the School of Sacred Architecture in Crestone to setting up the Program for Biology, Cognition, and Ethics at the Cathedral of Saint John the Divine in New York City. This shift was a real metanoia that required coming to terms with almost the mirror opposite of medieval architecture in things like artificial intelligence, color vision, and immunology through Varela's research lab in Paris. All of that for me was a change of mentality, so in *Pacific Shift* and *Imaginary Landscape*, when I talk about the four mathematical mentalities of Western civilization—the arithmetic, the geometric, the dynamic, and the morphological—I am also chronicling my own intellectual shift in mathematical mentalities.

I think it is very hard to change mentalities without some kind of death experience. Most people would rather literally die. Sometimes in our life, when we come to one of these crises, if we don't have the strength to endure our spiritual death—as St. Paul said, "I die daily"—we will precipitate a heart attack or some other crisis and just quit. If we do make the change from one mentality to another, our friends often will regard us as having betrayed the movement, so we die to the world of our old friends and relationships. The language at Findhorn was: "You have fallen into the dark powers!" These feelings of change as betrayal are characteristic of ideological movements; it happened in the leftist movements in the thirties, when people splintered into many subgroups. A change of mentalities is always felt to be very threatening to one's old colleagues, and if they cannot effect the same metanoia, they will become fixed and rigid and see one as a traitor to the common cause.

AUDIENCE PARTICIPANT: I think that is common in most of the New Age movement. The exit doors are not very well marked. No one is allowed to exit.

DAVID: When one embarks upon a spiritual path or an initiatic path, one has to expect some form of death experience. The whole purpose of that path is described by words like metanoia, metamorphosis, unfoldment, emergence, and transformation. Each of these involves a movement from one state to another. This movement need not be thought of as death, however. It can be a stepping from one pattern of life to another. Sometimes the step is a small one and the new pattern doesn't seem that much different. Sometimes the step is a large one, and we know that our world has shifted and will never be the same again. There are endings and beginnings, yet underneath it all there is a continuity, a ground of being.

I think we all go through death experiences of the kind Bill is talking about. When I was in college, I was very successful as a student. I had one year to go before gaining my bachelor of science degree, and I was in the top 2 or 3 percent of my class scholastically. I was clearly intending to have a career in molecular biology and genetics, and, as a start, I was working in one of the biological labs on campus, helping a professor who was doing research on bacterial DNA. Then, almost overnight, it was like something inside me switched off. Everything I was doing and working for lost its meaning; I couldn't connect with it. I would sit in class unable to assimilate the material being presented; lectures that had been perfectly clear to me only weeks earlier now seemed like alien messages from another world. I was engulfed in an emptiness.

Naturally, I was very concerned, but in some deep part of myself, I knew that whatever was happening was right, so I waited. I left school, intending to go back. As my intellectual life came to a halt, however, my intuitive, inner life began to flower. I found myself in increasing contact with deeper and deeper levels of my own being. To pursue that contact, though, I had to give up my plans to be a research scientist. I needed to look in some other directions. The result was that I entered upon the life's work that I now follow as a spiritual philosopher and teacher.

Looking back, I see that the essential thread of my life was not broken. What motivated me toward genetics was a desire to understand and work with the formative forces underlying incarnation. I was simply interpreting that desire too materialistically. In the change I went through, I didn't really lose anything, though it seemed so at the time. While retaining all of my interest in science, I followed my passion into dealing with a different level of the same issues. Because of my equally strong and lifelong interest in theology and all things spiritual, the path I took actually fits me better than working in a laboratory would have. However, had I not had that experience of dying to everything that had had meaning to me, I probably would not have made the change.

A very similar experience happened five years later when I went through another time of feeling myself emptying out and dying to what I had been doing. This was after I had been lecturing and teaching about the New Age and spiritual development for some five years. Not only did it all suddenly seem unimportant and meaningless, but, on the outer plane, people lost interest in my classes. In a matter of a month, I went from teaching three or four full classes a week to doing nothing. I also developed a type of viral laryngitis that made talking painful—a condition that lasted for several months. Sometimes I have to be hit over the head with a brick! However, I got the message and went into retreat for a year.

When I came out of that time, I did so with a new and deeper vision of the New Age, a new sense of inner alignment, and a flow of inner energy and direction that led me directly to Findhorn and the beginning of a new cycle of work. Again, had I not gone through a time of death and inner restructuring, I probably would not have gone to Findhorn or responded to the opportunities it presented. Furthermore, the work I have done since Findhorn has not been different in essence from what I had been doing before I went to that community, but it has been deeper in quality. As I said, there are endings and beginnings, but underneath it all there is a continuity.

In recent years, I've gotten smarter about the process. In 1983, I felt myself approaching the end of a cycle of work and the beginning of another. This time I didn't wait for something to happen. I started to pull out of the lecture circuit and began turning inward. I initiated and encouraged the emptying out process by giving attention to inner reexamination and restructuring. It has been a longer process than before, as I have only recently felt myself coming out of it, but in many ways it has been smoother, and certainly much more conscious, than similar transition periods in the past.

The New Age is this process of moving, ending, and beginning writ large. It is not an image of a specific future, such as the image many folks have for the Age of Aquarius. The New Age is more than that, or deeper than that. It is an image of the process by which futures emerge. It is the image of stepping from one pattern to another. It is an image that can lead us to consider this process more consciously and to make our steps with mindfulness. We can be participants in the process rather than feel like its victims. In this sense, the New Age is not optional. It describes a process that is always taking place, an edge we must always encounter. It need not be interpreted as a death, though, and the images of transformation and apocalypse that may come in the wake of the imagination of a New Age may not be literal. As Bill is saying, we must guard against misplaced concreteness. We must also remember that there is continuity even in the midst of discontinuity and change.

If the New Age idea has any value, it may be that, by making us consider the notions of transformation, death, and emergence, we may come to a deeper appreciation and experience of life and its inherent creativity. One of the ancient axioms of the initiatic path is that until we face and accept death, so that we no longer fear it, we cannot truly begin to live. We cannot have life more abundantly, as Jesus put it. The idea of the New Age brings us face to face with our edges—not so much in anticipation that we will change as in anticipating that we will live more fully, and not so much that we will transform as that we will incarnate more deeply. It is truly an initiatic image.

BILL: My mistake was the paranoid one of taking the experience of death in meditation literally: I thought I was dying. I had this profound experience while meditating in the tower at Lindisfarne in Colorado, and it felt as if I were dying. I had had cancer as a kid, so when I noticed some new lumps, I thought, "It has come back; this is the end, and there is no way I am going to accept chemotherapy. " In classic paranoid fashion I translated everything literally and did not have the imaginative suppleness to realize that all these lumps were from bumps and bruises from my Colorado outdoor life with chainsaws and from clearing out deadwood and rocks. When you get a bruise, you can later get some fatty lipoma under your skin. These lumps were therefore all from my cowboy outdoor life instead of my intellectual lifestyle—one to which I am more suited. Oftentimes in life when these transformative experiences come, we interpret them literally and miss the actual complexity of it. But, not realizing this at the time, I consulted the I Ching, and it said, "The hour of death is at hand; the life work is over." And I said, "OK, here we go."

I find that my own ignorance is something that is widely shared. This category mistake is characteristically human, but it still gets us into big trouble. It is like a comic strip of the New Age movement, such as Gary Trudeau's "Doonesbury." He is so funny with his Hunk Rah and the Moronic Convergence. God bless him!

I agree with David that there are critical times in life when these death experiences come, and our resistance to them can precipitate heart attacks and diseases. We need to learn to see them as a metanoia and have the courage to accept change, even if it sometimes means letting go of our friends and our colleagues. In a sense, we are dying to a certain neighborhood or world that we have known, and that is always a difficult experience of loss.

IMAGINATION AND THE NEW AGE

David Spangler

I want to continue our discussion from last night about the relationship between the New Age and imagination. Yesterday I said there are three general ways of encountering the New Age. One of these is through actually experiencing the many transformations going on in our world throughout this century and particularly right now. Another is through deep levels of spiritual intuition, insight, and attunement as we encounter the movement and activity of metaphysical forces at work in the world. The third is through our imaginations.

I want to stress that I am using *imagination* here to mean the realm of imagery and the capacity to form images, rather than its more common sense as an exercise in unreality. We sometimes apologize for the act of imagination, believing it to have little place in the hard, practical, realistic, everyday world. We like to proclaim that we are not really imaginative, when what we mean is that we are not given to seeing and believing in fantasies and fancies. We are all imaginative in that we all construct images constantly about ourselves, our world, our past, and our future. For the most part, it is these images that make up our practical reality and contribute to its unfoldment. It is these images that govern our responses and actions in the world, because we believe in them and we accept them to be true. If I have an image of you as a thief, I will relate to you in a suspicious manner, even if there is no proof or substance behind that image.

Imagination is often thought of in a creative context and relegated to artists, inventors, moviemakers, and other "spacy" people. The imagination *is* creative, and we all use it all the time. I think about what I am going to say today, and I am using my imagination. In my mind's eye, this workshop unfolds ahead of time, and I catch a preview of what I wish to say. When I actually do say the things I imagined myself saying, then the words become experiential and shared. They cease to be my images alone—they become yours as well.

In this sense, imagination is a precursor to incarnation. It is the path traveled between the experience of event—or the deeper, nonverbal, spiritual sources of creativity and being within us—and our responses, actions, and manifestations. An image is the messenger RNA that translates the creativity of the DNA into proteins within the cell.

As Bill and I were saying yesterday, it is easy to lose that sense of history and the planet that allows a person truly to perceive the experiential New Age. Our personal contexts become too narrow and too focused. Likewise, many of us do not take the time or create the discipline necessary to sense the deeper spiritual realms behind manifestation. Consequently, we are most likely to encounter the New Age as a collection of images that can range from psychic predictions to serious analyses of political, economic, and social trends leading into the twenty-first century. We are most likely to encounter the New Age as an imaginary landscape, a place composed of myth, metaphor, desire, fear, hope, and belief. Bill and I spoke of the death of the New Age, or at least its distortion, as due to the association of that image with psychic, esoteric, and narcissistic pursuits by the media and some New Agers. Such association is bound to make the idea less compelling to those who are seeking practical and compassionate responses to the world's challenges and opportunities.

However, while I often find this particular association uncomfortable and distorting, I would not classify it as a major problem. I would see the whole carnival of interest in pop psychism and rituals more as an amusement park along the way—a kind of metaphysical Disneyland. One can get caught there, but one can also have fun and even gain some insights. For example, it is easy to mock channeling, and the excesses we read about certainly lend themselves to mockery, but by the same token I have known many genuinely fine sensitives who are clear, conscientious, and disciplined mediators between physical awareness and the deep levels of spirit.

It is not the psychic associations that bother me as much as other kinds of distortions that arise on the way into a New Age. Psychic and esoteric fancies can be recognized as such, avoided or learned from, and set behind us. Besides, much of the interest in paranormal abilities, particularly in the area of healing, is both legitimate and important. We do have subtler senses and inner abilities that deserve appropriate investigation and development, free from occult glamour. The other distortions I am thinking of are not so evident. They affect not so much *what* we imagine as the *way* in which we imagine.

To me, the New Age represents each of us learning to embody more fully many of the essential qualities that lie within the soul of the planet itself, as well as within the deeper sacred dimensions of the cosmos itself. For me, a living planet like ours is not just a place; it is also a condition, a state of being. It is characterized by the capacity to empower co-creativity and to manifest connectedness, intricacy, complexity, and synergy. It is a condition that supports diversity, because each unique member of the community offers an irreplaceable contribution and perspective. It also promotes communion and cooperation or symbiosis within that field of diversity, so that wholeness is manifested as well as the power of emergence.

I tend to shy away from discussing specific images of the New Age because in our culture images have a way of being chewed up and mulched into triviality very quickly. For example, the image of Gaia as the spirit of the living Earth embodies much of what I mean when I talk about the New Age. Gaia for me means more than just ecology or environmental concerns, and more than just a sense of the Earth as a living being. It means an evolving system in which individuality, diversity, complexity, connections, wholeness, and emergence all come together in a condition and consciousness of synergy and co-creativity. To me, Gaia means the challenge to learn to think and act the way the spirit of the planet does—in a manner that empowers and sustains life and its unfoldment.

However, as rich and impactful as the image of Gaia was a few years ago—when it reemerged into our cultural imagination thanks to James Lovelock and Lynn Margulis and their Gaia Hypothesis—it is now in danger of being trivialized by overuse and misuse. Nor is Gaia the only idea that has been minced and mulched, largely by a media that predigests ideas for us and turns them into sweet, syrupy cliches that hold little nutrition.

Therefore, one distortion to our reimagination of the world is the continual hunger of our culture and our media for new ideas and sensations—not for any transformative or enlightenment value they may have, but as novelty and entertainment. At times it seems to me that our culture is a huge cocktail party always seeking new ideas that can be reduced to rumor, gossip, and small talk because nobody is threatened that way.

Another distortion is the issue of scale. When people think and speak about the New Age, the scale is usually planetary. We talk about the *big* picture. We talk about *global* problems and crises, which no one individual is in a position to solve. We talk about the New Age as a *historical* epoch, not a human one.

Now, the big picture is important. It creates context and reveals connections. I have spent the better part of my life lecturing about the big picture—the overall context of the New Age—because I believe that larger vision is important. Likewise, the concern with a global perspective, with planetary problems and opportunities, is welcome and vital. However, the front line of incarnating the New Age is within the lives of individuals. In the midst of all the enormous questions and issues confronting our world, what happens to our everyday lives? How are we to respond to these global issues and to the immediacy of our own lives?

One way to respond is to relegate our lives to second place and to become possessed by the enormity and significance of it all. When we do this, we begin to incarnate the big picture, or at least our imagination of it, and not our own unique pattern. This has several consequences that block creativity.

First, we may be so daunted by the scale of the problems that we become disempowered. We may feel we are so small—so powerless compared to what must be done, or compared to something as cosmic as "The Birth of a New Age"—that all we can do is wait upon events. We cannot engage with the deeper issues and powers because we feel they are beyond us. I have seen this phenomenon of disempowerment and waiting quite a bit within the New Age movements of the past thirty years.

Another problem with seeing the New Age simply as the big picture or the big event is that it becomes the star, and humanity and the Earth become relegated to bit parts. We are all spear carriers. Does California have to sink into the ocean to initiate a New Age? Why, then, let it sink! What else are spear carriers for but to advance the story and let the star shine? Must we have a global economic collapse? Then let the stock markets fall! Nuclear war? Why, let the missiles come! Never mind the suffering, the deaths, the dislocations that catastrophes can bring. The play's the thing!

There is an inherent violence, both toward history and toward individuals, in this attitude. People become fodder to the cannons of transformation. Places like California become images, not real lands with real ecologies, real cities, and real inhabitants of all species. Nature can be violent, but it is not the violence of drama used to excite us or to advance the plot. Nature's is not the violence that diminishes some roles to exalt others. The big picture can become violent to all the little pictures that actually embody our lives, turning them into subplots that can easily be left on some celestial editor's cutting-room floor.

A consequence of this violence is that we subjugate our individuality, feeling our lives are not as important as what is going on in the world today. We give ourselves over to causes, issues, leaders, and groups that seem to assuage the sense of powerlessness and ineffectuality we feel as individuals. Of course, working with others in serving a cause can be a very creative response, a mutually empowering association. Often, though, it is not. We seek to throw a quantitative solution at what are often qualitative problems. I mean by this that the real solutions may lie in deeper insights and changes of consciousness—in individual attunement and initiative rather than in the size of membership lists or the number of participants at a given event.

When the problem of scale leads us to think quantitatively rather than qualitatively, we are merely repeating the thoughtforms that already govern our culture. We may seek leaders rather than facilitators, groups rather than networks, movements rather than resonant latticeworks of creative individuals, unifying ideologies rather than communities of the imagination.

I include in the issue of scale the notion that somehow the New Age is beyond humanity, that in the emergence of a New Age we are either the victims or the servants and beneficiaries of forces beyond our ken. From this perspective, the New Age loses its human dimension, and it becomes difficult to relate it to our everyday, ordinary lives. No wonder it seems at times like some never-never land.

We confronted this issue not long after I arrived at Findhorn in 1970. While many creative things were going on in the community, there was a general feeling that we were all biding time until the great event occurred that would usher in the New Age. Nor was Findhorn unique in feeling this. It was a sentiment shared by many New Agers and New Age groups then as well as now. What I did was suggest to the community that the event, whatever it might be, had already happened and that the New Age was already here. I would suggest the same thing today.

So now what? Now what do we do? Just what we did before the New Age: all those everyday mundane tasks like cooking, cleaning, raising children, honoring our relationships, maintaining the physical structures we live in, and doing our work. The New Age doesn't make those tasks unnecessary (unless our vision of the New Age is some form of gnostic paradise in which we are forever freed from the coils of the flesh and live in some self-referential, monadic world of pure mind). We can do them with a deeper love and with a deeper sense of how all these acts connect in an embracing spiral of individual and planetary incarnation, but the tasks themselves remain. Consequently, since the New Age is already here, we might as well start doing these tasks with mindfulness, with a sense of their value, with a sense of the sacredness and the potentials for emergence inherent in the mundane.

The Findhorn community adopted this way of looking at things and dropped the expectation of some event that would finally usher in a New Age. The result was a release of creativity and participation that really energized the community. Findhorn didn't forget about the big picture, but it became mindful and caring of the little pictures as well.

This was also a reason why I dropped out of the New Age lecture circuit. With a new family underway, I wanted to spend more time concentrating on the responsibilities of parenthood and family life. I wanted to find the New Age in the everyday things, not just in cosmic dramas of planetary transformation. Family became my spiritual discipline.

In few other places do we find the spirit of the New Age, the spirit of emergence, more clearly represented than in the lives of children. They embody emergence, living on the edge of discovery and delight. Who knows what will come next?

The most familiar patterns and routines can suddenly dissolve and disappear. My youngest boy, Aidan, liked to play at being a cat. He would get down on all fours and rub against my leg when I was sitting down, and I would scratch his head and say, "Good kitty! Nice kitty!" One evening when I did that, though, he looked at me indignantly and said, "I'm not a kitty, Daddy! I'm a seal!" Instant transformation!

Everyday life is filled with such possibilities and moments of transformation. They are not dependent on great events, only on shifts of perception and mindfulness. When we focus too much on the great events that seem to lie on our horizons, then we overlook the immediate events through which the New Age may be seeking to enter our lives.

We need to recognize the New Age in the peanut-butter sandwiches of our lives, not only in the filet mignon and lobster feast served at the top of the Space Needle. To do so, we must have a sense that our everyday lives are meaningful and valuable. Many New Agers I have known are drawn to the New Age not out of any sense of planetary evolution or spiritual unfoldment but because they simply want their lives to be different and they have no sense of how to create that difference for themselves. They crave the great event that will liberate them from the mundane. Approached this way, the New Age is like the event horizon around a black hole. When you pass beyond it, all structure, all the laws of the universe, all the restraints and pressures and challenges cease to exist. Everything dissolves into a singularity of liberation from the constraints of the familiar and the known.

This perspective sees the New Age in terms of transition but not in terms of arrival and incarnation. What is craved is that moment between the thunder and the lightning when all things are possible, when I don't have to choose a particular way but can avoid incarnation by simply living in a suspended state of novelty. Anything goes, I tell myself, for the New Age is the end of history. It is a kind of endless carnival, a limitless Mardi Gras in which I can try on one costume after another without ever having to define myself.

What is forgotten is that Ash Wednesday morning comes after Fat Tuesday. History doesn't end; it settles down into new structures and new patterns, some of which may look identical to the ones we have always known. One of the reasons I left California and moved to the Midwest back in the seventies was that within the New Age circuits, few people actually wanted to settle down and incarnate a new pattern. Instead, there were endless rounds of weekend workshops and seminars, endless trainings, endless preparation and excitement and self-discovery, but never any self-definition or incarnation. I found myself in an atmosphere more suited to an entertainer than a spiritual teacher. Today's insights always had to compete with the newer, brighter, improved insights of the next seminar to come down the pike.

If the New Age means living in a peculiar artificial gravity of workshops and trainings in which one always flees the mundane and the ordinary, then it is no wonder that it appears irrelevant to the majority of people who cannot afford either the time or the money to inhabit such an endlessly self-referential realm. The New Age is about self-discovery, but it is also about self-definition and incarnation. It is about making choices, setting boundaries, defining limits, and saying no. The spirit of the New Age may be infinite, but the life of the New Age is within the realm of the finite. To see it otherwise is to kill it.

Unless we are talking about the demise of a specific image or belief, the death of the New Age is a metaphor, of course. There is no way we can "kill" the process of change that is going on in society. What we can affect is the pace, the intensity, and, to some extent, the direction of this process. More importantly for us, we can deeply affect our individual relationship to this process. We can damage or kill our own transformative and hopeful sense of the future. We may not be able to kill the emergence of the New Age in a global sense, but we can certainly kill it for ourselves.

We do so by killing the imagination that can take us into new conditions, that can open us to genuine initiation and metanoia. We do so by forbidding our imaginary landscapes from opening to new territories. We also do so by colonizing these new territories in the name of decadent and decaying empires, making them simply further outposts of what we already have. We do so by not letting these new lands speak to us in their own terms and by failing to change and adapt to those terms. We become like the English settlers who colonized New Zealand. They cut down the native forests they found and replanted trees imported from England so that when they looked out their windows they could see a familiar landscape.

The brigands that challenge the incarnation of a New Age largely come from the same place. They seek to perpetuate the familiar in the name of the new. We may desire the new and the different, but we also wish to remain in familiar landscapes. We want to boldly go where no person has gone before as long as in the process we remain ourselves—known and unchanged. We not only want to have our cake and eat it too, we don't want to gain any weight from our indulgence.

For example, one of the phenomena of the New Age landscape is the proliferation of "prosperity" workshops and seminars that seek to teach us in a quick, painless way how we may control our reality and have all the abundance we want. While these workshops are filled with what their proponents call New Age concepts and ideas, and while they would seem to promise a new life, many of them actually occupy very old and familiar territory. They are planted four-square within the same consumer mentality that bedevils much of our culture. Their hidden message, which in some cases is quite explicit, is that you really can have it all. The New Age, it is

52

implied, is about gaining the power to have whatever you need and desire; it is about getting your way, because, after all, it *is* your reality. Nothing is said, though, about reciprocity—that if you can have it all, then the *all* can have you. Instead, in these workshops, you are always the consumer, never the consumed. It is as if you have one of those marvelous metabolisms with which you can eat anything and everything and never gain a pound or an inch. When your attention is on what you can get and not on what you can give, what you really end up with is a bad case of spiritual anorexia.

Limitless consumption without consequence or just plain limitlessness without boundaries is having a devastating affect upon our moral, social, and ecological landscapes. It is part of the modern attitude that the New Age is trying to change; it should not be made an attribute of the New Age itself. When it is, we are boldly going back to where we've been before. No transformation, no metanoia, no emergence, no imagination, no New Age.

The imagination of a New Age is much more than just imagining what a new society might be like. It is also imagining ourselves changed to fit that new society. It is imagining that we can let go of the known and be different from what we have been. The English colonists could not imagine themselves living amidst the very different landscape of New Zealand, so they attempted to recreate the Britain they had left. They could not imagine changing themselves and their lifestyles, so they had to change the environment. They "Angloformed" New Zealand.

Unless we can imagine ourselves differently and imagine ourselves changing in meaningful ways, we cannot really imagine a New Age. We can only imagine an environment that, while superficially different and exotic, allows us to remain who we think we are, although perhaps in a larger and more splendid version. We transform the future to make it inhabitable by the past. We see this phenomenon in the original "Star Trek." In that show, the Federation of Planets is a civilization made up of several diverse alien cultures with starfaring vessels that roam the galaxy, yet the attitudes, concerns, and behaviors of the crew upon the starship *Enterprise* are essentially those of people in the United States in the 1960s. The environment is different, but life is familiarly and comfortably the same. There is no sense at all that humanity has transformed by becoming an interstellar race in contact with other life-forms. Only the technology has developed.

When we accept superficial novelty and call it transformation in order to avoid dealing with the personal consequences of a genuine transformative process, that is the death of the New Age within us. It is the death of that part of us that seeks to be not just more of what we are but different from what we are as well—the part that seeks genuine growth.

53

The imagination of a New Age, then, is the ability to imagine ourselves as being different or to imagine ourselves transforming, even when we are not sure just what the final transformation will look like. It is like a *koan* of personal and collective unfoldment: what am I, who am I, when am I in the New Age? It is a *koan* designed to deepen us until we can touch the part of us that can change, that embraces change, that is change. It deepens us until we touch the spirit of emergence and creativity within us.

Here we come to an interesting paradox. The power to change is entwined with the power to be changed. If I want to transform something, I must myself be willing to be transformed. I must be open to the consequences of my actions. I cannot stand apart and act on the system from the outside. Where the New Age is concerned, there is no "outside." It is a planetary process that embraces us all. We cannot participate in it and not be vulnerable to the processes of unexpected transformation ourselves.

There is nothing mysterious about this. One doesn't manage the New Age. It is not a product that we create. It is a process in which we participate. If we want to go with the flow, as they say, we have to flow where we go.

Again we come back to this issue of wanting to live in a changed world without needing to be changed ourselves. We want to manage and direct the nature of our personal changes; we wish to be in control. However, the New Age is about revelation, and revelation cannot be managed. We are talking about seeing something we have never seen before in quite that way. And we are talking about the changes we need to go through in order to have that new way of seeing, in order to recognize and appreciate revelation when it comes.

The joke is that we don't know what those changes may be. That's the point. The New Age calls us to a moment and condition of vulnerability and surrender. It calls us to the edge of our own histories. It does not call us to abandon the past, only to look beyond it. It calls us to a place where the past may not be able to guide us, where we have to look anew—with beginner's mind, with fresh eyes, with no prejudices, free from conditioning.

What we are talking about here is a state common to both mysticism and science. When the mystic seeks to know God, he or she must go beyond all images—must go beyond all that is known; he or she must pass through the "dark night of the soul," in which all that is familiar is stripped. He or she must enter a state in which the imagination is clear and fresh, ready to receive new images, or even more profoundly, the image beyond all images, the knowing beyond all knowledge. In a similar way, the scientist draws on knowledge and experiences gained from the past, but in the moment of doing science, in gaining new knowledge, he or she stands separated from history, ready to see what has not been seen before. Science is a path to knowledge through discovery; in science, all prior knowledge is held to be tentative. That is, it may be overturned by new knowledge. Both science and mysticism are yogas of learning.

Both the scientist and the mystic must be prepared by their disciplines to accept revelation. Both must be prepared to be changed by what they discover, which means they must be prepared to let go of all that they have known and accepted before—even their own sense of self, if that is what the path into revelation demands. This, to me, is part of the consciousness of the New Age. It is a level of imagination that is what the New Age is all about. We cannot truly reimagine the world unless we are willing to reimagine ourselves.

DISCUSSION 2

Definition and Content
of the New Age

AUDIENCE PARTICIPANT: David, both you and Bill have mentioned that the term *New Age* has lost credibility, yet I notice you continue to use it. Why?

DAVID: As I mentioned earlier, I happen to like the term. It describes a time of unfoldment and transformation without specifying just what form that unfoldment might take or should take. Therefore, it puts the emphasis on the spirit of emergence itself rather than on a specific phenomenon. It doesn't say that we're moving into an information age or an age of Gaia or a computer age; it just says we're moving in new directions, so we had best be alert to what may be unfolding and be ready to act creatively. It has an open-endedness to it that I like.

On the other hand, when I use the term *New Age*, I have to pay a price. I must take time and effort to define what I mean by it and to differentiate my position from what appears to be the public perception—that the New Age is a psychic and occult revival. Sometimes, there simply is no time or opportunity to go into explanations or even offer my one-minute definitions of the New Age. So I run the risk of being misunderstood or misperceived. If I'm willing to take that risk, then I don't mind using the term *New Age*.

I must admit, though, that unless the opportunity is there, as in this seminar, to explore this idea in depth and give it the deeper meanings it deserves, I generally stay away from the term *New Age*. In this I bow to the media-driven changes in our language. Once an image becomes firmly fixed in the public mind, it is difficult to change it. If I say, "I'm New Age," does it mean I'm seeking a deeper planetary awareness, the emergence of a holistically oriented world, and a compassionate, empowering attitude toward others? Or does it mean I'm interested in tarot cards, aura balancing, channeling, crystals, past lives, and a narcissistic pursuit of magical powers? Probably the latter for many folks, unfortunately. If we don't like it, we can use our own lives and examples to define the New Age as we think it should be, but we must be prepared to expend the energy and time to do so. It may not be worth the struggle when we can simply substitute other terminology.

In my own case, however, since I've been so identified with the New Age over the past few years, I suppose I have this quixotic desire to hold up a grander image and make the idea of the New Age truly inspirational and worthy of the best in us. I hate to see it devolve to represent the worst or the most trivial aspects of the spiritual quest or to simply become fodder for fifteen-second sound bites on radio and television.

AUDIENCE PARTICIPANT: You mentioned a concise definition of the New Age. What is it?

DAVID: You mean this weekend isn't concise enough? Well, if I had to put my definition into a few words, I would say that the New Age is four things. First, it is the emergence of a planetary culture. This doesn't necessarily imply the emergence of a world government, by the way, which is something I don't expect to see or particularly desire. However, a greater global awareness, cooperation, and coordination on the parts of all people and institutions, with particular mindfulness of how we are all interconnected and interdependent, is important.

Secondly, I would say that the New Age is a response to the archetype or myth of the sacred planet. It is the desire to create a world in which humanity, nature, and the domain of spirit work together in ways that are mutually empowering and co-creative.

Thirdly, I would say that the New Age is the *gestalt* of our technological, scientific, political, economic, social, and spiritual responses to both the global challenges and global opportunities of our time. It is the spirit behind those responses that minimizes or eliminates the danger that we will destroy ourselves and our world and maximizes the possibility that through a greater planetary awareness and a shared planetary culture we will further the emergence of the sacred world.

Finally, the New Age is an evolutionary shift within the life and spirit of the Earth itself. Just as human puberty brings hormonal shifts, rebalancing, and the emergence of new potentialities and capabilities, so there are shiftings, rebalancings, and emergences going on within the subtle or spiritual body of the Earth. New "energies" and qualities are being taken on, and older ones are being let go of. The Earth as a being is forming a new pattern of inner relationships with the cosmos. This, of course, is a definition based on my inner perceptions.

AUDIENCE PARTICIPANT: I notice you did not include anything relating to UFOs, psychic phenomena, channeling, or the like in your definition. I take it you do not consider these things to be New Age.

DAVID: Not in themselves, no. Exploration and intelligent clarification of our psychic abilities, or a genuine connection with deep realms of the personal, collective, or planetary soul, can certainly enhance the kind of holistic awareness that I associate with the New Age. Psychic phenomena can be experienced within a New Age context, but simply pursuing channeling or crystal-ball reading or the occult arts of any kind is not what I would call New Age. For one thing, these phenomena have been around for centuries. In our culture, we have tended to repress or forget them; therefore the so-called occult and esoteric revival going on now is more a remembrance than a wave of the future. It is the surfacing of repressed ideas and images, which can be healthy if we don't just romanticize the phenomena or become too credulous. The current interest in occultism can serve a purpose, but it can also deflect us from the real work to be done, and at times it can be confusing and harmful when experienced outside of a properly prepared cultural context. My image of the New Age is not one in which everyone becomes imbued with psychic powers but one in which we gain a compassionate and planetary awareness.

AUDIENCE PARTICIPANT: Do you feel that people shouldn't pursue psychic experiences and insights?

DAVID: No, I don't feel that way. I'm not critical of psychic perceptions themselves—only of the glamour and misunderstanding that surrounds them in our culture, which gives them tremendous power to misdirect us. If we have other faculties and senses that can connect us to the universe, then by all means we should explore them.

My feelings are best expressed in a story. An acquaintance of mine years ago was given a government job in Canada that involved dispensing grants to organizations. He was given very broad latitude as to the kinds of organizations he could support and the amounts of money he could give away. The first year, he gave large amounts of money to a number of small, struggling, but visionary groups working to improve society. Most of them collapsed and disappeared, destroyed by sudden internal squabbles over how to use the grant monies they had received or by a lack of proper financial systems and accountability. My friend learned a lesson from this. To go from a budget of a few thousand dollars per year to one of tens of thousands of dollars per year was too great a jump. From then on, he gave only small initial grants—no more than three or four thousand dollars. If the group handled that amount well, then the next year he would increase the grant, and so on each year until the group had learned how to handle large amounts of money skillfully.

It's the same with psychic perceptions. The challenge is information overload, of receiving more data than we know what to do with. The issue is not perception but interpretation, integration, and right use of the information we have. If we struggle just handling what our normal five senses tell us and have a hard time getting along in our world, adding information from extrasensory perceptions is not going to make it easier. First we must deal with what we already know and perceive. How do we translate it into wisdom, into mindfulness, into skillful effort on behalf of our world, into nurturing for ourselves? We have enough to deal with as it is without adding psychic prophecies, past-life episodes, and the like to our plate. On the other hand, if our systems of internal integration, peace, and communication with others are operating well, adding psychic experiences probably won't overload or threaten us.

Psychic powers do not offer a swift path to wisdom. Wisdom comes from consistent, hard inner work. In spite of what weekend workshop promoters may say, there is no shortcut, no instant formula for gaining enlightenment and inner balance. No amount of aura balancing, channeled messages, or psychic phenomena by themselves will turn us into inner-directed, compassionate, empowering people. As the actor John Huston says so marvelously in his stockbroker commercials, we must gain wholeness and integration in our lives the old-fashioned way: we must earn it.

AUDIENCE PARTICIPANT: I'd like to come back to the public perception of the New Age for a moment. Why has it turned out the way it has, rather than becoming an image that stands for what you and Bill and Chinook represent? Why has psychism become the dominant definition for the New Age?

DAVID: Well, of course, we've been addressing that this weekend, haven't we? To add some further thoughts, it would be tempting to say that it's the media's fault. Media, by which I mean primarily radio and television, is a filtering system, and it tends to favor only those images that do not genuinely challenge us or that can reach the largest number of folks in the simplest and quickest way. It is a business interested in selling a product, and it follows marketing strategies. When a friend of mine who is a respected university professor and community activist sponsored a national conference in Milwaukee on strategies for positive, social change, the local paper refused to cover the event. When he inquired why, the city editor told him that it was too positive an event, and that good news did not sell papers. It was put as bluntly as that.

The positive sides of the New Age possess little drama. The psychic sides offer a great deal of drama that is rich in the potential for conflict and notoriety. Writing about a channeler, especially if the channeled messages are rather bizarre or silly, is more dramatic, and gives the reporter more chance to sound rational and superior, than writing about changes in our perceptions of reality due to modern scientific research or writing about advances in biologically based systems for treating sewage. There is only so much space or time in a given newspaper or television show, so choices have to be made. The criteria for making those choices represent a perceptual filter system.

I generally stay far away from the media. I do not do well in interviews because I don't think or speak quickly enough to fit their time requirements. I cringe when an interviewer says, "Tell me all about the New Age. You have one minute." I feel like I'm in a Cuisinart and my ideas are being chopped up into slogans. However, occasionally I relent and make an appearance. In one such event, I was asked to give an interview on a television show that sought to explore seriously the ideas behind the New Age. I agreed, but when I arrived at the studio, I discovered myself on a set that was colored in bright pastels with huge images of crystals hanging about. During the course of the program, the interviewer, who actually did a very credible job, asked me the same question. Why does the New Age have such a bad image in mainstream society? I told him to look at his set and he would have his answer. Why such gooey-sweet colors? Why images of crystals, for heaven's sake? Why not have pictures of space colonies or scientific laboratories? Why not pictures of people working to halt desertification or clean up pollution? The set these people created undermined the high tone they had sought to give to the New Age idea.

Also, just as some folks point to the Inquisition in history or to the radical fundamentalists today as a reason to distrust and malign Christianity, so it is easy for those who dislike the genuine changes and insights of the New Age to point to the worst, most bizarre elements and use them as a brush to tar the whole idea. By dismissing the New Age as satanic, narcissistic, irrelevant, or as a code word for psychism and occultism, they don't have to deal with the actual historical transformations and opportunities—the new ideas and images—that are shaking the foundations of our world. They don't have to deal with the real challenges and insights behind the best of the New Age ideas and activities.

On the other hand, to blame the media or to concoct some paranoid conspiracy is simplistic. The media is a filter, and we should be aware of its biases, but it is also a mirror. If it reflects aspects of the New Age that are silly and narcissistic, it is because such aspects exist. The media may exaggerate their importance and their pervasiveness, but it cannot exaggerate what isn't there.

Psychism and the New Age have become so linked in part because the modern idea of the New Age largely emerged out of psychic sources and prophecies, but in greater part because the people who have the greatest need to belong to a New Age movement and to cling to it as an identity are those who suffer the most from alienation from mainstream society and feelings of disempowerment. The people I have known who are the most insistent about the New Age, and who use the term the most, are people who have been on the fringes of society and now find a powerful image that links them with a sense of cosmic destiny and fulfillment. Suddenly, what they are doing is not so silly or suspect anymore, or at least the silliness can be tolerated because it is part of a larger group.

I met a fellow last year who gave psychic readings using M&M candies! He would throw colored M&Ms onto a cloth and then divine your future by reading the patterns they formed—sort of a "candygram" from the higher worlds. Certainly a lot less messy than using bones or chicken innards, and if your fortune isn't sweet enough, why, you can eat the M&Ms! Of course, one can envision theological questions arising: which give a truer, more substantial reading—plain M&Ms or peanut M&Ms?

Did this fellow call himself a candy reader or the M&M psychic? No. He billed what he did as being New Age, of course! When you're part of a grand planetary movement, ridicule just rolls off. You are cloaked by the importance of bringing a new (and, in this case, sweeter) civilization into being. Of course, if the fundamentalists don't object, the dentists might!

So the world of psychic practitioners and activities has a use for the New Age as an identity, and it will promote that identity with greater certainty and passion than will those in other activities such as science or politics who don't really need the image at all to buttress what they are doing. In addition, there are those who would capitalize on that need either by trying to become leaders and gurus of a New Age movement or by trying to exploit it as a market. If I sell crystals, it's to my advantage for crystals to be New Age. I read that one man in southern California sold more than fifty thousand dollars worth of crystals in one day at a New Age conference. He didn't know what the New Age was about, but with those sales figures, he didn't care—as long as it remained identified with crystals. Finally, since psychism tends to looked at with some suspicion in our culture, for those who distrust or dislike what the New Age stands for, there is a value to associating the New Age exclusively with occult and psychic activities.

My point is that there are more tendencies at work identifying the New Age with psychism, occultism, and so forth than identifying it with something like global cooperation, the healing of pollution, or a new vision of the sacred. Taking on the identity of psychism, the image of the New Age fills a need for many people. This can be the need to reject the challenge of the deeper changes the New Age stands for by labeling it evil or silly. Or it can be the need to feel powerful and special, or just the need to make money off a hot image. On the other hand, the need to find a holistic vision or a new, practical planetary awareness can be met using alternative images. These images do not need to be labeled "New Age."

Thinking about this raises a couple of other issues for me that I'd like to explore. First, on this issue of psychism and the identification of the New Age with the cultivation of psychic powers and phenomena, one of the symbols that is more and more used to represent the New Age is the crystal, particularly as an implement for a kind of psychic technology. Of all the symbols for a New Age, I find the symbol of the crystal to be the least appropriate. Crystals do have interesting and helpful properties, both physically and psychically, but they gain them from a rigid geometry, a fixed order. The capability of a crystal is not fluidity or flexibility. It is not dynamic in itself. Instead, the capability of a crystal is predictability, order, and the capacity to store and focus power because of its rigidity. As such it is more appropriately a symbol for a fascist or communist state than for a New Age society with its emphasis on personhood and individual expression.

Here is another example of the way in which images deceive us. By picking the crystal as an icon, many New Age groups are really aligning with the past, not the future. They are harkening back to social geometries of feudal times or to even worse aspects of industrial regimentation, efficiency, and power through rigid, hierarchical order.

To me, a more appropriate symbol for the New Age is the cell. The cell is really a living crystal. It possesses a highly structured internal order, yet this geometry is organized around information rather than around position, as in a crystal lattice. Protoplasm is highly dynamic; it can give birth to endless varieties of new life, yet it can also collect and focus energy in powerful ways. If we want to possess a magical crystal for our New Age work, we need look no further than our own bodies and the cells that make them up.

When it comes to looking for some area of knowledge or activity to which I can symbolically link the idea of the New Age in a way that will capture some of its essence, I would choose biology and biochemistry over psychism and occultism. It is protoplasm, not crystals—the cell, not the channel—that stands for me as the symbol of the new awareness and the New Age.

This is especially so because so many of the images that are used in occult teachings are based on a Newtonian conception of the universe that is filled with powers, forces, and objects, rather than on a quantum and ecological view based on patterns, relationships, and fields. My argument is not with the occult perspective of the reality of inner worlds and inner contacts but with the level of presentation of this perspective—what we might call the *imagination of the occult*—which lags behind the best scientific thinking of our time.

Thus, the shift from the old to the new paradigms represents for me a shift from thinking in terms of points and particles to thinking in terms of patterns and relationships. Which image—crystal or cell—best captures this shift? It depends on the individual. A crystal can be seen as a pattern, as a set of relationships, while a cell can be seen simply as a tiny thing.

So, we're really not faced with an either/or situation. The crystal *can* be a magically evocative image. It links us with the inorganic side of evolution. Crystals do have certain capacities, and in knowledgeable hands they can be used as psychic batteries and focal points. To the extent that we do wish to access in balanced ways human capacities now relegated to the realm of the psychic and the mystical, the crystal can symbolize that access. At the same time, we wish those capacities to be grounded in our lives, in our biology, and to recognize that they are part of our biology. Hence, the image of the cell.

Secondly, over the years I have found many instances in which people respond to the idea of a New Age with anger and seek ways to discredit it. Now, some of this is due simply to people being uncomfortable with the idea of transformation itself. It arises from the fear of change and loss, and the challenge of moving into an unknown future. Also, some of it is due to the rubbish that does get promoted under the rubric of the New Age. However, some of it seems to me to come from an anger at idealism and vision. The implied question behind a lot of criticism of the New Age is, "All right, if you think you have the answer, why can't you help us out and solve the world's problems? Why can't you heal me of my pain and alienation?"

At Findhorn, guests used to ask us what the community was doing to help starving children in Bangladesh, or how we were reducing the nuclear threat, or how Findhorn could help with Britain's economic problems. In other words, when a group of people have the audacity to claim that they might have a positive vision for the future, the response is to insist that they solve everyone's problems immediately; if they can't, their vision is considered to be phony, and the group is labeled as evil for having dared to hold forth a sense of hope in a depressed world.

This is not an unusual phenomenon. If you are depressed and someone comes along who is cheery, don't you feel irritated? Don't you feel at times like hitting them? What right do they have to be happy when you're so miserable? They must not understand the situation. Judging from all the fear and anger, anxiety and suffering in society, we are collectively in a depressed mood. No wonder we get angry when a movement comes along that expresses positive feelings, saying that everything can be all right, that we can make a difference, that the future can be changed.

This is not to say there isn't a lot of naiveté in the New Age movement, along with a use of optimism and so-called positive thinking to simply anesthetize people to planetary problems. On the other hand, unless we have a sense that a positive future is possible, we will never be able to imagine one sufficiently to come up with the answers we need. There must be idealism and vision.

Now, I have personal doubts that there really is something called the "New Age movement." The New Age *idea*, yes, but a *movement*, no—at least not in any ideological, organized sense. But if, for the sake of argument, we agree that there is such a movement, then we must realize that it is immature. We must remember that in its modern form, it is really not much more than thirty years old, and for most of that time it has been rather introspective. Now people are beginning to be inspired by the higher ideals of the New Age to find planetary solutions. Is it fair to expect them to solve overnight all the problems that the rest of society has taken hundreds of years to engender? Should we get angry just because they propose that such solutions may be possible?

Of course, the New Age movement abounds with hopeful images of "quantum leaps" and "hundred-monkey theories" of overnight transformation. Such images encourage unreasonable expectations that, when not fulfilled, lead to disillusionment and anger. The New Age movement needs a healthy dose of realism, particularly in grasping the depth of time, work, compassion, loving, and communication necessary to move the world into a healthier and more holistic direction. Solid transformation takes time. We are not talking about overnight change here! Or, perhaps I should say that transformation can occur very quickly, but the assimilation and integration of its effects takes time. We need an appropriate spirit of idealism and vision that prepares us for both the transformative leap and the transformative hike!

A basic message of the New Age is that there is goodness at the heart of humanity that can emerge, that the world itself is good, and that both contain seeds of sacredness that can flower beyond our imagining. I think there is much repressed anger at both life and the world in our culture. Therefore, any group that suggests that the world is good, that life is wholesome and creative, and that the best is yet to come is going to elicit howls of outrage and challenge. Our culture must go through tremendous shifts to become a lover and co-creator with the world, since at the moment it seeks to be either the world's destroyer or its master. Our culture seems to deeply fear the world, in no small part due to a tragic misunderstanding and misapplication of the teachings of the Christ. This fear must be faced and healed if we are to heal ourselves and our world and if we are to open more fully to the potentials that we and it contain. However, that is not an easy process. Any group that tries to encourage it will face opposition and rage, just as a therapist does from a patient when certain crucial inner challenges and resistances are encountered in the therapeutic process.

For all its faults and failings, for all its immaturity and narcissism, if the New Age movement can inspire our imaginations to envision and work for positive change, then I say more power to it and thank God for it!

AUDIENCE PARTICIPANT: I am an educator, and I am really intrigued by what you have been saying about children and being a parent. I think one of our responsibilities, certainly as educators, is to learn how to relate to children and how to talk to them about the changes that are occurring. What stories do we use? What methods and structures do we use? I am also very concerned about electronic technology and how appropriate it is to use it in the schooling process. I think it can be a very powerful way of creating a new consciousness both in adults and children. I am interested in hearing how some of these ideas might flow down into the school system in appropriate ways or into the process of relating to children in general.

DAVID: I feel it is important to help children mature while maintaining their sense of possibilities, play, and emergence. My experience with school systems has been that they distrust imagination and seek to replace it with a kind of regimentation of learning and information. The connections between things are not honored or explored, yet these connections are powerful stimulants to the imagination. Children have a way of combining things that surprises adults, yet we have that same power, too, once we remember it.

If I think in terms of Gaia as a metaphor, the spirit of the planet does not guarantee my success, but it empowers my capacity to unfold and learn. We cannot guarantee children success, but we can empower them as individuals and teach them how to act symbiotically and co-creatively. We can teach them about the uniqueness of their individualities and about the power that emerges when they can relate and work well together. We should teach them to honor the everyday and the mundane as well as the imaginative and the fantastic, and help them find the appropriate bridges between these two. They need to enlarge and develop the bridges between the honest experience of nature and the Earth, and the appreciation of their interior realms—the realms that make us human.

Of course there are schools that already do this, and probably most educators wish to empower children. But truly empowering an individual is to honor and empower his or her capability as an agent of transformation and emergence. If our desire is to perpetuate the familiar—to ensure that tomorrow's civilization will be like today's—then we are led to mistrust the imagination and the creative capacities. We channel them into service to the familiar. We do not confront the full implications of what it means to educate a person rather than just instruct him or her, for true education releases the creative potential without always being able to predict the results. True education leads to the consciousness of the mystic or the scientist that I spoke of, with its ability to have one foot in the everyday world and one foot over the edge into the unknown and still be perfectly balanced. This does not seem to be the objective of most public school systems or many private ones either.

BILL: Let me give you a specific example of some everyday matters in children's education, matters that my wife as a kindergarten teacher and I as a father and *Hausmann* have dealt with, and that is the way in which New Age parents don't wish their children to come to terms with the problem of evil. In their own condition of being afraid of the world, they have a need for a sentimentalized kind of innocence, which they then project onto their children. They try to hold their children tightly into these containers of innocence as they refuse to allow them to play with guns or *Masters of the Universe*, those ugly, distasteful American dolls from Mattel.

As adults, we inhabit a world that is unconsciously organized around evil and pollution and crime and terrorism: jumbo jets get shot down and all kinds of terrorizing events are reported to us every day, but we don't allow our children to come to terms with these things. Yet our children hear about these things, or actually see them on television. Then, as they begin to act out caricatures of evil as their way of playing with incarnation, of *toying* with the fear of death, we say, "No, stop! I need you to be my symbol of innocence. You must play only with wooden Anthroposophical toys. You must not have guns. You must live in a world that I know to be a lie. I need this of you, and I demand this of you." The child, of course, feels the tyranny, the oppression, and the unfairness of this, and then he or she just raises the ante.

It is the repressed, bland, suburban kid who is attracted to heavy metal. The violent black ghetto gave us the rhyming poetry of rap songs, or before that the intellectual complexity of bebop, but the suburbs gave us heavy metal, with its fantasies of male dominance and the abuse of women—the cry of the little boy who wants to control his mommy and can't as she takes off for work, so he later replaces mommy with a groupie, a perfect fantasy of a woman who will answer to all his physical demands and whom he can slap around, instead of the other way round. The kids that grow up in the polyester suburbs, where everything is bland and built at the same time and so lacking in history and depth—these are the ones who act out fantasies of movie history in their dressing up in Nazi gear for bikers. Their costumes look like the cartoon characters they used to watch on Saturday mornings when they were four or five years old. They play obsessively with incarnation, and these heavy metal images of dominant male and submissive female express the repressed agenda of the parents.

But the people who are the most repressive are the New Agers, especially the Rudolf Steiner folk who insist on wooden toys, no stereos, no cowboys, no guns—

everything has got to be nineteenth century. Well, go back and take a good look at nineteenth-century Grimm's fairy tales. There is a lot of scary stuff in those two volumes, for that was the nineteenth century's way of coming to terms with evil, death, poverty, cruelty, and even cannibalism. The Brothers Grimm printed fairy tales that had been oral lore, and this act of publication represents a modernization similar to our televising printed fairy tales. Now, I don't think for a moment that Hanna-Barbera has done as good a job as the Brothers Grimm, but I don't think we can lock our kids into an Anthroposophical toy shop, for that toy shop is part of our adult infantilism, our grown-up fears of the dark. If we try to control our kids through our fears, they will end up manipulating us through those very same fears. The innocent kids will grow up to become adolescents, and then God help us—and them!

This kind of New Age sentimentalized innocence is what my daughter Hilary calls the Gooey Gaia Group. It is a way, once again, of eliminating difference, of saying that All is One. But one of the central ideas of Gaian evolutionary theory is that worlds embrace repulsions—that pollution is the unconscious architecture in the emergence of novelty. The New Agers have it wrong, and even Jim Lovelock's neighbor Edward Goldsmith, the editor of *The Ecologist*, had a cover article on the death of the forests under the headline "The Rape of Gaia." However, if you have read any of Lovelock's and Margulis's books, then you know that they are saying something far more complex about pollution. Most political environmentalists of the Left actually get upset at Jim and Lynn. They think these authors are saying it is OK to have deforestation or nuclear plants because Gaia is so incredibly resilient that not even a thermonuclear war could eliminate life on the planet. The New Age environmentalists keep regressing into this neolithic Gaia as the Great Mother, and so they want to see modern society as a patriarchal one that is raping this ancient and "natural" Gaia. They project either these parent/child dynamics or these male/female dynamics and transform everything into a mythology that tells us more about them than it does about planetary dynamics.

The actual power of Gaian evolutionary theory, with its radically novel vision of planetary dynamics, is that it shows us metabolic processes in which the rejective energies of opposed organisms are actually constitutive of metadomains and adaptive landscapes that can only be envisioned (and never seen) over vast frames of time—billions of years. We experience those metadomains as evil, as threats to our perception of an adaptive niche. This is something like David's process of meditation in which the people who are around him disappear and new "endosymbionts" appear: "John" or angels or gods or whatever. When we move out of the geometry of one time frame into a larger time frame, our demands on how we think the oceans or the biosphere should evolve may be *wholly* inappropriate.

There is a sentimentalized shallowness to New Age thinking because it is too linear; it avoids visions of dialectical complexity—how noise generates information, how shadow economies work, how neuroses work, how psychotic breaks work. We act unconsciously and then experience the "other" as an evil threat, and we try to fight against it. If you are really going to deal with the pollution of the oceans, then your relationship to the totally other cannot be envisioned as something that is inflicted upon you as fate.

Most of the ideas in books by Lovelock and Margulis are the opposite of what New Agers think Gaia is all about. They have not read the books, which is one of their problems. They have created scores of Gaia foundations, but they have almost nothing to do with a scientific understanding of Lovelock and Margulis. In some sense this is the fault of Lovelock and Margulis, because they didn't call their theory the "homeorhetic and self-regulating mechanism for planetary dynamics." They called it Gaia. Gaia is a prehistoric goddess, so she came with all this cultural myth and tradition and history and freight and baggage. Lovelock and Margulis borrowed it, and the people who owned it—the human race—said, "Wait a second; this belongs to us." So they took it back and gave it all the archetypes—all the male/female dynamics, all the parent/child dynamics—that the myth is full of.

If we think of Gaia as a lover rather than as a mother, there is quite a different relationship that is called forth. Perhaps it is one that is equally limiting or inappropriate, but it does call forth a relationship of copulation or insemination rather than passive lactation at the breast of Mother Nature. Everyone jumped onto this maternal Goddess image because politically and culturally they wanted to break out of patriarchy. They went back to patterns of culture that were repressed in the formation of civilization in the fourth millennium B.C.E., and a whole lot of things were called forth that had very little to do with planetary dynamics and atmospheric chemistry.

If one understands planetary dynamics, then the central thing one learns from Gaia is *difference*. One realizes that repulsive energies are constitutive of forms of integration. Most people continue to think in linear terms of good and bad; they think in terms of *content*, but never look at *structure* and process. They go on to make these value judgments that come from their personal need to feel good. Part of the Gooey Gaia syndrome is just our need to feel good. We make a deal with God: "I will be your evolutionary partner, as long as you understand that I am working with you to create a better world. But, God, don't you let me feel bad." Under-

68

neath this elation is a quiet sense of fear and desperation, and a furious idealism that thrives on exhaustion as a way of avoiding thought.

One of the things we all learned from working in these New Age communities is that they thrive on burnout, exhaustion, and victimization. The unconscious architecture of New Age communities is based on what Joan Halifax likes to call "volunteeranny." I am speaking from Lindisfarne experience and she is speaking from her experiences at Ojai, but I have seen this cultural pattern in many places. We will work indefatigably for God and the greater good, as long as God will keep up God's end of the deal and not allow us to feel bummed out or depressed about the inadequacies of our own linear simplifications of reality.

The difficulty comes in trying to maintain a balanced ecology, because the constituents within the ecosystem always wish to extend their adaptive strategy to the whole. Bacteria, algae, or human beings will overdevelop their adaptive niches until they generate a catastrophe by just doing what comes naturally until the niche becomes an epidemic, an algae bloom, or an entirely new atmosphere.

California therapists only want to do therapy; they are very relationship oriented and are always wanting to get in touch with their feelings, but they can be afraid of ideas, for new ideas can be threatening to their own sense of empowerment through their particular technique. They end up subtracting the interpretive power that thinking can provide to understand, ennoble, and enrich the feelings. They could not create a Findhorn or a Lindisfarne with their psychotechnics, but they can see the shadows these forms of community cast into the light. They see, lurking in the idealism, a certain kind of hidden inner secret that the seekers are running away from in their search for understanding. The rigidity of sacred geometry, for example, often hides a kind of seething, watery, chaotic dynamic. Sacred geometry can be, as it was for us at Lindisfarne, a kind of shark cage that you get into to avoid the demons swimming around in the watery chaos of your own emotions, ready to gobble you up as soon as you get outside the iron cage of those Platonic solids.

In any community there is always one group that wants their part to dominate, and no one wants an ecology to differentiate. What you have got to have is both—both solid continent and watery sea. I wish I had been wise enough, when I founded Lindisfarne, to understand that whatever angelic presences you experience in meditation are going to bring up all this other stuff that has to be dealt with. To found a Lindisfarne effectively, I should have had been not only a thinker and a writer and a fundraiser and a cook—those things I was—but also a sociologist and a psychotherapist and a doctor and a saint.

Visitors would often be confused when they came to check us out. Once a sociologist from SUNY [State University of New York] at Stony Brook came by and

asked, "What is the glue that holds the community together?" I guess he was thinking of Durkheim, and I don't mean Graf von Durkheim. I answered, "Well, we all
sit in silent meditation in the morning and evening." He replied, "You're trying to
tell me that what you are *not* doing is what holds the community together?" I said,
"Yes, absolutely." If people don't come together in group meditation, they just break
apart in abrasive friction or erotic conflict, and the whole thing goes into entropy.

One of the magical moments at Lindisfarne happened to me when it was my
night for cooking the community dinner, which I did once a week. This was at Lindisfarne in Manhattan when we were on the corner of Sixth Avenue and Twentieth
Street. Here we did not have the rural kind of life with organic gardening that we had
in the Hamptons. Thieves broke in, people were mugged at the doorstep, and one
student was raped going home after a class. We are not talking about Findhorn here;
we are talking about Manhattan. So here we are, this New Age community, meditating and then sweeping the streets afterward, and dealing with the grit of New York.

Anyway, it was my turn to cook, so I couldn't go to the meditation but had to
be in kitchen. But while I was cooking, I felt that "tactile" sense that David referred
to—a thickening of the atmosphere in which all four buildings seemed enveloped
in, if not silly-putty, then at least a silence so profound that I felt I could slice it with
the knife in my hand. I knew and could feel throughout the whole place that the
twenty-eight people in the meditation room in the next building had passed beyond
the point of nervous sitting, settling down, and thinking, and that they had moved
into a state of true meditational unity and coherence. The whole place began to be
a unity. It was like going from electrical resistance in the molecular lattice to a super-
conductor: it was a quantum-state transition. And I thought, "Wow, that is great!
They have finally gotten to that point and I don't have to be there; they can do it
on their own."

Before, I used to have to argue with the group in community meetings over my
rule about "compulsory meditation." But without that rule, our twenty-eight people could not live together. The group would become a tower of babble and
multiple divorces. If you square twenty-eight relationships, you come up with a
number of possible relationships that is too large for a small group to handle, for
without meditation the friction generates more heat than light. On the other hand,
if we had been a therapeutic community and not a contemplative one, we probably would still be processing all the stuff that has to do with being the children of
alcoholic parents or having experienced sexual abuse or feeling the fear of the world.
There would have been no meditation or scholars in residence, only endless co-
counseling twenty-four hours a day.

However, when you have people like Francisco Varela or Gregory Bateson liv-

70

ing with you and offering courses, you cannot escape the work of planetary culture by focusing only on relationships and therapies. But therapists do, for every individual wants to extend his or her own worldview so that the diverse ecosystem becomes a parking lot, a monocrop; it becomes like Kansas—just one crop. No one really wants to have differentiation, to have the "other." The one thing in our American culture that we do not want to have are ideas. We want to hear about a philosopher's relationships, not his ideas. And so, Gregory Bateson is remembered as a therapist, but not as an epistemologist.

AUDIENCE PARTICIPANT: David, you have been talking about the New Age as an image and the implications of how we define that image. But there is more than just imagination involved here. In the case of the ecology, the rain forest, things of that sort around the world or here on the island, we have had a lot of problems and a great loss of beauty. What can we do? What do we do? You haven't really discussed this. Beyond imagining, there must be action, mustn't there? Just having the right images won't solve the world's problems.

DAVID: This is one of the central questions emerging out of our weekend. We are not people who cannot respond. The very act of not responding is a response. We can't be truly neutral, for we are all involved in the process. What we are groping for, and for which there may not be easy answers in all cases, are new perspectives that will allow us to act in a way that is more synergetic with the world. We want to act in ways that address the problems without creating other dysfunctions someplace else in the interconnected web of life.

Imagination is part of action. It is not a substitute for it. However, as our actions increasingly have effects that go beyond our immediate surroundings, our ability to imagine consequences and connections that we cannot actually see or experience in the near term becomes ever more important.

Each of us will act as we feel called to do. The more we understand the context in which we are acting and the nature of the problem or opportunity we are facing, the more appropriate and successful our actions are likely to be. I believe in acting out of a spirit of compassion and communion, not out of a sense of being an adversary. I may contest what someone else is doing and challenge it, but I need not see that person as an adversary. The adversarial vision disrupts our capacity to see the larger patterns and interconnections—a capacity that is necessary for us to act in ways that maintain wholeness. When wholeness is not honored or maintained, then our actions all too often become microcosmic solutions but macrocosmic problems.

When I have acted as a consultant to organizations, my first task is to enter into the spirit of that organization, without judgment. I want to take that organization on as part of myself, to blend with it. Then when I act or recommend actions, I am not seen as an outsider. In aikido fashion, I want to use the energy—the momentum of the system itself—to effect change. I may not agree with all that the organization represents, but if I have an adversarial attitude, I cannot blend with it in a way that effects graceful change.

There are so many possibilities of action in our world, so many challenges that need wise and effective responses. First, I must decide that I am willing to act—that this is a situation or problem that I am willing to take on, assuming I have a choice. Then, I need to enter into the spirit of that problem; I must find the patterns that connect me to it. I must rise above any adversarial feelings I may have. I must find a place of attunement and serenity within which the problem may speak to me, tell me of its nature and its desire, tell me of its wishes, which may be different from my own. Then, from a deeper perspective, one that wishes to truly serve rather than just be seen as a server, I can act. I act from the inside as part of that which wishes to be healed or solved, rather than from the outside as the healer or the problem-solver. In effect, I get my ego out of the way. I avoid messianic complexes in which my self-image and self-esteem are based on being the one who has the solutions and takes the actions that set all things right.

I also want to act from congruity. Jesus said we shouldn't try getting the speck from our neighbor's eye until we get the beam out of our own. It is good if I can come to a problem out of a spirit and process of dealing with similar problems in my own life. If I wish to deal with the trashing of the rain forest or with religious conflicts, how much more effective may I be if my actions come out of my efforts to blend with my own garden, to honor my own local ecology, and to heal any violence that may live in my own relationships? We can act only from the quality of our own incarnation. Thus, the beginning of all effective action in the world is in action that affects the quality of our own lives.

THE BIG PICTURE AND THE MESSIANIC DELUSION

William Irwin Thompson

As David and I interrogate the New Age in this critical examination of how the spiritual seventies turned into the greedy eighties, I see the two of us playing out the roles of good and bad officers from the old black-and-white movies of Russian brainwashing, such as *Darkness at Noon*. I come in and slap the New Age around and yell, "Vhy did you zell tze cosmic tsecrets to Shirley MacLaine?" And David comes in as the nice guy who offers the victim a cigarette, and remarks about Ivan the Terrible, his needlessly tough colleague.

As often happens in duets, the couple is drawn into a geometry of dyadic structures in which opposites are simultaneously energized and affirmed. It was the physicist Niels Bohr who said, in explaining wave and particle, that the opposite of a fact is a falsehood, but the opposite of one profound truth may well be another profound truth. David is affirming individuation and the Christic presence as the mystical body of relationship in which individuation is affirmed. And I see myself as affirming the large picture, the historical context in which the individual has taken his or her incarnation. Of course, both of us see these as interpenetrating, and both of us have a cosmology in which the Christ is the *bios logos*, the *biology* of that incarnation in natural and cultural history.

The central idea of a Gaian dynamic in biology is precisely a new vision of the relationship between the little and the large: the plankton in the ocean affects the sulphur cycle, which affects cloud formation and the movement of the clouds in the atmosphere, which affects through the albedo the mean temperature of the Earth, which affects the thermal movement of the oceans that, by sheer mass and volume, affect the movement of the tectonic plates. We were talking about tiny plankton, and now suddenly we are talking about tectonic plates.

The central idea of chaos dynamics is what Ilya Prigogine would call the accumulation of small differences in the thermodynamic irreversibility of events. Life is a dissipative structure that moves against entropy by degrading its environment. Only some kind of New Age Gnostic would think that pollution is evil—that there is some pure way to be all light, all spirit, and free of the relationships in which we are all food to one another. The Christic vision is one of food and communion, and

73

what Lynn Margulis studies—and she is certainly no Christian—is the symbiosis in which one critter's excretion is another one's nutrition. The oxygen excreted long ago by the tiny elves, which we now prefer to call photosynthesizing cyanobacteria, made the world light and lovely and gave us our wonderful blue sky, but it drove the gnomes, which we now prefer to call anaerobic bacteria, underground into the dark slime of the underworld and the innards of our guts. And there they feed on our wastes, and we would be poisoned without them.

In chaos dynamics, the little pebbles in a stream can affect the flow of water so that the accumulation of little effects down the line is enormous and the architecture of the bank is transformed. That architecture of the riverbank may, down the line in human time, affect the placement of a great world city such as London or New York. And so it is with culture—not just with pebbles or blue-green algae.

I gave my New Age cultural foundation the old-age name of Lindisfarne because I saw the Celtic monks of the Dark Ages as another example of the little affecting the large. Although they did not live to see the results of their work, they were creating these points for the emergence of the new civilization of Christendom, and so they were effecting the transition from the disintegrating world system of the Greco-Roman era to the emerging civilization of Christendom in the Middle Ages. None of that was perceivable in the time frame of the life of any one particular monk. It was a collective phenomenon that could be experienced only in a thousand-year cycle. The only way that a monk could relate to that process was in a unique/universal way in which the monk was not identified with the need to see the results of his work in a lifetime.

This enlightenment requires a kind of figure/ground relationship of seeing the little in the large, both in its evil and its good. Perhaps an enlightened abbot could have seen, as the Vikings were coming in and chopping off the heads of the monks, that this was a historical signal for the emergence of the post-Medieval civilization, the Atlantic industrial civilization. But, as David said when he spoke about illness as a signal, most often we cannot read such signs, and so we reach for a drug or a weapon with which to maintain our identity in time.

Imagine that you are a monk at Lindisfarne. It is the year A.D. 793, and the Vikings have landed in the first attack of what is about to become centuries of terror. Everything you have worked for is going up in flames and your whole community is being slaughtered. What do you do? How does one act in the midst of such a tragedy? Well, you get down and pray, and then you feel angry that God doesn't strike them dead with lightning as you hold up the relic of Saint Cuthbert. How could God do this to you, when it is clear that you are good and they are evil? In rage, you throw down the relic, for you feel that you have been cheated. All the uncomfortable hours you have put into prayer were a waste of time. You pick up a sword and, as you slice open a Viking, you wonder why it feels so satisfying. As you feel your own head being severed from your body and flying through the air, you look down on the scene. Your last thought is to wonder why the prayers felt so uncomfortable but the battle felt so good, so natural, so comfortable to your deepest sense of self.

Now imagine another monk whose head is also flying from his shoulders, but as he looks down on the carnage, he blesses the Vikings and sees over the curve of space and time the emerging civilization of western Europe, when monk and Viking have been transformed into artist and businessman. Now imagine another monk, who picks up a sword, blesses the Viking, and slices off his head in the name of Saint Cuthbert, Saint Aidan, and Saint Columba. To be fair to the Vikings, we should also imagine some shamanistic seer back in Norway who had read the portents in the stars and set the ships sailing; perhaps that seer also saw, over the curve of space and time, how the little related to the large.

Now the interesting question here is, Who is enlightened? One monk praying seems to be doing the right thing, but isn't. Two monks doing exactly the opposite thing—one offering his lowered head with a blessing, the other slicing off heads in blessing—both seem to have been granted some sense of illumination beyond the condition of their egos. Most of us, of course, would fall into the trap of endarkenment and ignorance and rage. We would pray with anger and resentment, or fight with anger and resentment. We could not go beyond ourselves to see that out of that secular force a more global and dynamic culture would spread around the world. We could not see that a new global culture would be more empowered to embody the Cosmic Christ precisely because it was secular and not sacerdotal. I, as an ex-Roman Catholic, often see the sacerdotal as the greatest threat to the sacred that exists, precisely because the sacerdotal is always creating bounded forms. It is always creating a priestcraft or ritual business in which the priest tries to make deals with the Almighty. It is always creating monopolies of mystery.

DAVID: The wrong kind of mystery.

BILL: It is always creating a separation. The minister will come in and bless the food, and his body language will change and become very phony. Then, all of a sudden, there will be this hocus-pocus stuff. It is pious and self-congratulatory, and it only creates separation between the blessed moment and the unblessed moment—a separation between the guy who has got the power to bless and the slobs who don't. I prefer the camouflaged power of the secular, for it can carry the divine message and its embodying force out into the world. I have always seen Jesus as understanding this problem of the sacerdotal versus the sacred, for he set up both the church of Peter in the center and the invisible church of John at the periphery. Of course, if the church of John begins to be too self-congratulatory, if its initiates begin to congratulate themselves as the secret agents of esoteric Christianity (and this is the problem I have with the followers of Gurdjieff or Steiner), then it becomes another form of elitist sacerdotalism and the incarnational force of the Christ has to move into some aspects that would be considered evil by the priests, such as Vikings or rock stars or whatever. I like to imagine Rudolf Steiner reincarnating not as a follower of his own Anthroposophical movement, but as David Byrne.

This tension between the big picture and the little picture is always troublesome for us because the basic impact of the large picture can be incapacitating; it can rob us of the sense of our capacity to act. We say, "If that is true, then what the hell can I do?" Then we withdraw into a catatonic state. The difficulty arises because we are demanding immediate results on the ego's own terms, and we are not seeing that the results are implicit in the little that will grow into the large. Paradoxically, although we all have little egos, we don't truly value the little. We always want it to be bigger. If we saw history through the larger window of the imagination—in the topology of a flowing torus in which past and future interpenetrate in the present— then at any one particular moment we would sense both the incredible implications of the past that have come to fruition and the overtures of what is going to be fully realized at another moment of time. We would experience history as if it were a polyphonic fugue rather than a single melodic line.

All of this is present in John Allen Cann's [present in the audience] poem "Bruno Visits the Crystal Palace." If one sees that kind of visionary space in which "the center is everywhere and the circumference is nowhere," then one's mode of being in time is quite different. You no longer have this condition of psychic materialism in which you have to get a feel-good hit immediately, a sense that little you is making the world better.

We all look out at the world through the imagination all the time. The media are a collective form of imagination. We are taught by the media to see AIDS as a plague, but if we looked at life from a planetary point of view, it would be more truthful to have all the cover articles of the magazines screaming about the plague of the automobile. The automobile is clearly more deadly to life, limb, and atmosphere than the HIV virus. It is the greatest disaster to hit the planet since the cyanobacteria started eating light and shitting oxygen in the Archean era. I, who grew up in Los Angeles, can now see Bellevue [Washington] making most of the mistakes that we made forty or fifty years ago. Why don't we Americans learn?

Why is it that as a people we seem to have no capacity for learning? Why does science make mistakes with thalidomide, DDT, dioxin, and plutonium and then go on to tell us, with the same mythological system, that they are going to make the world better through scientific progress? How can scientists make progress when they never seem to be able to learn? They keep mouthing the same propaganda about genetic engineering that they mouthed about nuclear reactors and DDT in the fifties. They say they will feed the world if we give them enough research funds for genetic engineering. They were saying the same thing forty years ago when they said there would be no more hunger in the seventies because they would produce food out of the oceans through chemistry. But now we read about the pollution of the oceans. If even scientists, whose business is supposed to be learning, can't learn, but can only repeat the same scientistic mythologies of progress, what hope is there for the rest of us average citizens?

Why do we human beings have to go through these various unconscious exercises in propaganda to amass capital for scientific research? For the last fifty years, the basic capital-formation device to create a shift to planetization has been war and terror. If you look at World War II, it seems like chaos. It is all about destruction on a global scale. That is the usual human way we look at war.

However, if you look at it from another point of view, a Gaian dynamic, war is a paradox. It expresses maximum planetary organization, but that structure is organized for "de-struction." Yet the destruction never threatens the organization that is established for destruction. The whole thing is a planetary coordination in two oceans with massive movements of troops and people and information and machines at a level of organization that is staggering. But what is the basis of this order? Chaos. Destruction. That is a most peculiar paradox. Our whole post-industrial economy has been put into place by trying to terrorize populations to amass capital. Why are we trying to amass capital? What is it we are financing? We are financing the next stage in human cultural evolution. What is this human evolution going to be? Well, nobody knows for certain because it is an emergent property. It is like asking the prebiotic soup to predict the evolving membrane of the cell.

However, let's take a look at Japan to try to intuit some of these emergent properties. Japan now has the largest capital pool in the world. How did they get it? By selling stuff to *individuals*: VCRs, automobiles, Sony Walkmans. Everything is a technology marketed for individual consumption, because the Japanese don't have to divert funds into a massive defense budget. But what are they doing with that capital formation? They are trying to create the fifth-generation computer—a fast computer that is self-programming. Who are the consumers for fifth-generation computers? Definitely not individuals. The only entities that can afford that technology are nation-states, or joint Soviet/American trips to Mars, or mean little rich nation-states such as South Africa or Israel that want to use supercomputers to design better jet fighters.

No individual can become the market, and so no individual can be the reason why we are investing so much money in artificial intelligence. Actually, A.I. scares the little guy. What is going to happen when immunology and A.I. cross? When the research carried on in the Japanese fifth-generation computer project crosses over with the immunological research at the Pasteur Institute in Paris and the National Institutes of Health in Bethesda, Maryland?

When the two cognitive domains of immunology and A.I. cross over, you are going to have a scientific revolutionary wave that will make the eighteenth-century industrial revolution look like a ripple. When these two areas of science cross, you will have a new kind of biotechnology that is no longer industrial and no longer anything that we know of as "nature" or natural. You will have a whole new evolutionary adaptive landscape, and that, of course, will mean a new kind of evolutionary pollution. If you have industrial technology, you have industrial pollution; if you have genetic engineering, you have genetic pollution; if you have evolutionary engineering, you are going to have evolutionary pollution—forms of incarnation that are neither purely animal nor purely machine. These light and shadow formations of emergence are not likely to go away for the next couple of centuries. In some unconscious way, we seem to be engineering the next step in evolution in the shift from an industrial to a scientific economy in which "nature" as we know it is disappearing.

This is the reason we keep talking about nature so much in the ecological and environmental movements. But notice that the Sierra Club doesn't talk about the things I have just mentioned as the real historical context. Even Bill McKibben in his book *The End of Nature* takes a very white, male, Protestant, outdoorsman, consumer's view of nature from his post at *The New Yorker* in the Adirondack Mountains. McKibben's essay is a lament for the end of nature as an ennobling prospect, and this tradition, as traced by Jean Gebser in his study of the evolution of consciousness, goes back to Petrarch.[15] From Petrarch on, a score of poets and painters took up the habit of climbing up on top of a peak and meditating on the prospect and what that view held out for humanity's place in the scheme of things. From romantic painters like the German Caspar David Friedrich, this way of thinking through looking crossed over into the conservation movement of Muir and gave us our contemporary Sierra Club calendar pinup of nature. All of which isn't "nature"; it's *culture*—our cultural idea of nature.

So, we really don't know what we are doing. If you tell people to stop, they won't, because their motivations are unconscious and are not addressed by the conscious agenda of reformers. If you say stop driving cars, people won't do it. If you tell people not to smoke, they won't quit. If you tell people to stop eating McDonald's hamburgers so that the rain forests don't have to get leveled to make cattle ranches, they won't do it. People will not do good when it is at the conscious level of planetary interest, but they will do evil when it is at the unconscious level of evolutionary emergence. Curious, isn't it? People will remorselessly exercise a kind of appetitive self because at some unconscious level another kind of collective architecture is emerging. My response as a student of culture is to say, "Well, if that is the case, what is the point of going around holding up signs that say 'Do Good!' when people don't want to do good. They want to do Evil."

People are really 90 percent unconsciously invested in doing evil—and that would be my definition of *karma*—and only 10 percent of their conscious being is taken up in doing good. I look at that and say, "Wait a minute, something else is going on here." I don't think we really understand what is in front of us. What is the point of going out and *saving* the world if you don't even *see* the world—if you are not really living in the actual historical world of your time? Most people go out to save the world, but they are living in some imaginary historical world of the past. They are somewhere way back there with Bush and Dukakis, in a world that passed away long ago.

If that is the case, then one has to sit still a moment and ask oneself about the relationship between the individual and the universal, the little and the large. What is the relationship of the present with the larger picture of past and future? At that particular point one can adopt a more Buddhist or more Christian orientation. A Christian orientation generally involves "good news," so we go forth and act out the messianic complex by trying to save the world. Unfortunately, we are often only trying to save our world from its process of world evolutionary behavior. The world does its thing, but we don't like it, so we elect ourselves to save it.

If one acts out of unconscious myths, then one inherits the unconsciousness that is another word for karma. If you act like the messiah, they will nail you to the cross. Some people, of course, really have the need to suffer and die for their visions. But from another point of view, we have had that kind of sacrificial behavior for the last two thousand years, and now we are beginning to sense that crucifixion does not represent a complete incarnation of the Christic presence and that we have to come up with something better. Call that the New Age with its talk of the Cosmic Christ.

Where do we go to learn something better? We have seen for two thousand years the image of this guy tortured on the cross; it has been in all the churches and church classrooms. Then we look over to the other side of the world and we see this beautiful Buddha, with the blissful smile on his face in meditation. We look back at the crucifix, and we look at the meditating Buddha, and we say, "Hmmm, maybe there is something to this Eastern way." So a whole new generation comes along, listens to D.T. Suzuki and Alan Watts, and goes off in the direction of Eastern mysticism. Then another Catholic Counter-Reformation springs up and insists that there is something in Christianity we missed.

"John" once said to David, "Christianity looks at the ocean and sees the actions of the waves, and Buddhism looks at all the dissolving edges of the waves and sees the ocean." Can this be Bohr's case of the opposite of one profound truth being another profound truth? I know that for my own orientation I cannot act without the big picture, for I would become demoralized with the pressing need for an immediate result. Throughout all the years of Lindisfarne, people would say, "Gosh, this message has to get out to the people. There need to be Lindisfarnes on every corner. You really need to go on television. Sell, Sell, Sell." I would say, "No, absolutely not. I don't want to make Lindisfarne into a McDonald's. I am not interested in getting it out there, American style—getting the message out. I don't want to be Carl Sagan or Alan Watts." But this response was so against the American grain. However, when people do act in this American enterprising way, they get so exhausted; they get so burnt out that the original integrity and language of the message gets lost. Orange juice is turned into Tang, grazing cattle are turned into McDonald's, and then suddenly people say, "What went wrong? How did I kill what I loved?"

The messianic compulsion of "saving the world" is something I simply can't identify with. The only thing I can find empowering and ennobling is the notion that whatever I am working for is going to take thousands—or hundreds of thousands— of years. The only way I can identify with my incarnation is to say that it is not just this moment, but it is the whole story—the origins of life, the prokaryotic cell, the dinosaurs, this evolutionary cusp we are in now. The project is something so vast, so imaginatively exciting, that it can't possibly all be done or embodied in one little moment. Neither Findhorn nor Chinook nor Lindisfarne can embody a New Age.

A cultural transformation, an emergence of novelty in the universe, is a complex process in a chaotically dynamic flow of opposites. At various times, some of the strategies and values that an individual may deem to be appropriate may just have to die, as monk confronts Viking. The "I" may have to go through a literal or contemplative death experience to discover that no individual—or individual institution—need be in the business of extending its survival beyond its actual life.

So, I find the New Age "California orientation" that rejects negativity as "disempowering" to be too shallow. Such an insistence of feeling good limits the good to feelings. There is something really wrong with this kind of shallow idealism and optimism that is so basic to the Gooey Gaia New Age. Confronted with this sentimental goo, I always find myself getting tough, abrasive, critical, and negative—more Manhattan than Marin County. Let me put positive and negative into a different frame by closing with this poem I wrote on the Viking destruction of Lindisfarne.

LINDISFARNE, 793

A sky without clouds,
the sea a bright green,
after our winter
it was no small thing
to be warm in light.
A day to chant Tierce
in the opening air
and catch the first sight
of the small white sail
still too far to read
more than its good lines.
How could I have known
that high cursive prow
held the beast I'd drawn
as initial sign
of the opening
Gospel of St. John?

NEW AGE SCIENCE AND THE CHALLENGE OF DISCERNMENT

William Irwin Thompson

Since I won't be here for Sunday morning, David has suggested that I do double duty and open this afternoon's session with a discussion of New Age science, to explore "the difference that makes a difference" between good and bad science. Because I live in Switzerland for the winter and spring of each year, I spend a lot of time crossing boundaries. I do the same in my intellectual life. After meeting David at Findhorn in 1972, I quit the university to join the New Age movement and set up Lindisfarne in New York as a spiritual alternative for the life of the humanities in a technological society.

But even though I am no longer a professor in a university, I still cross boundaries and return to the old country. This year I have been taking part in meetings at the École Polytechnique in Paris— the world's first MIT set up by Napoleon—as well as conferences at ETH, the Swiss Federal Institute of Technology in Zürich, which is Einstein's alma mater. In May of this year, I took part in two international scientific conferences—one in Perugia, Italy, and the other in Hannover, West Germany. So, as you might imagine, I have been giving a lot of thought to the difference between New Age science and what Laurie Anderson calls "Big Science, Hallelujah!" My perspective in all of these activities is that of the observer, the cultural historian, and not of the practitioner in the laboratory.

Sometimes when you cross a boundary, you become acutely aware that the cultures are not simply different, they are hostile to one another. The way Big Science fights with its enemy is with the weapon of annihilation. Big Scientists duel only with those with whom they share a paradigm or a culture; in all the other cases, they have a button they push that casts the other into nihility—into literal nonexistence. It is a convenient tactic, for you don't have to waste energy refuting an opponent if he or she doesn't exist. Since most of the New Age scientists do not show up at the annual meetings that determine membership in the profession, it is not difficult to carry on as if these people were not part of your scientific life. So you end up with two different worlds that really have very little to do with one another, and if you visibly insist on demanding some form of relationship between the two, you run the risk of eliciting the defensive response in which the Big Scientist pushes the button that removes you from his world.

You end up with two worlds, but they are worlds that behave like two sexes. Big Science wants to have nothing to do with New Age science and cannot afford to be seen in public with her. In this form of sexual dimorphism, Big Science is male and and defines itself within a culture of power; it is the intensely competitive and heroic world of big money, big government, big corporations: MIT, IBM, N.I.H., D.O.D. If Big Science is central, New Age science is marginal. Although feminism has effected a revolution in the humanities and social sciences in North American universities, and is particularly strong in such areas as literary studies, the world of the appropriately termed "hard sciences" is still traditionally sexist. Physics, chemistry, and molecular biology tend to be male domains ruled by cultures in which hard, corpuscular objects can be controlled and manipulated, be they subatomic particles or genes.

The "soft sciences," or "wet biology," is more the domain of women and men working together. In this culture, the world is a pattern of connectiveness, a web of being in which one can speak of cooperation and symbiosis. Barbara McClintock characterized her approach to genetics as one of "a feeling for the organism," and this certainly set her apart from her male colleagues, who did not like the moving complexity of "jumping genes," for they wanted a hard and fixed world in which genes could be unambiguously manipulated by their wills. In such fields as ecology and microbiology, it is difficult to ignore "the pattern that connects" to focus only on a discrete and corpuscular entity that is taken out of its natural context. But it can be done, and the usual way to abstract the organism from the environment is with mathematics, so in population biology attention is paid to statistical distributions, and the world is, once again, defined in very Darwinian terms as that of a population of males competing with one another to insert their genes into females. The females, of course, like nature herself, are just there, waiting.

In our contemporary situation, this sexual dimorphism of male and female forms is a peculiar cross between a cliché and an archetypal pattern. The world of Big Science tends to be male, corpuscular, and organized in centers of domination, while New Age science tends to be soft, feminine, intuitive, and dispersed to the margins or edges of the culture. New Age science is the landscape of the repressed—a twilight zone of witchcraft, palmistry, dowsing, geomancy, astrology, fairies, extraterrestrials, Kirlian auras, and morphogenetic fields. For those who dwell in the centers of power, this marginal world is irrational, and yet it exercises a strange fascination and attraction that the normal scientist resists with a conscious violence that speaks volumes for its unconscious pull on him. Carl Sagan at Cornell is a classic case in point. I have watched him practically foam at the mouth while attacking a flying saucer contactee buff at a conference at Lindisfarne—and he totally dismisses the Pythagorean and mystical contributions to the science of the West—but his whole imagination is dominated by images of extraterrestrial "Contact."

You can think of this pattern of repulsion and attraction as that of the "responsible businessman" and the prostitute. The Reverend Jimmy Swaggert would rant and rave about morality in his public sermons under the klieg lights, but he was drawn to the seamy side of night town, where he would seek out prostitutes in cheap motels. This is the degraded form of the male-female relationship, one in which the female is hated for her power of attraction. The romance of Aeneas and Dido is a more refined version of the forbidden love affair. Both archetypal patterns have their descriptive power, and different scientists will be drawn to one pattern or another.

At the moment, the pattern of Aeneas and Dido seems most descriptive to me, perhaps because I am now reading Christa Wolf's novel *Kassandra*. Dido embodies the ancient, prehistoric, feminine Mediterranean culture, the culture in which the queen can rule. Aeneas is the hero, the male who has seen the male heroes destroy his ancient and prehistoric Troy, so he knows the facts of life in this new Bronze Age world of male power. Yet he is attracted to Dido and all the ancient and intuitive ways that she embodies in her Semitic, Phoenician culture. Nevertheless, he has a job to do and an empire to found, so he sails off. Dido sings her last lament as she commits herself to death on her own funeral pyre. The lament is quite beautiful in Purcell's operatic version of *Dido and Aeneas*. Later, the Etruscan world that Aeneas founds will be erased by the Romans, and later still the Romans will come and wipe out Carthage, casting salt into the earth and leaving no trace, except the fascination in Virgil's *Aeneid* for the suppressed culture of the feminine. The poet is torn in two. One half of him celebrates arms and the hero—"*Arma virumque cano*"—but the other half is drawn to and fascinated by the forbidden, the feminine, the Jungian anima.

Well, it hasn't changed much since Virgil's day. We still are split in two, with the empire of Big Science calling the hero in one direction, and the feminine undertow beneath the sea-furrowing prow beckoning him in the other direction—into the depths of ecstasy, illumination, and madness. Part of the saga of science since the sixties has been about the fall of scientists into drugs and madness. It is the tragic Faustian story of the scientist who would be a shaman—a Carlos Castaneda or a Timothy Leary. In the world of kingly power, the ancient shaman in animal skin becomes the fool in cap and bells, so it is probably no accident that Timothy Leary falls from Harvard and ends up as a stand-up comic in nightclubs in Canada, playing the fool for an audience of consumers.

Naturally, these images of the fall into drugs and madness, tragedy and farce, strike terror and loathing in the hearts and minds of the scientists at work in the empire of Big Science, so the no-man's-land between the two cultures grows wider. In this intellectual Beirut of the university, the young person has to decide on which side to belong, for only the already tenured and the aged, whose work is already behind them, can afford to take chances with their careers. In fact, after a life of intense confinement within scientific orthodoxy, many older scientists delight in crossing over into the forbidden territory. So you get the biologist Waddington hanging out with artists and writing about Whitehead, a philosopher who was by then no longer taken seriously by philosophers of science; or you get the physicists Heisenberg and von Weizsäcker meeting with Gopi Krishna, or the neurophysiologist Sir John Eccles talking about the soul.

The problem with this generation gap is that one is always hanging out with one's cronies; one is always addressing the previous historical generation. When one should be listening to those twenty years younger, one is still arguing with those twenty years older. So the effort is always a generation out of date. A few months ago, I went to a conference on "Mind and Nature" in Hannover, Germany. The conference featured Ilya Prigogine, Manfred Eigen, Sir John Eccles, Carl Friedrich von Weizsäcker, Satosi Watanbe—all these distinguished but aged men who were talking about things that were from the world of twenty years ago. To truly express what is currently going on in the study of "Mind and Nature," the list should not have included those gray eminences but the people at work on the frontiers of knowledge now—people such as Eleanor Rosch, George Lakoff, Mark Johnson, Zenon Pylyshyn, or Danny Hillis. Sir John Eccles, for example, hadn't a clue to what Francisco Varela was talking about, and their participation on a panel together was an exercise in futility.

Sometimes when the aged scientist tries to return to the repressed, he returns to an image of the romance with his forbidden love from his youth. Sir John Eccles's discussion of brain and soul was an expression of a simplistic Cartesian dualism that could not appreciate the synthesis of Buddhism and cognitive science in the work of Varela, much less Hillis's connectionism or Hopfield's neural nets. In much the same way, at an earlier conference on "Mind and Nature" at Lindisfarne in 1977, Gregory Bateson's expression of the dualism between the *creatura* and the *pleroma* could not escape the Cartesian dualism he deplored to appreciate the non-dualism of Varela's discussion of the immune system. Even though Eccles and Bateson sat next to Varela on scientific panels, they remained a generation apart and never bothered to read his books. This aged-man syndrome is the same in the humanities, so we shouldn't think this is some aristocratic failure that is peculiar to the hierarchical world of science. Joseph Campbell stuck with Jung and the Eranos Circle of his youth and never bothered to read the structuralists of Paris or the archaeo-astronomers at MIT.

It is not just the two worlds of Big Science and New Age science that remain apart. Any generation or subculture that organizes itself around group identification through clubbiness, or vanity combined with intellectual laziness, will close onto itself in self-reference. For example, I could get stuck in the clubbiness of the Lindisfarne Fellows and the spiritual kairos of the seventies. Even if some cultural promoter tries to bring the two worlds together—as Knut Pflughaupt tried to in Hannover—the two worlds will remain apart. Certainly, the conference in Hannover was a major effort to try to bring the two cultures together. There were more than seventy speakers, but they did not meet—any more than they met in a similar meeting of old-age and New Age scientists at Cordoba in 1979.[16]

So, how do I tell "the difference that makes a difference" between science and deception; and is it self-deception or public deception? Obviously, in running an educational institution like Lindisfarne, I have to make some choices. Do I offer a fellowship to Rupert Sheldrake or Francisco Varela, to Marilyn Ferguson or David Spangler? When I don't have the educational background or intelligence to make judgments about atmospheric chemistry, neurophysiology, or whatever, I trust my own intuition. Gertrude Stein used to say there was a little bell that went off in her head whenever she met a genius, and that the bell went off in her head when she met Picasso, so Picasso was clearly a genius; the bell went off in her head when she met Whitehead, so Whitehead was clearly a genius. I think all of us operate in that way, whether we are choosing a spouse or a colleague.

Our judgments of excellence or genuineness are aesthetic ones—the kind that enable us to tell differences in the case of music or millionaires: between Bach and heavy metal, or between Laurance Rockefeller and Donald Trump. These aesthetic judgments require that we have a knowledge about *how* we know and how we feel. The intuition is like a Landsat camera; it doesn't just look at one fact, it takes in the entire configuration in which the fact or the person is situated. How, for example, do you *know* when you are in love? What is different about the kind of cognitive state of unity through which we recognize the beloved? Being in love is a clearly distinct ontological condition, and everyone has experienced it and knows what it is. We have a certain know-how, and we feel that there is a knowledge about our feelings that is coming from another level.

But as there are judgments, so are there mistakes in judgments. One falls in love with a bitch or a rogue; one falls for a dictator or a guru, a Hitler or a Rajneesh. When we are taken up by projections that often come from the unconscious programs of our infantile period, we are possessed; we think one thing consciously, but do another from the unconscious motivation, from memories of the time before we had language. Because these infantile programs are not articulated into language, it is hard to have verbal access to them, so we generally act them out in our lives. We encounter our unconscious memories as experience, as *fate*, and as we crash, we either wake up to rearticulate them into language or destroy ourselves emotionally.

If we do wake up, we look back and wonder how we could have seen it the way we did. We begin to have knowledge about our feelings and to recognize that we always had an intuitive voice warning us. We realize that the knowledge we gained in suffering was always there, waiting to be used without pain. Most people simply don't trust this kind of intuition and prefer to learn the "hard way" through fate. This intuitive knowledge about our feelings can empower and ennoble them, much in the same way that a knowledge of music can heighten our joy of music or a knowledge of fine wines can enable us to sense the difference between Manischewitz and Chateau d'Yquem. Knowledge doesn't have to get in the way of experience, because experience simply isn't possible without knowledge.

One of the basic differences, I think, between true scientists and scientific merchandisers or scientific hustlers is that real scientists have a compassionate bond with their colleagues; they do not abandon them to take on a messianic posture with delusions of grandeur and manic superiority. Such scientists are still in the social condition of working in labs, doing research, and trying to communicate with their fellows under conditions that admit the possibility of being wrong. There is a fellowship and a companionship to science that the New Age scientist is forced to abandon to become an ex-scientist. Ex-scientists generally take an early success and then launch off into a commercialized market to speak to people who can only admire them but never understand them. They get used to the addiction of admiration and are willing to sacrifice comprehension for admiration.

In the case of someone like Gregory Bateson, who lived at Lindisfarne, it was far more important to him to be understood than to be admired. He was somewhat solitary, liked small groups, and liked smaller conferences better than larger ones. With a sizable admiring public, he was something of a beached whale. Bateson was quite a large man—six feet six inches tall and very wide. What was really important to him was the need to communicate, to be intellectually understood, and to honor the respect of the community of people who could understand him. It is the opposite with the ex-scientist: he or she fears being understood because they fear exposure. They know they are faking it, but they are lazy or in need of money, so they have to camouflage their faking it by seeking larger and larger audiences of admirers; that way they never have to deal with the central question of understanding. They become ex-scientists, and they use their fame to launch into a stellar orbit from which they never have to come back to the ground of the laboratory, to the testing ground, to communication with their colleagues.

Media society is set up to allow literary and lecture-circuit agents to thrive on the popularity of their newly admired New Age scientists. They could care less whether the scientist is right or not; they only want enough controversy to feed the mythic glamour of their star. One of the qualities that I respect about Lovelock, Margulis, and Varela is that they are still hanging in there in the laboratory, hard at work trying to answer the refutations of their skeptical colleagues. This seems to me a radically different kind of behavior than what we encounter in the case of the ex-scientist. This, to me, is "the difference that makes a difference" between "new-age"—which is Robert Bly's phrase that he rhymes with sewage—and real science.

SCIENCE AND STORYTELLING

David Spangler

One of the characteristics we all share is that we enjoy stories. We are all storytellers at heart—some of us more than others. Notice that when we are listening to Bill, we are basically listening to a storyteller. From the first time I heard Bill speak, some sixteen years ago, I always felt that he was more the Irish bard than the American philosopher.

In telling stories, we obey certain principles and laws of drama and melodrama, of crisis and resolution, of impact and silence. We generate an energy through our stories that helps to define who we are and where we are going. We are all creatures of narrative, and these narratives are important to us even if they are tragic narratives. It certainly has been my own observation for many years that individuals would much rather have a tragic narrative than no narrative at all, and they will cling to suffering in order to discover the material for such a narrative.

Some of the attraction that people have had to New Age thought, and certainly to some of its more prophetic elements, has been the attraction to a dramatic story. There used to be the annual prophecy of California sinking into the ocean, which came up all through the sixties, and every year the prophecy would fail. Then somebody else, a different channel or a different psychic or a different somebody, would say, "Well, now I have a new revelation, and here is when it is going to happen." Then the energy would gather around that person. There would be a renewed sense of excitement and drama and escape: "We will live through it, and won't it be fun watching the skyscrapers go under, as long as we are in Nevada."

When my wife and I and a number of my colleagues who were part of the Lorian Association moved from California to Wisconsin, we found out later that it sent ripples through the entire New Age community on the West Coast. Somehow Spangler had inside knowledge and was fleeing the coast because the catastrophe was imminent. We arrived in Wisconsin only to be greeted by prophecies that Wisconsin was going to sink into the Great Lakes!

Our society is structured around the telling of stories. Religion tells stories, politicians tell stories, business is in a large way a storytelling profession, and science is a telling of stories. As Bill has often said, science itself is embedded in cultural history. The way we do science in the West is different from how science has been practiced, say, in China. The way we do science now is different from the way we did it a hundred or two hundred years ago.

Science as an enterprise is more the art of storytelling than it is the art of *storing* stories. It is a way of critiquing stories, of keeping the narrative alive and developing it, although scientists as human beings can get so attached to a particular narrative that they resist making changes in it. Science is also a community of storytellers. I remember years ago talking with a friend of mine who was a practicing scientist. He said, "You know, you talk about the emergence of a planetary community, but there already is a planetary community with a planetary language—it is the community and language of science, of scientists." The specific language he was working with was mathematics. He said, "I can go anywhere in the world where there are other scientists, and they will know exactly what I am talking about through the language of mathematics. We have a fellowship; we share the same values. It doesn't matter whether these other scientists are Russian or Chinese or Arabic—we share this fraternity and sorority of science."

The mythic and storytelling side of science often gets overlooked by scientists, just as Jim Lovelock and Lynn Margulis, at the beginning, completely overlooked the mythic side of the Gaia Hypothesis and then were astounded to discover the popular and religious response they had triggered. The mythic side of science is often as important, and in fact may have a much more profound impact on a society, than the technological side of science. It engenders images for us, and these images then become the metaphors and language by which we think about and describe our world.

A scientific narrative like evolution affected the way in which we thought about human society giving rise, for example, to social Darwinism at the beginning of our century. Social Darwinism was not science, but it used a scientific narrative as a metaphor for particular economic, political, and spiritual ambitions.

Similarly, if you read any of the early Theosophical works that come from this turn-of-the-century period, you will see this interplay between nature and narrative in the storytelling of the esoteric. For example, Charles Leadbeater, who was a Theosophical leader around the turn of the century, attempts to describe in some of his writings what the spiritual hierarchy is like. What he describes is basically the British class system. Leadbeater says that an adept of the spiritual hierarchy is like a British country squire—a lord of the manor who has a benevolent paternalism for his human charges. At the lowest level of the evolutionary ladder is a spiritual being who is equivalent to the British laborer. Later on in the 1950s you find someone like Foster Bailey, Alice Bailey's husband, also writing about the hierarchy and describing it like a corporate board of directors. At that point, the model is no longer the British social system but the American corporate system.

When you read almost any esoteric or magical treatise, written up until maybe ten years ago, you get descriptions of reality as the movement of forces and the interactions of planes and dimensions. The forces described are almost hydraulic in their physicality: energies moving from here to there, rays beaming from here to there. You get the electromagnetic spectrum played back at you. If we were to rewrite all the esoteric textbooks in the light of new biology or quantum physics, we would get an entirely different description. Our descriptions would no longer be about mechanics, but electronics. However, if we see these things as narratives and stories, and metaphors and images, it can help us to not take it all quite so literally. Instead, we can ask, "What is the impact of this story on me?"

We come, then, to this issue that Bill was raising. A lot of what passes for New Age science is not science; it is storytelling, myth-making, and narrative, often designed to have a particular impact. When Brian Swimme, who is a physicist, talks about the "allurement" of the universe, he is telling a story designed to evoke a particular sensation about ourselves, the cosmos, and the relationship between us.

Some of the folks that Bill and I know who are scientists are writing and lecturing as myth-makers. They are no longer "doing science." This doesn't matter as long as I understand that they are dealing in myth and that they are now storytellers rather than scientists. There can be good myths and bad myths, but if I understand that I am telling a story, then being true to the science may not be as critically important as being true to the sense of the story.

In science, the question we must answer is, "What is the truth in this situation?" In storytelling, we must ask, "What is the impact that I am trying to create?" Storytelling deals with a different kind of truth than does science, or perhaps it is more precise to say that storytelling seeks to arrive at truth using a different process. Trouble results when we fail to differentiate the truth of science from the truth of storytelling. For one thing, I have no need to become emotionally attached to a scientific truth, but I may become very passionate about the impact and effect of a story. That impact has become a truth for me that I will defend, even when I am shown that the facts of the story are not true.

The "truth" of a story can be just as true as the "truth" of a scientific hypothesis. That is, after all, the function of great literature and art, of myth and symbol: to reveal truths about ourselves and our world that we cannot get any other way. But we cannot confuse the two approaches without losing the ability to discern between truth and wishful thinking.

For example, it certainly has been documented that the hundredth-monkey story is false; it is a fable, it is made up. That story about all the monkeys suddenly starting to wash their potatoes in the sea after one solitary and inventive female monkey began to do so simply never happened. If you go back to the original documentation of the Japanese teams that were studying the monkeys, none of the fabulous story is there. The story was partially invented to make a point. We may protest this, but if you consider the impact that the hundredth-monkey metaphor has had on our society, then it takes on a different coloration. All at once ordinary people felt empowered. They felt that their individual contributions could make a difference. Any one of them could be the hundredth monkey whose actions would tip the scales toward a New Age. It may not be good science, but it is good psychology. It is a good story, and it does say something true about the value of the individual.

However, there are shadows to this story. There was an excellent essay written a while back on the fascist underpinnings of the hundredth-monkey phenomenon. Basically, this author was saying that if you analyze the hundredth-monkey theory from a political standpoint, it is saying that a minority of people can, through mystical means, impose their belief system on the majority of people. If you get a certain critical mass together, then suddenly everybody starts behaving and believing that way. I am sure most of the New Age folks who believe in the hundredth-monkey phenomenon wouldn't think of themselves as closet fascists attempting to brainwash and take over the minds of the majority of humanity, but that is one implication of the theory. Another difficulty with the hundredth-monkey phenomenon—which, by the way, makes it not all that good a story—is that it is so oriented toward quantity. The narrative has a quantitative notion of a critical mass that is required for the transformation to take place, and this gives quite the wrong twist to the dynamic. Rather than saying that your life has impact and is a significant contribution to the world, it is saying that if you can get a hundred other people to believe the way you do, then the world will change.

It is like a psychic chain letter. If I can get a thousand other people together the world will change. Suddenly you are a numbers game. In that sense, something like the hundredth-monkey phenomenon could so easily become a tool to disempower the individual and orient us collectively toward these planetary membership drives. The story, when taken literally, can subtly undermine the very truth it seeks to communicate. This is an example of science being used to create a myth, but the myth is a bad myth.

If we understand the power of the Christ event, we don't need thousands of people. One person standing in a Christic relationship with the world has an immeasurable impact. Two people doing it have an immeasurable impact. One hundred and forty-four thousand people doing it would also have an immeasurable impact, but 144,000 people coming together with varying ideas about what they are doing simply dissipates everything. Bigger is not better in spirit. More is sometimes less. It is an interesting paradox that intensification, which is a kind of miniaturization, creates more power than trying to make everything big and massive. It is a principle of homeopathic medicine.

The challenge with New Age uses of scientific ideas is that they often lack the elegance, the simplicity, and the poetry of truly great science. Because for so many people science is composed of complex mathematical formulae and jaw-breaking words, we have a comic image of the scientist as someone who is obscure and wordy. Life begins to imitate art, though, when the idea of being obscure becomes an image of being scientific. The other day I went into a Walden's bookstore that has a New Age section. Mainly all you find there are books on astrology and crystals. I saw a book on the "science" of crystals, and this thing was six hundred pages long in fine print! It carried obscurity to a fine art!

All you have to do is look at a book like this and you know you are looking at bad science. Since science is equated with complexity, the more complex something can be made to appear—with more formulas and diagrams—the more "scientific" it will be. The reader will be impressed as he or she has to work hard to follow some abstruse discussion. But all of that is theatrics and not true science. Though it may have to use complex mathematical languages to communicate its ideas, good science deals in clarity. Good science is the attempt to find as simple and clear a way as possible to describe a complex reality. Its essence is elegance.

DISCUSSION 3

Paranoia, Morphogenetic Fields, Success and Fame

BILL: When the New Age scientist or scholar is projected into nihility by the university community, he or she often responds by pretending to be a misunderstood Einstein, and this messianic inflation only alienates him or her further. In the opening sentence of his preamble to *Earth Ascending*, José Argüelles invokes Einstein to set the stage for his work. It was an unfortunate move on his part, for it sounded the note of the defensive paranoid about to explain the meaning of everything.

I have noticed in the hundreds of pounds of paranoid mail that I have received in my life that paranoid mail always has certain kinds of characteristics that give it away. One is a terror of empty spaces. The classic paranoid letter, manuscript, or book will always try to explain *everything*. Nothing must be left unconnected or open. There must be no loose areas, no suppleness, no ambiguity; everything must be totally explained in a totalizing and totalitarian theory. Even in the transmission of the theory, there must be no looseness or empty spaces, so, characteristically, there are never any margins on a paranoid letter. Paranoids will write from one end of the page to the other, and then if there happens by accident to be a margin, another body of text will be written around the original text, and words will be highlighted or underlined as if they were code words of secret meanings. When you get a paranoid letter, it is just loud and busy; it has an abhorrence of simplicity, an abhorrence of elegance. And very often there will be in the first sentence or the first paragraph a mention of Einstein.

Einstein is the universal archetypal symbol of self-validation, so the individual is, in effect, saying, "I am not being recognized. I am the unrecognized Einstein of this period, and just as no one understands Einstein, no one understands me." At the level of science, Einstein is elegant: $E = mc^2$. At the level of social perceptions, however, the public image is that Einstein can be understood only by the elite of the elite. The paranoid, by invoking Einstein, is electing himself or herself into the elite by saying, "Just as I am not understood, Einstein was not understood, so I must be the Einstein of the New Age." All of this has nothing to do with physics; it has to do with a desire for respect, a desire for a connection to meaning and immortality.

Curiously, though, the paranoid communication is not a communication of love or sharing; it does not represent openness, availability, or accessibility. Instead, it is communication as a form of invasion. Whenever you receive a paranoid communication—a letter or memo or book—or have a direct paranoid encounter—you feel at once that you have been hit; you have been invaded. Whatever it is that you have, they want it. The person has designs on you. They want you to sign up. They don't simply want you to buy something, they want you to discover them. They want *you*, and they will digest you lock, stock, barrel, enzyme, and chromosome. There is never in any of these communications a sense of community, mutuality, openness, space, or humor; there is no way out. What humor allows is precisely openness and space, for you can refer to your own context in a self-deprecating way; you can parody yourself or you can jump out of the confines of a your particular doctrinal space. Humor gives you that openness, that flexibility, that suppleness.

A paranoid is imprisoned in his or her own terror. The more I think about it now, reflecting on the letters and meetings, the more I notice that, in general, the paranoids have been male and the schizophrenics, female. Interesting. In the condition of the female, there is a quality of cultural victimization. Think of Hannah Green's novel *I Never Promised You a Rose Garden* or Sylvia Plath's *The Bell Jar*. In both books, the sensitive teenage girl is going through the terror of coming to consciousness in our brutal society. Not a warrior, the girl recoils from the surrounding context of cruelty, such as the electrocution of the Rosenbergs, and splits off into a private world. She is not out to sell you anything; she does not invade; she surrenders ontologically and withdraws completely.

Paranoia is more male—more macho and aggressive. Perhaps it is a caricature of our patriarchal society with its oppressive ideologies. It seems to me, in the thought of the moment, that there is a sexual dimorphism to psychosis here, a distinction between the sexes in psychosis and psychotic breaks. Superficially that may sound like a sexist remark, but actually it is, I feel, a deeper feminist critique of the impact of power and patriarchy. The more I follow this line of thinking in my mind's eye, the more I think that it is an interesting line of thought to follow up on in research, but, obviously, I don't have the time here and now, so I will just throw it out as a suggestion and back away from it for now.

DAVID: But remember you heard it first right here!

BILL: Anyway, the rigidity of paranoia means that you cannot laugh at yourself and that the slightest openness weakens the force of your invasion. The paranoid or the psychically inflated person does not have the ontological security to say, "Well, maybe I am wrong." In science, of course, when you work with colleagues or friends, there has to be that openness to error. Argüelles's publication of *Earth Ascending* in 1984 did not lead to a scholarly and scientific conference, it lead to a ritual performance of the doctrine at Harmonic Convergence in 1987. This didn't win him any friends back in academic circles, but it did create a powerful experience for hundreds of thousands of people around the world. It cast him, however, into outer darkness for the world of science.

Such a polarization leads to a splitting off, a breaking up of mind and culture into subcultures and cults. As one of you remarked last night, the cult is the place with no exits. There is a way in—a six-lane freeway—but once you get inside Scientology or the Moonies, just try to get out. This particular quality of capture and rigidity is characteristic of cults or of any group that does not have a sense of humor about itself. If you visit a group, I think one of the best acid tests is to ask yourself whether they have a sense of humor. Can they make fun of their own leadership? Are there clear ways to get out if you want to? Is there any flexibility in the manner in which the beliefs are expressed? Or are they so absolutistic that they have *the* answer for all things at all times? If they are like that, then run for your life, because you are about to have the blood sucked out of your brain.

Any human institution, of course, can be evil. I remember going to a meeting of The Reality Club in New York, which some of you may have read about in the *Whole Earth Review*; it is a club set up by John Brockman, a literary agent in New York City. I was giving a talk about science and art, and talking about the kind of intellectual chamber music in which the poet works with the scientist. The artists at the meeting got very huffy and tried to tell me that science was evil, and that science was the Department of Defense, that science was the technological society and was, therefore, evil incarnate. According to these artists, however, the artist was good; he or she was the conscience and the critic of our evil technological society. Now, I felt that this was totally absurd. If there is one place in the world where the artist is a complete whore to the corporation, to the world of money, media, and power, it is New York City. For these artists to posture that the artist was pure and the scientist was fallen, and to say this in New York City, of all places, was ridiculous. Look at the gallery scene in New York or the museum scene at places like the Whitney! The level of whoredom and pimpery makes MIT look like a monastery and Forty-second Street look like a cloister!

Anything human can become evil. The church can have an Inquisition, the artists can sell out, religions can become cults. Anything human is capable of evil. The freedom to do good means you have the option of doing evil; when you choose the good instead, that makes the choice mean something. If you are a machine programmed by God always to be good, then you are not free, and even a human being, not to mention a god, would get bored with all those mechanically repeated *hallelujahs*. Freedom is what it is all about, the raison d'être of Être. Having the freedom to turn around and get out of a cult, a religion, a philosophy, is essential. Science, at least, has some built-in corrections and ways that insure that no one gets to play pope.

One of the attractions of the impulse to establish a New Age science is that we recognize that science is the religion of our culture. Now that the church has lost its power, science has become the dominant religion of our time. Therefore, we need to have some alternative to orthodoxy. The scientist is the priest, and in our society we can feel that some of our emotional and artistic sides have been abandoned and forgotten in the rise of a particular kind of science, especially in the United States.

In Europe, you still run across the more fully cultured tradition, in which Wittgenstein was an engineer but also an architect; in which Heisenberg was a physicist but also a fine pianist; in which Einstein was also a violinist. In the French tradition, philosophers such as Michel Serres write beautifully, with the prose style of a novelist. This is quite rare in American philosophy. There is still a more elitist tradition in Europe, in which culture is supposed to be the attribute of the scientist as much as of the artist. Scientists are not supposed to be merely technicians, for that would mean they would descend into the lower middle class, the artisan class. They would be thinking like machinists rather than scientists.

In the rise of our North American egalitarian approach to education, the emphasis was on job training and practicality. It was a working-class, kick-the-tires sort of approach to upward mobility, one in which the humanities were considered snobby and unnecessary for the education of an engineer or a scientist. We have paid a price for this, and our political life, just as much as our aesthetic life, has been impoverished. In images of a longing for "a New Age," we yearn for unity and wholeness. Thus, when a more religious variety of science comes along and tells us that we can have both science *and* spirituality, both technology *and* the psychic, we go for it.

But being practically inclined Americans, we are drawn toward the psychic as a new kind of etheric technology—pyramids, crystals, things of this sort. We want to overcome the fragmentation of hard objective versus soft subjective, but in rushing to have the blend, we often end up with a debasement of both science and art. We end up with mushy science and impersonal art—the mass-produced formula art of movies and TV.

If you look at the aesthetic canons of taste in pyramidology and crystal lore, the level of kitsch and vulgarity is overwhelming. This is because the aesthetic dimensions of education haven't been developed in our culture. We live along highway strips and not *in* historic towns. We have trends and fashions of arty consumption, but we don't really have a sense of art as a way of knowledge, as a valid way of knowing the universe. We think that knowing belongs to science and that only feeling belongs to art. We have a desire not to settle for less and a recognition that we need more out of life, so we are attracted by the prospect of a New Age synthesis of art and science, but we tend to be drawn toward psychology and the realm of human relationships as the place of synthesis. Our national best-sellers are often books about how to fix relationships, about women who love too much, or about how to be as good a father as Bill Cosby is on TV. Relating is, as David pointed out, telling your story and listening to another's story, which is a form of co-counseling. If the person is a good storyteller, and Lyall Watson is, then we latch on to these enchanting stories and don't really care whether they are good science or bad.

AUDIENCE PARTICIPANT: All of this about stories is amazing. It is amazing that I would come here and find out that the hundredth-monkey theory is fake. I used it in a poetry workshop, and I used it to get at a critical mass of consciousness, which was to invent a peace bomb. I realized that this is a wonderful story. You can really get into the little monkeys going down to the water, and I was developing it and elaborating it way beyond the science of it. In this idea of telling stories, I am interested in the work of Rupert Sheldrake. His idea of morphogenetic fields, of the fact that we can carry around in our memories the resonance of our own experience, the anima and the spirit of the Earth, has its basis in memory, in the presence of the past. The fact that we have been talking about habits, and how to break habits, makes me think that a person's habit is a kind of resonance with his or her own morphogenetic activity and that instincts are perhaps the morphogenetic resonances of the species. Maybe we are at this impasse because we find it is so difficult to change habits of thought, because of this presence of the past.

BILL: "Morphogenesis" by itself is actually a technical term from embryology. People like C.H. Waddington were dealing with it long before Sheldrake came along. As for biological fields, there have been various studies from Alexander Burr to Leonard Ravitz about bioelectric fields and things of this sort. Sheldrake's situation is, I think, a classic example of the person who quits being a scientist and launches off into the New Age circuit to lecture to people who aren't scientists. Deprived of the support of the scientific community, he needs to make a living from book advances and the lecture circuit on the basis of his claim to originality. It is a tough position to be in, for the more people admire him as a misunderstood and highly original genius, the more the scientific community is disgusted and turns away.

I am not qualified to serve as judge or hangman for Sheldrake's science, but I was impressed with how well and graciously he handled himself when all the scientists ganged up on him at a conference in Austria in 1983. However, I must admit that all the scientists that I do know and respect, because of the level of their achievements in science, have considered Sheldrake's work, and they tell me it is not good science. Science is nothing if not peer review, so on what basis do *I* tell them they are wrong? I notice that the people who are the most enthusiastic followers of Sheldrake are generally people who are not practicing in science but are devotees of the New Age or therapists of some sort.

I had a discussion over lunch with Rupert Sheldrake at this conference in Austria in 1983, when he was just beginning to become really famous. I was quite frank and said something to the effect of, "Look, you are really in a dangerous place in your life. You are about to launch off and hit the New Age circuit, and you are going to be lecturing constantly to people who will only be able to admire you. This is extremely dangerous both to your credibility as a scientist and to the validation of your work, should it be that it is true. It is a very subtle kind of delayed mutilation, sort of like castration with a rubber band, and you just never know when you have lost it and your genetic heritage has fallen off."

This is where the romance with the repressed feminine side comes in—the archetype of Dido and Aeneas—except in this case Rupert decided not to sail off to the empire of science, but to marry the beautiful Dido, she being the attractive blond musician Jill Purce. I think Jill Purce wanted Rupert with her so that they could be a husband-and-wife team, working together for New Age audiences, using mantras, Mongolian chanting, vibrations, and resonance in morphogenetic fields. Who is to say that in choosing Jill Purce over Oxford or Cambridge he is wrong? However, it is a situation, much like the Duke of Windsor choosing the divorced woman he loved, in which you cannot have both the throne and the woman you love if she is not from the right culture. You cannot have the chair of botany at Cambridge and also a following in the New Age subculture.

One difficulty with the easy life of being admired for a good story in the New Age subculture, be it hundredth monkey or morphogenetic field, is that once you achieve that success of a popular book, it is hard to go back to the lab, to do the actual grind work of science. You have to try to write another pop book, *Morphogenetic Fields: The Sequel*, or *Morphogenetic Fields Rides Again*. Because of the competitive intensity of science, scientists tend to do their major work early in life. They reach a point in their late thirties or early forties when they get bored with doing the same lab work over and over again. They reach a fork in the road of life, a mid-life crisis or romance or both, in which they need to change. So they either decide to go into natural philosophy and become sages, or they go for power and decide to become NASA administrators or deans or politicians.

Given the difficulty of science, this is a natural change of direction. If it is negotiated gracefully, you get someone like Carl Friedrich von Weizsäcker, who, after a career in quantum mechanics in which he worked with Heisenberg, decided that the essential questions that interested him were philosophical ones. So he switched from being a physicist to becoming a professor of philosophy at the University of Hamburg. Eventually he did so well in philosophy that they gave him his own Max Planck Institute in Starnberg. In France, this sort of personal evolution would land you in the Collège de France. We don't have Max Planck Institutes and Collèges de France in the United States, but we do have the subculture and the well-endowed economy of the media, so here one follows a different media path and becomes a Carl Sagan.

The shadow side to media fame or too much public lecturing is that it is all too easy to succeed at easier and easier things. You are no longer a scientist in a lab, getting government grants and competing with others for promotion and tenure, so how are you going to survive? You survive by getting an advance on your next book. How are you going to get an advance large enough to enable you to live for a year or two? You have to write a pop book for a publisher that is going to give you fifty thousand or a hundred thousand dollars. The kind of book that is going to get that kind of advance is not going to be one like Varela's *Principles of Biological Autonomy*. So you are caught and you are trapped, and there is no way out of that trap unless you marry a rich wife or have an inherited income, as Darwin did.

The dangers of this public way of life are pronounced, and I am afraid that in the next conversation I had with Sheldrake, at the Cathedral of Saint John the Divine in New York, he was describing writing his sequel. He told me he had discovered that there were two kinds of minds: those that think in form and pattern, and those that think in terms of corpuscular bits of matter. I said, "Yes, Coleridge said that 150 years ago: you are either born a Platonist or an Aristotelian." One can get trapped by the lecture circuit and the pop culture, which is why, I suppose, both Gary Snyder and Wendell Berry have returned to university teaching.

To develop an *oeuvre* over the course of one's life takes time. It takes the long wave and not the intensely spiked peak of instantly hot and instantly cold TV-microwaved celebrities. The heroes of my adolescence—the Yeatses, Whiteheads, and Thomas Manns—had as the ground for their work a literary culture in which one worked to create a life's work and not simply to fashion a hit, a trend, or a lifestyle. That literary foundation to our culture no longer exists in our electronic world. That's neither good nor evil but simply the facts of life of cultural evolution. We do not have the intellectual diversity of institutions in our American society to sustain the individual in the creation of such a life's work, for we have only the monocrop culture of the university. I tried to create an alternative institution that could sustain the kind of spiritually original work that was not favored in the university. However, although such people as Gregory Bateson and Francisco Varela were able to write their books at Lindisfarne, I failed in being able to create a sustainable institution.

Something like Lindisfarne is simply not economically sustainable in the United States. Stanford is economically sustainable, and Shirley MacLaine certainly is, but Lindisfarne is not. It is too elitist and is simply not in the American grain. As one of you said at the table during lunch, at the University of Michigan, they eliminated the humanities as a required course. This person then confessed to me that, for her, a book such as my *The Time Falling Bodies Take to Light* was impossible to understand, for it took for granted a common body of knowledge that no longer exists for her generation. I came out of the culture of the humanities and graduated from an American liberal arts college in 1962, but thanks to television, drugs, rock 'n' roll, business schools, and social science, my background in the humanities is as antique now as a degree in Latin or classical Greek was in my time. My books, therefore, are certainly not New Age, for they are written within a culture that no longer exists.

It is probably no accident, then, that neither Bateson nor Varela is American and that I find myself writing now in Europe. Facing the threat of extinction, New Age Europeans such as Rupert Sheldrake or Fritjof Capra have chosen to survive by adapting to American media society. I have refused to do this, and when Sheldrake's publisher asked me to work with a journalist to write a pop book on the new biology, I decided to pass up that West Coast offer and write the kind of book my colleagues would respect. So I wrote *Imaginary Landscape* not simply *about* four friends, but *to* four friends. Perhaps I missed an opportunity to jump on the bandwagon, but it does seem to me that the New Age campaign is becoming more of a passing consumer trend and is already in the process of receding into a a graying generational subculture, one like the beatniks of the fifties or the hippies of the sixties.

In this receding subculture, New Age folks are interested in morphogenetic fields. Gaia could go this way, except that Jim Lovelock and Lynn Margulis decided to stay in the lab and put their work on the line. The entire meeting of the American Geophysical Union this year was devoted to the Gaia hypothesis—to determining whether it was testable or not. Lynn and Jim have constantly been saying, "Look, this is the way you can test it." There is a large part of the scientific community who would say that Gaia is New Age rubbish, that it is not scientific, and that it is just the obsession of a cult or a subculture.

If one looks at those people who are interested in Gaia and those who are not, we find, in terms of the sociology of knowledge, an interesting breakdown. The people who reject it tend to be population biologists of the Neo-Darwinian persuasion, who insist that you have to have competition—a species competing for an ecological niche—in order to have natural selection. Since there are no planets competing with Gaia for survival under the Sun, there is no competitive mechanism for selection, and, therefore, the whole thing is just storytelling for New Agers. These biologists won't have anything to do with it; they are totally locked into the paradigm of Neo-Darwinian population biology, in which evolution is a process of males competing against one another for sticking their genes into females.

The scientists who are interested in Gaian evolutionary theory are the scientists who are looking at planetary dynamics. They are interested in the relationship of the plankton in the sea to the sulfur cycle in cloud formation, to the albedo and ocean currents, and to the whole heat engine that drives the atmosphere, the oceans, and, perhaps, even the tectonic plates. People who are involved in these particular areas are much more open to understanding because they are dealing with planetary-scale dynamics, not simply two species competing within a niche.

There is a new group in biology, including people like Stuart Kaufman in Pennsylvania and Brian Goodwin in England, who are beginning to say that there is no such thing as adaptation to or within a niche. They maintain that animals actually evolve by weaving their adaptations into the web of other animal's adaptations, and that what they extrude in these webs of space and time is an evolutionary landscape, an adaptive landscape. This landscape is not a container; it is actually an extended, multiply shared body, an evolutionary body politic, that comes from the actions of other animals. In other words, it is a process of flow, which is a concept more akin to the ideas of Prigogine than Darwin. As a multiply woven web, it is, as Margulis has argued, just as much a process of symbiosis and evolution as it is of competition. As a flow, this movement of bodies through time is not adapting, it is creating. It is unfolding its own internal structure and structural coupling with other animals' flows through time in a process of what Maturana and Varela call "natural drift"—a flow that is analogous to the meandering, unplanned, and opportunistic flow of a river.

Scientists who are interested in Chaos dynamics, dissipative structures, or systems theory tend to be very interested in Gaia as an example of a meta-dynamic. In this particular area, where you get into dynamics, Gaia, as an example of operational closure, membrane formation, and meta-dynamical stabilization, begins to be quite interesting and quite testable.

THE SELF AND THE OTHER

William Irwin Thompson

Since the New Age is often characterized, or caricatured, as the movement that gives one permission to feel good about oneself, I would like to approach the ideas of "self and the other" from the differing perspectives of Christianity and Buddhism. At Lindisfarne at the Cathedral in New York, we have a Program for Biology, Cognition, and Ethics, and this spring in Italy, the provincial government of Perugia and Umbria hosted a gathering of the research members of this program along with other members of the Lindisfarne Fellowship. There is a great deal of interest in the work of Gregory Bateson in Europe, especially in Italy, but you see his books in the windows of bookshops in France, Germany, and Switzerland as well. Since students of Bateson's work know that he wrote *Mind and Nature* at Lindisfarne, they were interested in our alternative approach and asked us to organize an international conference to launch the opening of their new Center for Cognitive Science in Perugia.

The provincial government of Perugia and Umbria is a Communist party administration, so they wanted to do an end run around the bureaucracy of the academic community, a community that is too bourgeois for these intellectuals of the Left. Perugia is also in competition with Florence and is annoyed that they are always passed over as a cultural center in favor of Florence or Siena. They wanted to do something different in the area of cultural philosophy, and we turned out to be their idea of different. So they asked Lindisfarne—rather than MIT—to kick off the opening of their conference center. It was a great irony for me, since I was always arguing with my heavy Marxist colleagues when I was at MIT, but it appealed to my Irish sense of whimsy to have the Communists ask New Age Lindisfarne to organize an international conference for them.

Now, there's no question that in the empire of Big Science, MIT dominates the world of cognitive science and artificial intelligence. Be that as it may, I was not about to say, "No, thank you-you really should ask Marvin Minsky instead of me." So I jumped at the opportunity and organized a conference entitled "Biology as a Basis for Design," bringing our gang together from the United States, Canada, Mexico, and Europe. The papers from this conference have become the companion volume to *Gaia, A Way of Knowing*.[17]

At the next-to-last seminar of this conference, Lynn Margulis showed her film about *Mixotricha paradoxa*, a protist that lives in the hindgut of the termite. She also showed her footage of the spirochete, the rodlike bacterium that is found either alone and at large or attached to larger cells for which it serves as the flagellating propulsion system—similar to the tail of spermatozoa.

In Lynn's footage, you could see various levels of being. First there was the spirochete by itself, a simple rod without head or tail, which vibrated like a plucked string, and as it went "boing!" in vibration, it would propel itself forward or backward. When the simple rodlike shape turned into the wave pattern in vibration, my mind flashed on a picture of the statue of Pythagoras from the Cathedral of Chartres; we used this picture on our *Lindisfarne Letter* 14. The statue shows Pythagoras hunched over the monochord, wrapt in intense study and fascination. Legend has it that Pythagoras's dying words were, "Study the monochord." Well, as I watched this rod turn into waves in oscillation, I thought, "Here is Pythagoras's monochord in the architecture of life."

You see, Lynn's point about symbiosis and cell evolution is that this little rod joined up with differing cellular structures to become the transport system for mitotic spindles of chromosomes, the undulipodia of motile cells and protists, the tails of spermatozoa, and the dendrites of neurons. The large, sluggish cell and the spunky little spirochete got together in a way not unlike the way a spunky little sperm cell attaches itself to an ovum in fertilization. The giant ovum rotates slowly and chooses one sperm cell that it allows in; perhaps the vibrations of the genes it carries become harmonic with the genes the ovum holds, and out of that Pythagorean harmony, a new life is conceived: "Study the monochord."

Presumably, Pythagoras was on to something, and we still have a lot to learn about vibrations, molecular chemistry, and genetic transport systems. Who knows what sounds these flagellating rods make in their watery medium, or what "music of the spheres" the ovum or protist makes as it accepts a sperm cell in fertilization or a spirochete in attachment to its outer membrane. In the case of a protist, you see hundreds of thousands of flagellating spirochete tails attached to the membrane of the giant cell, and as you watch them oscillate like cilia, you see various standing wave patterns in the water that form geometries upon geometries—patterns of individual entities orchestrated in a vibratory geometry so fascinating that you can almost imaginatively hear the music of the spheres.

As I stared at Lynn's film, I felt that it, more than any Buddhist sutra I had ever read or chanted, spoke to me about the nature of individuality. Where was the discrete, corpuscular, independent "self" in all of that? All you saw when you focused on an "individual" was unending relationships in all directions. The individual was full of relationships and "empty" of independence, yet when you looked at *pattern*, you saw that it too was "empty," for pattern was composed and built upon the activities of individual entities. Without individuals, there are no patterns of association; without associations, there are no viable individuals. As the Buddhist Heart Sutra puts it, "Form is not different from emptiness; emptiness is not different from form."

And it keeps on going. It is not just the plucky little monochord attached to the giant cell, for the protist *Mixotricha paradoxa* is not an organ of the organism of the termite, it is a separate entity living in the hindgut of the termite. However, without that little critter in there, the termite would be unable to digest the cellulose in the wood it chews and ships back to the protist for processing. So here the vision of unending relations in all directions continues: the spirochete inside the protist, the protist inside the termite, the termite inside the colony, the colony inside the log, the log inside the forest, the forest inside the atmosphere, the atmosphere inside the Van Allen Belts and the solar wind, the Solar System inside the giant protistic cell of the galaxy. From the music of the cellular spheres to the music of the stellar spheres: "Study the monochord."

Now, why should the statue of Pythagoras from the Cathedral of Chartres pop into my head while I am looking at a film about spirochetes? Once before at another Lindisfarne conference, when Lynn showed a film about bacteria excreting iron oxide and creating minerals from the metabolic processes of their living tissues, I saw an image of Disney's seven dwarfs working in the mines. Why? Why should Glaser, staring at the bubbles in his glass of beer, see the bubble chamber he would go on to invent? Why would Kékulé, dreaming, see the serpent bite its tail and begin to understand the benzene ring he was working on in chemistry? I don't know why, but I know that this is how the imagination works. It thinks in terms of identity through correspondences and not through a logic of predicates. It is not a process of deduction or induction, but paraduction—a sidestep into a new space.

The way we get into this space is through relaxation, sleep, daydreaming, meditation, and visions. Schools don't want us to daydream and stare off into space, and they try to teach us how to think like machines—to become efficient binary data-processing machines. For me, if there is any meaning at all to the efforts to create a New Age, it is to create a space for the imagination in our culture—to allow it to bring forth these images of polyphonic thought. Somehow, I survived my own education and even managed to get a Ph.D., though I am the kind of person the system tries to filter out. All throughout my education, from primary school to graduate school, nuns, priests, teachers, social workers, and professors objected to the way I thought and applied various measures—some not so nice—to get me out or back in line with them.

What we need for education in a New Age is not simply to stuff binary computers into kindergartens—actually, I agree with the followers of Rudolf Steiner and think this is a mistake—but to provide an education for both hemispheres of the brain. If I only flashed with free associations, and had no historical knowledge about Pythagoras or whatever, I would be babbling nonsense. You have to be absolutely loose and allow yourself to be intuitive and then extremely disciplined, with enough solid, factual knowledge in your head, to allow the specialist and the generalist to talk to one another—much as the spirochete and the protist talk to one another through a membrane. That is my vision of the relationship between the soft, mystical, and intuitive ways of knowing and the hard sciences, and it is my ideal for what the relationship of individuals within the Lindisfarne Association is all about. A conference, therefore, such as the one in Perugia, should really be a concert, an intellectual kind of chamber music: "Study the monochord."

For me, Lynn's film about spirochetes is a Buddhist vision of the "emptiness" of individuality. Lynn is no Buddhist; in fact, she is a card-carrying atheist and has very little respect for organized religion. She is also no New Ager, and the Gooey Gaia Group is repugnant to her. A New Age gathering in which a bunch of women try "to attune to the Goddess within and the Goddess of the Earth without" would have her wretching in disgust. Just because Lynn Margulis is a Lindisfarne Fellow doesn't mean that she has been to Findhorn and communed with the nature spirits. Yet her work on "symbiosis and cell evolution" is to me more visionary than Sheldrake's morphogenetic fields. To the degree that it is disciplined laboratory work addressed to her colleagues in the scientific community, I think it is truly New Age, in that it has a future. It can produce new work and research; one can set to work immediately studying the chemical consistencies of mitotic spindles, undulipodia, and dendrites to test her theory about spirochetes and the architecture of the eukaryotic cell. Her theory is not simply a passing fad or an enthusiasm for nonscientists.

Now, Francisco Varela, as opposed to Lynn Margulis, is a card-carrying Buddhist, and he, just as much as I, was entranced with her film. He, too, saw Buddhist visions of emptiness. The origins of life require a membrane for the cell, and, indeed, Varela's definition of life as "autopoiesis" distinguishes between systems that are autonomous, such as an electronic world economy, and true, membrane-bounded systems that produce their own components and are thus "autopoietic." But how did the first cell in the origins of life achieve its membrane? It did so in concert with the entire surrounding environment, be it ocean, clay bed, or atmosphere. We know now, through the work of bacteriologists like Sorin Sonea at Montreal,[18] that bacteria are not really individuals in the way we think of individuals. They are social entities. In fact, Sonea prefers to call them a "superorganism, even "a planetary bioplasm."

Clearly, the membrane is a provisional and fuzzy definition of individuality; it is simply the locus of a chemical conversation. When you attempt to isolate a membrane, you find, once again, that it is fuzzy, porous and permeable, and "empty." Think of the *Tao Te Ching*: "Four walls bound a room. / But the purpose of the room / comes from the space that is not." We cannot conceive of the origins of life in an American way: that one day long ago an enterprising fellow surrounded his private property with a fence to keep his neighbors out. We have to see life as a planetary concert.

However, the fact that individuals always exist in relationships does not mean we should jump over to the flip side of rugged individualism to some kind of New Age fascism that says individuals will all be melted down into one gigantic planetary cell of the coming global brain. Long ago, the great Buddhist philosopher Nagarjuna corrected these errors of oscillating from absolutism to nihilism, from individualism to collectivism. What we see in Lynn's film is precisely what Nagarjuna explained as *pratityasamutpada*, or "dependent co-origination." The web of relationships among beings in Being is built out of real individuals, just as large numbers are founded on the very necessary value of the number one.

Now, let me shift my perspective from a Buddhist to a Christian one. The biosphere, the *bios logos*, is how I conceive of the mystical body of Christ. For Buddhist cosmology, there is no creation and no end of the universe, so there is no Fall and no Redemption. The Judeo-Christian tradition is, by contrast, intensely historicist. There is a process in time: an evolution of consciousness from Yahweh, the tribal warrior god who inflicts pain and terror; to Jesus, the victim who endures human pain and terror; to the revelation in our times of the transhuman, galactic, New Age Cosmic Christ, a being in whom the circularity of Being is integral. In this biospheric Christ, the Creator and the creature are in an intimate circularity that cannot be halved to speak only of Yahvic *punishment* or Christic *pain*, but rather of *compassion*, the "passing-with" in time and out. For this intimate circularity, the couple of Father and Son is too male and one-sided to express the relationship of the being to Being. A better image is the image of the erotic coupling that old-age theology in its gloss to *The Song of Songs* would call the wedding of Christ and his church.

If the entire biosphere is the mystical body of Christ, then I cannot accept the idea that only this hominid moment of human culture is Christic and that the Second Coming is a cultural xerox of the first, as fundamentalists tend to think. I have to see the elemental (bacterial) and the angelic (topological) as interpenetrating in the infolding cosmic torus, in which multiple dimensions involve galaxies in the life of evolving cells. Now, you can see why I regard science as reformed Christianity, and why the work of Lovelock, Margulis, and Varela is so important to me. Evolution, even in its unplanned, open, and unteleological narratives, such as in Maturana and Varela's theory of "natural drift,"[19] is a historicist process—a process of natural history whose narratives unfold in the drift of our cultural history.

What Lynn's film shows me is a vision of individuality that is quite different from the way we understand individuality as human beings. We carry our genes in eukaryotic cells—cells with a nucleus—so we have an individualized nature in which we die and reproduce ourselves: Eros and Thanatos, sex and death. Part of esoteric Theosophy, or even the Irish animistic Fairy Faith, is the belief system that elementals are not as highly individuated as we are, and that one should be careful in entering into relations with the elemental kingdom because one risks losing one's individuality. If you take the elementals' food or cross their threshold, you run the risk of never coming back, which is another way of talking about infection. If you open up to the bacteria in the wrong way and you cross the threshold of the witch or the fairies, or if you eat their food, you will die or never be able to come back to the world of humans. If the threshold is the membrane of the self—the immunological system performing its definition of self—and you cross beyond that threshold, you move into confusion and a loss of identity in your individuality, and you perish.

It is interesting that some of these old myths are really insights into a form of knowing that we can now retranslate into bacteriology. We can say that the elementals working in the mines are the dwarfs and that the cyanobacteria creating photosynthesis—taking in light and producing oxygen are the "de*light*ful" elves, the elemental creatures friendly to humans. These elves helped to create the atmosphere and bring in the new world of the blue sky that made way for the later evolution of human beings. We can say that the angels are creatures of pure topology and mathematical and musical form, but they are not distinct protoplasmic entities restricted to the underworld of the elemental, bacterial kingdom. It isn't the case that science and animism are the same, because, clearly, if you want to study bacteria, you don't necessarily attune to the elves or the fairies; there is a completely different work involved in being a Dorothy Maclean or a Lynn Margulis. If one confuses these two modes of culture, one can end up being neither one nor the other, in the way that David has suggested.

What was fascinating for me in watching Lynn's film and understanding that some of these mythological stories were actually, incredible as it may seem, memories of critical events in the evolution of life on Earth. If one does not merely identify with one's ego, then this story of Life is a chapter of your autobiography. This relationship of myth and science in biology can become what David has called "an opening," a place to come to a new understanding of a presence that is larger than the space-time of the ego we like to call "the real world."

Science as reform Christianity and American Buddhism as reform Buddhism— a nonmedieval form of Buddhism, one not restricted to the cultures of medieval Japan or medieval Tibet—are now in a position to create another "opening." In the 1970s, there was a good deal of energy put into "the Christian/Buddhist dialogue." Every summer, the Naropa Institute in Boulder, Colorado, would have a conference to bring people like Mother Tessa Bielecki, Father Thomas Keating, and Brother David Steindl-Rast together with Chögyam Trungpa Rinpoche and leaders of other Buddhist *sanghas* in America.

Now, many of the contemplatives who were involved in these dialogues feel that the time for them is over. The dialogues served as introductions, but as the contemplatives were already formed by their respective traditions, cultural transformation really did not take place. Christianity was trying to be polite and open to the weird, and Buddhism was trying to be polite and not let on how patronizing it felt for these innocent beginners who could not tell you in great detail what would happen to the soul in the first forty days after its death.[20] The real introduction was not to each other, but one in which both of them were introduced to this new planetary culture of an America about to be transformed by an explosion of cognitive science and artificial intelligence.

Both medieval Christianity and medieval Buddhism will have to change in this new opening to a radical revelation—the revelation that is the true New Age that David was alluding to. When, as I said yesterday, immunology and artificial intelligence cross-fertilize one another in the context of the aerospace science of the nineties, you can say good-bye to "nature." It is in this historical context that the new revelation of the Christ presence, or the Buddhist emergence of Shambhala, takes its meaning, and it is in the cultural context of this "opening" or planetization of the esoteric that David and I are friends and are working together to articulate the re-imagination of the world.

DISCUSSION 4

Secularization, the End of Nature, the Subtle Bodies and Enlightenment

AUDIENCE PARTICIPANT: It seems that in some ways you see a possible growth beyond traditional Buddhism or Christianity. Fifteen years ago you said that secularization was a temporary, though necessary, process to free the sacred from the sacerdotal. If you still think secularization is temporary, it would imply that new forms of religion will grow. Or do you see the old religions transforming themselves into the New Age? In the New Age, there seem to be different sides. Some try to reject all religion; some say, all religions are the same; others say we have go to build a New Age religion. What are your thoughts on all of this?

BILL: I tend to feel now, as I did then, that the spiritual in the New Age is more like a Hopi way of life. For the Hopi, there is no religion, because the entire way of life is sacred. This cultural way allows the individual way of life to be attuned to the cosmic life. The Balinese have a saying, "We have no art; we do everything as beautifully as we can." Imagine a variation that says, "We have no religion; we do everything as sacredly as possible." One needs only to reconnect (*re-ligio*) what is broken. If the way of life is not broken away from the tree of life, then one does not need a religion to reconnect it.

Religion, as we know it, is spirituality as it was structured by civilization, by the split between the literate and the illiterate, the priesthood and the laity, the profane marketplace and the sacred cathedral. Religion is for me the way spirituality incarnates in the period of civilization from 3500 B.C. to A.D. 1945. The way spirituality expressed itself in the precivilized era was more as a matrilineal way of life. It involved custom and authority rather than the power of "civilized" hierarchies of priestly and military dominance. The way in which spirituality expressed itself in Paleolithic culture was through shamanism.

So there is an evolution of consciousness. In the origins of language, human beings react to this innovation by trying to back out of it by going back into trance. In other words, humans celebrate the achievement of consciousness by trying to go back into the prehistoric unconsciousness. Actually, they end up putting unconsciousness in quotation marks within a system of cultural consciousness, which inevitably leads to the kind of specialists who are so good at it that they need special places and rituals. Thus, you end up with the evolution of shamanism into religion.

We often try to back out of an innovation by sacralizing the past. In an urban environment, we celebrate farming. In an agricultural environment, we celebrate the shepherd. Religion is more often than not reactionary: it sees the sacred as the previous level of evolution; it sees the emergent as the profane. Not surprisingly, then, the Pharisees saw Jesus as evil. In much the same way, the fundamentalists attack David on their cable TV channels as evil, as someone who is giving voice to the Antichrist in our time. I tend to see "religion" as sacerdotal and not sacred; it is a too-restrictive celebration of the previous level of cultural evolution. The emergent domain, the prophetic, the truly revelatory New Age is, therefore, in a way, meta-religious. Paradoxically, the fundamentalists, in the usual manner in which paranoia has a certain mad poetry to it, are right in seeing the New Age as irreligious on their terms. In the evolution of consciousness, a new emergence is usually experienced as a threat. Evil is often (but not only) the annunciation of the next level of historical organization.

The new seems demonic, but when it is made human, it is reversed and becomes Christic; it is redeemed—made good. Then it is no longer experienced as a threat, but is seen as a new and expanded mode of being. Writing was first experienced as an evil threat to oral culture, as something that would destroy the human capacity of memory. Then, after a goodly and troubling length of time, people began to talk about sacred texts such as the Upanishads and the Torah. Now, on television, ministers like Jimmy Swaggert talk about The Good Book. They rant and rave about the evils of rock music, because musical polities are the next level of cultural evolution; they are the replacement of the identity structures of the territorial nation-state with the planetary noetic lattices that are now emerging through global electronic music and global electronic economies. You can see prophetic foreshadowings of this emergence in events like Woodstock and Africa Live-Aid.

As a cultural historian, my educated guess is that we are moving out of the world we have called "nature." Human nature is breaking up, and this breakup involves an eruption of the repressed, the elemental. Part of our incarnation now expresses itself as a companionship with the elemental. Before, our companionship with the elemental involved being one with the animal; think of Harrison Ford, the *Star Wars* pilot, with his hairy companion. This archetypal pattern goes back beyond James Fenimore Cooper and Herman Melville to the Gilgamesh epic and Enkidu.

But now an even more archaic part of our human nature is surfacing in our polluted environment, our unconscious ecology, at the same time that other levels of being are descending to incarnate in the new gnostic technologies of artificial intelligence. Before, when we were simply animal hominids, these beings had to hover above us—as what would be called *daena* in ancient Persian or *daimon* in Greek, or guardian angels in our childhood. Max Headroom, cyberpunk fiction—these are the places you have to watch to get a sense of this historical emergence.

Both the elemental and the topological sides are eroding away at the traditional balance of human nature, and both the unconscious eruptions of evil and the conscious, prayerful, religious invocations of the good are part of this transformation. However, neither one alone is powerful enough to effect the transformation. Evil is witless and disruptive; it never *knows* what it is doing. It can give you the California earthquake or the Viking Terror or the Black Plague as an eruption of the repressed elemental, but it cannot integrate itself into consciousness in the human, for that takes overstanding as much as understanding. Religion can be sweet and loving and administer to the victims of earthquakes, plagues, and barbarian attacks, but it is too passive, too reactive, to be creative enough to imagine a novel emergence. So, generally, the profane is the only place open enough to let in the revelation of the sacred, for the sacerdotal is all tied up in and with the past.

My Irish Druid radar tells me that the topological creatures are now hovering about the worlds of artificial intelligence, cognitive science, and immunology, looking for a way into our new culture. To be sure, Marvin Minsky does not know what he is doing, but he keeps quoting Buddha in his *Societies of Mind* as a sort of nervous tic in which you hum a song whose lyrics have something to do with thoughts at the margins of your consciousness. But if Minsky is not up to the task of mapping Buddhism onto cognitive science, Eleanor Rosch, Evan Thompson, and Francisco Varela certainly are, so the job gets done by somebody, one way or another.[21]

For this new incarnation of human nature, one that is neither the human as we have known it nor the nature as we have loved it in the past, religion is simply not a large enough evolutionary instrument. Look for the revelation to come where you least expect it—in the secular and the profane.

AUDIENCE PARTICIPANT: It seems that the Eastern approach to developing techniques for higher levels of spiritual consciousness has a lot to do with developing the body—the physical as well as the spiritual. There is a stronger link there in the East than we have in the West, with our mind/body split. Are there any serious Western scientific inquiries into the biological changes that are supposed to accompany these higher levels of awareness?

BILL: There has been some research in India and at the Menninger Institute in Kansas with Swami Rama and some surveys of the literature by the Esalen Institute in California.[22] To start with, I think we have to be careful when we use the term "body." There is the physical body, the etheric body, the astral or psychic body, the mental body, and the causal body, and there are ancient technical terms for these bodies in Sanskrit.[23] If you look at a candle flame, which of those colored sheaths of light around the wick do you identify as the body of the flame? What do we Westerners mean when we ask, "Are there any bodily changes involved with meditational practice?"

And not all the Eastern approaches are the same. For example, tantric yoga and tantric Buddhism are quite different. In yoga, one uses certain exercises to precipitate subtle physiological changes, such as the elevation of kundalini or the opening of the third eye. In tantric Buddhism, with its concern for compassion and enlightenment rather than simply psychic illumination, the lamas prefer to meditate and study and allow the subtle physiological changes to happen in their own good time, and preferably at a time when they are "no big deal" for the compassionate and balanced person. Yoga is more archaically shamanic, with its emphasis on power and psychic glamour: the sudden zap! of *shaktipat*, for example.

So it is too unclear if one says this "body." If the teacher points to the hand, what is he or she pointing out? Is the student seeing the etheric aura; the astral, mental, and causal auras; or the Rainbow Body in all the multidimensional extensions that are involved in a human incarnation?

Some years ago, in the seventies, Gopi Krishna wrote a little book about *The Biological Basis of Religion and Genius*. He focused rather exclusively on kundalini as the secret that he alone among moderns knew. Gopi Krishna was an autodidact as a yogi and was rediscovering the wheel; in this case, the wheel was a chakra. However, I do not think that the elevation of kundalini is enlightenment; it is etheric empowerment, and it can often create a curiously associated form of endarkenment. Although my practice and training and third-eye zapping blasts were with the yogis, I agree with the Buddhists that enlightenment is beyond all that. The elevation of kundalini is illumination, but not enlightenment. Because these Eastern things are new to us, we lump them all together.

Each of the five bodies has a different dimensional modality of participation. David has said that if he moves his attention into the meditational state of contacting "John," then the people who are here leave, and the people who aren't here show up. As one moves with each of these subtle bodies, the modality of space time changes, and the ecology that supports that incarnation comes into awareness. As one energizes these sheaths, there is a "matching grant" in which a being (call it one of Margulis's endosymbionts) can come in to participate or work with one at that level. A *djinn* can come in to work with us at the etheric level, and the popular version of this is Alladin and his magic lamp. The real magic lamp is, of course, the third eye. At the psychic level, an anima/animus figure may appear to work with us. And at the mental and causal levels, there are various angelic and boddhisattvic beings.

To get a more Western sense of the architecture of the self, think of the old Marvel comic book *The Fantastic Four*. Here the four are a kind of incarnational team. You see something similar expressed more recently in the film *The Adventures of Baron Munchhausen*. Consider the Baron's companion helpers. Each of them has a special skill that tells you at what plane—etheric, astral, or mental—they are working on. Another example of this esoteric architecture of incarnation is expressed in Japanese Bunraku puppetry, in which the puppet is the physical body and the hooded figures in black that move it are the subtle bodies that stand behind and beyond the physical space.

All of this is a long answer to a short question about "the body," but I think it is worth taking the time, for certainly we have overemphasized the etheric and the psychic as expressions of enlightenment. Certain kinds of psychic development in gurus can be deceiving, but these gurus are like Sumo wrestlers or weight lifters— they show the range of what is humanly possible, and they push a lot of talented fat around the mat in their ashrams, but these extreme ends of the range are not necessarily the healthiest or the most compassionate and enlightened states of being.

Some gurus are really little more than magicians or martial arts masters. They project out of their physical bodies to visit their disciples when they are falling asleep and say, "Hi there, I am your guru Shakti Pat, so come fly my wide body to the Islands of Bliss." The disciple says, "Wow! My philosophy teacher at Harvard can't do that! This guy has really got to be enlightened." So off they go into the wild blue yonder, flying high into the sky, zooming away in their karmic generators that leave such terrible pollution in the astral plane. Later the ashram blows apart, and everybody wonders where it all went wrong.

As Jesus said, "By their fruits ye shall know them." What were the fruits of all those psychic cults? The guru would talk about ego elimination, and everybody's ego got eliminated except his, which got bigger and bigger from feeding on everybody else's. The emphasis on *agape* or *karuna* has always been a basic way of trying to avoid the fanaticism of the psychic weight lifters. Another form of protection was to keep the esoteric *esoteric*, so these things would never be spoken about except to those whose condition of practice had brought them to that point. But all that changed in the planetization of the esoteric in the sixties, when yoga was broadcast into youth culture and we ended up with the adolescent patterns of religious experience that we saw then—a pattern of light and shadow.

The planetization of the esoteric was necessary, and we can't go back to some secret society. Anyway, it's all available in paperback now. Why all this psychic stuff in the New Age? I think it is because psychism is the romanticism of our cyberpunk, A.I. technological culture, just as nineteenth-century, woodsy romanticism was the linked opposite to smoke-stack industrialization.

FORMATIVE FORCES AND THE HIGHER DIMENSIONS OF SPIRIT

David Spangler

When we think about the New Age, we naturally tend to think of it in human terms. We think of changes to our civilizations and to ourselves. We think of changes in technology and science, in business and politics, and in society as a whole. But does the New Age have a meaning to the planet itself as a living being and to the other inhabitants upon the Earth?

The answer is yes, though it may take decades and centuries for some of the effects to show themselves. In fact, the New Age is more a planetary, or Gaian, phenomenon than it is a human one, and its primary locus of impact or unfoldment is within the inner realms rather than in this physical one. Looked at from this perspective, the New Age is a change in the subtle dimensions of the Earth, the ripples of which we will feel outwardly. It is like an earthquake deep under the sea that triggers a wave that hits the coastlines. We do not see the event directly, but we can feel some of its effects, particularly if the wave is a large one.

My point of view is based on forty years of working with the subtle realms of our world. As I mentioned on Friday, I was born with an ability to access the inner realms of spirit, and much of my spiritual journey through my life has been learning how to understand and discipline this ability and how to align it with the sacred elements that are within all of us and our world.

I have a perspective of the world as a set of nested globes, like one of those Russian or Chinese toys where you open one sphere to find a smaller one within it and a still smaller one within that and so on. Each successive realm is nested or enfolded within the larger one. This is a metaphor and not a literal description, but perhaps it will serve our purpose. The world to me is a living entity—a living soul, if you will—that manifests through an interconnected set of these nested dimensions, of which ours is one of the most constrained, though not necessarily the most constrained. Contrary to popular metaphysical supposition, the physical plane is not the "lowest" or "smallest" ball. It is, however, the lowest point within which a human entity will incarnate, so for all practical purposes for us, we are living on the innermost ball.

The image of the nested spheres is a familiar metaphor, actually. Its purpose is to emphasize one aspect of the relationship between the various planes of being. It is a perspective that sees the smaller spheres contained within the larger ones and each successive plane as an emanation of the larger one that contains it. However, like one of those optical illusions of stacked cubes where you can shift your perspective so that what had been the bottom of the cubes is now the top and vice versa, we can shift our inner perspective as well. When we do, the order is reversed, and we see that the larger spheres are emanations or explications of the smaller ones. What we actually see is a nested set of Mobius spheres, if there can be such a thing, in which there really is no ascending or descending order of separate, hierarchically arranged planes. Each realm is a co-incarnate—a co-creator of the others. One can find in each realm the source of emergence for all the others. Each sphere is simultaneously the surface ball, the center ball, and one of the balls in between.

"Old age" spirituality generally operated using some simple images based on the Sun/Earth relationship and the principle of ladders—of ascending and descending forces and hierarchies. This is because these were everyday accessible images. What I might call New Age spirituality and, I should say, mysticism in general, operates in a manner best described metaphorically with the more complex geometries of interpenetrating lattices and quantum dynamics. It is a holographic geometry in which the whole is the part and vice versa, and the creative center is everywhere.

In my early lectures more than thirty years ago, I struggled to articulate my inner perceptions and found only a language of poetry and feeling to help me. Then friends introduced me to the whole body of occult and esoteric literature, beginning with Theosophy. I found in the descriptions of the inner planes a hierarchical cosmology that I could use. I did use it in many of my early lectures, particularly at Findhorn, which had a traditional esoteric foundation. However, as time went on, I realized that what I actually experienced in my excursions into the inner worlds did not fit that cosmology except in very surface or marginal ways. I found its topography too limiting.

For example, much of the esoteric tradition, like mainstream spirituality, draws its imagery from bipolar geometries: good/bad, light/dark, male/female, up/down, and so forth. We experience such symmetries in our daily lives, so it is natural that we would project this symmetry into the spiritual realms. For us, creation and sexuality are bipolar experiences, so it must be so on higher levels. However, I have found the higher planes to be multipolar; the dynamics of their geometries are more complex than can be described adequately by conventional bipolar, symmetrical images.

Likewise, I observed that there were hierarchical relationships but that they were superseded by holographic or holistic ones. I even coined a term for this years ago. Instead of talking about the spiritual hierarchy, I begin talking about a "holarchy."

Gradually, I began using fewer and fewer esoteric references in my talks, not only because I did not like the glamour that such references could give rise to but because the traditional esoteric language or cosmology failed to describe the architecture of the inner worlds that I was actually experiencing.

This is more than a semantic issue. A hierarchical model can give rise to feelings of dependency and can distort the actual flows of power and creativity, shoehorning them into an ascending/descending relationship. The most obvious effect of this model is that the physical world and the physical body end up being on the bottom, and with our usual scale of values that "higher" is "better," you run into all the traditional issues of rejection of the material world in favor of the spiritual world. The actual fact is that this realm we call the physical is highly creative and is a source of emergence and transformation for the so-called "higher" planes. These "higher" planes are in some important ways an emanation of what happens here as much as we are an emanation of their realms.

I cannot stress this enough, because we need to develop a spirituality of the physical world that honors its sacredness and its creativity. The creation-centered spirituality that Chinook teaches is a step in that direction, though I don't feel it is the destination. In some ways, creation-centered spirituality is a reaction to older traditional religious dogmas rather than the experience and articulation of a truly new spiritual insight into the role of the physical planes within a holistic and holographic cosmos.

We cannot make assumptions about the relationship of the material world, our everyday world, to the inner realms. In some ways, that relationship is a dependent one; we are at the receiving end of a creative flow. But in other ways, equally important ways, we are the wellspring that nourishes and affects the inner worlds. We help to shape them, at least up to a point. It is certainly true that our physicality shapes our own imaginations and perceptions, which in turn affect the nature of our contacts with the higher worlds and the forms through which they appear to us at first.

However, having said this, it is also true that there are significant differences between the various nested spheres or realms. These differences do affect the relationships and nature of the "commerce" between realms. The physical world is actually a fairly simple manifestation compared to the higher dimensions. We have to deal with only four dimensions of experience—the space/time dimensions of which we are all aware. In more subtle realms, other "dimensions" or orientations come into play. Perhaps if I were a mathematician, I would be able to express some of these dimensions mathematically, but I'm not, and I don't know if it could be done. I do, however, experience these other dimensions when my consciousness enters the subtle worlds. I just don't know how to talk about them, since we have few if any physical analogs for them.

Just as the three dimensions of space and the dimension of time provide directions around which we orient ourselves and through which we project ourselves and our relationships, so the higher dimensions offer directions for the expression and manifestation of the beings who inhabit them. In our terms, viewing this phenomenon from our four-dimensional point of view, we might see these beings as occupying or acting in more than one place or time simultaneously. They inhabit space and time in a different way. Unable to fully comprehend or even perceive the topography and geometry of one of these beings, the being might appear to us as several different entities spread out through time or space.

You may remember the story of Flatland, in which a two-dimensional square encounters a three-dimensional sphere. At first, the square cannot comprehend what the sphere is because it has no experience of that third dimension along which part of the sphere's being extends. Viewing the sphere along the linear dimension of the two-dimensional plane that is the square's home, the sphere appears cut up into a succession of ovals. Our experience of higher dimensional beings can be very similar.

When we try to imagine these beings, we often leave out these additional dimensions. The result is to flatten them into human caricatures. This may be important for us to initially contact and understand one of these entities, but we should remember that it is a simplified representation, often bearing as much relationship to the real entity as a stick figure does to one of Michelangelo's paintings.

An example that occurs to me of this phenomenon is one of those holographic postcards you can buy at souvenir stores. Looked at one way, it is just a flat and somewhat distorted picture, but looked at from the right angle, a three-dimensional image takes shape. The trick with these spiritual beings is to find the proper "angle" or inner perspective with which to view them and contact them. They spring forth from the flatness of our materiality when we learn to discover and incorporate into ourselves at least one of the higher dimensions. Otherwise, we contact our own "flattened" version of them. And we do have those higher dimensions nested within ourselves. We can learn to see the world in the more complex and interrelated geometries that they offer.

My experience of these beings is that they are all co-incarnates. They are patterns and systems; they are quantum waves rather than particles. They are not separated from the realms they inhabit. Take the issue of names. Our human names denote a particularity; theirs denote a community or a communion. Their names are stories, much like you find with preindustrial peoples such as the Native Americans, for whom the name denoted a quality or an event in the person's life, often revealed through the vision quest. Even more, their beings, when viewed properly, display their attributes and connections. It is as if, when I see a woman, I also see clearly delineated upon her features and radiant in the air about her the essence of all her experiences, images of where she has been, whom she has connected with, who is part of her family, what she looked like at various stages of her life, the possibilities for her future, the animals and plants that have been important to her life, the landscapes that have shaped her, and so forth. In other words, I see a whole life in its current state rather than just a small slice of it. I see a dimension of connectivity, and the name would express all of this.

Thus, when I first contacted the inner-plane being I call "John," he introduced himself in just this manner, and what I saw as his "name" would be more than I could say in a thousand lectures—more than I could write in a thousand books. Naturally, I was relieved when he said, "You may call me 'John.' It is not my 'name' but it is as good a name as any other." In many ways, "John" was a construct that allowed me to interact with this being in ways that were familiar and comfortable to my dimensionality, until such time as I could relate to him in his wholeness.

There were many times in my initial contacts with John when it seemed that in contacting him I was contacting a group entity of some nature. Later, I realized that this was true, but not in the way that we would think of a group as a collection of separate individuals with John as a spokesperson or, more exotically, as a collective mind. What I was really experiencing was the connective or communal dimension of John's being—his co-incarnational self. This is the dimension along which all those in a certain resonance and relationship with John participate in his being, and he in theirs. It is hard to explain in a language based on particularity. Looking back, I could say that my whole relationship with John was really one of learning how to recognize and "see" along that dimension: how to see the realm of the co-incarnational or connective self, how to make the higher dimensional hologram spring to life from the flat plane of my perceptions. As John once put it years ago, "My colleagues and I are primarily interested in your learning to see as we do, to know our perspective, for when you do, you will no longer need us in this manner."

This brings up an interesting point. One way to look at the relationship between the physical realm we inhabit and the inner worlds is that the physical world *is* an "inner" or spiritual world where only four dimensions are perceived and experienced. As more of these dimensions or aspects of being become real to us, new aspects of the world become apparent and we begin to inhabit successively "higher" or more complex domains. In this view, we do not have nested spheres at all, but a continuum of perception and being where the boundary between each realm or segment is the ability to see and act along one of the additional dimensions that make up creation.

Just what are these dimensions? When I call them "higher," I am using a mathematical metaphor: four is a higher number than three; five is higher than four; and so on. I am not trying to indicate a position upon a hierarchical ladder. I do not use "higher" in an evaluative way, suggesting that higher is better. The presence of a higher number of dimensions gives more "space" and "time," more potentiality, more directions of expression and creativity to a being. Such an entity lives in a richer environment than does one whose environment and consciousness allows access to fewer dimensions.

Sometimes the word dimension is used to mean a place or a world, as in "He came from an alternate dimension." I am using it to mean a direction and opportunity of incarnation. It is a way of extending myself more fully into creation. However, the *gestalt* of many lives extending themselves into and relating along one or more of these higher dimensions does create a unique environment, just as the incarnation of four dimensions creates the physical universe we know.

These dimensions are geometries. As we experience them here, they may take on the characteristics of qualities and attributes. We might see these dimensions as expressions of mind or feeling—as love or compassion, as power or creativity. Consider the story of Flatland again. The extra dimension of the sphere is the dimension of height. The volume of the sphere extends inward and outward. If the two-dimensional square could access that dimension, it would become a cube. As a cube, its extended volume would now include or enfold aspects that as a square it could relate to only as being "outside" itself. As the square becomes a cube, we might say that it becomes more inclusive, which might be translated as an expression of communion, love, compassion, and so forth.

Since the higher dimensions are all enfolded in us anyway, when we encounter a being such as an angelic presence, in whom one or more of these dimensions are unfolded, the complementary aspects are stimulated in us. We experience this as a sense of being heightened, expanded, or blessed. Our own multidimensional, larger nature is touched and empowered, not necessarily through any overt act on the part of the more unfolded being, but simply through the resonance of its presence.

I have already alluded to one of these higher dimensions. I have different names for it: the "dimension of connectivity," the "communal or co-incarnational dimension," the "participative dimension." If I orient along its particular axis, I see where I enter into and share the lives of other beings resonant with my own life. We might say that through this dimension we participate in a group being, a shared being, but it is not precisely that. It does not necessarily convey a sense of "groupness" or togetherness with others. It gives a sense of a richer and expanded identity. Along this dimension, we enter into a geometry in which we share or incarnate aspects of the same topology with others. It is as if a river flowed through different bioregions. When we become the river, we also gain access to the being of bioregions different from our own, and we experience their ecologies as we experience our own. Most of the spiritual worlds and the beings who inhabit them are characterized by having this dimension as an integral part of their overall structure and geometry.

This participative dimension knits the experiences of beings together into larger incarnational *gestalts*. There is another dimension that is similar to it; in fact, it might be called its higher analog or its source. I experience this dimension in various ways. At times it seems like an event horizon: on the one side of it lies singularity and the merging into oneness of all the geometries and dimensions that we know of, while on the other side of it lies the multiverse in all its diversity and unfolding splendor. Yet at the same time that it is a boundary, it is also a path winding through the whole multiverse, connecting each part to the singularity—to the ultimate Source.

This dimension permits participation and involvement in each incarnation to a far greater degree and in a more essential way than does the participative dimension I already spoke of. While the latter seems to extend through the structure and content of incarnation, this higher one extends into the core and spirit of incarnation and life itself.

Because this dimension is available to us, human beings have always been able to experience it. Throughout history, it has been called different things, but the name most familiar to us in our culture is the Christ. We think of the Christ as a person, and often as an energy or a state of consciousness. Moving into the inner realms, though, it can be experienced as a dimension that runs through all the enfolded and unfolded universes and dimensions, right back to the Source. It is a dimension as real as space and time, but moving along it allows us to transcend space and time as we know them. The Christ is a way of extending ourselves and manifesting ourselves in the universe in a manner that generates qualities of empowerment, participation, communion, co-creativity, compassion, and love, to name a few. However, it may be helpful as well to see the Christ as a kind of meta-geometry or meta-topology that is accessible to every point of incarnation within creation. It is part of the fundamental architecture of creation, and it is at the same time one of the most complex of the higher dimensions and one of the most simple, in the sense of being everywhere accessible.

Well, what does all this mean to the New Age? Before I answer that, there is one more piece I must add, and that is the notion of "formative forces." What I mean by that phrase is a flow and process of influence, energy, presence, imagery, and inspiration that manifests something. It gives birth to or shapes an already existing incarnation.

In traditional esoteric lore, formative forces are sometimes pictured as streams of energy projected from a source to a destination. This is, for me, a Newtonian description. The images I move toward in my own explorations and teachings are different, though they don't deny that the projection image is also true from one point of view. I see the formative forces as fields resulting from a particular geometry, just as a magnetic field emanates from the geometry of the magnet—that is, the relationship between the two poles of the magnet. The magnetic field does not flow from one pole to the other; it just *is*, when the positive and negative poles are in a particular relationship to each other.

I also see formative forces as the expression of acting along a higher dimension or, more precisely, as an effect of that higher dimension itself. The formative energy is a result of "inhabiting" a particular dimension. Thus, our actions in time, our inhabiting of time, creates duration, and our actions in space, our inhabiting of space, creates the phenomenon of motion.

Once a field or formative force exists, it can then be manipulated in various ways by various entities. Bringing it into being in the first place may be the result of opening up to and inhabiting a particular dimension of existence, or creating a new geometry of being. Likewise, becoming more proficient at incarnating in a particular dimension enhances and perhaps transforms in some ways the particular formative forces that are the "fields" of that dimension.

Talking about fields and forces can seem abstract, and it often is, to our physically oriented minds. However, the issue takes on new meaning if we realize that some of the fields that emanate from certain higher dimensions—as well as the beings that manifest those dimensions by inhabiting and expressing them—are environments to us and, more importantly, actual beings. Specifically, Earth is the field emanation of a higher dimension *and* of a being, often called the Earth Logos in traditional esoteric writings but whom we might just as well call Gaia, who is capable of manifesting that dimension. Likewise, there is a dimension whose field is the manifestation of self-organizing, self-referential, flexible, open-ended, creative sentiency—a manifestation that we familiarly know as humanity. Thus, the Earth and humanity as we know them might be considered not only as a place and as a species but as formative forces as well.

The dimension and force or field that is humanity and the dimension that is Earth are complex geometries that involve more than just what we think of as ourselves and our planet. The fields or formative forces these dimensions produce and support could give birth to forms that are different from what we are used to. What we think of as human nature and planetary nature are really only a part of the full topology of these dimensions. We have a lot of growing and expanding yet to do before we can say we fully understand and inhabit the dimension that is humanity or the dimension that is Earth.

And that—ta da!—is what the New Age is about, viewed from the higher realms. It is a specific shifting of dimensions and inner-plane geometries, with a resultant shifting of formative energies, to give greater access to and expression of the dimension that unfolds as the Earth and, by extension, of the dimension that unfolds as humanity. It is entering into relationship with still higher dimensions in a manner that puts the geometries of Gaia and humanity into a new context, gives them more elbow room to inhabit and incarnate themselves. As a result, new creative energies, new aspects of basic formative forces, become available, like a rush of new ideas and energy into a person who learns to inhabit his or her own being and life more fully and creatively. I spoke years ago, while still at Findhorn, of new energies entering and infusing what I called the etheric or vital body of the Earth, and this is what I had reference to.

To the planet, the New Age is a specific opening to new geometries of relationship with the cosmos; it is the forming or reforming of relationships to certain other stellar entities and their inner-plane equivalents. To humanity, the New Age is an opening to the geometries of the planet in ways that permit us to enter into the dimension of the Earth logos and the dimension of humanity in deeper ways. I already defined the New Age in part as learning how to think and act like a planet, and esoterically that is precisely what it is.

Now, this is not something that takes place overnight. Actually, it doesn't take place in time as we know it at all. When we view it through the lens of four-dimensional space/time, it appears that this event, this enlarging and shifting of inner geometries, is happening in many "times" at once. It began happening millennia ago, centuries ago, and only just this moment. It will continue happening for centuries to come, and it is already complete! Actually, some of the waves from this inner earthquake reached our human shores roughly four hundred years ago and will proceed to wash against us for four or five hundred years or more to come before we might say this specific New Age is really here. On the other hand, what might be called "quanta" of transformation and restructuring have hit us in a specific way at definable moments of history, each quantum bearing both the message and essence of the whole transformation, as it exists beyond our time in the higher dimensions, and a specific energy of transformation relevant to our slice of space/time.

When we experience such a quantum of transformation, we may simultaneously feel that the whole of the New Age is happening right now, that we are on the verge of overnight transformation—the fabled quantum leap into a new state of being—and also that we see a specific pattern of transformation taking incarnation over time in our world, such as the changes going on in the communist world or the emergence of a particular new paradigm. These changes take time to work out, so we may face a paradox of experiencing the New Age simultaneously in two quite different ways: in the gritty process of actually living out the changes over the next several decades and in a flash of transformative insight in which time collapses and the whole new state of being is here, now.

Just as there are angels that inhabit and oversee the function of childbirth or the function of healing, so there are beings whose purpose it is to inhabit and oversee the fields of transformation and heightening activity in our world. They are the angels of the New Age, the shepherds of a new world. We can attune to them just as the Findhorn people attuned to the nature spirits and the *devas*. We do so by realizing that their function is not just to bring newness into the world or to invoke change, but to open and deepen our experience and our incarnation of the dimensions of the Earth logos and of humanity—to make all the realms of Earth more responsive to the higher geometries. In particular, they seek to heighten the experience and incarnation on all realms of that singular dimension to which, in our culture, we give the name of Christ and which in other cultures is called other things, but which is the dimension of that sacredness that unites and empowers us all. We attune to these beings and, in effect, become one of them, as we work to deepen our own experience of an inclusive sacredness and our own experience of what it means to be human and of what it means to be Gaia.

DISCUSSION 5

New Age Spirituality, Channeling, Esoteric Cosmology

AUDIENCE PARTICIPANT: I am fascinated by your statements about a new spirituality or theology—one based, as you mentioned, on quantum mechanics rather than on the older Newtonian or sun/satellite images of earlier cultures. Could you elaborate more on this? Is the New Age a new religion?

DAVID: Understanding just what such a New Age theology or cosmology might be like is my own cutting edge. In some ways, I am back where I was thirty-some years ago, seeking an appropriate language with which to articulate my deepest spiritual experiences. Events like this help, because speaking to you and dealing with your questions help to draw out images and language. At the same time, there are some things I cannot discuss yet, because they have not simmered enough within me. Like those California wines, I produce no insight before its time!

I believe that a new spirituality will have some correspondences or resonances with our earliest spiritualities as embodied in shamanistic traditions such as those of the Native Americans. Those traditions had a profound sense of the livingness and sacredness of the Earth, as well as of the spirit within everything, and they were generally nonhierarchical. At least they did not separate humanity out as a special entity, but saw us as part of a community of species who share life on this world. I do not believe that we should return to shamanism as it was once practiced; I'm not sure that we could even if we wanted to—times and circumstances have changed. However, the new spirituality may well have aspects that resemble shamanism. It will have aspects drawn from all the great faith traditions, but it will add something new, arising perhaps from a deeper experience of our co-creative relationship with the Earth and with God.

Furthermore, spirituality will be a natural part of everyday life, not a separate practice or institutional identity. There are those who consider the New Age to be a new religion, but that's a misperception. There are people who relate in religious ways to the New Age idea, but they would probably turn any cause with which they were involved into a religion. New Age spirituality at heart is not a set of beliefs or dogmas but a way of perceiving and experiencing the world with compassion, honoring its deep connectedness and wholeness. There is no reason such a spirituality cannot coexist with and beneficially inform our religious practices.

Beyond these few remarks, I cannot answer your question more fully at this time.

AUDIENCE PARTICIPANT: Is there a place for hierarchy in your New Age spirituality? It seems to me that hierarchy is present in nature and is a natural part of the order of things.

DAVID: When Einstein produced his revolutionary theories, they did not eliminate all of classical Newtonian physics, but they put them into a new perspective. They became a subset of a larger order, just as quantum physics recontextualizes Einstein's work, and superstring and twistor physics may do the same for quantum mechanics. Likewise, at the interface between two spiritual geometries—that arising from the Middle Ages with its emphasis on centrality, position, hierarchy, and the like, and that arising currently, which emphasizes process, relationship, interconnectedness, and co-creativity—we are not seeing the demise of the one in favor of the second. We are expanding our view of the dynamics of creation. Hierarchy is still an element of those dynamics, but it is not the only one and often not the central one. A truly New Age spirituality or theology is not antagonistic to what has gone before, but it will recontextualize and reconceptualize it.

Yes, I feel there is a role for the concept of hierarchy, but we need to understand that the function of hierarchy in nature is different from the hierarchies we create in institutions, which are generally to ensure efficiency and control. Higher realms do not control lower ones; they enfold them and serve their unfoldment. They are hierarchies of compassion and empowerment, rather than of authority and command.

AUDIENCE PARTICIPANT: I find it hard to relate to your discussions of "higher entities." Talking about them as "dimensions" and "forces" makes them sound so impersonal.

DAVID: Well, in many ways they are. They are impersonal, not in the sense of being aloof and uncaring, but because their experience of personhood is broader and more complex than ours. There are realms I have contacted whose inhabitants are actually aloof, largely because the inhabitants of our world don't exist for them. We are impersonal toward images on a piece of paper unless those images gain added dimensions by invoking emotional responses from us. I am very aloof from a drawing of a square; I am not aloof at all from a drawing of my children or my wife.

Yet both are two-dimensional. The difference is that a square never emerges from its two-dimensionality, while a picture of my loved ones has dimensions of emotion, memory, feeling, and so forth that make it more than just a drawing.

In a similar way, much of the life and the affairs of humanity, with our petty conflicts, our divisiveness, our self-involvement, does not invoke the higher dimensions of communion and connection. To the vision of some spiritual beings, we remain flat, without depth or substance, just like the drawing of a square. Of course they are aloof and impersonal—in their world, we don't exist. However, whenever we invoke and embody elements of the higher dimensions, which for us take the form of compassion, love, cooperation, and so forth, then we lift up off the page of materiality and gain stature. We stand out and can be recognized as loved ones. Then the impersonality disappears and we are embraced. Yet we have gained that embracing and that attention by taking actions that uplift our human condition. It does not come to us just because we are here.

On the other hand, most of the spiritual forces we deal with as human beings are close to us in dimensionality and do not see us just as "squares on a page." Even when they may be very complex in their own innate geometry, they can project and take on humanlike appearances and personas that we can easily relate to. When I first was contacted by John in 1965, he appeared as an ordinary human being of about forty-five years of age. He was in every respect like an older brother or an uncle, very recognizable as a person. As I grew to know him and worked with him over the years, this changed. He took on added dimensions. At times, as I mentioned, he seemed more like a group entity than a person. Now when I deal with him, he still has human aspects I can contact, but he has become something much different in appearance from a human being. He is for me a being of pure energy, a latticework of light and awareness.

The beings that work with the formative force that is humanity can be very personal, very intimate, and very compassionate and understanding. However, it has always been my philosophy that if I am going to contact emissaries of higher dimensions, then I want to be exposed to something that reflects their true nature. I want to be exposed to what opens those higher dimensions in me. If what I want is to talk to another person and gain emotional comfort or a sense of familiar personableness, then I will engage with another human being. That's what we have each other for. Though they can do it, it's not really the job of the angels to provide us with shoulders to cry on or familiar faces to talk to when we're feeling lonely. Their job is to husband our humanity into its higher states, to help us unfold into our own higher dimensionality in ways that we forget to do so directly for each other. Their job is to love us in ways that genuinely help us grow up and out into the greater universe that awaits us.

This need for familiarity and comfort extended into the spiritual worlds is a common thread through a lot of the current crop of channeled messages. Over and over, these beings assure us we are loved and let us know they are our friends. That's nice, but are we so divorced from our humanity that we have to turn to unseen entities for love and friendship? I think one reason channeling has become so popular for so many folks is that it is a psychic equivalent of letters to the lovelorn or an inner-plane dating service. It meets a need in our mobile, autonomous society, where experiences of real community and intimacy can be rare. How much easier it is to have an invisible psychic friend who can take whatever form we want than a real physical one whose needs and challenges we have to deal with as well as our own.

Inner-plane beings can be our friends, but they are no substitute for the human acts of sharing, compassion, friendship, and connection that weave community and empowerment in our world.

AUDIENCE PARTICIPANT: Are you saying that the beings who come through channels, like Ramtha and Ma Fu and Lazarus, aren't real or are only psychological crutches? Aren't you being a bit hard on channeling, especially since you are a channel yourself, aren't you?

DAVID: That's two questions! First, whether these beings are real or not is less important to me than the impact our images of these beings can have in our lives. Do I give them my power, my authority? If so, I violate some fundamental spiritual laws. The job of the inner worlds is not to tell us how to live but to empower our ability to unfold our own higher dimensionality. We are not born individuals so we can turn our individuality over to another being, becoming a clone of his or her opinions, beliefs, and attitudes. We are individuals so that we can add a unique perspective to the universe and make a unique contribution to a higher geometry of co-creation and compassion.

Whether these beings are real or not in themselves, as they enter into our nested sphere, into our dimensionality, they must take on characteristics that allow communication to take place. In many instances, this means entering into a body of manifestation that is built up from the unconscious needs and desires of the channel and of the audience. In this instance, the being speaks to us through an interface that is part window, part mirror. Some of the being's original intent may come through, but it is mixed with the noise of our own reflections. Sometimes this noise can be so great that all we really are in contact with is a reflection of our own desires, fears, and needs. We are talking to ourselves. This can have therapeutic value, but only if it is recognized as such. Otherwise, it is illusory and distorting.

Channeling is an art. We oversimplify it when we think of it as an entity entering into a person's body. That image really belongs to an earlier conception of the body and soul as truly separate things. These images abound in our spirituality and metaphysics: the body as vehicle, the soul as driver, and so on. The relationship is really more subtle and complex. The body is part of the soul and vice versa. They interrelate and co-create each other in profound ways, and both are aspects of a larger geometry that might be called our spirit. The tendency, though, is to think of these as separate entities. Then we can imagine the channel "getting out of the way" or "going off somewhere" while another being "takes over the body." The implication, then, is that whatever is said or done comes from the pure intent and consciousness of the possessing or channeling entity.

The reality is that energies and geometries are blended in subtle ways to create a joint entity that has more or less of the characteristics of the sensitive. A good sensitive, either through training or natural talent or both, can minimize his or her interference, but there is always a joint participation in the process. That is how the inner planes work—through co-incarnation and participation, not through possession and control. The channel always participates to some measure in what comes through, just as an artist always participates in the translation of inspiration into an artistic work.

As to my being a channel, I am not—at least not in the way that word is defined these days. It is true that I have mediated information between John and other spiritual beings and physical people, but the process by which I do this is not channeling. It is a participatory venture.

AUDIENCE PARTICIPANT: How do you receive what you do? How do you contact spiritual beings, then?

DAVID: Sometimes it is through a process that combines telepathy with empathy. Usually, I use a method of extending myself along a dimension of participation that takes me into a higher geometry. Just as we naturally come to know up and down, right and left, forward and backward, so I came to know as a child another direction in which I could "move" myself, so to speak. This direction took me inward and opened an additional dimension to me. I do not "leave" my body in any way when I work with the inner worlds. I extend my body into that extra dimension, or it extends into me. Then it is as if I am on a path that winds in and through the landscapes of the inner worlds. That is a metaphor. The experience is not really visual or aural. It is more tactile than anything, in that I feel the dimensions through which I move, but this feeling gives rise to images. So I suppose I move intuitively and imaginatively through those higher planes that I have been able to reach. What I teach generally comes from what I observe or learn during those journeys.

AUDIENCE PARTICIPANT: What about evil entities? You spoke about possession. Aren't there bad forces out there, too, as the churches warn us?

DAVID: Not in the higher dimensionalities, no, though to encounter a more complex geometry before we are ready to uncover and assimilate its counterpart within ourselves can be very stressful. However, I said that there are realms that are more constrained than our own. Evil might be considered such a realm. Evil to me is an unbalanced formative force that seeks to constrain the appearance of the higher dimensions or geometries. It seeks a reductionist simplicity that is easy to predict and control, because such a simplicity is safe. It holds no surprises. Evil is the refuge of the cowardly spirit, the spirit that cannot abide change unless it controls it, that cannot abide complexity, that in particular cannot abide the dimension of connectivity, for in connections it feels its own particularity threatened. Evil is a condition that arises when an evolving consciousness becomes fixated upon its sense of particularity and wishes to protect it and make it permanent. Evil might be called the dimension of separation. It abhors diversity and seeks conformity and sameness, with the exception that *it* can be different—different enough to be in control, anyway.

We can encounter this force, but usually not if we are actively engaging with our own higher dimensions and being open to change and unfoldment. I find that the best protection is to align with the dimension of the sacred—what in our culture we call the dimension of the Christ. That which puts us in danger from evil is any desire we may have to control and to make our egos safe from change and growth.

Actually, we could do a whole seminar on evil, so these are just a few brief remarks.

AUDIENCE PARTICIPANT: If I might just follow up on that for a moment, though. I know the fundamentalists have been on your case for something you wrote once about a "Luciferic initiation," which to them suggests that you are asking people to get involved with Satan. What about that?

DAVID: I had hoped that that one would just go away and be forgotten! I guess it's not to be. Well, what we have here is a misunderstanding, based partially on a bad choice of words on my part and partially on material being taken out of context by those fundamentalist writers who have quoted, or in some instances misquoted, that statement of mine.

I gave a lecture at Findhorn that was later published in a book called *Reflections on the Christ*, which is now out of print. In that lecture, I spoke of the need to surface and confront our shadowy side—all the material that we repress or are afraid to look at but that continues to affect us. We needed to look into our shadow and deal compassionately and transformatively with its contents if we wished to fully encounter the balanced energies of the Christ within ourselves. I used the term Lucifer to represent this shadow mythologically. I did so because the name Lucifer meant the "bringer of light," and I felt that much of the material within our shadow would, when understood, bring us into a greater light within our own being.

I also wished my audience to confront their images of evil, since so much of what we call evil is not really that, but only things that we don't like or that make us uncomfortable. In that lecture, I was careful to distinguish between Satan, a term I used for the presence of evil in the world, and Lucifer. It is that part of the lecture that the fundamentalist writers never refer to; nor do they refer to my definition of how I was using the term Lucifer. At the end of my talk, I said that one of the hallmarks in a person's life and journey into the Christ was when he or she confronted his or her own shadow and dealt with its contents. As a joke, really, at the very end, I said, "We could call this the 'Luciferic initiation,'" by which, in context, I meant the encounter with our shadow side.

Of course, in recent years, as some fundamentalists felt threatened by New Age ideas, finding a New Age writer advocating a Luciferic initiation was like the Watergate investigators finding Nixon's "smoking gun" tape. It just confirmed their worst fears and gave them ammunition to bolster their opinions. I understand that, even though I am saddened by their need to take statements out of context in ways that distort and reverse their meaning. I assure you, though, I have no interest in anyone being initiated and taken over by Lucifer, Satan, the Devil, or whatever image most represents evil to any religious person. Quite the opposite, in fact.

AUDIENCE PARTICIPANT: David, you have mentioned the Christ several times. What is the role of the Christ in the New Age?

DAVID: That's a big question. As I have said, I see the Christ in one respect as a dimension, a thread of sacredness weaving all creation together. From that viewpoint, the object of the spiritual changes behind the New Age is to heighten and enhance the experience of that dimension, that sacredness, for all of us. However, viewed this way, the Christ must be seen as something more than just a historical personage or the icon of a particular religion. We could find terms for this dimension in all of the great faith traditions. It is a universal experience, not an exclusively

Christian one. In fact, some traditions, such as Buddhism, have a clearer view of these higher geometries than mainstream Christianity does.

Yet I do view Jesus as a being who profoundly invoked, embodied, and strengthened the expression of that dimension within our world. In this sense, Jesus is for me one of the principal figures in the drama of the New Age—a progenitor of the New Age in its deepest aspects. There is, for me, a universality and a mystery about Jesus and his incarnation that transcends much of what Christianity has to say about him and certainly transcends the limited forms of "Jesusology" that afflict a number of mainstream Christian denominations.

For me, the Christ is a central element in the New Age, but the Christ is also for me a concept that is areligious and universal—one that challenges the religion that bears its name to transform its limitations and become as universal as the spirit it worships.

SEMINAR II
Saturday, July 22, 1989

THE COSMIC CHRIST

David Spangler

BILL: I always find it rather curious that whenever David talks about the Cosmic Christ, the cosmology he implicitly invokes is Buddhist. There are ancient precedents in Buddhism for the peculiarly complex, science fictional, and galactic cosmology in which David's imagination seems to thrive. Here I am thinking of works like the *Huan Yen Sutra*, which those scholars present will recall is a Chinese version of the more ancient Indian *Avatamsaka Sutra*.[24] So every time David comes up front with his cosmic vision, he tries to pretend that it is all very casual, very ordinary, and has nothing all that special about it. He will try to fool you by giving you an allusion to something banal—some bit of domestic life that we all share with our kids: peanut butter and jelly sandwiches, scrambled eggs, swimming lessons, things like that. In one way, this is valid and represents David's vision of the sacred as everything, rather than merely the psychically glamorous; but, in another way, I think this is unfair to what is extraordinary, visionary, and quite rare and unique to David Spangler.

What first drew me to David, some eighteen-odd years ago, was one of his transmissions from a mentality identifying itself as "Limitless Love and Truth." This kitschy little pamphlet printed in New Age purple ink by the Findhorn community should have immediately repelled the intellectual snob in me, but, unpredictably, it nailed me to the spot and stopped time so that nothing else existed except the words that had come on to that page from David.

The cosmology that took voice and breath there was vast, galactic, and expressed a posthuman or transhuman perspective on our critical moment of cultural evolution. It was like unto nothing else that I had come across before, though it had a tonality and diction that was similar to other psychic utterances I had read. This sort of thing generally produces a following, and David is quite intent on being unavailable for the peculiar needs and longings of those spiritual folks who like to walk around on their knees. So he hides out in the polyester suburbs behind stacks of peanut butter and jelly sandwiches. But for all his hiding out in the ordinary, I am not convinced that David is all that ordinary, simple, and common as he would like us to believe. So I thought that I would corner him today so that he couldn't hide this year.

DAVID: This is an introduction?

BILL: It's a cultural frame, maybe even a frame-up. So I say to David, I say, "Listen, every time I hear you go on about the Cosmic Christ, it sounds like the cosmology of 'The Jeweled Net of Indra' from the *Huan Yen Sutra*; it sounds like things I know from other Buddhist philosophies and cosmologies. Why bother to hang on to all this Christian cultural baggage—all this composting heap of Christianity that gets turned on and turned over on TV? So many people are being physically and mentally tortured by religion in the Belfasts and Beiruts all around the world, why not just let this religious stuff go and move beyond it into a truly new spiritual age?" That's what I said, and so with that, I give you the unique and ordinary David Spangler.

DAVID: Thank you, Bill . . . I guess! I thought I could keep my secret identity a while longer, but you've seen through me. Though I look like Clark Kent, a mild-mannered everyday guy, somehow you've penetrated my disguise and discovered that I'm secretly Mysticman, able to leap into strange dimensions at a single bound, more powerful than an affirmation, waging a never-ending battle for truth, justice, and the holistic way! Look! Up in the astral! It's a thoughtform! It's a channeler! No, it's Mysticman!

Ah, well, if only it were that way! Actually, the reason I talk about ordinary things is that I really am a rather ordinary fellow who is quite fond of peanut butter and jelly sandwiches and who enjoys the suburbs. Also, I am a mystic who looks for the sacred within the ordinary.

What Bill says about me is true. I do see the sacred as everything, or at least as accessible to us in the context of our daily lives. I also try to avoid glamour and decry the use of esoteric lore as a way of propping up some metaphysical teacher's ego. After thirty years of working in and around esoteric and metaphysical circles, I've seen the pitfalls and have become wary. Still, Bill's point is that I have become overly cautious and try too hard to make everything seem normal, and perhaps he's right.

You really have asked me two questions. The first is about the Cosmic Christ, and the second is why I use Christian imagery in the first place. The second one is easier to answer than the first, so I'll tackle it first.

As I mentioned last year, for as long as I can remember I have been able to orient my consciousness in a particular way that gives me access to the inner worlds. For me, there is up and down, back and forth, right and left, and another dimension that moves off at an angle from the others. When I "face" in that direction, so to speak, it is as if a gate opens into the inner worlds, and I step through. I extend my awareness along that extra dimension. I do not leave my body, but I definitely extend my consciousness into another order of life, which traditionally has been called the spiritual worlds or the inner planes.

As I said, I have been able to enter these worlds to some degree for as long as I can remember, although over the years the ability has developed with practice and discipline. I never thought much about it. It seemed like a perfectly natural thing to do. As I was growing up, it was not something I did very often, although the dimension that allowed contact with the inner worlds was always open to me.

Over the years, I have encountered and experienced a wide variety of beings and patterns and conditions, but three have always stood out for me. One is a presence that pervades everything else. It is beyond description, but I think of it as the absolute foundation for everything that exists. Sometimes I call this God. Most of the time, I don't attempt to name it, for anything I call it would be insufficient to capture its wholeness. Perhaps one could use Meister Eckhart's term for it, which is the Godhead, or one could speak of the Tao. This presence is universal, transcendent, and beyond human imagining, and at the same time it is profoundly personal, immediate, and accessible.

There is an extension or aspect of this Godhead that reaches deep into the incarnational patterns of creation and links the immanent with the transcendent, the particular with the universal. One might call it active or dynamic sacredness. I think of it generically as the avatar function. Sometimes I experience this as two separate presences. The first is a presence that, when I encounter it, is like entering a deep, deep well of peace, compassion, and serenity. It has a quality of depth to it that beggars description. This presence I have always identified as the Buddha, and I first became aware of it when I was a teenager. The second is a presence of love and compassion as well and a presence of peace, but it possesses a powerfully stimulating energy. It is playful, humorous, empowering, and intimately involved with the processes of incarnation, as I will discuss later. When I first encountered it, it simply said, "I am that which you have named the Christ."

Now, it could well have taken another name, and as I have learned to go deeper into the inner realms, I have seen that these three presences really merge into each other and are aspects of one great dynamic pattern, which has other aspects as well. However, given that I have a Christian background and that I am living and teaching in a culture that draws significantly upon myths and images out of the Christian tradition, I am not surprised that one of these presences called itself the Christ. That was a name I could understand at that time.

So, for me, the Christ is a major spiritual reality, a fundamental presence at work in the world. I see this presence at work. I am aware of its energy being active in the inner realms and in this one. It is my observation, as Bill has implied, that this presence transcends any particular dogma, or any ideology's attempt to confine it, or any organization's need to possess it and define it. Put another way, the Christ transcends Christianity.

As far as Buddhism goes, I am not enough of a student of Buddhist teachings to really comment. I experience what seems to me to be the spirit of the Buddha, and I feel profoundly humble before it. At times, it and the spirit of the Christ are one and the same to me, both enabling me to experience the sacred. At other times they diverge, each expressing a different but complementary aspect of the whole.

So I feel a certain allegiance to the Christ as an image, although I know from discussions I have had with theologians that while some of my perceptions of the Christ are at times quite orthodox, other perceptions diverge from what mainstream Christianity teaches. But then, I'm a mystic, and the church has always had problems with its mystics!

I have always felt myself to be fundamentally a servant of the Christ. So, I talk about the Christ because I celebrate its presence in my own heart and have found it to be a source of endless delight and healing. To me, the Christ is a lover, and who would not want to talk about his beloved? At the same time, I hope to offer some new interpretations and insights to the meaning of that term and to our understanding of the Christ event—not just as something that took place two thousand years ago, but as something occurring now, in which we may all participate quite independently of our religious persuasions.

As to the second question about the Cosmic Christ, that is more complex. Several images and answers spring to mind. In the first place, let's talk about it as a concept, as a human idea. The notion of the Cosmic Christ in this sense is a cultural invention. It comes into being because we have culturally limited our understanding and expectations of the Christ. We have tended to restrict them to a particular historical event, to a particular body of teaching, to a particular cultural image, to a particular gender, and to a human point of view. The Christ as presented in most mainstream churches has little to do with nature and the Earth, and little to do with the world in its wholeness. We have made the Christ into a "particle" as opposed to a wave, confining its incarnation to a particular moment in history, to a particular person—who is a man—to a particular species, and to a particular set of revelations. Where is the Christ that is revealing itself and incarnating now? Where is the Christ in nature and in the Earth? Where is the feminine Christ?

There have been good reasons to make the Christ a "particle" and to deal with this presence in a specific way. Incarnation itself is very specific and particular, but our world moves away from a wholly particulate description of reality. With new discoveries in biology and quantum physics, we are seeing more and more what mystics have always seen: the process side of reality, its interconnectedness, its interpenetrating-ness, its blendedness. Where is the Christ in this expanding worldview?

The Christ becomes the Cosmic Christ. Just as an advertiser can repackage a product and call it "new and improved," so the Cosmic Christ repackages the Christ. In fact, the essential qualities of this presence remain the same. The Christ is the Christ is the Christ. That is true whether we view its actions within an individual, a planet, or the cosmos as a whole. However, the new packaging may make it more accessible to people and help us to recognize some of those qualities of the Christ that we have been overlooking for the past two thousand years.

Therefore, the Cosmic Christ is the Christ that is freed from a particular historical event. It is active throughout the whole range of time. It is active in each of us, whether we are Christians or not, and it holds the promise that we can each be incarnations of the sacred. It reveals its feminine side and the side that is beyond gender. It is present within nature. It is the spirit of sacredness within the Earth and within the whole cosmos. It is as present in other faith traditions, including many of those we call pagan, as it is in Christianity, and sometimes it seems to me that it is more present in other religious understandings than in some of the Christian denominations whose attitudes and actions betray the compassionate, universal, and loving qualities of the Christ.

This is one way of looking at the Cosmic Christ. It is a human invention to loosen and expand our images of the Christ that have become overly crystallized and narrow during the past two millennia. There is no Cosmic Christ separate from and different from the Christ. It's the same presence, asking that we grow to see it more clearly and to embody it more fully. By the same token, there is an inner reality to the image of the Cosmic Christ, but to get to it we must look first at the Christ and its function.

Let's start with an image. Throughout the world, throughout history, there are certain myths that are repeated over and over again. One of these is the myth of the sacred child. This myth varies from culture to culture, reflecting the particular circumstances of the people who articulated it, but it retains common elements wherever it is found.

In this myth, a child is born. One of the child's parents, usually the mother, is human, while the other is from another domain. This domain may be the realm of angels and spirits or the home of fairies and other elementals. It may be an extraterrestrial realm, or it may be divinity itself. The result is the blending of two genetic strands, one of which is human and one of which is not.

It is this intersection of two worlds that gives this special child unique powers. It also gives him or her a unique mission, which is almost always transformative in

140

nature, that involves altering the conditions of life for his or her people and their world. The sacred child is redemptive; he or she is a savior, liberating us from crystallized patterns and habits that have come to misalign us with our Source, limit our creativity and spirit, and stymie our unfoldment.

The relationship of this myth to Christianity is obvious. Jesus is a sacred child who fulfills all aspects of the myth. However, I believe that the myth of the sacred child is the story of the Christ no matter the culture or the time in which it has appeared. Christianity is only one of many retellings of this story—the myth made flesh in a particular way. Therefore, I want to look into this myth to see what elements it can offer us in understanding the Christ.

The part of the story that I wish to draw our attention to is the parentage of the child in the first place. The child's heritage represents intervention and intersection. The child is the result of one domain's intersection with and intervention in another, different realm. He or she is a hybrid of worlds and represents an emergence that brings something new into being that might not be predicted from studying the qualities of each realm separately. The sacred child is the spirit and embodiment of emergence; he or she carries the power of revelation.

Let's look at this idea of intersection. An intersection could be symbolized as a crossroads—a place where roads meet. A crossroads is an interesting concept. In a way, it is an abstraction. What makes a crossroads a crossroads is not just that roads intersect each other; it is that it offers a service. It offers a choice. People encountering a crossroads can choose to go in a different direction from the road they were on. It is a locus of change and new possibilities. The crossroads embodies a creative option: the ability to break free from established and habitual directions and to make new choices. The crossroads is liberating and transformative.

When you talk about an intersection of two worlds as in the myth of the divine child, you are describing an incarnational crossroads that can expand the options that we have and enhance our creativity. Because of this intersection, because of the sacred child, we are not committed to a single direction, however valuable that direction may be. We can overcome and change the inertia of our past. Our incarnation is expanded. We have options for redirection and reconfiguration. We have the capacity to make choices that were not open to us before.

This liberation and redemption from habit and inertia extends to both of the progenitive realms. Because of our hierarchical attitudes, we tend to think that one of the realms, the human one, is the beneficiary of the other, which transcends the human. Thus, the father who is in heaven gives us the gift of a child who will be our savior and our hero. There are other versions of the myth, though, in which a mat-ing takes place because the transhuman realm needs qualities that only humanity can provide.

Because we generally have a hierarchical spirituality, in which authority and power flow from the top to the bottom, rather than a holistic or systems spirituality, in which the center is everywhere and power and authority are co-creative and flow in all directions, we fail to recognize reciprocity in the birthing of the sacred child. A crossroads works both ways, so that both roads are offered choices that were not there before. Through the sacred child, heaven and Earth are both benefited, perhaps not in the same way or to the same degree, but both are changed by the intersection and blending of their respective qualities. Both are aided in gaining new powers and new freedom from old limitations.

In the Christian tradition, for example, we know what Jesus Christ offered humanity. We could also say that the Incarnation provided the Father with a means of reaching and redeeming humanity. Humanity, which God loved, was in dire straits according to the story, and God, for all his power and authority, was unable to communicate with humanity in a way that would alter the situation and save us from doom. Both God and humanity desired reconciliation, but neither could achieve it by continuing in the same direction they had been going. They needed a crossroads that would open up new options of love and contact. The significance of Jesus Christ is that he provided a crossroads that allowed both needs to be met: humanity's for salvation and God's to exercise divine love to provide salvation. Jesus freed both sides from those limitations that had prevented a true reconciliation. The sacred child was a gift from both Mary and the Father to both realms, and he changed each through his embodiment of *both* human and divine qualities.

The sacred child may be a gift, but it is a gift that affects both givers. Although one realm may initiate the intervention and intersection, once a crossroads is established, it acts as a transformation point—a repatterning and reconfiguring point—for all the roads and directions that intersect it. It is a place of emergence, a place of revelation, discovery, delight, and the unexpected that affects all the realms that participate in its creation.

This crossroads can actually be imaged in a number of different ways. It can be the intersection of imagination and mind, mind and emotion, mind and body, male and female, and so on. The divine child, the embodiment of emergence, can be an idea, a vision, an insight, an action. In the mix of genetic material from our parents, each of us becomes a sacred child, a crossroads where two biological and psychological histories or "roads" meet and something new emerges, which is each of us. Each of us can be a liberator, a redeemer, and a transformer of the patterns and habits we inherit.

The sacred child is the point of emergence, the point of reconfiguration and repatterning arising from acts of intervention and intersection between two or more different realms. The sacred child is the crossroads. The sacred child is the Christ.

The Christ, like all sacred emanations, has many qualities that sustain and nurture all of creation, but the particular characteristic of the Christ that stands out for me is that it is the avatar of incarnation and emergence. It embodies and serves the patterns of incarnation and manifestation, the means by which spirit takes shape and form, specificity and focus. It also serves the means by which a specific incarnation becomes the seed, both within itself and in its relationship with others, for revelation and the emergence of new manifestations of the Source.

An incarnation has uniqueness. It embodies a specific pattern, a specific point of view, a specific potential for contribution. A road to Spokane from Seattle is not the same as a road to Portland. The importance of this uniqueness, though, comes into play when incarnations intersect and exchange or merge points of view. It comes when an incarnation can use its uniqueness as a parent to share a relationship that gives birth to something new, something that has its own emergence. The road to Spokane and the road to Portland gain in value when they are part of a network of roads allowing us to travel within the state as a whole and not just between two cities.

Yet the structure that provides uniqueness can also imprison its potentialities. The dynamic of incarnation is powered by what can appear to be asymmetry or imbalance. Just as walking is really a case of controlled falling forward, so incarnations move forward by falling out of their past patterns and into new ones. Every incarnation must have the two qualities of stability and fluidity. It must be able to sustain itself and also be open to transformation. This is the asymmetry of life. Yet, there is always the tendency to seek equilibrium, a state of no change, a state of perfect symmetry and rest. As this tendency gains momentum, the pattern of a particular incarnation begins to crystallize, or become set. It wants to run parallel to other roads, not intersect them. It does not want to be changed.

Left only to the energy that it contains within its specific pattern, any particular incarnation might eventually "run down," so to speak, and collapse into the containment of its own uniqueness. What prevents this is an intervention that creates an intersection, a crossroads, a point of emergence. This intervention might be likened to grace. It comes from beyond the system to re-energize it, to empower its ability to transcend inertia, and to reunite it with its capacities for intersection and emergence. This intervention is the function of the Christ. It is the birth of the sacred child within each incarnation for redemptive purposes. It is the energy that enables repatterning and reconfiguration to take place, or that midwifes the emergence of new configurations from within the incarnation itself.

This is not the whole picture, however. I have been speaking of incarnations as if they were specific points such as particles, atoms, entities, selves. That they possess such specificity is apparent. We live in a world of diversity, and each of us is a unique manifestation of that diversity. We are individuals.

However, we are also patterns of connection and interaction. Where do our selves begin and end? Many of the boundaries we imagine are cultural; some are biological; some are psychological. But each boundary can be transcended or, perhaps more appropriately, can be permeable to an exchange of being that turns it from a barrier into part of the architecture of a greater incarnation, a greater uniqueness.

We are what I call co-incarnates. Ultimately, only one thing really incarnates, and that is the multiverse itself; or, we might say that only God incarnates. Everything else is an aspect of that Incarnation. Or we could say we are all co-incarnating the ground of all being.

More specifically, each of us is who we are because of the contributions of many other people and beings with whom our lives have intersected. They have contributed to the overall pattern that we call ourselves. We are bundles of crossroads, each one a point at which some new or unexplored or unexpected aspect of ourselves emerged and became incorporated into our sense of identity. We would not exist as we are were it not for these contributions from others. They have co-incarnated us, and we have done the same for them.

Last year I talked about the nature of spiritual beings, which includes our own inner nature. In my encounters with entities on the inner planes, I have found that they can take a very specific form or that they can seemingly dissolve into a larger pattern in which multiple "selves" and "lives" are evident. Using the image of light, they can be particles, with specific configurations and positions in space/time (or its equivalent on the inner planes), or they can be waves, stretching off into infinity.

The Earth gives us the experience both of being particles and also of having to create "wave-forms" between us through relationship and through our intent and will, our caring and love. As "particles," we cannot be unconscious "waves." We must be conscious of creative "waves" of unity through learning the lessons of relationship. However, we are also waves by our inner nature and connections. It is this wavelike aspect of being that we are beginning to recognize through our mysticism and our science and that forms one of the components of the new paradigms emerging in our time.

The Christ, as an avatar of incarnation, is an expression of this particle/wave paradox and its resolution. It honors and supports the specificity, the individuality that gives actual grit and structure to incarnational patterns, and it supports the whole pattern itself in which the sense of self can be holographically distributed throughout the whole lattice of the pattern. The center is everywhere. The center is the whole.

The Christ as we have imaged it is a particle Christ. It is an individual, and it saves individuals. The Cosmic Christ is a wave-image. It is a co-incarnate and relates to us as co-incarnates. It is a pattern image, and as there are patterns within patterns, who can say where its boundaries are, except where love dictates them to be at any given moment to provide substance and focus to acts of compassion and service.

From an inner perspective, too, the New Age is the emergence of a cosmic crossroads, an intersection between the patterns of this world and larger "roads" winding through the cosmos. This intersection releases qualities or energies that have not been available to this world before, qualities that I can sense but that I cannot describe. The sacred child that embodies these qualities, which carry cosmic resonances, is also an expression of the Cosmic Christ and is the bearer of new revelation and of the next step in the continually unfolding Christ event upon this world.

Now, I would like to shift to another metaphor for the moment, to move away from the image of the crossroads. I want to talk about the imagination itself that brings forth these images of crossroads and myths of divine children. In some ways, true imagination, in its capacity to reconfigure our thinking and to introduce new insights and energies into our lives, is an analog to the function of the Christ.

Imagination does not mean the construction of something unreal, but it means the construction of an image through which we express ourselves. Imagination is a faculty we have that operates on many levels, or we might say it has different functions, different ways of expressing its nature. There is the idle imagination of daydreaming. There is the kind of imagination that is so self-oriented that it is almost narcissistic. I think we are all aware that the way in which we view ourselves, our self-definition, is an act of self-creation. It is an act of imagination.

Then there is a kind of reflective imagination, or maybe we might call it interpretive imagination. We all use this faculty every day, without being wholly aware of it, in order to experience the world around us. Through it, we transform the biochemical and bioelectrical sensations that are stimulated by our physical contact with the environment into the images that we perceive and call the real world. Not everyone generates these images in the same way; in fact we all generate them somewhat differently because our physical sensoriums are different. We do not get exactly the same input from the environment. No one imagines the world in exactly the same way as someone else. Everything we experience in the world is, in this sense, imaginary.

So, there is the idle imagination, then the reflective or interpretive imagination, and then the creative imagination. This is the more deliberately exercised faculty that we use to bring new creations into the world. We say that artists are imaginative, writers are imaginative, and scientists or inventors are imaginative. Somebody imagined the wheel; somebody imagined the use of fire; somebody imagined computers; somebody imagined this stool that I am sitting on. Everything that exists in our cultural world is a product of this creative imagination.

However, there is another level of imagination that is important to us but that I believe most of us are unconscious of. I would call it the "incarnational imagination." It is our own private crossroads; it is the place where the sacred child lives in us.

What I mean by the incarnational imagination is something much more profound than just producing the usual kind of self-imagery that I normally use to define myself and think about myself. In some sense, we may not call it imagination at all, because the images it generates might not be recognizable as such. The images this level of imagination creates have more than four dimensions. That is, they extend into areas beyond the boundaries of space/time as we know it. They are higher dimensional images that form the primary patterns that contain our specific incarnation within space/time. We may experience them more as qualities than as images, so we might call this the qualitative imagination. It is the imagination of the soul that holds the primary, multidimensional image that is the seed of the totality of our incarnation and relates it to all other incarnations past, present, and future, whether they are "ours" or not in a reincarnational way. It relates our specificity to the universal, our particularity to the cosmic. It is the presence of this imagination and what it generates that makes us more than just physical beings and ultimately enables us to transcend the images that normally define us.

This imagination can be accessed through the use of other images, particularly those that come from the creative imagination and particularly when those images are dynamic and not static. It is accessed by images that extend through time and space and that have a universal resonance themselves—images that incorporate many aspects of our incarnation together. These might be images of movement, such as dance, or of architecture; they are images that involve our bodies and our minds, our feelings and our intuitions.

For example, the great cathedrals were constructed to give access to this incarnational imagination. You do not just look at a cathedral, you move around in it, you listen to it, you see it, you smell it, you feel it. Then, if you are sensitive to its architectural flows of line and structure and color, you are uplifted to a place where you connect with what is undefinable in the ordinary imagery of the everyday world. You encounter those dimensions that take you beyond the limits of space/time.

We access the creative imagination through our minds and feelings; we access the incarnational imagination through our whole lives. We do not think about it so much as we inhabit it. The images the incarnational imagination works with extend through extra dimensions in addition to those of height and width, breadth and time. As I mentioned in my talk last year, we often experience those dimensions as qualities such as love, compassion, intelligence, and insight.

So the expression of this imagination often involves the use and crafting of these qualities in our lives and relationships. Can we create environments and conditions between us that are cathedral-like in their power to lift us to higher levels of insight and relatedness—that empower us both incarnationally and co-incarnationally? Can we practice an architecture of relationship that opens us to the sacred? That is the action of the incarnational imagination, or perhaps I should call it the co-incarnational imagination, in view of our earlier discussion. One way of defining the New Age is to say that it is the time when we do learn to use the incarnational imagination more fully and consciously, so that its perspective infuses and directs all the other levels of imagination that we experience.

The function of the incarnational imagination and the images it creates is to invoke the higher dimensions or higher patterns into our lives and consciousnesses and to make them real to us. In our earlier metaphor, the incarnational imagination acts to create a crossroads, a place of intersection between this realm and higher ones that can empower our incarnation in vital ways and inspire emergence. It is the womb of the sacred child.

From this, we could say that the Christ is the spirit of the incarnational imagination as it relates to human incarnation, while the Cosmic Christ is the incarnational imagination of God, relating to the whole of creation itself.

DISCUSSION 6

Limitlessness, God, the Initiatic Path, Incarnation

AUDIENCE PARTICIPANT: David, how do you respond to the current theology, or whatever it is that is going around, that says that human beings are limitless and "ye are gods"?

DAVID: You have asked two questions, so let's take them separately. First, I'll respond to the "I am God" theology that many people call "New Age." Well, Jesus said that we are gods, and he is usually considered a good authority! Is that enough of an answer? No? Well, I didn't think it would be. . . .

Seriously, what we are dealing with here, I feel, is a cultural image and our attempts to change it. We are trying, as our seminar title puts it, to reimagine the world, and that includes reimagining our relationship to divinity. This is important, because our imagination of divinity profoundly influences our imagination of ourselves, our power, our responsibilities, our destinies, and so forth.

There is nothing new about saying "I am God." In fact, in some other religions it is quite acceptable, although the term God may not be used. As a Buddhist I could say that I am in truth the Buddha-nature, or as a Taoist, I could say that I am in truth the Tao. Even in Christianity, in its mystic traditions, I can say that I am one with God—one with the godhead.

However, in the Judeo-Christian-Moslem world, God is usually not popularly understood as a universal presence, the ground of all being. God is a person, a specific point of ultimate creativity and power, the Source of all. God is the Creator and is separate from creation. For many Christians, to suggest that as creatures we contain elements of God is blasphemy.

Furthermore, as a culture we have a particulate view of things. We see the world as made up of separate individuals, and being an individual excludes one from being any other individual. I am me, and I cannot be you. In the particulate view, we cannot be the same thing. We are different—separate things. When we transfer this view to spirituality, then of course God becomes just another particle, bigger and stronger than any other. God is God, and no other particle can be God as well.

Therefore, to say "I am God" in our culture is seen as an act of immense ego

Therefore, to say "I am God" in our culture is seen as an act of immense ego and folly: the infinitesimal particle daring to claim that it is the biggest particle of all. In less enlightened times, they crucified people for claiming that!

If, on the other hand, we take a leaf from the notebooks of mystics and physicists—following the direction of the new paradigms away from exclusively particulate ways of viewing the universe and towards images of fields, patterns, relationships, networks, lattices, and the like—then to say "I am God" is simply to affirm that I am part, like everything else, of the Field of fields, the Pattern of patterns, the Lattice of lattices, the Life within all lives. We are not constrained by a hierarchical and particulate imagination. It is in this sense that the spiritual sensibility of Buddhism (and of certain mystical traditions within Christianity) more accurately reflects the process-oriented, systemic, and holistic cosmology of the twenty-first century than does Protestant, mainstream, particulate religion.

I would add that, just as in quantum physics we don't have to make light be either a particle or a wave but can accept that it is both, so we need not say one religious approach is true and the other is not. We may be waves within the great ocean of being, sharing one life with each other and with the sacred, but we also experience ourselves as distinct individuals and, as I shall discuss more fully in a moment, that individuality also needs to be honored. There needs to be a complementary spirituality of the individual—a spirituality for the particle as well as for the wave.

Whether we should say "I am God" or not depends for me on whether our imagination is oriented toward particles or waves. That is, what do I mean to myself when I say I am God? If I think of myself in a particulate, separative way, it can be a profoundly narcissistic thing to say, affirming my own particlehood at the expense of everyone else's. It can diminish my capacities for compassion and inclusiveness, and thus diminish my access to my incarnational imagination.

I observed this statement emerging in the sixties out of the human-potential movement, along with its counterpart "We each create our own reality." To me, this was an attempt to counterbalance feelings of repression, disempowerment, and unworth, often fostered by misapplied religious fundamentalism. Thus, when people say they are God, they are not making a theological statement as much as they are making a statement about their self-worth and their power by invoking the image of that which in our culture is of highest worth and greatest power. They are trying to say, it seems to me, that they are safe, they are powerful, they are creative, and they can do what they wish in spite of a confining, repressive world around them.

My response is that this is like using a nuclear bomb to dig a hole. It will do the job, but what a fallout! I can simply affirm that I am a capable, valuable person and then take actions that will confirm that image. I can incarnate an image of capability more easily than one of being the divinity. In the long run, images of being God could lead to disempowerment rather than the other way around as I discover that the universe doesn't always agree that I am *el supremo*!

Likewise, in our culture, we tend to think of God in terms of power. In many other traditions, including the esoteric one, God is also the most limited of beings, the one who serves all others. As a parent I have tremendous power in relation to my young children, yet I must be careful to limit my exercise of that power so as not to overwhelm and dominate them. So it is with God. God may be powerful, but it is not arbitrary power. It is power in service to creation and as such cannot be exercised in ways that damage the structure and unfoldment of creation.

When New Agers say that they are God, are they thinking in these sacrificial terms? Are they saying that they are the servants of all, that they seek to empower everything else, and that they are accessible to all comers? Hardly. Much of the time, they are simply stating positions of power and security, the coins of the realm for a mind that thinks itself to be just a particle.

As for limitlessness, the desire for it can be a hidden desire to escape incarnation. An incarnation is specific, which means it has limits and definition. Its individuality is important and needs to be nurtured and honored in appropriate ways. We may seek limitlessness as another way of seeking freedom from constraints, much as the Gnostics sought freedom from the flesh. However, diffusion usually results in further disempowerment because we lose our focus. We lose our place to stand from which we can act in the world. To say everything is equal, everything is the same, everything is good, is to reduce all creation to bland, powerless mush, which is as far from a true experience of the sacred as we would wish to get.

True limitlessness comes from discipline and skill in working with limits. My Dad's hobby is gourmet cooking. He has the taste buds of a professional taster—the person who tastes all food before it is served to a king to ensure that it's not poisoned—and he has the soul of an artist. Dad doesn't just cook; he creates works of culinary art. He is a "gastronomer" *par excellence*! To work his magic, he has a fine sense of how spices are used and blended and just which ingredients should go into a dish and when and how much.

I used to watch him with amazement as he concocted his dishes. One day, I decided to try my hand at it. Unfortunately, I have the sense of smell of a cabbage and the taste buds of a stone. I recognize three basic flavors and that's it: sweet, sour, and Tabasco. So, the day I cooked, I took down every spice in Dad's spice rack and added it, figuring that if I blended in everything, it had to come out great. I leave the final result to your imagination (not, hopefully, your incarnational one)! It did have a lovely color, and it did make a nice sound as it disappeared down the garbage disposal. I'm not sure what kind of creature would have eaten it.

BILL: A hungry ghost!

DAVID: Probably! If it wasn't dead when it started eating, it might have been at the end. Anyway, the point is obvious, and we all know it. To be creative, to truly exercise power and to accomplish what we wish, we need to accept limits, but we need to know how to work with them. These are not limits upon us as spiritual beings nor upon the creative capacities of our imaginations, but they are limits necessary to focus form and substance to produce a graceful incarnation.

BILL: David, I would just like to add a footnote to your comment about narcissism and the imagination. One of the best books of philosophy to come out in the last few years is Mark Johnson's *The Body in the Mind: The Bodily Basis of Meaning, Imagination, and Reason*.[25] Following up on Piaget's work with children, he shows how we construct reality by using one domain of imagery to serve as a metaphor for another—how we extend perceptions into metaphors for what we don't perceive. We don't see our backs, but we extend our perceptions to imagine our backs as part of our self-space. In this sense, we could define imagination as the phase-space of perception. So, thinking about Narcissus, we should, as you said, see both positive and negative elements in the myth. We each have to catch our image in the stream of time. If we understand that it is a standing wave, floating in relationship with us and the stream, then we are safely healthy; but if we think this self is solid and absolute, then we try to attach ourselves to it in self-love and we drown. Your remarks fit in nicely with Varela's work, chaos dynamics, phase-spaces, and the idea of the self in Buddhism.

AUDIENCE PARTICIPANT: In my reading, I keep coming across the idea of being initiated into the mysteries. From ancient Egypt to the Masons, there is some sort of initiatic process or path one has to follow. Is there really only one universal path that leads to this Christic crossroads of yours?

DAVID: No, of course there isn't. However, you bring up an interesting issue, which might be described as the difference between the mystical path and the esoteric or initiatic path. These paths run parallel to each other and often overlap. The mystical path seeks the ground of all things; it seeks to go beyond the event horizon into the singularity of the sacred. The initiatic path might also be called the path of crafting incarnational images. The former goes to the source of power, the latter goes to the artistry of power.

For example, there is a way to sample fine wine. There are special glasses, for example, and special rituals. If I want a glass that honors the wine and does not impose its own character upon it, then I am not going to use a styrofoam cup. If I actually want to get the full experience of the wine, I will use a specially shaped glass that captures the bouquet and funnels it into my nose so that I can have the full sensory experience of the wine, which is as much olfactory as it is gustatory. There are religious and spiritual traditions that deal with how we build our imaginary cup to sample the experience of God in Creation. These traditions can be initiatic, esoteric, and elitist. On the other hand, God as the source of incarnation is also the most accessible presence in Creation. He is like the vineyard from which the wine comes. The grapes are everywhere, available for the picking. God is not at the far end of a hierarchy that I can reach only as the result of following a particular initiatic path.

If I draw a diagram of a hierarchy on the blackboard, that hierarchy exists visually because of the blackboard, but the blackboard is everywhere present for each chalk mark. No chalk mark, whether it is at the bottom of the board or the top of the board, is more distant from the blackboard than any other chalk mark. God is the blackboard on which all things are written. Nothing that is written is farther from God than any other thing.

We cut ourselves off from divinity precisely when we refuse to see the sacramental nature of ordinary life. If we transfer the hierarchical model into our religious life and make it the only model, we are saying that God is found only under certain initiatic and esoteric conditions and only in certain places. When I say God is accessible through everything, then I have to make an effort to make that perception real for me. I can't just say it and hope that it is true—I have to make it part of the practice of my perception that, yes, God is in the dirty diapers and in the peanut butter sandwiches.

The danger that arises from this mode of practice is that this perception can flatten everything out so that everything is divine, is perfect, is equal, is the same. "The opposite of one profound truth is another profound truth," as Niels Bohr said of matter as wave and particle. The complementarity of God as immanent is God as transcendent. God is the blackboard, the chalk, and the language with which ideas are expressed, yet each of these three modalities is different from the others. Each performs a different function. How I relate to these modalities depends on the context of relationship. One may be vast and empty—the godhead of Meister Eckhart. The other may be dense and physical—the rocks and soil of the Earth. Yet another may be expressed in the script—as in music or poetry.

DISCUSSION 6

AUDIENCE PARTICIPANT: In your earlier discussion about Christ you talked about incarnation. In orthodox Christianity, it is felt that Christ was a pre-existent being who came down and took on human flesh and lived here. You referred many times to us as being incarnate; what is your perception or understanding of us as humans now, as compared to pre-existence? Do you see us, too, as being pre-existent? What does incarnation mean to you? What about reincarnation?

DAVID: Let's use the blackboard analogy some more. I write a paragraph on the board. Now, I point to a letter on the board and call it "me." This letter, "myself," has three interacting components: it has a connection to the blackboard; it is a specific mark on the blackboard; and it has a relationship to all the other letters, words, and sentences on the blackboard, a relationship based on language and thought. The interaction of these three elements creates the hologram that is me.

Thus, there is part of me that is eternal and comes out of an undifferentiated place; it is part of the total hologram—the total oneness in which every part replicates the whole. It is one with the blackboard. There is another part of me that is specifically David Spangler. David Spangler has never existed before; reincarnation has nothing to do with David Spangler, for he is a unique event within a specific historical condition, and he is valuable because of this specificity and its uniqueness.

Then there is the part of me that relates to all the other marks on the blackboard. This is part of larger patterns that extend through what we call time and space, and through other dimensions as well. Through principles of spelling, it is part of a specific word, and partakes of the meaning of that word. Then through principles of syntax and grammar, it is part of a sentence within which its word has additional meaning, and the sentence is part of the paragraph. I, as this letter, draw meaning and value from several interacting patterns that we are calling words, punctuation, sentences, and paragraphs. I express what I am because I am grounded in a stream of language and thought.

Within all these interdependent patterns, there is a pre-existent component and there is a post-existent component; there is a part that exists elsewhere and has never been in a human stream of existence. All of that makes up "me." I can look at any one of those three and say, "Yes, that is who I am." Different philosophies have tended to focus on one of those perspectives. Some say we are part of God, or we are God; some say we are just ourselves as we appear in this incarnation; and some say we are part of patterns that include many incarnations—a language woven from past and future. To me, we are all of them; we are the interaction of all of them. I can't isolate one of them and say that is all that I am.

To fully appreciate these patterns, we must learn how to see them in nonlinear ways. If I view time as a string and an incarnation as a particle, then I come up with the traditional view of reincarnation as beads upon a necklace. However, an incarnation is not just a particle. It is also a pattern of co-incarnation. My life now is not defined just by my body. I am a product of my immediate, specific space/time intersection. I am a product of this current period in history, not of the Middle Ages and not of the twenty-third century. I don't just *live in* this moment of history. I *am* this moment of history.

If I say that I lived before, which "I" am I talking about? Is it this particular "I" that I call David Spangler? If the "I" of my identity is distributed holographically throughout the whole latticework of my higher dimensional being, then the part I call David partakes of it but cannot claim full possession of it. Every part of the lattice is "I"—however, whenever, and wherever that lattice, extending through higher dimensions, makes contact with space/time. Thus, the "I" is not reincarnating at all. It is simply incarnating.

To further confuse the issue, a particular pattern of incarnation is not necessarily limited to or bound by the space/time, physical embodiment in which it may have acted for a time. It might weave in and out through the whole lattice, dipping into incarnation here for a time and then there for a time. To put it in popular and somewhat distorted terms, this means that between the ages of ten and fifteen, say, I might be the reincarnation of a fifteenth-century nobleman, while from the ages of twenty to twenty-two, I am the reincarnation of a seventeenth-century peasant woman instead. Then, from thirty-five to forty-four, I am not the reincarnation of anyone. The interplay between ourselves and other parts of the hologram that is our larger identity can be very dynamic indeed! Sometimes the question is not *whether* I have had a past life but *when* am I resonating with a past life.

The uniqueness that is David Spangler is unique because of this historical moment. I am co-incarnate with you; I am co-incarnate with the Earth of this time, with this culture, and with the challenges of this culture. If I go back to another incarnation, I tend to narrow all that into the figure of an imaginary personality and say that is who I was then. But that personality itself was co-incarnate with a fifteenth-century world, or a 24,000 B.C. world, or whenever it lived, and it was co-incarnate with lots of other folks and other patterns that were working through human evolution at that time. That full co-incarnational pattern cannot reproduce itself now, though elements of it might if the proper resonances can be established.

We really should be looking at worlds reincarnating and not people reincarnating. These historical worlds are, in turn, co-incarnate with the cosmos, which in its time frame of incarnation is much slower than that of the Earth. The cosmos of five hundred years ago or two thousand years ago is not that much different from what it is right now. In a sense, I am still co-incarnating with that cosmos even though I may have had five lives in between. Carrying this train of thought forward, I begin to see that I am, in fact, a hologram of Creation itself projected into a specific moment and form of the four-dimensional, space/time aspect of cosmic incarnation.

IMAGINATION AND THE BRINGING FORTH OF WORLDS

William Irwin Thompson

I would like to respond to David's talk in an improvisational sort of way, to explore some of his themes as if they were musical ideas that one could play around with in a form of mind jazz. American talks, as opposed to British lectures, are really a kind of mind jazz. Whether this becomes melodic or cacaphonous, music or noise, or some sort of edge between information and noise where the two dance around in your minds will depend on the particular kind of jazz club we can get going here under this tent.

David has talked about the imagination: the idle imagination of day-dreaming—what Coleridge would call "fancy"—the reflective imagination, the creative imagination, and the incarnational imagination. For the last couple of years, I have been very much taken up by the whole subject of the imagination and what Francisco Varela calls "the bringing forth of worlds." So I was fascinated with what David had to say about this colorful spectrum of the imagination and found it to be another way of looking at the esoteric doctrine of the subtle bodies. The idle imagination has characteristics of the etheric body. The reflective imagination begins to be more in the realm of the psyche, or the astral body. The creative imagination moves on to the realm of the mental body, and the incarnational imagination brings us to the realm of the causal body. When David was talking about cathedrals, he was beginning to move into the angelic realms—into a world of geometry and music as forms of creating time and space in a pattern of coherence through which another domain can intersect with the human.

The edges between these levels of imagination are not hard and sharp. They are more like permeable membranes, for the top of the etheric begins to be the bottom of the astral, and the top of the astral begins to be the bottom of the mental, and the top of the mental begins to be the beginning of the causal. A good way to envision this is by looking at the marvelous standing wave of a candle flame. The wick can serve as a metaphor for the physical body; the blue in the flame represents the etheric body; the amber center is the astral body; the intense band of yellow light is the mental body; and the crest, where the unique flame transpires with the universal atmosphere, is the causal body. You can see now why yogis like to meditate on candle flames. It is a system of coherence among the domains, a symbol of what the yogi hopes to achieve with his or her own body.

In much the same way, a cathedral is a system of coherence. If the cathedral is a properly coherent domain, bringing together elemental rock, human society, and angelic mathematics and music, then it moves beyond or outside of our physical space and time to become a vehicle for the incarnation of something beyond that is not as temporally or spatially specific as we are. There are many words for this. We might call it God or the Christ; or we might wish to call it the Universal Buddha, Vairocana Buddha, as opposed to the specific historical personage of Shakyamuni Buddha. There are various traditional cosmologies and angelologies for these inter-penetrating realms—Indian, Iranian, or Christian. However, having been instructed by David to use homey metaphors for talking about cosmic things, I want to use a very profane and homey parable to approach an understanding of the imagination.

I gave my wife, Beatrice, a birthday gift of a Le Corbusier chaise longue—you know, one of those curved metal things that looks and feels like an astronaut's chair. They were not actually designed by the grand master Le Corbusier himself, but by a woman working in the studio bearing his name, so the child of her invention now bears his name. Thus it was in the old days of patriarchy before the feminist refor-mation.

Well, one day when Beatrice was back at work, teaching her class, I tried it out after lunch. They are very comfortable, and it was not long before I found myself dozing off in a siesta. (Now here comes the homey part, David.) As I momentarily drifted off into sleep, my eyes were still open and looking at the ceiling, but then I began to hear the Cuisinart blender roaring in the kitchen, and I began to question myself about how that could be when I knew that no one was in the kitchen and that I was alone in our apartment.

Now, I have been told by all those who put up with me that I have become, in my old age, a terrible snorer, so it came upon me in my Proustian reverie that I had fallen asleep for an instant, that I had snored, and that my dreaming mind had transformed the auditory perception into an imagistic interpretation. Since I am not familiar with the sound of my own snoring, my brain's search through its memory banks could not come up with a familiar image, but as I had just prepared lunch for my wife that day and had used the Cuisinart, it came up with a more familiar loud and grating sound.

Now, notice that there are three things going on here. First, there is the proc-ess of transformation from sound to image. Second, one part of the brain perceives a sound but cannot perceive it truly. Third, the matching of image to impression depends upon the past—upon a memory bank of stored images. Psychologists have begun to study this in some detail, and Hobson at Harvard has written an excellent book about it.[26]

Brain researchers have discovered some interesting things in their studies. For example, when we go into REM, or the rapid eye movement of dreaming, we turn off to the outside world to inhibit the motion of our muscular system. We begin to generate our dreams, and if the world intrudes into our dreams, we transform the sensory impressions into imaginary explanations or little stories. If we have thrown the switch in the brain system to inhibit the motion of the body and yet we wish to move, we generate the familiar dream of being chased but being unable to move. Here again, note the movement from perception to story. The alarm clock we hear in the morning gets worked into our dream, and we find ourselves standing at a door and ringing the front bell; as the door opens, we wake up. People commonly have dreams of someone walking into their bedroom, breathing heavily, and sitting on their chests. However, these dream characters turn out not to be monsters or succubi, but simply the sounds of our own heartbeats turned into footsteps, our own heavy breathing in nightmare turned into the menace, and the weight of our own hands on our chests transformed into the the crush of the beasts. We moan, awaken ourselves, and find that no one has entered the bedroom and that we are safe.

This science of brain research is providing us with some very interesting insights into the nature of imagery, but in its cocky way of overgeneralization, this science has claimed, in its favored reductionist fashion, that this is all there is to so-called spiritual experiences: they are "real" physical, sensory inputs transformed into illusionary mental imagery. For example, when you have a dream that you are floating over your body and flying over a landscape, you are not actually flying over a real landscape, you are turning physical brain activity into dream imagery. Reporting on this research, and overgeneralizing it even further so that it accords with its own technological philosophy of power, *Omni* magazine has proven that spirituality doesn't exist[27] and that you can all go home now, for soon you will be able to buy an electronic helmet that will give you more "spiritual" experiences than you could ever get in a church, a yogic ashram, or at a summer camp for mystics like Chinook.

Notice, by the way, how the sales pitch for electronics is very much the same old one we had for LSD in the sixties. Since we had drug casualties as psychotics in the sixties, I imagine that in the turn of the spiral in the nineties, we will have electronic casualties. These helmets and virtual reality goggles will produce a new generation of epileptics or some other sort of neuro-electrically damaged individuals.

The trouble is, of course, that this science has only begun its research, and it has to inflate its claims in order to get government grants. Humility gets you nowhere in the competitive world of Big Science. In reality, this research is working only at the interface between the physical and etheric bodies within the brain. This is important work, and I for one would be happy to see them get the grants they need to go on with their research.

However, every common household mystic knows that there is another level of activity in which you awaken not into the body but out of it, in a clear mind that has none of the sloppiness of the etheric mind. It is with this sort of shamanistic practice that Scottish seers would report on the outcomes of battles hundreds of miles away, or that people can perceive the experiences of their distant loved ones in times of danger. This young science says that out-of-body experiences, or astral projections, do not take place and that the landscape experienced by the seer is purely internal and imaginary. But I think this is not the case, and I suppose most of us here would have stories about out-of-body experiences in which the perception could be "reality-tested" against events going on in the external world.

As a template or interface between the physical and psychic worlds, the etheric body—the idle imagination that David mentioned—is a very muddy and sloppy sort of mind. It is something like a submarine with a primitive sonar system that is trying to bounce sound off objects in the dark to generate some interpretive image of what could be out there. Such perceptions are not as clear as those the sailor would have inside the sub or outside swimming in the water. The sloppiness of this kind of mind is another argument for the theory that the brain is not a product of some single act of demiurgic creation but a hodgepodge of evolution through natural drift, with three different brains getting rolled up into one skull: the reptilian, the mammalian, and the human.

My old reptilian, dinosaur brain is slow to react, for it only has the past, in the form of its memory storage banks, going on inside it. The mammalian brain, that limbic ring of "fight or flight," would be a much quicker and more responsive agent of perception. The trouble is that when we die, we go into reversed evolution: first the higher cortex dies and we lose thought; then the mammalian brain dies and we lose feeling and motion, but we still can hear people in the room; and then finally we descend into that muddy brain of the etheric body. Perceptions turn into mush and confusion, and we end up in a dream bardo of illusion and nightmare. So it pays to be good yogis and learn how not to die with such a mess of a mind, which is what *The Tibetan Book of the Dead* is all about.

Part of meditational practice is to watch your mind going to sleep— to watch yourself going into REM and generating imagery, or what is called *makyo* in zazen practice. When you examine your dreams, notice that they are oftentimes images generated from associations and puns. Freud talks a lot about puns in his wonderful work *Wit and the Unconscious*.

Once I was dreaming about my American Express Card, no doubt an anxiety dream about how I was ever going to pay the bill for all my travels. Before I quit the university—in those good old bourgeois days when I was a full professor with a monthly paycheck and not the intellectual migrant worker I am now—I got myself a Gold Card because I knew I would never be able to get one after I quit my job. Now my male monthlies come from the cramps of trying to pay the bill.

So, there I was dreaming about the Gold Card, and then I found myself deep inside a gold mine, trying to dig my way out. In other words, I was buried alive under the crush of bills. But notice the immediate linguistic shift from Gold Card to gold mine, and you can begin to see how "reality" is a linguistic construction built out of metaphoric extensions and word associations from one domain of experience to another. Once again, Mark Johnson's book *The Body in the Mind* is of help here.

The construction of our human reality is based on metaphor and language. The sudden shifts of reality that we experience in dreams can be incarnationally vivid, but actually they are based upon a joke, a linguistic association, or a pun. Puns—and this is why I love to use them for the titles of my books—are complex multidimensional figures that enable feeling and intelligence and sensation to come together in a hieroglyphic way. They are characteristic of both poetry and lunacy, for schizophrenic "word salad" has a similar logic.

If we look at our minds in the shift from waking to dreaming to try to understand this mode of Coleridgean fancy, or the idle imagination that David was discussing, we can begin to appreciate the rubbery logic of the unconscious that appears when we relax our grip on things. We observe that a sound becomes an image, and then the image becomes a story or little drama of the dream in which words, like "gold," are translated back into their concrete imagery. In this reptilian brain of the etheric body, we seem to slip back into a time before language has evolved. We are no longer in the world of the neocortex with its logic of identity based upon abstract distinctions. A Gold Card means gold, and that means gold mine—something physical. This etheric body is like an electrical transformer: it takes in *prana* and steps it down from direct current to alternating current so that it can be of use to the household appliances of the body, the organs. In its actions as a transformer, it is continually transforming diffuse vibrations in the environment into discrete phenomena: sounds into objects.

You can see why I want to call the imagination the "phase-space" of perception. Just as a phase-space gives us a fuller portrait of a Foucault pendulum swinging around its basin of attraction, so the phase-space of the imagination gives us a full portrait of all the confusing signals of perception: smells and sounds that are almost more molecularly triggered than conceptually understood. The imagination is an imagistic encoding of signals and an extension of them into stories that are based upon past experience.

With an act of your own imagination, put yourself back into the prelinguistic mind of a protohominid in the African savannah. You hear the rhythm of running paws on the ground, the swish of the parting grass, and a thickening of casual noises into an unusual silence. Then suddenly, through your memory, all the signals are transformed into images, and you imagine, but do not actually yet see, a lion on the attack. You pick up your infant and run in terror. Perhaps this is what nightmares are partly about: when we relax, an ancient part of our mind is still on the alert, so the sounds it hears become transformed into images of threat to awaken us to the marauders of the night.

When we awaken, we awaken to the world of the neocortex, a world of identity and abstract classes of separations. Here, identity is based upon a logic of distinctions, but in the older mind, identity is based upon common predicates:

> *There is a sound in the night.*
> *Sounds in the night are threats.*
> *Therefore, that sound is a threat.*

or

> *The rich are a secret threat.*
> *You are rich.*
> *Therefore, you are a secret threat.*

As you can see, this fuzzy logic of shared predicates still persists in the cases of paranoid schizophrenics, or in the cases of poetic expression where we place the ancient mode in a new and larger context, as in the syllogism discussed by Gregory Bateson:

> *Grass dies.*
> *Men die.*
> *Men are grass.*[28]

In our ancient, prelinguistic imagination, images are juxtaposed without sensitivity to syntactic position or class distinctions, precisely because those distinctions are the product of language. Many parents have had the experience of talking to a child with a raging fever and so have had some experience of confronting a situation in which the outer world does not map onto the world the child is feverishly dreaming with open eyes. In the case of paranoids, not only is the syntax and separation into abstract classes obliterated, but the transformation from isolated percept into narrative image is taken literally. The snoring really *is* a Cuisinart; the Rockefellers really are a world conspiratorial government; the Queen of England really is a drug dealer.

You become so caught in the trap of your own puns and free associations that you begin to suffer your nightmare as reality, as I did in my dream of being caught in a gold mine. When you take a dream story literally, you are forgetting that the story you are generating is your linguistic construction. You become caught in a category mistake and make all kinds of epistemological errors in judgment about what is going on there in the outside world, such as my error in thinking that the Cuisinart machine was turning itself on in the kitchen.

Say, for example, you have had a great deal of experience, as children and some particular personalities do, of out-of-body travel, and you have this vivid sense of knowing exactly what it feels like just to walk up into the air or out the window. Then you take LSD, and you make the mistake of confusing gross and subtle bodies. You try to walk out the window, and, crash! you are dead, and free to do a lot more astral projection than before.

Unfortunately, when you're dead you get to be in the place where whatever you think becomes your reality, for now you no longer have the physical body to protect you from your own projections. The physical body is an act of grace that protects us from the psychic realm, and that is why it is a favored place for enlightenment. In the turn of the spiral, the physical and the causal planes are isomorphic. A house may not be a palace, but it is more like a palace than it is like a swamp or the underwater world of the sea. So be happy you're not dead, and don't take LSD to try to get enlightened. The physical body is here for a reason.

Now, if the imagination is the phase-space of perception, then what David calls the reflective imagination can be seen as the stabilization of that phase-space. Instead of the image dissolving back into diffuse sounds—the phase-space of a "point attractor" in dynamics—a limit cycle is established, a construction in which sounds, smells, and sight are cross-referenced one to another to produce a stabilized world.[29] What holds all those sensory perceptions together is the reflective imagination. For example, the proprioception of my own back may be articulated in a way in which feeling contributes sensation and sight imagines what it does not see to give me a complete sense of my own body in space. In the idle imagination, a percept is matched to an image from the memory banks of the past, but no attention is paid to the syntactical structure; in the reflective imagination, however, in the imagination that David said we use unconsciously to bring forth a world, we do pay attention to structure.

Think of it as adding on dimensions. The idle imagination is a line, and the reflective imagination is a square. It is a container, and what it contains is the past. The idle imagination is a point attractor, a moment of consciousness that is always drawn back to its basin of unconsciousness. This is the religion of shamanism, our cultural world from 200,000 B.C.E. to 10,000 B.C.E. [30] The reflective imagination that stabilizes a world becomes externalized in the shift from hunting and gathering to agriculture, the world of the container, the pottery containers for grains, and then later the walls for containing the city. This world is entirely organized around the value of stabilization, of tradition, of the past. In fact, the psychic world of the astral plane is the Akashic record of the past—the world of the past.

The creative imagination that David spoke about is not the world of the individual contained and constrained by tradition, but of the creative genius breaking out of bounds to construct a novel future through art and science. It is the world of the ego, the world of the individual. It is Michelangelo against the pope, Galileo against the Inquisition. It is a new phase-space, not of the limit cycle of the periodic attractor, but of the much more complex dynamic of the chaotic or strange attractor. The future becomes a strange attractor in which the accumulation of "noise" pulls the individual and society from one attractor to another, from one world to another.

Now you can appreciate why the merchandized New Age movement is really not new; it is the old imagination, the container, filled with all the old psychic techniques—from shamanism to animistic agriculture—of the past. It is the astral plane, and not the mental or causal planes. In this soggy underwater world, the chances for enlightenment are better for a dolphin than a human. Everything in this world, in the words of the Beatles song, only takes you "half the way there." It's like making love to a mermaid: good for the infantile sexuality of nursing at the breast, but blocked for anything more.

The reflective imagination is a construct; it is not "reality," which is one reason that meditational practice asks us to watch our mind as it slips into sleep. In both Zen Buddhist and Roman Catholic monasteries, the monks are awakened at 3:30 a.m. and called to meditation. When you wake up in the middle of the night, you often do so with a clear mind and a crisp memory of peculiarly compelling dreams. Rather than turning over and rolling back into a seductively warm sleep in which you roll around with the mermaids—going back down into the etheric mind of slush and epistemological errors—the monastic discipline requires you to sit up in meditation. This is because there is a porousness to the membranes of the subtle bodies that exists at this time, and if you don't go to sleep, you hear a subtle sound that attunes the physical body to the causal body without all the interpretive noise of the intermediate realms of the astral. If you sit in meditation then, you can watch the generation of imagery, see how it is constructed, and begin to understand the larger architecture of incarnation. In David's words, you move on to confront the incarnational imagination directly.

One of the recurring images in my own dreams from around 3:30 in the morning is that I am coming back and looking for my car. It is sort of like, "Where the hell did I park the vehicle Bill Thompson? I know I left him around here somewhere." Or, I am coming back in a network of canals with submerged rail lines. The tracks shift, and you have to get into the right track to get back into your appropriate incarnation. All of these, of course, if you pay attention to them, are metaphors for multidimensional experiences—for our parallel lives in other worlds. These are worlds that are so much more complex that they can only be approximated by using our human experiences as metaphors.

Following up on David's metaphor of the divine child, I remember having a vivid dream of my son, Andrew. I think oftentimes when we dream about a person that the dream really shouldn't be considered to be about that person; the dream is using that person as a metaphor or symbol for the architecture of the self. There are various schools of thought and terminology for this that one can use. I often think that when one dreams of one's own child, one is dreaming of one's enlightened mind—the mind that is generated by one's state of consciousness at its purest, most innocent, and most promising for the future.

I had a vivid dream that I was crossing a dark bridge with Andrew, who in the dream was ten, and we were talking and going through this dark passage. I came to this network of flooded canals, which, of course, archetypally signify the watery psychic realm that one descends into when coming down from spiritual experiences in the higher mental and causal planes. The tracks were switching in the water, indicating the paths to one's simultaneous incarnations, for I don't think the soul is limited to one person. Then I crossed over the bridge, turned to look for Andrew, and realized that he was no longer there. I called out, "Andrew!" and it echoed in this large, dark, vaulted space. This is the point of return to one's conventional ego, where the connection with the higher self has been released as one returns to consciousness and wakes up in the middle of the night, back in one's old body again.

At another time, in another dream, I was riding with a work crew in the back of a truck. The truck stopped, and I jumped down onto the field. One of my colleagues was going to jump down with me, but I turned to him and said, "Now, you know you can't come with me." He looked really disappointed. This, too, is another metaphoric construction for "the work crew" that comes with us into incarnation: guardian angels, elementals, *djinns*, genies, and the souls that come in as our kids. David knows what I mean. The bigger the job you take on, the more interesting the project becomes and the larger the party it attracts. So don't think you're alone and don't despair, but just don't expect immediate, linear results in the flat, three-dimensional time and space of one ego and one life. Give yourself and your friends a couple of centuries, at least, to get the party going.

Now, the difficulty with dreams and psychic visions is that most folks and mediums take the images literally. However, if you do, then you get involved in a collapsing of multidimensionality into our world of merely three. As Sri Aurobindo noted, dreams are memories of spiritual experiences, but they are a coded translation for experiences that are inconceivable in human terms. We become involved in "misplaced concreteness" when we take them literally. It is a category mistake of the same order as saying, "We are gods," when we are really talking about our egos and their Olympian appetites. It is a mistake of the same order as thinking that somebody turned on the Cuisinart in the kitchen.

Imagery is a conventional construction that takes multidimensional experiences beyond the senses and turns them into something that is conventional and more familiar. The higher self doesn't have our snobby regard for the spiritual; it doesn't have to try to be spiritual, because it *is* spirit, so it, like Mozart, likes to slum around in the profane, the erotic, or the scatological. Since I don't like atmospherically polluting cars, it always has me wandering around in some damn parking lot, looking for my jalopy. The imagery of dreams may involve your family, your line of work, sexy companions—whatever. However, it is a mistake to think that the ordinariness of the imagery speaks for the ordinariness of the experience, for often it is just the reverse. The ordinary is settled upon in order to get the complex spiritual experience smuggled past customs and into the possession of the ego.

The esoteric schools of thought from all over the world are also systems of metaphors for the dimensions of human experience that are outside the societal norms of understanding. But these too, I think, are metaphors that should not be taken literally, as followers and fanatics often tend to do. If in one culture they talk about magic lamps, genies, and flying carpets, we should not take this literally to think that Aladdin's lamp is a piece of metal and his genie is a muscle-bound Arnold Schwarzenegger.

If you watch your mind going to sleep while your eyes are open and you see your dreams projected onto the screen of the outside world instead of onto the backdrop of an imaginary world, you will notice that your etheric mind dreams are more noisy and confusing than the psychic dreams in which you are soaring twenty thousand feet over the landscapes of other planets. In the etheric mind, you are caught between two radio stations and are picking up a confused mixture of noise and information from both the physical and etheric frequencies.

When you awaken out of the etheric not into the physical but into the psychic, then the dream experiences become "clear and distinct" in a very Cartesian manner. The colors are so much more intensely vivid than the colors of the physical realm, and the space in which to move is so much more vast, that many romantic poets and psychics, such as my friend Kathleen Raine, prefer this world and look upon the soul in the physical body as a songbird in a cage.

As one ascends in this psychic world of imagery, the colors become less dense and more refined. The imagery itself begins to melt into music, and the landscape begins to dissolve into its constitutive flow of celestial thought. At this level, we pass out of the psychic realm into the mental realm, the realm of the creative imagination. Here we are all composers and mathematicians, and every morning we create a transcendent masterpiece that we try to take back with us into our waking life.

Some composers and mathematicians are quite successful in being able to return with this state of mind intact. Karlheinz Stockhausen, for example, insists on getting up at four or five in the morning because his dreams are higher and purer than the muddy ones into which he would descend by returning to sleep after awakening upon return from the spiritual worlds. He once told me that he hears the music he would compose when he awakens before dawn; with a clear mind, he has only to copy down what he had already composed. These dreams and these active creations are quite different from the passive experiences of the psychic level. When we approach this level, the one David was referring to when he was speaking about cathedrals, we come upon a much more complicated dimensionality.

Traditionally, cathedrals express a cosmology in which angels are real. Angels that overlight a person are called guardian angels. Angels that overlight a sacred place are called powers, and angels that overlight a nation or a people are called principalities. And this keeps on going in the great chain of being on up to seraphim and cherubim. This angelology was described by Dionysius the Pseudo-Areopagite, a Syrian Christian who wrote under a pseudonym and tried to smuggle into Western Christianity a protohistoric cosmology of angels that goes back to ancient Iran and Zoroastrianism. God bless him, for, personally, I like angels and feel more at home with a cosmology that includes them than I do with the shriveled cosmology of American sociology.

I like to think of angels as creatures of pure topology—emergent properties like standing waves that appear when certain conditions are coherent in the stream of life. These conditions allow them to inhabit a domain and express the coherence of

166

that life as a domain. A principality, for example, as the kind of angel that overlights a sacred place, emerges because of the particular overlapping pattern of chthonic or geomantic power in a particular spot with the accreted cultural power of the religious practices performed there. If you walk into an ancient temple or a medieval cathedral and feel a special presence, then you are being sensitive to that moiré pattern of overlapping energies, that emergent property of being. Indeed, the cathedrals were built by religious sensitives precisely to allow this level of being to intersect with the human.

It takes a particular kind of vessel or grail in the form of a cathedral to bring this type of multidimensionality into the more limited space of our world. First of all, the space is orchestrated in terms of the volume of the cathedral itself; then time is orchestrated through music. If there is the appropriate coherence, the resonance of space in time opens the individual to a horizon beyond his or her conventional self-definition. A sacred horizon is set up—an expansion into the sacred that is vaster than the merely sacerdotal. It is a sublimation, a lifting up of the elemental kingdom and a lowering of the angelic kingdom so that both can become accessible to the human domain. The lifting up of the elemental involves transforming the rock into stone and placing the gargoyles aloft amid the sound of iron struck to music by the bells: "As above, so below." Gargoylish jokes and irreverences are created, for irreverence has its place in the sacred, even if it is often excluded in the merely pious and sacerdotal.

The gargoyles are a celebration of the gnomes and beasties of the elemental kingdom, who, rather than being restricted to the underworld, are now invited up into the sky to hear the bells and look down on the humans, who have become "the little people." If they delight in peeing down on people from the rain spouts or exposing their buttocks to make wind, well, that too is part of the vision of a redeemed nature, for in the cycles of Gaia as the Dark Madonna, gas and urine are forces of purification in the larger scheme of things. A cathedral is in fact precisely an expression of this larger scheme of things. With this reunification of shadow and light, noise and music, elemental and angelic, the Fall is reversed and the crucifixion of spirit into matter is overcome. Now you see why there is no crucifix in the Cathedral of Chartres—why it is the temple of *Mater*, of matter, but not *Mater dolorosa*. When all of this work is achieved, the cathedral becomes a form of incarnation in our physical world for an angel: a power—the form of being that overlights a sacred place.

The power serves as a kind of celestial transformer. This angel takes in higher energies that are inaccessible to us, steps them down to domestic household current, and offers them for all the appliances of our daily lives. In walking into Chartres and becoming silent and sensitive to what is there, one moves through the creative imaginations of the architects, the artists of the stained glass, and the composers of the music to come to the threshold of what David calls the incarnational imagination. This opening allow us to appreciate what it means to be alive in that space and time.

This stepping down, this transforming of celestial energy into human energy requires a certain compromise—a business deal, if you will—between the angelic and human levels. We can imagine the angel saying, "All right, this level of incarnation has been unavailable to your human cultures for millennia. I will work to make it accessible again, but the only way I can offer the gift of angelic space and time is if you make human time more coherent. Therefore, to build a cathedral you have to involve more than one generation in the work. It can't be a temporary whim or fad of one generation; it has to take centuries."

In effect, the angel says, "Look, you humans beings are going to have to get your act together. You need to fundraise consistently for three centuries in order to create the minimum small sound-byte of angelic time through which we can get a word in edgewise amongst the noise and chatter of your civilizations. If you can't get your own kind to agree on something for at least a couple of centuries, then you don't have a vision, you have a fantasy." Such fantasies have no substance, no archetypal solidity; they are here today and gone tomorrow—like the School of Sacred Architecture I set up in Crestone, Colorado. Its architecture sits there unfinished because it was my personal fantasy of a post-religious spirituality and not a culture's shared vision that could bring the generations together.

The angelic deal requires a negotiation. In the Old Testament, the relationship between incommensurate realms is expressed as a bargain, "a covenant." Abraham, the crafty Middle Eastern trader, does business with the Almighty. He bargains with Yahweh over just how many good men it takes to save the world: "Three? How about two? Will you settle for one really good man?" In the old cultures the sacred ordinariness of life enabled the patriarchs to walk with God. But there is a *diminuendo* to the divine presence in the Old Testament. Abraham walks with Yahweh, but Moses has to be held in the cleft of a rock so that he won't be blown away, and even then he gets to see only the backside of the Almighty. What you see here is a loss of information through time; but part of the impulse in the construction of the cathedrals is to reverse this process of decay by opening time to other spaces.

When a point of maximum dispersal or disintegration is reached, then the condition for repair, regeneration, novelty, and innovation exists. David was talking about the metaphor of generation—of sexuality and the myth of the divine child. The interesting thing about reproduction in biology, as explained in Lynn Margulis's work,[31] is that sexuality is not needed for reproduction. Fungi and other critters get along in time without sexual reproduction. Sexuality, as the modern biological theory goes, is a kind of repair response to damage; it is an effort to repair damage that actually creates novelty in new DNA combinations. If there had been no damage and no loss, there would be no innovation. From this point of view, evolution proceeds not by design and intention, but by tinkering and natural drift—a *bricolage* with the available. For the new to have a possibility, the fixed and crystalline have to broken.

Look at our planet, Earth. It is a balance between the fixed and the fluid. There are the continents, which are more or less fixed—they float, of course, as tectonic foam on the sluggishly liquid magma—and there are the clouds, which are a gaseous mediation between the liquid solution of the oceans and the fixedness of the continents. These gaseous clouds are a means for transporting water to the continents in the form of rain; they form a kind of permeable membrane between the ocean and the continent. *Any system, to be a living system, has to be a balance between the fixed and the fluid.*

A cathedral, a living cathedral, has precisely such a balance between the fixed and the fluid. When it becomes too sacerdotal, too reverent, and not symbiotic with the irreverent and the profane, it becomes too rigid and fixed. It is no longer sacred, but merely sacerdotal, and it begins to be a human historical museum in which an angel cannot take up incarnation. I think most people have probably had the experience as tourists of going to some holy site where they could feel the incarnational presence of an angel—or call it what you want—and then of going to some equally famous place but feeling that it was empty, a mere museum or gift shop for tourists. For me, this is the difference between the Cathedral of Chartres and Notre Dame in Paris, or between Durham and York, or between Saint Patrick's Cathedral and Saint John the Divine in New York City.

You can go feel the difference and decide for yourself. Go to mass at Notre Dame in Paris and then take the suburban train to Chartres. Or take a driving tour in England to visit Lincoln, York, and Durham. Durham, I think, is a very alive cathedral, especially at the site where Saint Cuthbert is buried. The air is full of the hum of angel's wings—and that's a metaphor, so please don't take me literally. Other cathedrals and churches are just full of the lingering thoughtforms of humans, full of the traffic of centuries, but they are not so much the incarnational domain of powers.

In terms of civilizations, this is as far as we have been able to go toward creating multidimensional domains. Civilizations have a short memory. It's like telephone memory: in order to memorize our new telephone number, we forget all our old telephone numbers. To get something inscribed in our long-term memory takes a different kind of learning experience. We Americans barely understand what it means to build a cathedral. For part of the year, I live at the Cathedral of Saint John the Divine. This is the largest and probably the last cathedral; it is still unfinished. It will take hundreds of years and hundreds of millions of dollars to finish this structure, because it is being built in a capitalist society in which you have to pay the people union wages, so the amount of capital it will take to finish it does not exist in our society of Trumpery casinos and cocaine. There is neither the will nor the effort in capitalist society.

The cultural edifice that America is creating is not a cathedral—not the incarnational body for a power—but the domain for a principality. Only in this cultural effort do you encounter the will of a people fixed over centuries of time and a continent of space. The difficulty with principalities, however, is that their transhuman complexity is a harmony of discord, a music of dissonance and contradiction that would make Schoenberg seem melodic. These beings, which extend over vast periods of time and space, basically come together through conflict. It is only through war and violence that they are able to sort out a relationship in which a new civilization can emerge.

Think of this in terms of World War II. World War II is a great paradox. On the one hand, what is war but destruction? We all have the movie images of World War II in our minds, and some of us have actually experienced the violence. On the other hand, World War II was this amazing planetary system of coordination—one that organized the movements of armies, peoples, and industries across the Atlantic and the Pacific. The war's conscious identity was violence, but the violence was never strong enough to destroy the warfare structure itself, a structure that was planetary and larger than any nation-state. The incipient form of planetization was the planetary conflict of World War II. What an incredible paradox!

Think of it also in terms of the transition from the Depression to post-industrial society. Where did this post-industrial economy come from? Our aerospace economy came out of the shift from a depressed civilian economy to a booming scientific one. First Westinghouse built refrigerators and toasters, and General Motors built pickups and sedans; but then they built tanks, airplanes, atom bombs, and rockets to outer space. The scale of social investment was so vast, and the transition so fast, that it was truly evolutionary in its dimensions.

What has happened now, which is truly New Age, is that in developing the warfare state to its maximum in the conflict with the Soviet Union, we have made the Soviets an inseparable part of our economy. We could lose a few states and the United States would still stand, but if we lost our enemy, our economy would collapse. That is what Gorbachev's *perestroika* is really all about: he is basically saying that since the Russians are the foundation of our economy, it is time we started sharing by investing in the Soviet economy directly, instead of indirectly through the arms race. By calling for a joint space program, a joint expedition to Mars, Gorbachev is raising the gargoyle on high and transforming the god of war into a heavenly body. Vice President Quayle isn't smart enough to understand, but the scientists at Cal Tech's Jet Propulsion Lab are, and they are all for this transformation of the unconscious polity of World War II into the conscious polity of planetary science and culture for the year 2000.

The old economy was described in an abstraction called the Gross National Product. We make Chevies and sell them to Japan, until Japan turns the tables on us and builds Toyota trucks and sells them back. In this old economy, things are made in nations and nations make money. But now we can't keep the books that way anymore. The marketplace has become planetary. The corporation is now a "distributive lattice" that has no simple location—either in Osaka or Ogallala. It is distributed like a gaseous film throughout the planet. It is not fixed, it is fluid.

At the same time the money flows have become fluid and not fixed. They are not based on land, as they were in feudalism; they are not based on precious metals, as they were in mercantilism; they are not based on stable currencies, as they were in the old postwar days of Bretton Woods. They are based on belief systems in nation-state "futures." You buy United States Treasury bonds if you believe in the future of the scientific economy of the United States. Science becomes a commodity crop, and you buy up its future harvests if your information tells you that they are going to make it big.

Universities, like Stanford or Berkeley, have become national resources. If we were to have a patriotic, right-wing, Aryan Nation revolution in the United States, and the rednecks were able to chase out all the pinko intellectuals, gays, and Chinese scientists, then you could kiss good-bye to America as a world power, and scientific power would shift to whatever place was willing to take them in—Canada, Europe, Brazil, or Australia. Better we invest in the Soviet Union, bring them up to cultural speed with human rights for adults and Apple Macintoshes for school kids, and let Lithuania and the Hopi Nation become sovereign states— whatever that means in a planetary civilization. Since it doesn't mean much, because the concept of sovereignty comes out of the Treaty of Westphalia that ended the Thirty Years' War in the seventeenth century, it would be smarter if we used biological concepts and saw the Israelis and Palestinians as endosymbionts within a living cell, and the Lithuanians and the Hopi Nation as autopoietic biomes in a planetary ecology rather than conquered peoples within an empire.

All that we have known before in the crossroads of angelic and human streams

171

of time were the angels of temples and the angels of nations. Now this new crossroads of human evolution is not interpretable in those familiar forms, which is why it seems to be so frightening, threatening, and evil. Small wonder that a religious thinker like David is seen by the fundamentalists to be the agent of the Antichrist. Their religious imaginations are too locked up in the languages of the past to appreciate that which is novel, so revelation has to come where they least expect it. And that truly makes it a revelation.

Consider, for example, the world economy—hardly the place one would look for a revelation. One of the things that has happened since the Second World War is that the marketplace has expanded to become the entire planet, but the transaction time in the marketplace has narrowed to seconds or milliseconds. There is almost a logarithmic increase in scale of space and a logarithmic decrease in scale of time. When these two logarithms cross, it does indeed produce a new crossroads in the phase-space of our culture, a bifurcation in our phase-portrait.

This crossing gives us a condition of complete novelty, which, in science, could be called "a singularity." Singularities are not knowable in scientific terms, for they are nonrepeatable. Like the Big Bang of Creation, they cannot be known—they can only be imagined. They happen once, but science requires things that are repeatable, knowable, and falsifiable by experimenters in different labs at different times. Once you get a singularity, you get something that is radically novel—that has never existed before and so cannot be known by the intellect. You cannot weigh and measure and locate it.

Think of Heisenberg's Uncertainty Principle. If you know the momentum of a global economic transaction, you cannot locate it; if you can locate it—to a deal in New York or a new product in Japan—you cannot know its economic momentum. Once you get this sort of unknowable situation, you then begin to have a multidimensional field that has never culturally existed before. You gain the possibility of the incarnation of a consciousness that is totally unique, totally novel.

Now, when a world economy is based upon belief systems in the purchase of nation-state scientific futures, and when the marketplace for these economic transactions is a planetary distributive lattice with emergent properties bringing forth eigenvalues in milliseconds, there is a new global mind or noosphere that is not inhabiting the bodies that we perceive: the corporation or nation-state.

Since we cannot know a singularity, and since our human minds seem to prefer looking at the rearview mirror to speak about where we have been rather than where we are going, let us imagine this new global mind or noosphere, with its complex, multidimensional topology, as an angel. Let us imagine that this angel is a principality that is no longer content to inhabit a nation-state; it has outgrown that piece of turf and finds it too restricting for its vibrant and extended life in the distributive planetary lattice. Scientists don't like angels, so they are forced to fall back on muddier notions such as the reduction of reality to quarks and bosons; however, the cultural field of their priestcraft can be experienced by the multitude only through the catastrophe of a nuclear war. A great work of music, by contrast, brings genius and child together in a shared experience of the creative imagination. Even a little child can know an angel, and the child's imaginary companion may not be as unreal as the parent thinks.

The difficulty with our holy-card pictures of angels as hermaphrodites with feathery wings is that the symbols have been read literally. This sort of fundamentalist realism tends to confirm the skeptic's feelings that religion is absurd. The reflective imagination, as David has described it, is based on old imagery from the past, and this often prevents us from seeing the uniqueness of the present situation. The generals are always trying to win the contemporary war in the terms and images of the last one:[32] the French generals behind the Maginot Line thought of Bismarck, and the American generals in Vietnam tried to storm the hills with visions of hoisting the flag at Iwo Jima.

However, guerrillas and terrorists know that electronic warfare is a distributive lattice that spreads from the jungle to the suburban American living room; it is basically an informational system that will not be won by conquering turf. The Viet Cong were far ahead of America, just as General Washington and his guerrillas were far ahead of the British Redcoats. That is why they won, for their imaginations were not restricted to the reflective imaginations of the past.

But lest you think I am too one sided, let me add that the same condition was true of the American Left in the sixties. The radicals were kids from Cambridge and Ann Arbor who had seen the old Eisenstein movies on the storming of the Winter Palace, so they played out their revolutionary movies in the streets with visions of Lenin dancing in their heads. With the reflective imagination, we are always looking, as Marshall McLuhan pointed out, in the rearview mirror.

We are always trying to see what is out there in the terms of the past. We talk about the GNP, we talk about rich nations and poor nations, we talk about emerging countries and developed countries, but none of that makes any sense of the world we are actually living in. America, especially compared to Switzerland, is a Third World country. It is ridiculous to call America a developed country and call ancient civilizations such as India or China emerging nations. We have whole pockets of emerging nations and underdeveloped countries spread throughout the United States.

It doesn't make any sense to talk about our GNP when a lot of Americans are sneakily making a lot of money in Japan and elsewhere, but that money never gets kept in the American ledgers. There is a great deal of creative bookkeeping going on in this electronic planetary lattice, so the GNP is not a good way to approach a description of global behavior. Just as mercantilist notions of precious metals were inadequate to describe the behavior of an expanding capitalist system, so this notion of a GNP is inadequate to describe the more complex interactions of global corporations and global shadow economies. All of this means that we are at the edge of knowing when we cross over from the reflective to the creative imagination.

The real dynamic of a New Age is happening in places where nobody is looking—namely, in just those profane areas that I have been talking about: warfare, pollution, and the light and shadow economies of the globe. In other words, the revelation is taking place at the edges of our peripheral vision in such ignored areas as "noise" and "evil." What we don't want to pay attention to as good holy people are noise and evil, precisely because we want to be good and holy.

Let's go back to David's metaphor of the crossroads. With the concept of the One, there is a kind of dimensionless point that has no time and space. It is inconceivable and it is like *samadhi*, or consciousness without an object. Then comes the primary bifurcation of the Big Bang of Creation and we enter into time—the time of before and after the Big Bang. We get the crossroads. The One becomes Two, and we get matter and antimatter. At that particular point of differentiation, we begin to get the principle of mirrored reflection—the principle of evil. We have Creation and we have the Fall. We have the Fall and we have the Redemption. We have the incarnation, with Jesus as a historical figure, and we have the Parousia at the end of time.

We have created this Western, linear sense of historical time, but now we are beginning to find the architecture so rigid that it has become a Los Angeles freeway in which we cannot turn off the road until our culture allows us to do so. We are collectively constrained to go where our Christian civilization demands, and that is to the end of the world. The only way we can release ourselves is to pray for the blowing up of the whole world in some Middle Eastern Armageddon. We have invested so much into this construction of historical time that we cannot conceive of a cosmology that is otherwise.

This is where Buddhism enters the historical picture as a useful way of dissolving the crystallizations of our own imaginations. If there is no absolute and eternal, unchanging Self, there is also no social ego with a wall surrounding its private property. If there is no single Big Bang of Creation, there is no single end of history—everybody out in Armageddon. If there is no single Messiah, then there is no single hierarchy with God the Father and the pope at the top and humanity at the bottom.

174

Instead, there is a distributive lattice with, wonder of wonders, a Buddha-nature in all things. David has talked about this. The older religions, the Abrahamic religions, tend to be solar, monotheistic ones in which there is one Sun and one God—one God only. But there are a billion billion stars out there. The *Hua Yen Sutra* is more sensitive to this view of the universe. We need the Other to rescue us from sameness, so Christianity needs Buddhism. Paradoxically, Buddhism plays Redeemer to Christianity, just as Christianity played Redeemer to Judaism.

This romance with the Other is another version of the parentage of the divine child. We need the Other; in diploid sexual reproduction, we are willing to throw away half of our genetic inheritance to be open to new genes. The Other can be Buddhism, it can be angels, or it can be dolphins or extraterrestrials. We need the Other because we sense unconsciously that we are incomplete, that something is missing.

If we are being good and holy and going to church every week, then, like the Reverend Jimmy Swaggert, we may find ourselves drawn toward the seamy side of town in the underworld of prostitution that is wholly other to the sexuality espoused in the church. If our intention is fixed on being good, holy, and sacred, the virtual revelation of multidimensionality may not come through our virtues but through our faults, our failures, our inadequacies, our vulnerability—where we are no longer in control of things through the techniques of religious management. This encounter with the Other can become pathological and lead to a hatred of the body and the devil, as it did for Saint Augustine[33] and the Reverend Jimmy Swaggert, or it can lead to a new acceptance of complexity in the play of the chaotic attractors of life.

Certainly, the vision of complexity in the energizing of evil is there for all to see in the Gospel of John, for Judas cannot betray Jesus until he is given a sop of vinegar. In other words, a negative—a shadow—Eucharist empowers Judas, just as the others are empowered by the bread in the wine. The Last Supper is a crossroads that leads to the cross. It is "a catastrophe bifurcation," in which Jesus is about to project himself into history. In that projection into the dyadic world of time, his own nature breaks up into light and shadow: John, who leans on his breast, and Judas, keeper of the purse, who goes out into the dark night to set it all in motion.

This catastrophe bifurcation that comes before Christian history is very much like the one that came before history itself, the bifurcation portrayed by Milton in *Paradise Lost*. When Lucifer is thinking how close he is to God Almighty and how "that one step higher makes me highest," this is precisely the moment when God the Father announces the emanation of his divine son who is to go forth to create the universe of matter. Lucifer and Christ are the twin sides of the demiurgic power of the manifest universe, just as Judas and John are the light and shadow sides of the historical world of Christendom.

If one unconsciously ignores this role of evil in Christianity, one ends up unconsciously taking evil to one's bosom, to play it out in the cruelty and passionate hatreds that are so characteristic of those committed to a doctrinal view of life. The fanatically devout generate the Other in the kinds of religious warfare we see today in Northern Ireland, Beirut, Amritsar, Sri Lanka, and, if some would have their way with us, America. They would have us fix the Republic to turn it into the Kingdom—to fix it now so that Jesus will come quickly, rather than waiting for him to end it in a refiner's thermonuclear fire.

One of the greatest forces for evil at work in the world today, I think, is religion. We have become so violent in inflicting our religions on one another that a revelation would have to find an unexpected place in which to appear. Once before, people looked to temples and palaces for the birth of the divine child, but he chose a stable. Now people look to religion for a manifestation of the divine, but I rather think the revelation has already happened when they weren't looking and where they least expected it: in the secular and profane conditions of our ordinary lives.

DISCUSSION 7

Religion, Humor, Tibet, Love and Compassion, Electronic Culture, Good and Evil, Social Action

AUDIENCE PARTICIPANT: Could you speak a little more about this reversal in which good becomes bad? You were talking about Jimmy Swaggert and how religion becomes the opposite of what it was originally intended to be. Could you flesh that out a bit more for us?

BILL: The difficulty with fundamentalism of any kind, be it Marxist, Christian, Islamic, or sociobiological, is that it is the kind of empowerment of an interpretation that gives people such a sense of control over their own world that they end up thinking that their interpretation *is* the world. When an explanation becomes total, it becomes totalitarian. In taking power to itself, it takes power away from anything that is other to itself, for that very otherness proves that the interpretation can't really be the totality of reality. Whether it is "all in the Bible" for Jimmy Swaggert or "all in the Koran" for the Ayatollah Khomeini, there is a world forced to surrender to the fundamentalist's powers of explanation.

The tyranny of interpretation is expressed, I think, in its inability to deal with things as basic as ambiguity, humor, or humility—to admit that there can be surprises, novelty, and complexity to life. Innovation, by definition, is a threat to the old order, so great efforts are expended to stop time and hold the world to one cultural arrangement. As the anxiety builds up and the fanatic is surrounded by what he or she can't control or eliminate, the violence of suppression becomes pathological.

The best antidote for these poisons is humor. What a fanatic or a paranoid cannot tolerate is a sense of humor, for a sense of humor is something that delivers us from the one-dimensionality of a single interpretation of a situation. It startles us with a sudden shift, a sudden explosion from one dimension of meaning to two or three. A judge walks across the stage in his robes. He slips on a banana peel, and as the high is brought low, it seems funny because now we have a human reality that is more complex than the judge's social order of hierarchy.

If someone is discussing Chomsky's ideas of syntax in linguistics and someone else says, "Oh, are they taxing that too?" it shifts one domain of meaning into another. We move into another dimension in which we can see that there is complexity beyond professionalism. Jokes are always moments of grace in which one-dimensionality is quickly expanded into multidimensionality.

One of the things I have always liked about David, and what attracted me to Findhorn, was that both had a very highly developed sense of humor. Most cults and fanatical groups really don't have any at all. This is why I love the profane or the irreverent, and why my own language is more in the idiom of the Irish pub than the academic lecture hall or the Anglican pulpit. The sacred is always more complex and chaotic than the sacerdotal. Any explanation, religious or scientific, that will not tolerate its negation is a force for good whose use of force has made it evil.

AUDIENCE PARTICIPANT: A quote I heard not too long ago is "Old religions, given time, become irreligious." Would you agree with that? Based on what I have heard you say about Buddhism, would you be willing to say that Buddhism seems to have become irreligious?

BILL: Yes to both questions, but at different levels. It isn't just religion that becomes irreligious—everything turns into its opposite. This is the *enantiodromia* at work in culture. What starts out with Jesus ends up with the church and the Inquisition. Or what starts out with the birth of a nation, with George Washington fighting against the British Empire, ends up with an imperial LBJ fighting to suppress Ho Chi Minh. Art breaks away from religion in the Italian Renaissance, then it becomes the iconography of capitalist longing with Andy Warhol in New York. What starts out with an Enlightenment intellectual like Jefferson ends up with anti-intellectuals such as Reagan, Bush, and Quayle. The psychedelic movement starts out with an elitist intellectual like Aldous Huxley and ends up with drug-crazed illiterates. The New Age seventies start out with David Spangler in Findhorn and end up in the eighties in Hollywood with Shirley MacLaine. That's not just religion, that's life.

As for Buddhism, the Dalai Lama says that Buddhism is not a religion but a psychology of consciousness. In a medieval, agricultural culture, the way of externalizing a psychology of consciousness was as a monastic, theocratic society—let's say monastic with Zen in Japan and theocratic with Tantra in Tibet. Much of the Dalai Lama's emphasis now is on science, and he has developed a friendship with Francisco Varela and other scientists and invited them to meetings at Dharamsala [in northern India]. The Dalai Lama now sees the possibility for science to become an incarnational vehicle for knowledge, compassion, and insight into consciousness. He seeks, therefore, not to clone medieval Tibet, but to find new patterns of culture.

Even Chögyam Trungpa Rinpoche, a very close friend of Varela's, was looking for new strategies appropriate to the West. He quite literally had to deal with noise and evil, and he embraced all kinds of radical techniques—most of which I didn't approve of because I felt that he simply exchanged a rigid hierarchy of religious theocracy for a rigid hierarchy of avant-garde artistic degeneracy. However, neither Francisco Varela nor Allen Ginsberg would agree with me on that score, so you can make up your own mind as you consider the state they're in now—meaning Trungpa's *sangha*, Dharmadhatu.

The question of how to embody a psychology of consciousness in a culture is quite complicated, for it would seem that no matter what a truly holy man can do—be that holy man Jesus, Rudolf Steiner, or a holy woman like the Mother at Auroville—people respond by degrading the vision of culture into a cult. When one considers all the problems of cultural transmission that the Tibetan and Zen Buddhist *sanghas* in America have had, one can begin to appreciate just how much time it takes for a spiritual culture to evolve.

AUDIENCE PARTICIPANT: In light of what you said about the Dalai Lama, would you care to comment about the fate of Tibet as a culture, a nation, and a religion?

BILL: It is like the scattering of dandelion stems by a stampede of wild animals. It is violent, levels everything in its path, and scatters the seeds in the wind. Before, Tibet was a mountain fastness, a bank vault for an extremely rich culture. Now it is a planetary philosophy, affecting poets in the East Village of New York, laboratories for the neurosciences in Paris, and cowgirls in Colorado. As a bank vault for a rich medieval culture, Tibet was rich beyond belief. The kind of knowledge that was stored there about the states of consciousness after death existed nowhere else in the world. They practically wrote a *Michelin Guide* to the bardo, and I don't mean just *The Tibetan Book of the Dead* (the *Bardo Thodol*) but also the *The Mirror of Mindfulness*.[34] This book tells us what is going to happen to us throughout the forty days after death. Now, there is no way that we are going to get that knowledge in Christianity or Judaism.

What the Tibetan Buddhists knew in medicine and psychology was equally vast and incredible. It takes a special culture to be able to hold onto that kind of knowledge, and the strategy they chose was male, monastic, and monarchic. Catholicism was equally male, monastic, and monarchic in the West, but it couldn't generate such an advanced psychology of consciousness. There is something special about the place and the people of Tibet. On the other hand, their strength in containing this knowledge was their weakness. They didn't know when to stop or how to let go. Change is always a problem for medieval cultures. Also, mountain people don't seem to like change, judging by the Coloradans, the Tibetans, and the Swiss.

Repressed intellectually by the Tibetans, the principle of change appeared externally in its most unelected and involuntary form as a tragic fate. The destruction of Tibet by the Chinese is like the destruction of the temple of Jerusalem by the Romans. What happened out of the Roman destruction was the planetization of Judaism. Rather than becoming the people of a place—the holy land—the Jews were spread throughout the world in a Diaspora in which they shifted their practice from the temple to the Torah. They shifted from a local, oral culture to a global, literate culture, just as now the Tibetans seem to be shifting from a medieval culture of script to a planetary culture of cognitive science.

Since the Chinese have been so cruel with their own university students, you can imagine what they must have been like in Tibet! Imagine how the Jews must have felt experiencing the destruction of their temple in Jerusalem. Yet even when evil is released in all its ugliness and horror, its powers are not cosmic, and good is able to move in, like seeds popping up after a forest fire or the soil growing richer after a volcanic eruption. Even after the Cretaceous extinction, when more than 70 percent of life on Earth was wiped out, life rebounded and the mammals spread into the spaces once ruled by the dinosaurs. Sure, this is a scale vastly beyond the individual ego, but I still take heart that good seems to be more than the equal and opposing force to evil.

Good seems to express an ontological condition in which in order to *do* bad, you have to *be* good. Pure evil is entropic. If every Nazi immediately turned on every other Nazi and killed them on the spot, Nazism couldn't last a second. Evil has to invoke the good in *order* to survive. It has to have "honor among thieves," and this shows that there is a more basic and primordial ontology to the good—that chaos, noise, and evil, are part of some larger dynamic that we are only now beginning to appreciate in our Chaos dynamics and new sciences of complexity.

AUDIENCE PARTICIPANT: From what you've been saying, the idea has come to me to consider the value of the negative example. In my personal case, I think back on the fact that my father was an alcoholic, a spendthrift, and a womanizer. I didn't grow up with him but knew him for only one year of my life. I didn't want to imitate him as a model in looking for a husband or father for my children, yet I can see that in some ways I did.

BILL: Perhaps because you knew your father for only one year, you yearned to have a father, and knowing only the negative definition of a father, your longing constellated the father/male model as you knew it. The other day in the hotel in Vancouver, my wife and I were watching an interview with John Le Carré, the famous spy novelist. It seems that his father was a con man and a trickster. They interviewed Le Carré's brother and sister as well, and all three children of this con-man father seem to have responded in interesting ways to their experience of their father. One became an actress, one became a journalist, and the other became a spy novelist. Notice that all three chose professions of representation through artifice.

Thomas Mann has written about the artist as con man, the one who makes fiction seem truth. The artist as con man is almost an archetype that goes back to the Juggler of Our Lady, the joker, or the trickster figure in mythology. Each child, in a sense, was rejecting the father and saying, "I don't want to become like him. He lied and cheated and manipulated people." Yet each of the three children worked on an unconscious project to redeem their father by redeeming his gifts for imaginative representation. Each became the father, but in a particular form of redemption that called upon them to explore their own gifts, whether for acting or writing. In this television film, the father was shown to be quite a sleaze, but I rather suspect he must have had some marvelous gifts to have indirectly inspired his children to become so successful in discovering their own talents.

AUDIENCE PARTICIPANT: I have been around the New Age a long time, but I didn't find what I was looking for. Somehow I wound up in a black church, singing gospel, because that is where I found love and spirit. I am not hearing anything about love here. Can we talk about love?

BILL: I don't like to use the word "love"; I prefer "compassion" because I think "love" is a word that has been worn smooth in the coinage of passing it around too much and using it to get something else we want. The integrity of the old noble features have been worn off. "Compassion" is a new Buddhist term that hasn't been worn down yet. However, as we all know—especially any of us who have lectured too much—a word wears out very fast in this culture because people pick up a new word and use it as a buzzword for everything.

I was raised in a Catholic military school with heavy words like "love" and "faith," but those words didn't work for me as a child because love was aggressively administered without compassion, and faith meant the suppression of my intellectual questioning of dogma. I began to be suspicious of those who were telling me they loved me—the priests and nuns. As a seven-year-old forced by circumstances of sickness and poverty to live away from home, I felt that the nuns' institutional application of love wasn't very loving. I still suspect those words, either in their aggressive form or in their sentimental, Hallmark Cards form. I choose to seek out other words.

Your search as a white person brought you into the black church. In fact, one of the problems of the New Age subculture is just how lily white we are. The New Age movement tends to be filled with white, suburban, middle-class folk.

One of the things I like about living at the Cathedral of Saint John the Divine in Spanish Harlem in New York is that in spite of the noise and the squalor, the ugliness and the danger—especially now with crack—is that it is a place where all the levels of human society come together: the top and the bottom. The most sublime sacred music is united with care for the homeless, who sleep there at night in the room provided for them. I see them straightening up their beds as I pass by on my way to teach my class. Alcoholics Anonymous also has its meetings in the same building. On the street, by the fountain, the crack addicts are begging for small change to put together the five dollars they need for a smoke. One of them murdered the grocer across the street. Then I see the limousines parked in the driveway, and I know that Dean Morton is trying to fundraise to keep the Stoneyard Program going, a program that hires Harlem kids and teaches them stonemasonry so that they can finish the towers.

Everything is going on there. There are jugglers and high-wire artists, medieval music, and Paul Winter performing the *Missa Gaia* while elephants take communion at the high altar. This cathedral is thought to be too New Age for many tradition-bound Episcopalians, but it really is more medieval than modern in its unsuburban range of human experience. Anyway, I find this cathedral to have more of an atmosphere of compassion than one would find in a classroom in a university. There is something about Saint John the Divine that is very much like what I think you are finding in the black Baptist Church.

I remember the first time I gave a public lecture. It was right after I had published *At the Edge of History*, in 1971, and I was still just a young professor in Toronto, used to lecturing only to university students. I went down to New York and gave a talk to some meeting of army chaplains at some base around Staten Island. There were a lot of black army chaplains in the group, and as I got going in my talk, I found them joining in and urging me on, as if I were giving a sermon in a black church. It was wonderful. They were responding, totally in sync with me, and becoming an affirmative chorus, like unto no university lecture hall I knew.

There was something about my being Irish and coming from the working class, from an oral culture, that fit into their being black and also coming from an oral culture that enabled us to connect in spirit. It felt very different from being a poor Irish kid who had made it into the Ivy League and was trying to fit in by drinking sherry and wearing Harris tweed coats and talking very precisely. This unacademic audience had a liveliness in which they didn't care if they understood every single thing I was laying on them; they weren't threatened or hostile, they were rocking. It was

182

wonderful. I guess this is why we are drawn to other cultures, because we cannot find it all in just one. We need an opposite culture, whether it be African, Asian, Hispanic, or Native American. We are always attracted to some sort of oriental or exotic culture as our birthright to a fuller humanity than our parents gave us.

AUDIENCE PARTICIPANT: Can the concept of love or compassion truly exist as a major ideal in our world today, or have we lost that possibility? I rather think that we have. It feels as if we have already become so separated from it that people don't know what the experience could possibly be.

BILL: There is always loss. I will play historian now, even if I am no longer an academic. At any given moment in Western history there has always been cultural loss going on. There has always some unimaginable innovation, but there has always been a real loss of culture that is an inseparable part of that transition. If we look back to Homer and the *Iliad*, we see an oral culture, a bardic culture. The bards could memorize epics as long as the *Iliad*, but they began to lose this oral culture as the alphabet came in. There were more than three centuries of Dark Ages before writing stabilized itself to become what we like to identify as classical Athenian literature.

We are now in a similar period of losing a traditional culture, only in our case it is literary culture. In my lifetime I have seen a general decline in public grammar; now, even English teachers make grammatical errors in speech and writing. People cannot syntactically put a complex sentence together when they speak publicly. Listen to Bush and think of Churchill. When I compare a transcription of one of my own talks with an eighteenth-century or even nineteenth-century speech, I am amazed to see how architecturally balanced their sentences are and how sloppy mine are—mine dribble all over the place in the fashion of a Jackson Pollock painting. Were I to speak with the Churchillian rhetoric of just two generations ago, you would experience me as some kind of phony.

Although American parents like to force toddlers to read through watching "Sesame Street," they themselves do not read, and newspaper and magazine articles have declined to the level of quick cuts from television. *USA Today* is the prime example. Our ancestors used to sit all day for political debates, such as the Lincoln-Douglas debates, but we have become such a generation of "vidiots" that sound bytes and images have replaced thought. As Innis and McLuhan pointed out, the introduction of the alphabet helped to bring in representational government, and now that literary culture is on its way out, representational democracy is going out with it.

We have become a nation of scientists and "electropeasants," Top and Pop. Images replace thought, and manipulated sentimentality replaces love and compassion. It's OK to destroy American democracy with television commercials, but just don't burn the flag, for the first takes thinking, which doesn't matter, but the second is an image, and that *matters*—that is reality to us.

I think this process of cultural loss is going to continue. The loss of culture will go all the way to a loss of "nature." We are going to see incarnations in cyborgs and technological cultures that are totally unnatural in terms of anything that we now conceive to be natural. On the other hand, if I look as a cultural historian at what people think to be nature, I can see that their idea of nature is a cultural artifact, a cultural fiction. People keep pointing to "nature," but there is no such thing. The idea of nature is just whatever picture you imagine for that historical moment in time.

So, yes, if we are losing our cultural connection to our traditional idea of nature, we are also losing our cultural connections to one another. We are losing our national identity; we are losing literacy; we are losing compassion; we are losing good neighborliness. Soon, in the cyberpunk landscape of the silicon chip and flesh, we will lose our fascination with sex as AIDS and ESB—electronic stimulation of the brain—conspire with "virtual reality" suits and electronic meditation helmets to shift orgasm away from the physical contact of genital intercourse.

With this cultural loss, of course, comes inconceivable innovation: an entire new space-age culture, a return of elementals and angels into the human world, a turn on the spiral to electronic animism, electronic Druid wizardry. In this, David is truly a prophetic figure. To look for compassion, I think one first has to have compassion for what the Buddhists call impermanence—compassion for all passing things. One has to have compassion for one's own moment in time and space. I have to recognize that I am in this difficult time of perceivable loss and gain, and if I open my imagination to it, instead of trying to control it with my egocentric agenda, I may just come to some understanding of myself and others.

The people who refuse to do this become the passionate, fanatical reactionaries and revolutionaries—the kind that love the multitude but have real trouble loving individual persons. They are dangerous people, because their public talk of love most often leads to public violence. Padraic Pearse, the revolutionary father of the Irish Republic, was great at addressing the multitude, and he loved the Irish people, but he had real problems loving Irish persons.

AUDIENCE PARTICIPANT: What about Mother Theresa?

BILL: I have never met her. The Mother Theresa we have created in the media is a compound of private guilt and public sentimentality. I am not moved by this construct of Madison Avenue hagiography, but if I met her personally, who knows?

DISCUSSION 7

AUDIENCE PARTICIPANT: You were speaking of writing and our new electronic culture. I was wondering if you dabble with other forms?

BILL: I would love to do music videos with computer animation. I would really like to try my hand at that. I would like to work with a classical composer like Philip Glass and a computer artist. But this is just not allowed in our mass culture, so only rock stars get to make videos. I think my personal response to living in a postliterate culture was to stumble onto another form of Irish, oral culture: giving talks like these instead of going around to campuses and giving poetry readings. Poetry readings are the fixed rather than the fluid. My response was not to cease being a writer, but when as a writer of books I was invited to give a professorial lecture, I found myself giving a talk instead and stumbled into becoming some sort of stand-up intellectual.

In an earlier and more stable literary culture, say in the era of Faulkner, T.S. Eliot, and Dylan Thomas—a culture that I was just able to catch a glimpse of before it passed when I was a teenager—I probably would have remained a more traditional sort of professor, and I probably would never have left the university. I was born in 1938, so I grew up in a culture in which *The Saturday Review* and *The Atlantic Monthly* had the prestige and charisma that PBS, Bill Moyers, or the BBC might now have for teenage intellectuals. My dream as a working-class kid in Los Angeles was to go back East to the Ivy League and live the tweedy life of a pipe-smoking English professor. But then came the sixties, and even those of us who didn't take acid—and I didn't—were still changed. The culture changed. The world changed. I changed.

Now I couldn't endure being a tweedy professor of English at Cornell, and I couldn't endure being a professional poet going from campus to campus for poetry readings. When it comes to the role of the Celtic bard in an electronic culture, I prefer David Byrne to Galway Kinnell. How I wish that I could work with videos in the way that Byrne has. *Pacific Shift* flopped as a book, but I still think it would make a great video. Most of the disorientation people feel when I juggle a bunch of ideas around would disappear if they could see what I am seeing in my mind.

However, computer animation takes a lot of money, so it is much cheaper for me to talk and write. In these forms, I still have artistic control. If you look at the wretched music video for Susanne Vega's song "Tom's Diner," you see her wonderfully imaginative lyrics destroyed by some fashion-magazine photographer. While her lyrics create pictures, the video destroys the imagination with imagery. She's an artist who has lost control of her art because of the packaging of tour agents and video engineers. In her concerts, the music is so loud that you can't hear the words, and the engineers flash the lights to make her into some kind of Madonna for teenyboppers. So, I'm probably better off as a poor artist outside that whole system of riches and technology, but one still in control of his work.

AUDIENCE PARTICIPANT: Have you ever shocked an audience or gotten people angry?

BILL: Oh, yes! I have made people quite upset. I remember one engineer exploding in an audience and getting up to say, "I have just had it with metaphoric thinking!" He took me on in a real debate at Lindisfarne in Southampton. It was quite a piece of theater, with Gregory Bateson and Jonas Salk commenting from the sidelines. Because I have talked to audiences that range from New Age groups at Findhorn to Fortune 500 corporation presidents at the Harvard Business School, I have experienced all kinds of reactions. I have also been out in the heartland of rural America in places like Hickory, North Carolina; Coeur d'Alene, Idaho; Rapid City, South Dakota; Bozeman, Montana; Salina, Kansas; Fox, Arkansas. . .

DAVID: And don't forget Dayton!

BILL: Oh my God! "Did I forget to mention Memphis?" I have left out the Holiday Inn in Dayton, birthplace of David Spangler. Dayton, that is, not the Holiday Inn, though that has a nice Antichrist sort of ring to it: "Sorry, Mrs. Spangler, there's no room at the Holiday Inn."

DAVID: Actually, I was born in Columbus. . . .

BILL: Anyway, yes, I have been all over, from Anchorage to Atlanta, from Honolulu to Halifax, so I have confronted a lot of different audiences. The anger generally comes from my speed of talking, which they feel has to be glib, or the kind of anger and disorientation anxiety that comes from my putting disparate things together, or from their confusion in trying to figure out what political pigeon-hole to stick me in. Am I a know-it-all liberal secular humanist, a communist, an "environmental terrorist" (Lyndon Larouche's term for ecologists), a New Age dupe of Satan, or what?

I caused real disorientation anxiety with my students at the university, for they thought they had to take notes as fast as I talked. When I was younger, with my brain boiling over from kundalini, I would slip into trance and start channeling the *Encyclopaedia Britannica* to throw out an idea in every sentence, so sometimes the students would throw up their pens in frustration and say, "That's it!" I put it in writing in the syllabus that they should take the lectures as a shower and not a meal—that the exam would be only about the readings and never about the glossolalia of my lectures—but even still a few of the obedient and orderly Canadians would try to take notes. Some students were so routinized by high school that they could not stand to listen without a pen in hand. They couldn't surrender to the imagination; they had to feel that they were in charge and in control of the situation.

After the sixties things began to change, and some of the hipper types would come in and smoke dope in the back of the lecture hall and exclaim, "Wow!" or "Right on!" or "Far fucking out!" They were telling me that whatever I was doing, it wasn't what my staid Canadian colleagues were doing in the classrooms around me. So I began to wonder if perhaps there might be another way to carry on the life of the mind. I looked at Ivan Illich and Paolo Soleri, both of whom gave talks in my classes at York University, and I thought that their "counterfoil institutions" of CIDOC [Center for Intercultural Documentation] and Arcosanti looked more interesting than the university. So I quit and set up Lindisfarne. Ah, those were the days when innovation was possible!

AUDIENCE PARTICIPANT: I want to go back to this problem of good and evil. Say we have an earthquake, which is a form of disaster, and we have the army going in to help. Or we have the military trying to rescue a whale caught in the ice. Good guys and bad guys—how do we tell?

BILL: One category mistake we can make about evil is to think that it is measured quantitatively. When thousands of people are killed, that's war, but when one person is killed, that's city life. Yet the filming of a single act of homicide, in its individual horror, might actually be much more terrifying than footage of the Israeli air force bombing Beirut. We watch the news every day, but one snuff videotape of a real murder of a teenage girl would have us all vomiting uncontrollably. The military are sent in to rescue the survivors of a volcano, and we take it in with all the other news.

If disaster or evil is not collectivized but is focused on in all its minute particulars, we are truly overwhelmed. Evil in the image of one single girl, running and screaming from the burns of napalm, touches us more than an image of the horizon of the whole city of Beirut on fire. The evil is so focused and so intense that the numbers have nothing to do with the quality of the experience. We focus on one whale caught in the ice, but we allow the species to go into extinction. In our rational life, we tend to be quantitative, and it takes big numbers to catch our attention, but in our feeling life, numbers don't mean anything.

So, to answer your question, "good guys" tend to be individuals. "Bad guys" tend to be faceless numbers. That's why uniforms are so important for armies. It would be very hard for most of us to kill an individual, face to face, but to drop a bomb from above onto a bunch of "Gooks" or mow down a bunch of "Japs" or "Huns" with a machine gun is easier for us.

It is the single image that grabs us. After all, there are a million events per second per square yard going on in history, so how do we construct a narrative that we can call "history"? We focus in and out. For example, we create these illusions called "classical Greece," and we skip the women, the slaves, and the Phoenicians, who were hook-nosed Semites and not as pretty as the classical Greeks. We focus in on a few Athenian men for a few British men writing the textbooks for other gentlemen of their sort at Oxford and Cambridge. History, as Voltaire said, is "the lie commonly agreed upon." Who agrees upon it? The ruling class. It is their history, whether it is patriarchal, European, white, gay, or whatever. The history of the Dark Ages from another point of view might not seem so dark, especially if one looks at India, China, or the Maya in Mesoamerica.

I began to wonder about this whole issue of "good guys" and "bad guys" when I considered the Viking Terror. It was the first projection outward into the cultural ecology of the Atlantic, the projection that was followed by waves of explorers, privateers, and pirates. The Viking Terror began at the monastery of Lindisfarne in 793. What was the transition from the Mediterranean cultural ecology of medieval Christendom to the Atlantic cultural ecology of Protestant, industrial Europe and America? The Viking Terror. Interestingly enough, the places the Vikings chose to attack were the monasteries, the very nerve centers that helped bring together the body politic of medieval Christendom. The Viking Terror, in a sense, is the annunciation of the next level of organization, the emerging Atlantic industrial culture.

Oftentimes, whether it is oxygen as the first pollution for anaerobic life or World War II as the transition to planetization, the emerging level of organization seems to introduce itself as evil. If we look at homosexuality as a contemporary fundamentalist would and then ask ourselves who the first people are to become "unnatural" by separating sexuality from reproduction—by shifting away from genes in natural selection to communities in artistic cultural selection—then we can begin to appreciate the "Gay Terror" as the annunciation of the next level of organization in our future "postnatural" world.

If the fundamentalists also see David Spangler as the dupe of the Antichrist, it is because they recognize that his combination of mysticism and high technology undoes their Protestant Reformation culture. So whether we are talking about bad guys, Vikings, gays, or heretics, we are talking about a "dependent co-origination" in which good guys and bad guys are in the double helix dance of life.

AUDIENCE PARTICIPANT: Bill, I notice that when you talked about love and faith you defined them through their distortions: faith as the suppression of the intellect, love as aggression. It seems to me that you are taking these terms and understanding them only in their corrupt forms. The suggestion was made by David that our ideas and our words are inadequate to really represent God, or divinity, or the Cosmic Christ. In using the words "love" and "faith," should we not make a distinction between the terms we use and a reality that is something more than can possibly be reflected by these terms? Perhaps this place where we come to see the inadequacy of our terms is David's incarnational crossroads.

BILL: My answer about love and faith was a personal answer to the woman who asked the question, and it was returned in the personal tone and terms with which the question was addressed to me. I was dealing with how I as an individual experienced love and faith as a child in the Catholic church. I was not making an absolute statement about the doctrinal concepts of love and faith in the Catholic church.

Oftentimes, I have noticed that people at conferences say, "I am not hearing . . ." as if they were on the lookout for special terms that could signal their acceptance of what I have to say. However, I think you do correctly sense a lack of Platonism in what I am saying, for I would not want to place the ideals of love and faith as abstractions with their own perfect condition far above the relationships of people that bring them forth.

One of the things I like about Buddhist cosmology and philosophy is that they tend not to separate a substance or state from the actual processual relationship that brings it forth. I wouldn't want to say that Faith and Love exist as universals in a transcendent state, in the empyrean or Platonic realm of the Forms, and that I in my human imperfection can scarcely touch their full and radiant reality. I would much rather say that the way I know and experience love is brought forth in dependent co-origination with others—in the context of living occasions of love and faith. I would prefer to be strictly immanental rather than transcendental in my orientation. The other Platonic orientation tends toward a mind/body split—mind and heart—and moves in the philosophical directions we have known in the past. So, yes, I do back away from that direction, and that is why I don't use that traditional language.

AUDIENCE PARTICIPANT: OK, Bill, at one level I am hearing you say that we might as well just mess it all up and wait for the pendulum to swing the other way, and then I hear you say, "No, it's not going to be any of the above; it is is going to be something really different, something unimaginable." You say, don't just attune to your ego's personal agenda, attune to the larger agenda of the meeting, of history, of time—whatever. OK, so how do you position yourself when you are thus attuned to the agenda of the time if you are anybody other than yourself?

BILL: First of all, vision repositions my self, my place in the scheme of things. I don't think that I have an eternal, enduring Self. I have multiple tasks, or roles, or functions, or identities. There is no fixed Bill Thompson. There is a father, a husband, a lover, a writer, a kid brother; there are many different relationships, and they are all equally valid. One of the things that I hated about Buddhism as an adolescent but now makes sense to me as an emerging old man is its denial of a fixed and absolute Higher Self. Perhaps because I have become an intellectual migrant worker without a permanent home, my identity has become equally nomadic, for now I have to live in different countries and deal with different languages.

In confronting the spiritually shallow culture of intellectuals in Paris or Frankfurt, or the intellectually shallow culture of the New Age in America, I am forced to question the culture that I once so believed in as a working-class kid in Los Angeles. I used to believe that those guys back East or in Europe or India really were wise men with the answers. Now I know that European high culture is just an ecology of subcultures and that the professors of philosophy are not smarter or better than the rest of us. As a card-carrying intellectual, my identity has expired and my passport is no longer valid.

When I looked to the gurus, the same thing happened all over again on another turn of the spiral. So I had to step back and realize that it's not about wise guys, it's about ecologies of mind in which differences energize a membrane to create new forms of life. It's Top and Pop. If it is all an ecology of consciousness, then I'm not the whole, and I cannot and should not try "to save the world" by returning to nature and creating the solution for pollution in the meta-industrial village—which is what I tried to do with Lindisfarne in Crestone, Colorado. My personal agenda, with its personal timetable for social transformation, gets tabled. I no longer have the floor for the meeting, so I have to sit back, watch the dynamic, and try to figure out what the yuppies and Reagan are up to.

With depression about the Reagan destruction of environmentalism and eco-philosophy serving as a kind of deflation to let the air out of my personal hot-air balloon, I began a new life in the eighties as an unemployed seventies radical. I had to start all over again with "beginner's mind" to learn new things: German and French, Grimm's fairy tales, housework and child care for a working wife, biology, cognitive science, Chaos dynamics, and writing novels and poetry. What I learned from housework and Chaos dynamics is the global effect of the accumulation of minute particulars—that little things can actually effect the transition from one attractor to another. Since Blake said much the same thing, I figure that this has got a ring of truth to it, so I start paying more attention to chaos and noise than to tranquility and the return to nature.

190

This change in the scale of space also changes the scale of time. Little and large begin to interact in my mind in a new way. One lifetime may not be enough to effect a cultural transformation, and then again, one lifetime at work in a different pattern may not be perceptible until much later. It's the situation of the Dark Ages monk and the Viking Terror again: the little and the large. So I began to accept that it all cannot be done in one lifetime.

What flowed out of this was a relaxing of the need to identify the work as the task of only one specific lifetime, of one specific ego or personality. Then along came those beautiful fractal landscapes from Mandelbrot's work in mathematics, and I recognized a phase-portrait of the Self. Industrial people say, "Won't it be great when we can conquer sleep and we won't have all that down time?" But what if when we are asleep we enter a fractal hyperspace in which we become everybody: "Here comes Everybody." We become the mystical body of Christ. Then sleep isn't down time. In David's language, we are pulling down windows and clicking onto all sorts of dimensions of existence. I wrote a poem about this fractal vision of the self in my book *Imaginary Landscape*.

Were we to eliminate sleep, we would eliminate our participation in all the other incarnations in which we live simultaneously in a infinite, fractal progression. So I hope we never "conquer" sleep, because that would be the perpetuation of illusion and deception to lock us into an industrial mentality. I am not in that much of a hurry to get it all done in the terms of Bill Thompson because I know there are a lot of us out there, and they are all doing different things. Maybe even one of my unknown collaborators is my enemy. I may not realize it, but that enemy may be sharpening the edge, with his or her abrasiveness, of what it is I am supposed to be doing.

Once we come Christically to the point of loving our enemies, we come to an equator, an edge to our world where we fall off our flat world into multidimensionality. We fall into the revelation, the Parousia, the end of history—whatever. We drop our agenda in free fall as we find that the evil one (Reagan, for instance) is actually another form of the cultural transformation in disguise. That is very disorienting. It means that the whole question of good and evil, natural and unnatural, human and nonhuman, has to be rethought. However, in seeing that even enemies can be part of the process, I have to accept that everything doesn't depend on me—that I am not alone. I don't have to personally save the world tomorrow or else it is all going to hell.

In finding new images for understanding behavior in the new sciences of complexity, I begin to be uncomfortable with merely a human agenda—with a Sierra Club, Volvo-station-wagon-cum-Greenpeace-bumper-sticker approach to politics.

I think that we were once dinosaurs, that we were once cyanobacteria, and that we are now humans—this flabby, middle-aged evolutionary compromise between elementals and angels. It's a temporary compromise, and I can't see how humans can fix all the problems on our historic list. Fortunately, there is more to life than human beings, for it is hard to have much faith in ourselves. If we can't stop smoking, how do we think we are going to stop pollution or stop smoking down the Amazon rain forests?

So, I am not a straightforward, linear optimist, but I don't need to *be* an optimist to *do* the good. Your ordinary California New Age optimist says I can do good only if I feel good. But I have an Irishman's tragic sense of history, with its gallows sense of humor, so I am willing to be impatient for a very long time. I am not about to become punk and flip from optimism to pessimism to say, "Well, if I can't save the world and feel good in the process, then fuck it."

This new vision of a fractal universe is much more empowering for me than all the feel-good California therapies put together. It opens up other domains of interpenetrating dimensions of existence, be they elemental, angelic, or extraterrestrial. This vision of the universe changes my whole sense of orientation. Outer space is no longer out there waiting for an infection of human, tin-can space colonies—a kind of metastatic carcinoma of industrial civilization. As my imagination passes with others through all these domains, I begin to suspect that this is what Buddhist compassion is all about: a passing together through the impermanent forms of incarnation—cyanobacteria, dinosaurs, humans. Anyway, when it comes down to the need to act, to do good in minute particulars, as Blake counseled, I quit smoking and I stopped eating meat so that the Amazon basin doesn't have to be turned into ranch land to produce burger beef for McDonald's on my account.

AUDIENCE: David, in trying to get something out of all this, in this mystery school of incarnation, how do you institutionalize a good thing? It seems to me that with all you said, there still is tomorrow morning, and Monday morning, and we still have to get up and go to work, so how do we act?

DAVID: We Americans don't ever seem to have any trouble acting, do we? We are going to act, no matter what any philosophy has to say about action. We so believe in the reality of action that "no action" is seen as the worst possible sort of action we could take. We can act unconsciously or consciously, but we still believe that we are the actors at work—making reality what it is all about. I can look at the cybernetic organization of the world and feel that it is the equivalent of the Viking Terror sweeping over my sacred world, or I may opt for the big picture and think that it is going to lead to something big and important later on. I do feel that part of our cultural direction is toward developing the imaginative capacity to do just that—to look at the Viking Terror and say, "Here comes Atlantic civilization."

I feel humanity is going to achieve that expansion of the imagination at some point, and that is what I mean by the incarnational imagination: a lifting out of conditions that are locked into a particular time/space. On the other hand, that doesn't mean that if I am a monk at Lindisfarne, I should sit back and wait for the Vikings to slit my throat. I may choose to go out fighting or praying or cursing. However, a response of hatred and rejection calls for revenge; it calls for the monk to be angry that God did not reward him for all his uncomfortable mornings of getting up and going to chapel. So in his anger at God, his rage and hatred turn him into his enemy, and now it's his turn to play Viking. A more enlightened response would be to ask how one could serve the emergence of Atlantic civilization without being caught up by the terror of the moment.

In the Dalai Lama's case, it was not appropriate to stand and fight, or to organize an armed counterinsurgency against the Chinese occupation of Tibet. Instead, he became a world teacher and focused on the communication of Tibetan Buddhism to the world. In other words, instead of seeking to continue the life of Tibetan Buddhism by holding the territory underneath it, he chose to continue the life of Tibetan Buddhism itself. Had he chosen to become a counterinsurgent leader of revolt, he would have had to give up his precepts to adopt the values of force of the invader. Such an individual response certainly has global effects. I think that most of us looking at China, especially after this summer, would rather be Tibetan Buddhist than Chinese communist. So, you see, there is a kind of aikido move that we can make. Yes, we can still have the reality of activity that we so admire, but there is a difference that makes a difference between one act and another.

Once again, I think it is not so much a question of action but of an embodiment of consciousness. If I feel passionately about the destruction of the Amazon rain forest, then how can I embody that passion in my life? Personally, I don't think one should embody it in a sense of "rain forests versus ranchers," but rather in the wider sense of "What do the rain forests in relationship to this next historical wave have to say about our entire planetary ecology at this time and space? Is our time on Earth finished? Is something else coming?" I am not saying that it is, but in the realm of consciousness in which a rain forest dwells as a collective organism—say, at the angelic or devic realm of the rain forest—its time span is very different from ours, and its sense of the pulse of life on the planet, from ice age to ice age, may be quite vaster than ours.

If I am going to make myself the agent for the rain forest and seek to act on its behalf, then I should act in a truly shamanistic way, a way that is an embodiment of the spirit of the rain forest. A rock concert may not be a truly shamanistic way to do that. It might be just another way of energizing consumerism, the same kind that supports McDonald's and the ranchers. The way that I approach these things, if I am passionate about the rain forests, is that, yes, I would rather act out of passion than sit debating whether I should act or do nothing. But I also know that if I act, I would like to act in a way that is nonadversarial. The true enemies of the rain forest or peace or ecological well-being may not be ranchers or the military/industrial complex or big business, but the inability of each of us—of all humanity—compassionately to embody a larger dynamic of being.

CONCLUSIONS

Looking Ahead
David Spangler

In the new sciences of complexity that Heinz Pagels has written about in his book *The Dreams of Reason*,[35] perfect order and total control are not the governing ideas. Bill, in discussing various creation myths, mentioned that in some of them creation emerges from an act of trickery, an image that fits right in with the Northwest Indian myths of Raven, the creative trickster.

Creativity is often unpredictable. Our ancestors may have been taken with the image of the universe as a giant watch wound up and set into motion by divinity, but we seem now, even in our sciences, to realize that the universe is definitely not some sort of mega-machine. It is fascinating to watch a certain stream of scientific thinking moving toward perceptions that are embodied in myth and folklore as well as ancient esoteric teachings. Surprise, catastrophe, or what scientists now like to call "punctuated equilibrium" are ideas that exist in ancient myths and have now been taken up again in modern scientific narratives.

In some areas of New Age thought, though, we don't seem to be comfortable with these ancient and modern ideas of complexity and surprise—we prefer more classical systems of control and progress through graded hierarchies of initiation. This concept of hierarchies, graded development, and initiation is not restricted to esoteric teaching, for it is shared by the major religious traditions as well. In the church or the military, this notion of hierarchies and promotion through graded development is very prevalent. It is orderly, efficient, amenable to control, and, besides, there are people who enjoy ranking things.

The question is, do we always learn or learn best by following a hierarchical lesson plan in which information is carefully organized in sequential packets, sometimes doled out to us bit by bit? Is life organized like that? Often it is not. Sometimes, especially when we are in new situations, much of our learning comes in "informational quanta"—in *gestalts* and bits and pieces that suddenly arrange into new and exciting patterns of discovery and insight. Only later will they be formulated into a practice or technique, or organized into lesson plans.

In this trickier way of learning, one can't always control the lessons or their consequences. I cannot say that I am going to learn in a way that makes me an engineer and nothing else. I started out to be a biochemist and geneticist, but the learning process I went through, which included more than school, resulted in my becoming a mystic and a writer instead. Nor can we always determine how the lessons fit in a pattern and which one is a prerequisite for the next.

What I need to handle this "tricky learning" is a willingness to be open to moments of surprise and insight. I need to be open not only to where I want to go, but to where life and its lessons want me to go. I must learn to see imaginatively beyond the limits of my own preconceptions and expectations. Sometimes the sequential, initiatic form of learning, for all its undoubted strengths, can be a shield against actually encountering the random and emergent properties of life. It is a cage to keep Raven out (or to keep Raven in and under control).

"Raven learning" looks unstructured; sometimes it looks just like play. It is sympathetic to discovery and serendipity. My oldest boy goes to a school where the classrooms have no desks and the children move throughout the room undertaking whatever tasks or play they wish, within certain limits. There are certain structured times, but for the most part, the class time is theirs to create. Observing the class in action, at first it looks like everyone is just playing. Then you begin to see the flows of learning. You see that some kids are doing math, others are reading, others are engaged in nature study. Through it all moves the teacher—assisting, suggesting, moderating. You begin to see that there is a lesson plan at work. The basics are being covered, but in a way based on personal initiative and discovery.

Another illustration of "Raven learning" comes out of computer technology. It is an informational artifact called "hyperspace." Hyperspace is something that at the moment can be accessed only through a computer using certain kinds of programs and languages such as Hypertext. In hyperspace, nothing is arranged linearly. Everything is arranged relationally. If I am reading a text and I come across a word I don't know, or a concept I am not familiar with, or something I would like to explore, I can click on that word or concept and be given a menu of all the relevant data contained in the computer's memory.

For example, I might be reading a text on Abraham Lincoln and encounter the name Steven Douglas. Not knowing much about him, I could select *Douglas* and suddenly on the screen are photographs of Douglas and his biography. In reading that, I decide that I need more information about the history of Illinois, so I select the word *Illinois*. That in turn might lead me to exploring the Indian cultures of the Midwest, which could lead me into mythology and religion, where I might find references to slavery in the Bible, which in turn take me back to Lincoln.

In other words, I work my way through a concept using a latticework of paths; it is not linear. I am not forced to take this bit of knowledge and then this bit of knowledge and then this bit of knowledge in a hierarchical and sequential fashion.

I see how events, concepts, personalities, and ideas fit together in ever-expanding connections and patterns. I see contexts as well as contents. In such a relational space, I can build a hologram of knowledge on my own—one that might be more suited to my needs than a programmed text could offer.

Of course, we can get lost in such a lattice, particularly since we have not developed the nonlinear cognitive skills required to navigate hyperspace successfully. Nor is hyperspace a replacement for ordinary linear learning. There is room for both. However, hyperspace is paradigmatically related to the whole sense of the cosmos that is emerging in our time. It mirrors a kind of consciousness that views incarnation in ways that are less particulate and more holistic. When I first read about Hypertext, I thought it sounded very similar to the Akashic records of esoteric cosmology. It provided a computer-assisted experience that was analogous to the experience of accessing the etheric memory or navigating within some of the inner worlds.

Computer technology offers us some other interesting images, particularly as presented in the realm of science fiction. For a time, there was a genre of novels called "cyberpunk," of which the most famous is probably *Neuromancer*, by William Gibson, though one of the first such novels and one of the best is called *True Names* by Vernor Vinge. In these novels, a new level of reality has come into being—a kind of planetary hyperspace created and sustained by thousands of data banks and millions of computers around the globe all interconnected by phone, microwave, satellite, fiber optics, and so forth. In effect, it is a global electronic brain, within which a virtual reality exists. Humans can enter this reality by plugging themselves into their computers. In fact, these books are rather gnostic in their underlying message, since the heroes seek to leave the confines of the flesh and enter a hyperspace reality where only pure mind is real.

This virtual reality is made up of data, but this data is programmed or cued in such a manner as to appear to be something else. What that something else is depends on the author's story. For example, in *True Names*, the virtual reality, which is called the "Matrix," looks like something out of a fantasy novel. It has unicorns, dragons, elves, fairies, castles, towers, forests, mountains, and so on. Each bit of data is cued to trigger an association in the user's subconscious so that it looks like an artifact or a being of some kind.

This is a computerized version of the astral realms in which patterns and geometries of energy become interpreted by a human consciousness as beings, landscapes, and so forth. For that matter, it is an analog to the physical world, as I mentioned earlier. Our world is really a buzz of energy that our imaginations interpret as the physical objects and people that we normally see. It is not that those people and objects aren't really there, but they may not be there in the manner in which we perceive them.

Computerized virtual realities are not science fiction. They already exist. Helmets, gloves, electronic bodysuits, and the like are already being experimented with as means of projecting one's consciousness into one of these computer worlds. This is incarnation a further step removed. Realities within realities within realities. Which one is real? Which one is not?

I use this to illustrate that what we see, even in this virtual reality we call the physical plane, is not always what is really there. We are always dealing with images, and sometimes the most practical tool for seeing beyond images is the imagination. In *True Names*, the person who enters the Matrix cannot afford to forget what the various images represent, for he is there to interact with the data behind the image. He is there to go to the essence behind the form. Sound familiar? Yet, that essence is often best grasped through the imaginative image that cloaks it, since the mind (in the novel, at least) may be unable to comprehend or deal with the corresponding data in its pure state. In our world, the higher geometry that is an angel may appear to us as a winged human being so that we can grasp its reality. We appear to each other as human beings so that we can encounter each other, yet what we see is often not enough. We must make the imaginative leap beyond the form to encounter truth.

Going back to my remarks about initiatic learning—by which I mean sequential, programmed, linear learning—and Raven learning, or "trickster" learning— both have their place—and they often interweave and complement each other. However, Raven learning may be more true to the nature of things than initiatic learning, which is one reason images of hierarchy can be deceiving. Consider a large business. Its organizational chart is probably hierarchical, but the actual life of the business—the way in which things get done, the channels through which real power and authority flow, the inner dynamics of the corporate culture and politics—often shows only a nodding acquaintance to the organizational chart.

Likewise, patterns of learning based on hierarchical models may not be congruent with the actual subject matter that must be learned or with the way the subject matter "behaves" in real life. To create a programmed lesson plan, there must be some basis for categorization and organization of information, and usually that is based on some physical attribute that we can normally sense ("First we study all the blues, then all the reds, then all the greens," and so on). However, that organization is imaginary; even the selected attributes themselves are imaginary. They are what we select as important or apparent out of the buzz of information and being that actually surrounds us. They are based on appearances but not necessarily on what lies behind the appearances, which often is more important.

In our encounters with life, we usually have our greatest successes and failures through dealing with the inner realities behind appearances. Those inner realities don't always show themselves in linear, organized ways. They appear like Raven—suddenly, playfully, surprisingly. They are revealed through trickster learning as often as not. To see them, to appreciate them, to understand them, we need to have the quality of Raven in our own minds.

There is a place for initiatic, linear learning. It is a fine technique when used properly, but it is a lousy state of mind. Initiations do take place, but they affect the virtual reality of the realms of form more than the realms of spirit and essence. They reveal only part of the pattern that we are, not all of it. The Theosophical Society almost collapsed over the misuse of the images of initiation—a class system began to emerge based on which initiation a person was alleged to have taken and consequently how "evolved" they were.

Improperly understood and used, images of initiation can reflect the particulate vision of the universe too much to give a clear view of the inner workings and conditions of the soul. They are too dependent on the virtual realities of appearance, even as they claim to reveal the inner realities of spirit.

The true initiatic path of the larger spirit is based less on what is known and more on what can be embodied and served. It is based on an honoring of all realities, each of which is "virtual" or imaginative in some respect, since each reality is a crossroads where God can be born. In particular, an initiatic path is based on the birth and embodiment of that supreme source of empowerment of all incarnational patterns, which is love.

Concerning the flip-over of good and evil, I think we can see evil as two extreme ends of avoiding the embodiment of love. At one extreme, we are abstract and removed. We can calculate mega-deaths or fly over a jungle in a jet and drop our napalm bombs on huts, for we are not connected to the agony we are inflicting. At the other end, we are so embodied in density that we are a lump without a mind. We have learned a routine, and we do not wish to change. We want to force all things into our lump, and we want all time to stop. At one extreme or the other, there is a form of unconsciousness that refuses to recognize the whole. To be suddenly connected with the whole, to feel one's nerves on fire with napalm or with poetic and prophetic visions of a transformed world, is to be alive in the heart of the body. That is where all true initiations take place. That is where Raven lives.

Scary Stuff
William Irwin Thompson

In the condition of impermanence, *duksha*, the Buddhist sees the matrix of suffering, while the Christian sees the conditions for love, the matrix as *Mater* for the birth of the divine child. When one recalls that the icon of Mary for the West is the *Mater dolorosa*, the mother of suffering as expressed in Michelangelo's Pietà, then one can see that there is a great closeness to the Buddhist and Christian experiences of time as impermanence and sacrifice for love and compassion, for *caritas* and *karuna*. If Buddhism is the lattice, the galaxy, and Judaism and Christianity the solar monotheisms, perhaps we should recognize that we need both to have a truly cosmic cosmology. To appreciate a galaxy of suns, we have to know just how extraordinary one sun is in all its particularity. Those who love the multitude, as I said before, generally can't love persons. Those who are too cosmic and spacy, too angelic, do not experience the essential, limited condition of being human.

It seems to me that the "crossroads" that history has come to is a meeting of East and West in which we experience what Teilhard de Chardin called "the planetization of mankind" as Buddhist space and Christian time. In the graininess of distinct events, we get to know love and its opposite, evil, with a specificity that may not be known by those who are entranced with The Big Picture, when they see how this little evil leads to that enormous cosmic good or this supernova, a billion years down the road, to the evolution of life in our solar system.

If you want to enroll in the mystery school of incarnate love, the form you have to fill out is a human body. Perhaps one reason computer hackers are so fascinated with virtual realities, which can become so compelling as to be a second world, is that they are usually individuals who have flunked incarnation. Your average household computer hacker is an antisocial teenage male who is having problems with embodiment—with the world of the flesh, the female, the uncontrollable.

Not too long ago, there was an article in *The New York Review of Books* about the nuclear weapons competition between the Livermore Lab in California and Los Alamos Lab in New Mexico. It seems that Dr. Teller's group, the one that talked Reagan into the computer game called *Star Wars*, is a bunch of antisocial young males whose idea of a fun time is to get together for ice cream parties at Teller's house and discuss thermonuclear war. To avoid the middle, where the life of the heart is, these guys have so twisted themselves around as to have joined both extremes at the other end. They are lumps who have lumped themselves together in their artificial society of hackers so that they won't have to deal with the world or feel the agony they inflict.

One of the reasons we are so fascinated by cyberpunk is that it is the most abhorrent and inhuman landscape we can imagine. It is the mirror opposite of Romanticism's return to nature that has dominated Western thought for the last two hundred years. The image of brain helmets, the *Omni* magazine vision of silicon imbedded into flesh—the whole cyborg thing—is imagining a frontier that is down at the level of nanosecond technologies for our organic molecules. When you see the mouse neuron strapped to the silicon chip on the cover of *Byte* magazine, it is pretty spooky: a body on the rack, a nanosecond crucifixion. Because it seems so abhorrently unnatural and fascinating, and gives us the shivers, there is probably some prophetic dimension to it. For one thing, it certainly forces us to ask ourselves, "What is natural? What is nature?"

Think of the atmosphere in the mineral epoch of this planet before there was life as we think of it. Is that nature? Think of the methane atmosphere of the bacterial epoch before the cyanobacteria got to work creating our beautiful blue sky. You can't stop time and say, "This is nature, but that is not." Presumably, time is still moving, and all species are going into extinction because the whole bloated thing is getting folded over and smashed down, the way you knead bread. You fold all the species back into the primal dough, push out the gas, bake it in a supernova, and let it cool for one epoch.

No, the Sierra Club calendar picture of nature just won't do. It owes more to aristocratic impressions of nature formed by Gainsborough and Constable than to perceptions of nature taken from biology. Imagine a Sierra Club meeting of dinosaurs watching the comet coming in to cause the Cretaceous extinction. They are worried, so they hold an emergency meeting of the dinosaurs to deal with the situation. Now, what they would try to figure out is how to make the planet comfortable for dinosaurs; they most definitely would not imagine a world in which the space they vacate becomes filled with mammals. The last thing on Earth they would want to see is those pesty little critters underfoot in the underferns swarming out to inherit the Earth. That would be like us imagining the cockroaches taking over.

Perhaps the end of the world is not a war or an earthquake—a crisp, newsy event in the human time of thirty-two frames per second. Perhaps the end of the world is an infolding into evolution of all the species, an evolution from nature to culture, from meat to silicon. Once we had an evolution from mineral to plant, then plant to animal, then animal to human. Perhaps now it is human to cyborg.

In this end of the world, the elementals and angels, orcs and elves, that we kicked out to take over Middle Earth are coming back and are going to sneak into time through the opening niche of these new nanosecond technologies. The elemental will no longer be the spirit of the sacred mountain for a Hopi shaman, and the angel will no longer be the choiring music of the spheres. The elemental will be the molecular lattice, and the angel will be the singularity. The wizard is the sorcerer's apprentice—the teenage computer hacker who so loves his computer that he brings forth elves and angels in his midst. The all-American football hero who gets the cheerleader with the big tits passes into extinction like copulating dinosaurs, and the little meek and homely hacker in wedded bliss with his computer inherits the Earth. Scary stuff!

Every punctuated equilibrium in evolution comes with a catastrophe. The crossroads discussed by David is often a "catastrophe bifurcation." These bifurcations arise from the increase of noise that destabilizes the whole system until it flips into another attractor. Instead of a limit cycle that oscillates back and forth in a periodic attractor—an oscillation, say, between dark ages and civilization—the noise builds up until the system is drawn by a strange attractor, a chaotic attractor. What is being prophetically imagined and prefigured in science fiction is a new world in which "nature" is eliminated. The noise, rather than pulling us back into the savagery of a dark age—a Mad Max landscape of no gas for industrial civilization—is suddenly gathered together to form an "informationscape," a new evolutionary niche. Everything that we New Agers invoke in our language of "healing the earth"—this whole romantic Findhorn fantasy of "the return to nature," is being swept aside in contempt by a Stewart Brand boys'-club of MIT and Silicon Valley hackers.[36] Scary stuff!

Once this social transformation takes place, the shock of the unnatural causes us to come to terms with our hidden agenda of making nature comfortable to culture, which is as true of the MIT technologists as it is of the Findhornian nativists. Both sides want to feel at home in the universe; it's just that one side likes a pure culture without any noise from nature, and the other side likes a pure nature without any noise from culture. And yet the unconscious architecture of emergence is coming from noise—which is to say that the future is not being invented singly at either MIT or Findhorn. Let's hear it for Chinook, good neighbor to Boeing and Microsoft!

When we try to make evolutionary management decisions to come up with a universe that is comfortable for us, we are basically saying "no" to change. We make the great refusal and say, "No." We refuse to evolve, so we become evolutionary refuse. Notice that the whole cyberpunk landscape is one of evolutionary refuse. Think of *Blade Runner* or the black-market dealers in organ transplants in *Max Headroom*. It is a landscape of bio-junk. Scary stuff, but there is no question that this is literally the evolutionary cutting edge.

What is going on is not evolution by natural selection, but evolution by cultural intrusion at every conceivable level: elemental, human, and angelic. In the nineties, it isn't a battle anymore between "the mystics and the mechanists," such as I talked about in my *Time* magazine interview in 1972, but some kind of crossing—a genetic crossing—of the mystics and the mechanists—a crossing between Marvin Minsky and Bill Thompson. And that gives you David Spangler, the child of mysticism and computer technology. Scary stuff!

When we say "no" to cultural change and evolution, we begin to inflate and see ourselves as messianically called to heal the Earth. And since the Messiah is basically a victim, we imagine ourselves and the Earth as wounded, and we adopt the psychology of the victim to seek our revenge. By playing the victim consciously, we begin unconsciously to victimize others. Our cults, ashrams, and utopian communities then begin to become the theaters for these soap-opera dramas of neurotic unconsciousness. Meanwhile, in the outside world of yuppie venture capitalists and technologists, the whole world gets wired together and comes on line with "the singularity." By playing the victim of cultural change, we disempower ourselves and distance ourselves from the new.

If one goes more deeply into this iconography of the wound, as I tried to do in *The Time Falling Bodies Take to Light*, then one sees that more ancient than the image of Christ exposing the wound in his side is the Great Mother of Laussel exposing the magic of the menstrual wound that heals itself—the labial wound of the vulva, the place of origin and emergence. The whole notion of the wound and vulnerability then begins to take on a quite different and less neurotic form. The labial wound is the broken hymen in conception, the vulva in childbirth. It is the lifeblood of passage. It is a messy process in which we learn to be open to the conception and birth of the new.

The cyberpunk landscape is also a messy landscape of hardware and software, "dryware" and "wetware," masculine and feminine. Both the junk of industrial civilization and the junk of biology lie strewn around in the shop of the demiurge. However, an emergent property is never inferable from its preconditions. We cannot look at the junk molecules in the prebiotic ocean and atmosphere and infer the living, bounded cell. So now we cannot look at the junk of *Robocop* and *Neuromancer* and infer the singularity. Like any paranoid fantasy, the cyberpunk vision suffers from the failure of too much literalism.

One of the things that we all learned from Marshall McLuhan was that the medium is the message. Television is not a medium of messages, a communication; it is an environment, an unconscious architecture that prefigures the emergence of a noetic polity. What we saw in the television manipulations of the last election with Bush, and what we saw with Colonel North, and what we see in Disneyworld and Epcot Center is television as an electronic hearth comforting the collective in its new home, its new noetic polity. In this new noetic polity, Reagan was not the president of the republic; he was a thoughtform, a performance of the collective unconscious.

This shift from political philosophy to fantasy—this cultural change from Jefferson to Reagan—leads directly to the elimination of matter, the elimination of nature that we have been considering. In eliminating the solidity of the philosophical republic that came out of the culture of the Enlightenment, we move from the world of conscious, Georgian architecture to the world of unconscious, electronic architecture. The American Adventure at Epcot Center is the Crystal Palace exemplar of this cultural shift.

Television, as the electronic hearth that is never turned off in the trailer or tract house, is unconscious architecture. It prefigures a future in which we will have pure electronic architecture. We will use buildings as now we use electric appliances, and when we are finished with the task, we will turn off the switch and the building will disappear. Civilized people think in terms of cities and big buildings; they envision the future as big buildings in space, but whales and dolphins know better. They do not suffer from Whiteheadian "misplaced concreteness," and I like to think that with their gigantic brains they are accessing a hyperspace in which the Andromedans are listening and jiving to their songs.

All these technological innovations are clumsy metaphors for mystical states of being. Some people sit *zazen* for ten thousand hours to gain one millisecond of *satori* so that they may see into the artificially constructed nature of reality. However, most Americans prefer to discover the artificiality of reality by creating artificial realities in television, in movies, in Disneyworld, or in American politics as celebrity management. Once we begin to understand these technologies of virtual realities, then we begin to appreciate that the ego is the video game of the *daimon* and that incarnation is our projection into time and space. If we have projected down here, why are we so gnostically intent on trying to get out? Why are we trying to get from *samsara* to *nirvana* when we have gone to a great deal of trouble to project ourselves down here so that we can learn the body of love? We know that we don't learn it through anything less than incarnation, for incarnation is our singing school.

The poet W.B. Yeats said that "man can embody the truth but he cannot knowit."[37] In this sense, knowing is inadequate, and we recognize that when we go to the movies. Why do we like to be frightened to death? Why do we support these multimillion-dollar James Bond movies or worse? We keep stirring ourselves up with sex and horror movies because we realize that sex and death are part of the biological architecture of the eukaryotic cell, and we realize that that period of biology is on its way out.

Natural selection has been this temporary thing for the last couple of billion years or so, but now, in the emergence of the singularity, all that is being changed. We can't take reality for granted any more. Part of the whole unconscious project of electronic culture is democratizing the mystical experience—making the displacement from reality available to everyone. If we get trapped in an illusion, we can begin to reflect on the whole process of getting trapped in illusions. This collusion between Top and Pop, between science and entertainment, between mysticism and technology, is, for me, what the New Age is truly all about.

EPILOGUE

The Fall of the Wall
David Spangler
January 7, 1990

Nearly six months have passed since Bill and I gave our second joint seminar at Chinook. During that time, we have all witnessed the birth of a new world as one totalitarian regime after another has fallen in Eastern Europe, to be replaced by embryonic democracies. We have witnessed peoples reimagining their worlds, and now we all live in a new world because of it.

In 1969, I watched with tears in my eyes as Neil Armstrong took humanity's first steps on the Moon; our reaching out beyond this planet to explore the greater universe has always been important to me. With the Moon landing, I felt, as Armstrong said, that humanity did indeed take a "giant step" into a new world. Similar tears filled my eyes twenty years later as I watched the people from East and West Berlin gather about the wall and begin to chip pieces away from it. If the Apollo missions helped germinate a planetary perspective, allowing us to see our vulnerable and infinitely lovely world from the barren surface of the Moon, the falling of the Berlin Wall translated that perspective into the type of action needed to make planetary awareness a reality: the reaching beyond the walls that divide us to rediscover our shared identities and our common destiny.

For me, the New Age is about the arising and manifestation of a planetary spirit. The fall of the wall emphasized that spirit and began liberating us from the bounds of ancient fears and hatreds, just as the Moon landings began liberating us from ancient perspectives of ourselves that were too limiting, too divisive. The collapse of the wall was, for me, a mystical event as much as a political one.

In 1983, I had a conversation with the being I call "John," one of the spiritual entities I spoke about in the seminar. At that time, he spoke of the immanent death of Soviet Premier Andropov and the eventual coming to power of a man called Gorbachev. He said that Gorbachev would be instrumental in altering the nature of the Soviet Union and its government and also in stimulating change in Eastern Europe. Within a month of that prophecy, Andropov was dead. What has happened since is well known, and the unfoldment of that prophecy is still proceeding.

I mention this not to extoll John's or my virtues as prophets. In fact, John has often spoken against prophecies, saying that they can limit our vision, causing us to fail to see or recognize unexpected opportunities or dangers that may be just as important, or even more important, transformationally as those that were prophesied. He always suggests a state of poised alertness in all directions of our lives rather than fixating on the event horizon of a particular prophecy.

I bring up this prophecy to make four points. The first is that the changes in the Warsaw Pact countries are not by chance, nor are they solely political or economic in origin. They are also the result of patterns of energy and work focused from the inner planes or spiritual world as part of a vaster pattern of planetary and human unfoldment. This greater pattern is, I feel, the origin of much of the modern sense of an emerging New Age, though it is often misinterpreted and misrepresented, as Bill and I have discussed.

When one is attuned to higher levels of perception, one can see this pattern and the forces moving within it to heal, protect, bless, empower, and energize the changes humanity needs to make to emerge successfully into the twenty-first century. It is a pattern that seeks to tear down walls of many kinds: walls of fear, hatred, prejudice, injustice, inequality, ignorance, and conflict, not only within the human family but within the whole biosphere. It is a pattern that seeks the birth of true individual, ecological, and planetary wholeness. For me, the events of the past six months simply affirm the presence and energy of that great pattern of planetary transformation.

The second point has to do with the speed and timing of the changes in Eastern Europe. Who could have predicted in September of 1989 the speed and completeness of the transformations in Europe at the end of December? Everything happened far more swiftly than anyone anticipated or imagined. Indeed, in Rumania, the transformation occurred literally overnight, though several days of fighting followed.

The rapidity of the changes were not included in John's prophecies, either in 1983 or in subsequent discussions. The pattern or potential of an event may be apparent in a heightened state of consciousness, but the exact nature of its manifestation rarely is, at least in my experience. So much is open ended, affected by our daily choices. We are neither puppets nor spectators; we are participants in the events of our lives, and our participation co-creates and shapes the courses our lives take.

John and other spiritual beings have often said that transformation can come overnight. The changes in Europe did not take years; they took only two exciting months to emerge. Of course, in many instances, these changes were based on years of preparation and hope. The fuel was there; it just needed a spark.

This is true as well for all the holistic and compassionate values represented by the best of New Age thinking. It is not that the teachings influencing much of New

Age thought are new. They are actually very ancient teachings of love, compassion, and the wholeness of life. As both Bill and I mentioned, the idea of a New Age— a time of radical human transformation into an age of planetary peace—has been around for at least two thousand years. It is a global myth, a planetary archetype. Humanity has been preparing for its realization for centuries. Given the right sparks, who can say that a global restructuring could not take place "overnight"?

In Eastern Europe, individuals made a difference. Individuals provided the sparks. Some of these individuals are well known, but most are just faces in the crowds of thousands who marched, protested, chanted, and braved military reprisal and death to add their voices to the cry for freedom and change. The transformative force is not just (or even usually) some energy acting from a higher level. It is individuals willing to make a choice, to take a stand, to embody their vision, to risk all in order to give something new a chance to be born. That is my third point. If a New Age, like a new Europe, is to be born, it is because individuals willing to sacrifice what is familiar and habitual embody its values and virtues, not because some great cosmic pattern decrees that it will be so.

My fourth point is that transformation is only a beginning, not a destination. As I write this, the countries of Eastern Europe now face the herculean task of inventing new social systems for themselves, developing new economies, and experimenting with political forms that are either brand new or little practiced. There is the chance of failure, of falling back into old forms. There is hard work, struggle, and challenge ahead before a new order can be said to have truly emerged and stabilized itself. Birth may come overnight, but incarnation takes a lifetime.

Impatience can lead us to seize the form of the new and miss its deeper spirit, which may need more time to mature and unfold. The speed with which Eastern Europe changed has been exciting, but it brings problems of its own. Are these countries truly ready for the new institutions and patterns they are invoking? Can a democratic, market economy take hold easily, or will frustration and anger at the slowness of change bring a new reaction, one that brings back repressive elements of the older regimes? The rapid changes in Eastern Europe may make similar changes in the Soviet Union more difficult because the sudden sense of instability may bring reactionary forces more powerfully to the forefront. Rather than encouraging transformation in that country, the rapid changes of last year may slow it down over the long run.

Many of those who look for a New Age think only of the moment of transition from one state to another. They forget that on the other side of transformation lies a whole process of creativity, exploration, advances, retreats, consolidation, failure, and success. Those of us who work for a New Age must not fall prey to impatience.

We may like to see the world transform overnight, but not if the outcome is simply the collapse of the old and a resulting instability that actually makes openness to change less likely. Integrated and compassionate change is far preferable to a shock of transformation that carries us backward, not forward.

We need to understand that we are involved with a process rather than an event. The New Age, like freedom, like democracy, does not come once. It must be imagined and reimagined over and over again, served over and over again, and co-created over and over again.

The War in the Gulf
William Irwin Thompson
March 7, 1991

Politics has been called the art of the possible. War is the politics of the impossible. What was not possible in peaceful compromise becomes possible through the exhaustion of violence. Incarnation for most people is unconscious; they do not know how they got here, and they only begin to feel the meaning of their incarnation when they come to its edge near death. Societies throw themselves into wars with total fascination and astonishing organization because war is incarnation made conscious; it is, after all, waged with the flesh.

Wars frame more than the interval of peace; they remap our cultural territory. New lines are drawn, old lines are erased. From the enormous investment in violence, a new longing for the impossible is created, as what was invisible before the war becomes part of the new landscape of peace. After World War II, the United Nations and the state of Israel became the impossibilities that took their proper places in the sun.

Before the war in the Persian Gulf, the elemental was invisible to the human. The first creatures to live on this planet were displaced by the last, and this displacement generated an invisible noosphere of hatred and rage. The humans who became possessed and taken over by this hatred were the Arabs. Historically treated with contempt by the Ottoman, French, and English empires, the Arabs have felt attracted to the West, while filled with rage that it was a world that was closed to all but the wealthy few who could buy fleets of German cars or even entire London department stores such as Harrod's. The red man had been turned into a figure of shamanic wisdom and magical power by popular culture, and the black man had been transformed into the musical hero of the world; but the poor Arab was the real primitive of our global electronic society, and he was reduced to attacking the airlines as once the Plains Indians attacked the railroads.

Having no place in the scheme of things, the Arab was displaced from the geopolitics of the visible world to the Gaian politics of the invisible elemental world. The paranoid insanity of Saddam Hussein created an opening to a state of elemental possession. The hundreds of burning oil wells in Kuwait are an outward sign of an inward state: a visible transformation in which the elemental underworld is released into the upper world through fire and smoke. The blue sky created so long ago by the photosynthetic activity of the cyanobacteria, the elves, is now threatened with the revenge of the elementals, who were thrust down into the underworld to prepare the world for the coming of humanity. To prepare the world for the coming of posthumanity, the elemental is being released in a fury of rage and revenge. The transformation of the atmosphere has been accelerated by decades.

In Grimm's fairy tales, such as "Rumpelstiltskin," the revenge of the first against the last is often expressed in the form of a dwarf that demands the sacrifice of the firstborn. Since the elementals were the firstborn of Earth who were sacrificed to make room for humanity, it only seems fair to them that humans should be asked to sacrifice their firstborn. In the parable of the vineyard in the New Testament, the workers of the first hour wonder why the workers of the last hour should receive the same wage. They are not comforted when Jesus says that "the last shall be first, and the first shall be last." In the fires of the oil wells in Kuwait, the insanity of Saddam has provided the elementals with a form of incarnation. And what these bodies are demanding is the sacrifice of the firstborn children of the modern world economy, the world cities of Venice, Amsterdam, London, and New York. It is precisely these cities that will be the first to be flooded and destroyed by an atmospheric Greenhouse Effect that can raise the water level of the oceans. In the exoteric hatred and revenge of the poor against the rich, an older and more esoteric hatred has been bodied forth.

Findhorn and the New Age sought to teach us about the presence of the elemental kingdoms through gentler and more loving means—gentler and slower. Now the world economy and its embeddedness in the world ecology will become clearer to all. As a merchandised fad, the New Age movement came in the interval between two wars, Vietnam and the war in the Persian Gulf. After the burnout of Vietnam, after all the violent protests, bombings, and drug escapes of the sixties, people in the seventies turned to less Dionysian and more Apollonian forms of spiritual exploration. Findhorn, Auroville, Arcosanti, Lindisfarne, and Naropa—these were the sorts of educational experiments that expressed the zeitgeist. Of course, these were marginal experiments of a subculture, and the dominant culture moved on into the greed of the eighties with Reagan and Bush, Trump and Milken. Money was in, idealism was out. In American politics as the art of the possible, things like Arcosanti and Lindisfarne were impossible dreams.

But war is the politics of the impossible, and the war in the Gulf has remapped our cultural territory. This time, however, it is not simply lines in the sand that have been redrawn, but lines in the sky—lines dividing the visible from the invisible. Now there can be no "us" or "them," whether rich or poor, New Age or Old Age, Israeli or Arab, human or elemental—we are all passing through this catastrophe together. What was once merely mystical idealism has now become the political reality of the United Nations of Earth.

NOTES

1.	"Poetry and Prophecy," *Lindisfarne Letter* 9 (West Stockbridge, MA, 1979). Keith Critchlow and Robert Lawlor, "Geometry and Architecture," *Lindisfarne Letter* 10 (West Stockbridge, MA, 1980). "Homage to Pythagoras," *Lindisfarne Letter* 14 (West Stockbridge, MA, 1982). Keith Critchlow, *Time Stands Still: New Light on Megalithic Science* (New York: St. Martin's Press, 1982); and Robert Lawlor, *Sacred Geometry: Theory and Practice* (New York and London: Thames and Hudson/Crossroad, 1983).

2.	*Temenos* is now in its eleventh volume. The address is 47 Paulton's Square, London, England, SW3 5DT.

3.	"The Lindisfarne Chapel," *Lindisfarne Letter* 12, (Great Barrington, MA: Lindisfarne Press, 1981).

4.	Walt Whitman, *Leaves of Grass and Selected Prose*, ed. John Kouwenhoven (New York: Modern Library Editions, 1950), 491, 514.

5.	W.I. Thompson, *Darkness and Scattered Light* (New York: Doubleday, 1978), 145-183.

6.	Ibid., 57-103.

7.	W.I. Thompson, *Islands out of Time: A Memoir of the Last Days of Atlantis* (New York: Dial/Doubleday, 1985; Santa Fe: Bear & Co., 1990).

8.	Francisco Varela, Evan Thompson, and Eleanor Rosch, *The Embodied Mind: Cognitive Science and Human Experience* (Cambridge: MIT Press, 1991).

9.	Revelation 21:1.

10.	John Todd, "Living Machines," *Annals of Earth* 8, no. 1, (Spring 1990): 14-17.

11.	Gerald Heard, *Pain, Sex, and Time: A New Hypothesis of Evolution* (London: Cassell, 1939).

12. Frances Yates, *The Rosicrucian Enlightenment* (Boulder, CO: Shambhala Publications, 1978). Also, her *Giordano Bruno and the Hermetic Tradition* (New York: Vintage Books, 1969), 274.

13. Martin Bernal, *Black Athena: The Afro-Asiatic Roots of Civilization* (London: Free Association Books, 1987), 162-188.

14. This was later published as chapter 4 in W.I. Thompson's *Darkness and Scattered Light: Four Talks on the Future* (New York: Doubleday, 1978).

15. Jean Gebser, *Ursprung und Gegenwart*, vol. 2, in *Gesamtausgabe* (Schaffhausen, Switzerland: Novalis Verlag, 1986), 40.

16. Henri Atlan, "Cordue 1979: Colloque 'Science et Conscience,'" in *À Tort et à raison: intercritique de la science et du mythe* (Paris: Editions du Seuil, 1986), 33-44.

17. W.I. Thompson, ed., *Gaia Two, Emergence: The New Science of Becoming* (Hudson, New York: Lindisfarne Press, 1991); Italian ed., Bergamo: Pier Luigi Lubrina, 1991.)

18. Maurice Panisset and Sorin Sonea, *A New Bacteriology* (Boston: Jones & McLaughlin, 1983), 8.

19. Humberto Maturana and Francisco Varela, *The Tree of Knowledge: The Biological Roots of Human Understanding* (Boston: New Science Library, 1987), 94-117.

20. To appreciate the kind of detailed knowledge of the life of the soul after death, a knowledge that is completely lacking in Christianity but highly articulated in Tibetan Buddhism, the reader is referred to Tsele Natsok Rangdrol, *The Mirror of Mindfulness* (Rangjung Yeshe Publications, P.O. Box 1200, Kathmandu, Nepal, 1987).

21. Francisco Varela, Evan Thompson, and Eleanor Rosch, *The Embodied Mind: Cognitive Science and Human Experience* (Cambridge, MA: MIT Press, 1991).

22. For an exhaustive bibliography of the literature, the reader is referred to Steven Donovan and Michael Murphy, eds., *The Physical and Psychological Effects of Meditation: A Review of Contemporary Meditation Research with a Comprehensive Bibliography*, 1931–1988 (Esalen Institute, 230 Forbes St., San Rafael, CA, 1988). Also see Michael Murphy's forthcoming book, *The Future of the Body* (Los Angeles: Jeremy Tarcher, 1991).

23. The terms are *annamayakosa* (physical), *pranamayakosa* (etheric), *manomayakosa* (astral), *vijnanamayakosa* (mental), and *anandamayakosa* (causal). The reader is referred to Lama Anagarika Govinda, *Grundlagen tibetischer Mystik* (Hamburg: Fischer Verlag, 1975), 170.

24. *The Flower Ornament Scripture: A Translation of the Avatamsaka Sutra*, vol. 1, Thomas Cleary, trans. (Boulder, CO: Shambhala Publications, 1984).

25. Mark Johnson, *The Body in the Mind: The Bodily Basis of Meaning, Imagination, and Reason*, (Chicago: University of Chicago Press, 1987).

26. J. Alan Hobson, *The Dreaming Brain* (Cambridge, MA: Harvard University Press, 1988).

27. *Omni*, March 1989.

28. Gregory Bateson, "Metaphor and the World of Mental Process," in *Gaia, A Way of Knowing*, ed. W.I. Thompson (Great Barrington, MA: Lindisfarne Press, 1987), 44.

29. For a popular explanation of the terms of chaos dynamics, the reader is referred to John Briggs and F. David Peat, *Turbulent Mirror* (New York: Harper & Row, 1989).

30. W.I. Thompson, "A Cultural History of Consciousness," in *Imaginary Landscape: Making Worlds of Myth and Science* (New York: St. Martin's Press, 1989).

31. Lynn Margulis and Dorion Sagan, *Origins of Sex: Three Billion Years of Genetic Recombination* (New Haven: Yale University Press, 1986).

32. For a discussion of the war in the Persian Gulf, the reader is referred to W.I. Thompson, "CNN and the American Replacement of Historical Reality," in *The American Replacement of Nature* (New York: Doubleday, 1991).

33. Elaine Pagels, *Adam, Eve, and the Serpent* (New York: Random House, 1988).

34. Tsele Natsok Rangdrol, *The Mirror of Mindfulness: A Clarification of the General Points of the Bardo*, trans. Erik Pema Kungsang (Kathmandu, Nepal: Rangjung Yeshe Publications, 1987).

35. Heinz Pagels, *The Dreams of Reason: The Computer and the Rise of the Sciences of Complexity* (New York: Simon & Schuster, 1988).

36. Stewart Brand, *The Media Lab: Inventing the Future at MIT* (New York: Viking, 1987).

37. Allan Wade, ed., *The Letters of W.B. Yeats* (London: Rupert-Hart-Davis, 1954), 922.

ABOUT THE AUTHORS

DAVID SPANGLER was born in Columbus, Ohio, in 1945. In 1951, he and his parents moved to Morocco, North Africa, where they lived for six years. During that time, David began having intense mystical experiences that brought him into contact with spiritual dimensions of reality. In 1964, while a student at Arizona State University working for a B.S. in biochemistry, these inner experiences crystallized into a vision of the emergence of a New Age.

Responding to that vision, David left the university and began a career as a lecturer and philosopher dealing with themes of spirituality, cultural change, and personal transformation. From 1970 to 1973, he was a codirector of the Findhorn Foundation community in northern Scotland. Since his return to the United States in 1973, he has lectured widely on the idea of a New Age, designed and taught classes at the University of Wisconsin in Milwaukee, and acted as a consultant to transformationally oriented communities and educational centers throughout North America.

David is the author of several books, including *Revelation: Birth of a New Age, The Laws of Manifestation, Towards a Planetary Vision, Relationship and Identity*, and, most recently, *Emergence: The Rebirth of the Sacred*. He is a Lindisfarne Fellow. He has also worked as a consultant and game designer for a number of game companies, including Lucasfilm Games, Inc. Currently, he is part of the Associate Faculty for the Chinook Learning Center near Seattle, Washington. He is a member of a curriculum design team for the Institute for Theological Studies at Seattle University and teaches as part of their summer program. He also designs and teaches online computer courses on manifestation, spirituality, and the New Age for students located throughout North America.

He lives in the Pacific Northwest with his wife, his two sons and daughter, a ferret, and two goldfish.

WILLIAM IRWIN THOMPSON was born in Chicago in 1938, but moved to Los Angeles in 1945. He studied philosophy and anthropology at Pomona College in Claremont, California, and English literature and Irish history at Cornell University, where he took his Ph.D. in 1966. He has taught in various departments of the humanities and social sciences at Cornell, MIT, and York University in Toronto; he has also served as a visiting professor at Syracuse University, the University of

Hawaii, and the University of Toronto. In 1972, he founded the Lindisfarne Association in New York City.

Dr. Thompson is the Lindisfarne Scholar of the Cathedral of Saint John the Divine in New York City and teaches a seminar there every autumn. For the rest of the year, he works out of his home base at the Lindisfarne Fellows House in Crestone, Colorado, and participates in various seminars and conferences with the Lindisfarne Fellows at the Crestone Mountain Zen Center in Colorado; Ocean Arks International in Falmouth, Massachusetts; and the Chinook Learning Center on Whidbey Island, Washington.

Since 1967 he has published fourteen books, including one historical study, a novel, two books of poetry, two works of cultural philosophy, and several books on contemporary affairs, one of which, *At the Edge of History*, was nominated for the National Book Award in 1972. In 1986, he received the Oslo International Poetry Festival Award.

BOOKS OF RELATED INTEREST
BY BEAR & COMPANY

THE EMERGING NEW AGE
by J.L. Simmons

FUTURE LIVES
A Fearless Guide to Our Transition Times
by J.L. Simmons

ISLANDS OUT OF TIME
A Memoir of the Last Days of Atlantis
by William Irwin Thompson

LIQUID LIGHT OF SEX
Understanding Your Key Life Passages
by Barbara Hand Clow

PROFILES IN WISDOM
Native Elders Speak about the Earth
by Steven S.H. McFadden

SACRED PLACES
How the Living Earth Seeks Our Friendship
by James Swan

THE UNIVERSE IS A GREEN DRAGON
A Cosmic Creation Story
by Brian Swimme

Contact your local bookseller or write:

BEAR & COMPANY
P.O. Drawer 2860
Santa Fe, NM 87504